Miss

LIZZIE

Also by Walter Satterthwait

Wall of Glass

Miss

LIZZIE

Walter Satterthwait

St. Martin's Press,   New York

89- 989341

Design by Holly Block

Library of Congress Catalog Card Number: 89-35115

ISBN 0-312-03400-8

A THOMAS DUNNE BOOK

First Edition
10 9 8 7 6 5 4 3 2 1

This book is for Bobbi

Acknowledgments

In Thailand, I'd like to thank Joe West, Dusty Rhodes, Igor and Buayem Studnar at Buayem's Books, and, for his help and chili con carne, Gabe Vallicelli at The Fountain restaurant. Anyone who finds himself with a hankering for American or Italian food while stranded on Koh Samui is advised to check out Gabe's place.

In the southwest United States, I'd like to thank Jim and Donna Ballin in Phoenix, all the staff at the Coronada Waldenbooks in Albuquerque, and the librarians at the Wyoming branch of the Albuquerque Public Library. Chuck Fair, of Office Incorporated, Santa Fe, has once again been extremely generous, and I'm grateful. Dr. Roger Smith-peter, vascular surgeon and man about town, has been a good friend.

In particular, I want to thank Jeanne W. Satterthwait (Hi Mom) and Jonathan and Claudia Richards, without whose help this book might never have been finished.

Lizzie Borden took an axe
and gave her mother forty whacks,
and when she saw what she had done,
she gave her father forty-one.

Yoshitsune was a famous warrior who lived in medieval Japan. Because of the situation of the country at that time, he was sent to the northern provinces, where he was killed. Before he left he bade farewell to his wife, and soon after she wrote in a poem, "Just as you unreel the thread from a spool, I want the past to become present." When she said this, actually she made past time present. In her mind the past became alive and *was* the present. So as Dogen said, "Time goes from present to past." This is not true in our logical mind, but it is in the actual experience of making past time present. There we have poetry, and there we have human life.

SHUNRYU SUZUKI,
Zen Mind, Beginner's Mind

Book
ONE

Chapter
ONE

THE DAYS WERE longer then, in that long-ago summer at the shore, and the air was softer, and the sunlight more golden as it winked and wobbled off a bluer sea. The men wore immaculate white linen and jaunty boaters of straw as they sauntered, hands in pockets, up and down the boardwalk; the women wore white lace and white bonnets, broad-brimmed and gay. The dress I wore most often that summer (yet felt I had not worn enough, *could not* wear enough) was in fact my very first lace, and to this day I can hear the whisper it made when the breeze, warm and sweet and smelling of salt, came fluting in off the water. And I can hear the rustle of the crinoline beneath; and, at my throat, as precise and real as though it were happening at this moment, I can feel the flutter and tickle of the bonnet ribbons. Time does not really pass away; people do.

There must have been other women that summer, besides Miss Lizzie, who wore mourning; but for the life of me I cannot recall them. Perhaps they kept themselves and their griefs indoors, never ventured out into that bright white sunswept world where grief would have seemed beggarly, derelict. Or perhaps, so self-involved was I that season, so intoxicated by a sense of my own, and the world's, infinite possibilities, that I simply never noticed them.

For, two years after the end of the War to End All Wars, the country had at last unbuckled its belt and loosened its tie. Women had obtained the vote; and, with it, they had helped replace the Democrats—represented by sad somber Mr. Wilson and his would-be successor, Mr. Cox—with the Republicans—represented by the hearty handsome Mr. Harding. There was everywhere a feeling of expectation, of Something Wonderful trembling just around the corner. Little wonder, then, that a thirteen-year-old girl (having just arrived, so she saw it, on the shores of womanhood) might have failed to notice anything so shabby, so offensive, as mourning.

Difficult it would have been, however, not to notice Miss Lizzie. She was, for one thing, our nearest neighbor. She rented the white clapboard cottage next to ours, and every morning from the parlor I would watch her bustle down the steps and across the small sandy yard, tufted with weed, to the gate of the picket fence. She would unlatch the gate, slip through it, then turn and latch it once more, carefully, deliberately, like someone who took care against intruders. And then she would set off down the street, a short squarish figure, her hands folded into the sleeves of her black dress, her purse hanging from her forearm like a padlock. She moved with her shoulders hunched and bent slightly forward, leaning into a private wind, and she wore her black, I thought, almost proudly: as though it were a uniform, as though she were on march.

For another thing, of course, she was notorious. I doubt there was a single child in all New England, in all the country, who had not heard the famous bit of dog-gerel about her and the axe. I remember my disbelief, and my secret thrill of excitement, when Father re-vealed to me that, yes, the woman next door was in-deed *that* Lizzie, the woman who had been tried, almost thirty years before, for the awful murder of her par-ents. And had been found, he added gravely, point-edly, not guilty.

"So the truth," I said, hugely disappointed, "is that she didn't do it?"

"The truth?" Father smiled sadly and stroked his mus-tache. As on every Sunday after-church afternoon, part of the *Boston Herald* was spread out across his lap, while the rest of it—except for the Katzenjammer Kids, whom I had appropriated to my nest on the sofa—lay scattered about the floor around his easy chair. Music was waltzing from the gramophone, outside the sun was shining, and the day was one of those lazy Sundays, now extinct, that seemed filled with time enough for everything and everyone.

"The truth," he said, "may never be known, Amanda, except to Miss Lizzie and the Lord. But legally she is entitled to our respect, and—"

Across the parlor, working methodically on her needlepoint, my stepmother sniffed once. Loudly.

Father sighed. With a patience that had over the years been drained of its original fondness, he turned to her and said, "Yes, Audrey?"

"They arrested her, didn't they?" she said, her lips set

in the thin grim line they assumed whenever she ex-pressed what she knew would be an unpopular opinion. "Where there's smoke, there's fire." This she delivered, nodding her head slightly, with the absolute conviction she reserved for all her platitudes; and then she took a chocolate bonbon from the box that lay (as always) on the coffee table, plopped it into her mouth, and bent once again over her needlepoint.

"Legally," Father said to me gently, "she is entitled to our respect. And spiritually she is, like everyone else, entitled to our compassion."

My stepmother sniffed again and said, without looking up, "Nothing good ever came out of Fall River."

No people are more provincial than the metropolitan middle class. Had Miss Lizzie come from Boston, instead of Fall River with its mills and its tradesmen, my step-mother would have asked her over for tea. Had she come from Back Bay, axe murderer or no, my stepmother would have been camping on her front porch.

———

This conversation took place, as I say, on Sunday. With a neatness of coincidence that in fiction would seem suspicious, but in real life (when you are thirteen) seems inevitable, I met Miss Lizzie face-to-face on Monday.

Annie Holmes and I were in Drummond's Candy Store on Broad Street, ostensibly to buy licorice whips but actually to display our summer finery to Roger, the son of the owner. He was tall and lean and dark, and he had poetic hollows below his cheekbones and fine black hairs along the backs of his long tanned fingers. (And also a sleek black Shaw motor-bicycle.) He was our Heathcliff, Annie's and mine, and both of us would have gladly let him ravish us; even, I am sure, if we had known exactly what that meant.

As we left, I turned at the doorway and drawled over my shoulder—with the insouciance, I believed, of the born coquette—"So *very* nice to see you again, Roger."

Annie snorted explosively beside me, and for an instant I was furious, and then suddenly the giggles were upon us both, overpowering, and Annie pushed me quickly out the screen door. Directly into Miss Lizzie and an armload of packages that went soaring abruptly off in every direction.

I stood there, immobilized, while Annie scuttled around me to help the woman. There were fewer parcels, only three or four, than their eruption had made them seem, and in only a moment Miss Lizzie had collected them all. Then she turned to me and said, "Why the open mouth, child? Catching flies?"

I closed a mouth that I had not, until then, realized was open.

She narrowed her eyes. Behind the pince-nez clipped to the bridge of her nose, they were a very pale blue, almost gray, and large, which made them seem expectant, waiting. "You're the Burton girl," she said. "Next door to me."

I nodded. Her hair, pulled back into a chignon beneath her black bonnet, was silver-white. She must have been in her late fifties or early sixties, but her skin was fine-pored, neither wrinkled nor freckled. Like most women in the first few years of the 1920s, before rouge and lipstick became emblems of chic, she wore no makeup.

"Well then," she said, and she smiled, "do you have a first name?" It was really quite an extraordinary smile, creating two deep dimples in her cheeks, transforming what had been a stern, severe face into one of great liveliness and charm.

"Amanda," I said, finding my voice. It was raspy, threaded, as though I had not used it for years; I cleared it and repeated, "Amanda."

Her left arm grasping the packages, she held out her right hand for me to shake. At thirteen, I had received few offers of a handshake, and I felt very sophisticated accepting hers. (And very grateful to her for giving me the opportunity to demonstrate this sophistication.) Her hand was small and plump and dry.

"Lizzie Borden," she said, and if she was waiting for a reaction from me, a flinch of horror, a gasp of surprise, she gave no sign of it. Nor did I provide such a reaction. Unaccountably, I felt a sense of kinship with the woman.

Annie, however, reacted. Her body stiffened and her eyes grew wide. She held out her hand reluctantly, as though putting it into a flame, took Miss Lizzie's, and jerked it back immediately after whispering her own name.

With a small smile, amused and inward-looking, Miss Lizzie turned to me. "And how is it, Amanda, that you haven't come avisiting?"

I smiled back, and already it seemed to me that we were sharing some private joke; although what it was, I could not have said. "But I haven't been invited."

She laughed. It was a full laugh, almost a man's laugh, loose and easy and up from the diaphragm. "Well then," she said, "we must rectify that at once. Would you care to come to tea at four o'clock?"

"Today?" I said, and I think some disappointment slipped into my voice. Annie and I were planning a swim at four (the time at which, by happenstance, Roger Drummond habitually took his).

"If not today," said Miss Lizzie with a small shrug, "then perhaps some other time."

"No," I said, suddenly deciding. "This afternoon would be fine. I'd love to. Really."

She turned to Annie. "Of course you're invited as well, dear."

Annie nodded numbly.

"At four, then," said Miss Lizzie to us both. She adjusted her packages, turned, and went bustling down the street.

When she was out of earshot Annie clutched at my shoulder and whispered frantically in my ear, "That was *her*! That was really *her*!"

Casually, I shrugged. The cloak of sophistication still lay, regally, upon my shoulders.

"Lizzie Borden," Annie hissed, jumping up and down beside me. "Lizzie *Borden*! Took an axe and gave her mother forty *whacks*!"

"The jury in the trial said she wasn't guilty."

Annie stopped jumping and stood back. "Oh no," she said, horrified. "*Amanda*. You're not really going to go there? *Amanda!* You *can't*! Are you screwy?"

"Legally," I announced, "she is entitled to our respect."

———

If Father had been there that day, I am certain that I would have asked him for permission to visit Miss Lizzie's house, and I am equally certain that he would have given it. But he was in Boston, back at the office where he did something immensely important but rather vague with stocks and bonds, and would not be returning to the shore until Friday.

There was no question whatever of discussing the visit with my stepmother. She would have flatly refused. Not because she feared for my safety (I think that by this time in our lives she would have gladly handed me over to a bona fide witch, providing she received in return an iron-clad guarantee that I would be roasted and eaten), but because the neighbors might learn of it and be scandalized. She dreaded the idea of scandal attaching to herself, probably because she was such an assiduous collector of the scandals that attached to others.

———

I shall have to talk about my stepmother for a moment, for she will play an important if unwilling role in the events which follow.

It was said during that August—although by no one who actually knew any of us—that my brother and I hated her. This was simply not true. Hate, like love, requires an acceptance of the other, a recognition of his or her reality. What we felt for our stepmother was something worse, something far more shameful. It was contempt.

I never knew my natural mother; she died shortly after my birth. When I was five years old, Father was diagnosed as tubercular and shipped off to a sanitarium in the dry therapeutic Southwest. My brother William and I were sent to my father's parents, to live with them in a rambling stone mansion built before the Revolutionary War, a conflict which, from the way my grandmother spoke of it, displaying an easy familiarity with its participants, I assumed had occurred some few short months before.

It took over a year for Father to regain his health, and, in the process, he gained a new wife while my brother and I gained, so he told us upon his return, a new mother.

She had been his nurse, out there in the Wild West of cowboys and Indians and recuperating consumptives, and before me now I have a photograph, brown-edged and brittle, that shows him sitting back on a chaise, gray mountains folding and unfolding off into the background, a blanket around his legs and a smile across his lips that seem so absolutely radiant with vitality that it is impossible to believe he was ever in his life unwell. She stands behind him in her medical whites, her hand upon his shoulder, and the smile she wears (or so it has always seemed to me) is at once relieved and triumphant, that of the cat who has, after a long-sustained and wearisome stalk, finally snared the canary.

In an attempt, no doubt futile, to avoid cattiness myself, I must say that I believe she made an honest initial effort (and probably much against her natural inclinations) to like my brother and me. That first day, I remember, she beamed at me and, bending down, swept me up against a broad buoyant bosom smelling strongly of lilacs. "Amanda!" she said against my ear. She squeezed and released me, abruptly, a woman uneasy with children, with touching them, and she held me out at arms' length, her head cocked to the side, and said, "We're going to be great chums, *aren't* we, dear?"

The strain behind the smile was so obvious, even to a six-year-old girl, that I looked up in confusion to Father. Surely he could see that this blowsy woman, overdressed and (even then) overweight, was acting a part? That her affection was, transparently, affectation? Father stood looking down at us happily—proud, I think, of both of us, his wife, his daughter.

I looked to William, four years older than I, and he, at least, had seen what I had. Arms tightly crossed atop his chest, he pursed his lips at me and rolled his eyes heavenward.

I turned back to my stepmother and with the effortless cruelty of childhood I said, "I don't think so."

For only a second her smile flickered; then, immediately, she relit it. "Now, dear," she said, "you must give me a chance. After all, you know, Rome wasn't built in a day."

Petulant, willful, I pushed her away and screwed up my face and shouted, *"No!"* Then, chanting it viciously, *"No no no no no,"* I turned and ran from the room.

———

I wince now, thinking of that moment, and of others. At our cruelest, William and I laughed outright at the clichés and the narrow-minded strictures around which she structured her life and around which she expected us to structure ours (*ours*, two children who had learned, from a year of doting and wealthy grandparents, that we were unique, privileged: *anointed*). At our kindest, our politest, we pretended to ignore her; and I suspect that our kindness was far more cruel than our cruelty.

Our obvious scorn did nothing to improve her relationship with Father, who was trapped between two loyalties. But I truly believe (trying neither to minimize our awfulness nor to seek forgiveness for it) that the marriage would have deteriorated in any event. He and she were no longer playing the roles in which they had met and first loved each other; and, without the starched white uniform and the coarse woolen blanket, they were merely two (very) dissimilar individuals who happened to be living under the same roof. Father came from a tradition that believed that nothing but death could terminate a marriage, even a bad one; and so resigned himself to his lot. And she, I think, knew this, and so resigned herself to hers. She retreated into a sullen silence, nibbling her bonbons and lancing her needle in and out that taut circle of fabric, while her bosom, harking (as all flesh must) to the croon of gravity, slowly grew broader and less buoyant.

If there was no question of discussing the visit to Miss Lizzie with my stepmother, there was equally no question of my not making it: I had told Miss Lizzie that I would; I had given my word. And so, at a quarter to four that day I left our cottage by the back porch, slipped through the hedges at the rear of the yard, turned right, and trod across the warm sand for the distance of a half a block, past the parasols and the scurrying children and the recumbent adults. The breeze had the bite of sand to it, and tugged at my bonnet. Breakers curled and thumped and swooshed against the shore. Three houses down, I followed the path that led through some azaleas back to Water Street, turned right once more, and walked down to the Borden house.

All of this was unnecessary—my stepmother was taking her usual afternoon nap. But I possessed (and regrettably continue to possess) a fondness for intrigue and mystification.

I unlatched the gate, latched it behind me, went up the flagstone walk, up the wooden steps to the front door, and rang the bell.

Chapter
TWO

"PICK A CARD," said Miss Lizzie, peering at me over her pince-nez. With one hand, she fanned the deck of blue-backed Bicycle playing cards and held it out across the table. I leaned forward, around the teapot, over the plate of scones, and plucked one from the deck.

"Look at it carefully," she said, shuffling the deck. The cards clicked and whirred between fingers that were, despite their plumpness, remarkably nimble. "Don't let me see what it is, but you memorize it."

It was a seven of clubs. I had played gin rummy with Father and knew the names of the suits.

"Will you be able to remember it?" she asked.

"Of course," I said, pique putting an edge along my voice.

Miss Lizzie smiled. "No insult intended, Amanda." She squared the deck on the table, left it there, sat back, and said, "Right. Put the card back in the deck. Anywhere you like."

I slipped the card back into the deck about a third of the way up from the bottom, and then made quite certain, proud of my caution, that all the cards were carefully aligned.

Miss Lizzie took a sip from her teacup. She said, "Right. What we're going to do now is make that card move through the deck, and then all the way through the table so it comes out underneath."

"You mean," I said, "that it's going to go through the wooden table."

"Exactly," said Miss Lizzie, with a single crisp nod.

I was too polite to express my disbelief out loud (like most people I was rude and cruel only to those I knew well), but my expression must have revealed it.

Miss Lizzie smiled. "It takes a good deal of concentration, and you'll have to help, but I think we can pull it off. Notice, now, that there's nothing up my sleeves." She held up her hands, turned them back and forth for me to see that they were indeed empty. I nodded. She placed her left hand under the table and said to me, "All right, you press down on the deck. And concentrate." She closed her eyes.

Warily, watching her closely, I pressed my fingertips against the deck.

After a moment, Miss Lizzie opened her eyes. "Hmmm," she said. "It's not working."

I laughed.

She looked at me sternly. "*Patience*, Amanda. Here, try pressing the deck like this." She put her hand flat atop the deck in demonstration, pressed, and then sat back. "And try to concentrate more."

"I *am* concentrating." Hardly my fault if a silly playing card refused to violate the laws of nature.

"Well," she said, "try it again, then." Closing her eyes,

she reached under the table again with her left hand. "Don't forget, press *hard*."

I pressed hard, still suspicious, still eyeing her.

Suddenly she smiled, sat back, and moved her hand up above the table. "There we are," she said. She was holding the seven of clubs.

I frowned at her. It was a trick, I knew that; the card had not actually passed through the table. But I had no idea how she had worked it. "Do it again," I demanded.

And Miss Lizzie laughed.

———

I had stood there on the front porch for a few minutes before Miss Lizzie opened the door. When she did, she seemed harried, slightly out of breath and slightly out of focus. Her pince-nez was a shade askew and a few fine strands of white hair had escaped her chignon. She ran her right hand back over her scalp, smoothing them into place, exhaled elaborately with her left hand to her breast, and smiled at me. Once again, the smile transformed her face. "I'm sorry, dear, I was out back." She looked around the porch, looked back at me, raised her eyebrows. "Your friend didn't come?"

"She had a previous engagement," I explained.

"Ah," she said, smiling again. "Well, come in, come in."

She stood back to let me enter. She was wearing the same clothing she had worn earlier, or its duplicate, a full-length black dress with buttons climbing up the bodice to her neck. With more presence of mind now, I noticed that the cut of the dress was very fine, and that the material was brocaded silk. As before, she wore no jewelry and no makeup.

She led me down the hallway and through the house.

("And this," I remember saying to myself behind her, with a strange but very real sense of accomplishment, as though I were somehow responsible for her existence, "is *Lizzie Borden*.") Passing the parlor, I caught a glimpse of a dark polished mahogany coffee table, a large wall mirror, a Persian carpet, three red plush chairs, and a red plush sofa, all of them antimacassered, and the sofa supporting a very large fluffy white cat who was either fast asleep or quite dead. Everything (including the cat) looked a great deal more substantial and expensive than any of the things in our cottage next door, or, for that matter, in our house in Boston.

"I thought we'd have our tea out here," Miss Lizzie said as we reached the rear porch. "There's a nice breeze today."

Like ours, her porch was enclosed with screening, but unlike ours it had at its center a square mahogany table. The table was set with enough food to feed a small battalion. There was a Wedgwood teapot, a Wedgwood platter heaped with sandwiches, a silver salver piled high with scones, a small porcelain crock of strawberry jam, another of marmalade, and a plate of brightly colored petit fours. If Miss Lizzie had prepared all this by herself, in the time since I had seen her last (and I knew, from my surveillance, that she had brought no servants with her to the shore), she had good reason to look harried.

"Sit, sit," she said, sitting down herself and directing me to the chair opposite her. "Tell me all about yourself."

"Where shall I start?" I asked. I sat down, watching her so as to learn what to do next. This was my first Afternoon Tea, and I was not entirely sure of the Rules.

She lifted the damask linen napkin from the placemat

before her, unfolded it, draped it across her lap. I did the same. "Well," she said, "tell me where you'd like to be ten years from now."

"In an airplane," I said.

"An airplane?" She smiled.

I nodded. "I want to be a flyer."

"An aviatrix." She nodded. This was the first time I had heard the word, which would not, and then only because of the remarkable Miss Earhart, come into common usage until the next decade. Pouring tea into my cup, she said, "Would you be carrying the mail?"

"Passengers," I said. "Father says that one day airplanes will carry more passengers than the railroads do."

"Cream or lemon?" she asked me.

"Which one are you having?"

"I'm having cream."

"I'll have cream too. He says that one day it'll be possible to go from New York to California in a single day."

"I'm sure he's right," she said, "but whyever would one want to?"

Caught off guard for a moment—why indeed?—I frowned. "Well," I said finally, "they might be in a hurry."

"No, dear, I meant why would anyone want to go to California at all. From everything I've read, it's a dreadful place. All cowboys and oranges. Sugar?"

"Yes, please. He says they'll cross the Atlantic too. People will be able to fly from New York to London and Paris."

"Now that *would* be nice," she said. "I'd love to see Paris again."

"You've been there, you mean?" This summer's trip to the shore had been my farthest journey away from Boston.

She waved a hand dismissively. "A lifetime ago."

Somehow I knew immediately that, despite her easy dismissal, the trip to Paris was something about which she would enjoy talking. Certainly it was something I would enjoy hearing. "What was it like?"

"It was," she said, and smiled, "very French."

We talked for over an hour, sipping at our tea and nibbling at the sandwiches (cream cheese and watercress, the bread crusts neatly manicured away), and she told me about Paris, about strolling down the sun-dappled Champs-Elysées and sitting at a sidewalk café and talking, through a drunken and probably unreliable interpreter, to a bearded red-haired painter from Holland who reeked of absinthe and despair. Miss Lizzie had expressed, in passing, a liking for the work of Constable; the painter, furious, indignant, had leaped from his chair, knocking it over in the process. In a few raging moments he had dashed off a sketch of her, torn it from his notebook, and hurled it spinning to the table. Then, scowling and mumbling, his arms conducting an invisible orchestra, he had staggered off toward the river. As a memento of her Grand Tour, she said, she had kept the sketch with her ever since.

She left the porch to fetch it, returned with it in a small but elegantly wrought silver frame. The hair was darker and fuller; and the smile, slightly bemused by the antics of this mad Dutchman, seemed more an integral part of the younger face than, as it was to the older, a pleasant afterthought. But she was recognizable, this other Miss Lizzie; the artist had gotten the large gray expectant eyes exactly right. He had been a talented man: despite the manic swiftness of the pencil he had captured a quality that was at once innocent and mischievous. Down in the right-hand corner he had scrawled his name and underlined it with a flourish that had nearly rent the paper: *Vincent*.

We were eating the scones, and very good they were too with the Irish marmalade and the English jam, when all at once Miss Lizzie leaned forward and asked me, "Do you like card tricks, Amanda?"

I had never once seen a card trick. I said, "Of course."

She smiled, sat back, reached into the side pocket of her dress, and pulled out a deck of playing cards. With a practiced thumbnail she split the cellophane wrapper, flicked open the package. She adjusted her pince-nez, shook out the deck, held it up, riffled it with her thumb so that I could see the cards' faces and know that the deck was normal, then fanned it with one hand and held it out to me. "Pick a card," she said.

———

"Do it again," I said.

Miss Lizzie laughed. "A magician should never repeat a trick, Amanda."

"But how'd you *do* it?" I felt stupid and clumsy. Everyone said I was smart, I *knew* I was smart, and yet here, now, something had happened that I could not explain.

She shrugged, smiling slyly. "Just magic, I suppose."

"One more time?" I pleaded. I could hear the whine in my voice, and I hated it; and so, deliberately, calmly, I added, "I'd be very grateful."

"All right," she said, nodding. "Once more. But only once." She fanned the deck once again, held it out across the table. "Pick one."

I did. It was the six of hearts. Hawklike, I watched her shuffle the cards. So far as I could see, she used, but more smoothly and quickly, the same shuffle Father used when we played together.

She set the deck on the table and said, "Right. Put the card back in."

I did so, making certain, as I had last time, that the edges of all the cards were aligned.

"Right," she said. "Now press on them. And remember, *concentrate*."

Frowning, I pressed on the cards as Miss Lizzie moved her left hand beneath the table.

After a moment she shook her head. "Here, Amanda, remember? Press on the cards like this. . . ."

She was moving her right hand to the deck when suddenly I called out, "*Wait a minute!*"

Her hand stopped in midair and I slapped my own hand down upon the deck and shouted, "You did that the last time!" Quickly, before she could stop me, I flipped over the top card of the deck.

The six of hearts.

But she had not touched the deck since I had returned the card to it. . . .

I looked up at her. She was watching me intently, eyes narrowed and a smile growing.

I said, suddenly understanding, "There's more than one of them."

With an explosive laugh, almost a bark, Miss Lizzie rocked back in her chair and clapped her hands together, delighted.

I picked up the deck, turned it over, examined the cards. Immediately I saw that this was not a standard deck.

This particular deck, as Miss Lizzie told me later, is called the Mene Tekel deck. Magic supply houses sold it (and still do), but you can make one yourself easily enough by selecting twenty-six identical pairs of cards from two separate decks, and shortening one card of each pair by shaving from it about a sixteenth of an inch. Arrange all fifty-two cards so that the short card is the top card of each pair. Now, wherever the pack is cut, the cut will always be made at one of the ordinary cards, and its duplicate will lie directly above it. When the deck is riffled, only the long cards appear, and the deck seems perfectly normal.

When I selected the seven of clubs, Miss Lizzie, knowing that the card above it was identical, brought that card to the top of the deck and kept it there with a series of false shuffles. Then, under the pretext of demonstrating the proper way for me to handle the deck, she palmed the second seven and dropped it into her lap. It was from there that she produced it after it had "passed through" the table.

I explain how this trick was performed because it was the first such trick I had ever seen. It will also be the last such trick I shall explain. Over the years I have learned that most people do not want to learn how a magic trick is accomplished. They may say they do, may even believe they do; but almost invariably, when they do learn, they are disappointed. They know that they have been deceived (part of the pleasure of magic—and this is true of few other human activities—lies in the *certainty* that one is being deceived), but they wish for the deception to be something more than sleights of hand and gimmicked props. They wish for it to be less simple, less pedestrian; they wish for it to be truly magical.

But to me, to the girl I once was and whom, alas, I still carry about with me, the simplicity of the trick *was* truly magical.

I asked Miss Lizzie if she would show me another.

Smiling, she told me to wait a moment, and she left the porch.

When she returned she was carrying a flat, dark, wooden box. Sitting down opposite me again, she set it on the table. "Do you mind if I smoke?" she asked me.

"No," I said. More and more now, one saw women smoking cigarettes in public, something that would, before the War, have been unthinkable.

Miss Lizzie lifted the lid of the box, took out another pack of cards, a small silver penknife, and a long black panatela. She put the cards down on the table and opened the knife. She cut off the panatela's tip, put the cigar in her mouth, took a kitchen match from the box, struck it cowboy-fashion on her thumb, let it flare for a moment, then held it to the cigar. She puffed for a moment, getting the thing going, then sat back and blew a cone of blue smoke off toward the screen, toward the sky and the sea. She sighed happily and looked down at the cigar in her hand with something like admiration. "It's a terrible habit," she said, shaking her head, "but I don't know what I'd do without it."

I nodded. I was astounded.

Leaning forward, she stabbed the cigar into the corner of her mouth. "Well now," she said, picking up the deck, fanning it, holding it out to me. "Pick a card."

———

Throughout that June and July I spent a part of nearly every weekday afternoon learning about magic from Miss Lizzie. We would sit out on the porch at the mahogany table, the ocean breezes gently rustling our hair as she explained and demonstrated the manipulation of cards. Sometimes her big fluffy white cat—whose name was Eliot, after a former president of Harvard—would condescend to join us, lying in a chair to himself, watching us with bored green eyes.

No one, or so I thought, ever knew about these afternoons. They were, I told myself, my secret, the first real secret all my own that I had ever possessed. Once in a while on the weekends, delighted with my new knowledge, my new skills, I almost told Father. Yet always I hesitated, telling myself that I would lose the secret. And, of course, without really admitting it to myself, I was afraid that he would not approve of his daughter's learning magic. Looking back on it now with hindsight's wisdom, I know he would not have disapproved, and I wish I had told him. If I had, perhaps things would have happened differently. But hindsight also teaches us, as Miss Lizzie once said, that there are no *ifs* in this world, that we cannot remake history. And, given the individual characters of the people involved, perhaps there was nothing I could have done to alter what was about to happen.

But I did learn magic. Every afternoon on Miss Lizzie's porch, she taught me something new. I learned about the Svengali deck, the marked deck, the stripper deck. I learned how to crimp a card, how to slick one with paraffin, how to make one sticky with diachylon. We spent a week on sleights: the false shuffle, the false cut, the glide, the jog, the palm. I learned how to deal seconds and bottoms; although I was never able, as Miss Lizzie was, to deal middles.

Few people were; few are. Since that summer I have met hundreds of card handlers, amateur and professional, and I think that of all of them only a handful begin to approach her level of expertise, and only one, John Scarne, might be said to have matched it.

Skill of that caliber requires an enormous amount of time to develop, and it was not until much later that I realized that Miss Lizzie had had that time precisely because she was Miss Lizzie; because she had lived, since the death of her parents, most of her adult life by herself. And it was only then that I understood that the skill might signify (by its practice having been used to avoid) a terrible lifelong loneliness.

But at the time, as we sat out on the porch, the cards before us, pale blue cigar smoke curling across the table, it did sometimes occur to me that, whether or not she was responsible for their deaths (and I could not then believe that she was), this woman had seen the battered and bloody bodies of her father and her mother. How had she felt then? How did she feel now? Was it something from which you ever truly recovered?

I was to learn the answers to some of these questions soon, for in August, with the awful heat, came the first of the murders.

Chapter
THREE

IN THE THIRTIES, before World War II, my second husband and I lived for a while off the coast of Kenya on an island called Lamu. It was a beautiful place of palm trees and acacias and of sand dunes over two hundred feet tall parading back from a beach five miles long. For most of the year, the weather was perfect; the breeze off the Indian Ocean was so constant and firm that you could very nearly lean against it, like a wall. But just before the rainy season, sometimes a month before, sometimes less, the breeze would disappear, and from then until the rains finally arrived you knew that you were living within a hundred miles of the equator. The sunlight had a weight to it, oppressive, relentless, and the air took on substance, thickness; you could feel it slide apart to let you pass, and then close almost audibly behind you, like a jelly as the knife withdrew. In all my life this was the only weather that approached, in intensity and unpleasantness, the heat of that first week in August at the shore.

The wind that week, as it would do some fifteen years later in Lamu, simply died away. The sun hammered down upon the sand and the flat glaring silver sea, and unless you were actually bathing, the beach was unbearable: you could not walk across it, even in leather boots. In the town, everything seemed to stop. The streets were empty, their tar surface soft and spotted with shiny bubbles; the shops were shuttered. It was a time of long naps and short tempers.

On Tuesday morning, the second day of August, after a night of shallow sleep punctuated by breathless awakenings, I woke for the last time at eight o'clock.

I lay there for a while on the damp sheets, my hair pasted to my forehead, my skin oily with sweat. The air was still, the curtains at the open window limp. The room smelled of dampness and mold. I did not want to leave the bed, I did not want to move.

But finally I rolled over and pushed myself off the mattress, stood and peeled away my sodden nightgown. I sponged myself down at the wash basin; for an instant, the lukewarm water against my skin provided an illusion of coolness. I toweled myself dry, slipped into a chemise, brushed my hair at the dressing table, and then found a dress in the closet, a cotton wrapper, shapeless but offering in this heat at least the hope of comfort.

Downstairs the house smelled of last night's cabbage. My stepmother was in the kitchen, sitting at the breakfast table with Mrs. Mortimer, her neighborhood confidante.

"Morning," I said, nodding to them both.

My stepmother nodded curtly back and took a bite of

toast. She wore her gray cotton housecoat, its loose sleeves rolled up along her fleshy arms.

Mrs. Mortimer, tall, brittle, birdlike, was wearing a navy blue frock printed with tiny red fleurs-de-lis. She smiled at me, blinking rapidly. "Hello, Amanda. And how are *you* this morning?" Childless herself, she was one of those women who spoke to children as though they were advanced housepets.

"Hot," I said, "and awfully sweaty. How are you, Mrs. Mortimer?"

"Very well, thank you." She bobbed her head.

Strictly speaking, as the wife of the local tavernkeeper, Mrs. Mortimer was not my stepmother's social equal; particularly not now, with the tavern, in this first year of prohibition, being operated illegally. But, strictly speaking, my stepmother had no social equals: She saw the world as divided into those above her—the very rich—and those beneath her—everyone else. What Mrs. Mortimer lacked in refinement she made up in subservience and availability.

"Horses sweat," my stepmother announced, "and men perspire, but women glow."

"Well, in that case," said I, spiteful child, "I'm glowing like a pig."

Mrs. Mortimer tittered.

I walked over to the stove and lifted the lid off the pot sitting there. Oatmeal. Again.

"Don't encourage her, Esther," my stepmother said. "Amanda, why do you insist upon being disgusting?"

Obviously it was not a question that could be answered without starting a fight. I took a bowl from the cupboard and scooped into it some of the glutinous oatmeal. "Has William come down yet?" I asked.

"No," said my stepmother. "And if he doesn't get himself down here soon I'm going to go upstairs and pin his ears back."

I was careful not to snort: William, over six feet tall and weighing nearly two hundred pounds, was an unlikely prospect for ear pinning.

I opened the icebox door, lifted out a bottle of milk, pried off the cardboard cap, started to pour some over the oatmeal—

"Shake the bottle first," said my stepmother.

"But I *like* the cream," I said. This was in the days before homogenization, and at the top of the bottle there was always a small sweet conic section of cream.

"*You* like, *you* like. Don't you ever think about anybody but yourself?" She wanted the cream, of course, for her coffee.

Sighing, I put the cap back on and shook the bottle. I took the cap off again, poured the milk over the oatmeal, put the cap on once more and returned the bottle to the icebox. I carried the bowl to the table and sat down opposite my stepmother, with Mrs. Mortimer to my right.

Mrs. Mortimer asked me brightly, "Are you having a nice summer, Amanda?"

"I was until it got so hot." I spooned sugar over the oatmeal. "How is Mr. Mortimer?"

She bobbed her head again. "Very well, thank you."

"Can I have some coffee?" I asked my stepmother.

"*May* I have some coffee."

"*May* I have some coffee?"

"No," she said, "you may not." Her face was expressionless; one of the differences between adults and children is that adults do not admit the pleasure they derive from petty triumphs. "If your father wants to let you have coffee on Sunday," she said, "that's his business.

He knows I don't approve. But as long as it's my responsibility, I refuse to damage your health. It's a medical fact that caffeine can stunt your growth. Look at your brother."

"But William never *drank* coffee."

She nodded, smug. "Exactly."

A sudden loud clatter at the front of the house told us that William himself was hurtling down the stairs. A few seconds later he came rushing into the room, dressed all in dazzling white—shirt, slacks, shoes. His black hair slicked back with brilliantine, his smile agleam, he looked (to a sister at any rate) like a younger, taller version of Douglas Fairbanks. "Sorry, folks," he said. "Can't stay. Hi, Mrs. Mortimer. Gotta run over to Andy's. We're taking his jalopy up the coast for a picnic."

"Sit down for a minute, William," said my stepmother.

"Gee, Audrey, I can't, I haven't got—"

"You sit down," she said, and her mouth was grim, "or you'll regret it."

She had never spoken to either of us that way before. William looked at me, puzzled; as surprised as he, I shrugged and shook my head.

He winced with impatience, then lifted one of the wooden chairs, spun it around, and sat down on it next to me, his arms folded along the chair's back. "Okay. What is it?"

She looked from William to me. "The two of you think you're very clever, don't you?"

William looked at me, I looked at him. He grinned and said to her, "Well, Audrey, I guess we do."

"You two have had things your way for a long time now. Daddy's little darlings. Daddy's little angels. Well, I know a thing or two about you, about both of you, that Daddy *doesn't* know."

Mrs. Mortimer cleared her throat. "I really ought to go now, Audrey. I've got so much—"

"You stay there, Esther. I want you to see what a wonderful pair of brats I've got here."

William was still smiling, confident he could handle whatever she was about to offer.

But it was to me that she turned first. "Do you think I haven't seen you sneaking over to that awful woman's house? Do you think I don't know what you're doing?" From her housecoat pocket she pulled a pack of playing cards and slapped it onto the table. She reached in and pulled out another pack, slapped that beside the first. "How do you think your father's going to like it when he hears that you've been *gambling* with a *murderer*?"

I was so surprised at how wrong she had got it that I burst out laughing. "Gambling? That's crazy!"

At my laughter, my stepmother's face had closed like a fist. "Crazy? You think it's crazy? What're the cards for, missy? What're you doing when you sneak over there to see that woman?"

I shook my head, petulant. "I don't *sneak* over there."

"No?" Her upper lip curled with scorn. "Then why haven't you told your father about it? Why the big secret?"

Unerringly, she had located a pocket of guilt, and prodded it. I switched from defense to attack: "You took those out of my dresser. You had no right—"

"Don't you tell me about *my* rights, missy. This is *my* house and it's *my* responsibility to watch you two." She leaned forward. "They say she smokes too. Does she give you cigarettes?"

"No!"

"And they say she's not right, she's not normal. Does she touch you? Do you *let* her touch you?"

My anger had become confusion. *"What?"*

Her face was twisted. "Do you take your clothes off, do you—"

Angry, William said, "Stop it, Audrey, goddammit. Leave her alone."

"Oh no," she said, rounding on him, pointing a finger at his face. "Oh no you don't. You don't tell *me* what to do. You think I don't know about *you*? You think I haven't seen you and that cheap little Grady slut? Grabbing and groping at each other out on the lawn like *animals*?"

William flushed, his face turning bright red. I did not know (and do not, to this day) whether it was fury or embarrassment.

My stepmother's eyes were narrow slits. "Are you giving it to her yet? Are you sticking it in her? You must be, or you wouldn't need *these*." From her other pocket she pulled a small cardboard package and flipped it onto the table. Although I did not know it then, what the package held, of course, was prophylactics.

William said, "God *damn* you, Audrey."

She laughed—a hard, dry, bitter cackle. "Curse me. Go ahead, you curse me. Your father will hear about that too. He'll hear about *all* this. His little angels. His little darlings. He's going to learn what you're *really* like."

Through clenched teeth, William said, "You're a rotten bitch."

"Don't you *dare*," she said, standing up and moving around the table, toward him, "don't you *dare* call me that, you sneaky little *bastard*." Next to him now, she slapped him viciously across the face. In the tiny kitchen the sound was as loud as an explosion. I heard Mrs. Mortimer gasp. William shut his eyes and his fingers clutched at his forearms, knuckles turning white.

She hit him again. "*Bastard!* I'm not good enough for you, I was never good enough for you, I'm just fat old

Audrey, *stupid old Audrey.*" She hit him again, back-handed. *"You bastard, you bastard, you bastard."*

William stood up. He towered over her and still she hit at him. He turned and, without a word, moved toward the rear entrance to the house. She stayed close behind, hitting at him with both hands now, left, right, smacking at him. I stood up and followed them. I was afraid that William might strike back at her—strong as he was, he might have killed her. I think I believed that I could stop him.

Out on the back porch, her arms still flailing at him, he opened the screen door. He turned to her. She stepped back—suddenly afraid, perhaps, that at last he would strike back. He said, "You'll be sorry, Audrey," and then he went down the steps, closing the door behind him.

She slammed the door open and went down the steps, stopped at the bottom and called out after him: "You *bastard!*"

Without turning back, walking slowly, in no hurry, he disappeared behind the hedges. Then my stepmother turned and saw me standing there in the doorway.

For a moment, I think, she was going to hit me. Her eyes narrowed and her body tautened. But she hesitated. Perhaps she considered how Father might have reacted if he learned of it.

She took a deep breath, exhaled, and snapped at me, "Get out of my way."

I stepped back, and she tramped up the stairs and passed me.

Mrs. Mortimer was almost at the front door. My stepmother called out to her, "Esther!"

I stepped into the kitchen. Quickly, I sneaked a gulp of coffee from her cup: I would get *something* for myself, despite all this melodrama. Then I left the kitchen and ran up the back stairs to my bedroom. I locked the door behind me.

I pulled open the bottom right-hand drawer of the dresser. The two decks, a stripper deck and a marked deck, had been underneath a box of stationery. The box looked untouched. She must have come up here last night, while I was reading in the parlor. Which meant that she had probably known for some time that the cards were there. For how long?

I felt as though I had been violated. The woman had no right to go through my things, no right to take the cards.

I shut the drawer, crossed the room, flounced onto the bed. What would Father say when he learned that I had been going over to Miss Lizzie's nearly every day?

I heard the front door shut, heard my stepmother moving around downstairs. She was alone.

From the bottom of the stairs she called out my name. I did not answer. For a few moments I was afraid that she would come upstairs; but she did not.

What was it that William had done with Marge Grady? What was it that Marge had done that made her a slut? And what was in the package that my stepmother had thrown to the table? What did it have to do with him "sticking it in her"? What had my stepmother meant by that? And why had the woman been so incensed?

It was as though all these questions were too much for me. After a while, lying there, I fell asleep.

———

I awoke out of a dream, one I can no longer remember. But it had been one of those dreams—we all have them, I think—which seem so foreign that they might have been dreamed by someone else, with us acting only as a means, a medium. And, because shreds and wisps of the other still cling to the wisps and shreds of ourselves, we are appalled and frightened at how frail a thing our personalities, our identities, truly are. (After we regain ourselves, of course, we forget the truth and dream, once again, that we are immutable.)

I looked at the clock on the nightstand. Twelve-fifteen. I had slept for almost two hours.

I sponged my face again at the washbasin, then went downstairs to find my stepmother. I knew that I had not gambled, had never gambled, and I wanted my cards back.

Usually at this time my stepmother would be in the parlor, doing needlepoint, or up in the guest room taking a nap.

The parlor was empty.

I climbed up the front stairs to the guest room. Its door was at the top of the landing, opposite the door to William's room.

In the air was the smell of lilacs—my stepmother's favorite scent—and it was mingled with another smell, this one heavier, metallic, vaguely remembered but for the moment unidentifiable.

The guest-room door was open and she was lying on the bed.

The eye can see, and the mind understand, only what they already know. (This is of course the principle upon which magic is worked.) Confronted with a thing which is new, a thing which is impossible, they will perceive it as something else, something with which they are familiar.

And so at first I thought, absurdly, that the thin dark striping that covered her heavy body was a piece of netting, of the kind the local fishermen used, and I wondered what she was doing with it. And then I saw that her face was quite literally falling apart. Her forehead was sliced open, pink brain showing through the bloody rent, and a flap of skin hung loose from her cheek, exposing the white bone of her skull. Her left eye was gone and her right stared sightlessly upward. And I saw that the striping that covered her was, in fact, her own blood, and that it was everywhere, the walls, the ceiling, the bed. The pillow beneath her head was black with it, soaked through, and this was the smell that hung in the air behind the smell of lilacs, the stench of blood, and, backing out of the room, I could no longer breathe that thick dreadful coppery reek, my throat had closed against it.

I tottered down the stairs and unbolted the front door and went reeling from the house. Numb, my vision narrowed to see only what lay directly before me, I staggered across the lawn, seeking out the one person nearby who might help me. Seeking out Miss Lizzie.

Book
TWO

Chapter
FOUR

MY RECOLLECTION OF the next few hours is a jumble of images, some so clearly defined that the outlines of things, of people, of furniture, of the everyday realities of matter, seem sliver-edged, sharp enough to slice open flesh; others so dim and gray that they might have been seen from afar, through a window rimed with frost. Time, during this period, no longer moved in sedate measured intervals; it lurched and wobbled, leaped and stumbled; occasionally it altogether stopped.

I remember Miss Lizzie standing at her doorway in the white glare of sunlight, her mourning dress as black and starched as a nun's habit. I remember her wide smile of greeting fading away as her large gray eyes widened in concern. "Amanda?" she said, and in her voice was an uncertainty like that with which we greet long-ago friends now barely recognized. And then, more insistent: "Amanda, *what is it?*"

"Dead," I said, the words uttered by some other, distant, self. "The blood. Everywhere."

There was no slow dawning of comprehension; there was not even an instant of bafflement or disbelief. Her eyelids shut and she rocked back as though slapped. She must have wished desperately, I believe, to flee this stricken creature on her doorstep and the horrors that all at once she represented. But she opened her eyes, took a deep breath, firmed her mouth, and reached forward to touch me, her fingers steady, and steadying, along my upper arm. "Who, Amanda?" she said softly. "Where?"

"Upstairs," I said. "Mother." This was the first time in my life, and it was to be the last, that I called the woman by that name.

Miss Lizzie took another deep sharp breath, almost a hiss, and then her plump arm encircled my shoulder, pulling me toward her. "Come in. Come in, dear." She led me into the parlor. As I shuffled along, legs weak, feet heavy, I felt the palm of her hand against my forehead, and her skin seemed neither warm nor cool; I had lost the ability—had lost the desire—to distinguish between sensations.

"You're freezing, child," she said.

And so I was. Despite the viscid August heat that hung about me, I moved within an envelope of dense, impenetrable cold. My teeth, I noticed, were clattering.

"Here," she said when we reached the red plush sofa. "You sit down, child, and I'll—"

"*No!*" I cried, and hurled myself into her, clutched at her. Beneath my grappling fingers I felt the stiff whalebone stays of her corset, against my face I felt the swell of her breast and smelled the scent of her, of oranges and cinnamon and cloves. She was warmth and substance, softness and strength; she was real. She was alive.

"Amanda," she said gently, after a moment; gently she stroked my hair. "Amanda. Amanda, child."

For a long while—I cannot say for how long—she held me, crooning my name as her hand caressed the nape of my neck. I wanted nothing more, forever; and nothing less.

At last I felt her body gathering itself, stiffening, as though preparing for some enormous effort. She put her hands along my arms. "Amanda, you must be very brave now, and very strong. I want you to sit down on the sofa while I fetch you a wrap."

I made a weak protesting sound and shook my head against her.

"Hush," she said quietly. "Hush now." Slowly but steadily she eased me away. Her gray eyes stared unblinking into mine, and possibly for the first time I recognized the intensity of purpose she possessed; her will, beneath the kindliness, was almost palpable. "You're in shock, child," she said, "and there are things that must be done. Be brave now, Amanda. Can you do that for me?"

Mutely, helplessly, I nodded.

She nodded back, once, crisply. "I know you can. Everything will be all right, I'll see to it, Amanda. I promise you. You sit down now."

I sat, boneless and slack, my hands limp atop my lap. And then, with a whisper of petticoats, Miss Lizzie was gone.

All around me, slowly, inexorably, like falling snow, the chill began to deepen.

———

. . . from very far away across the Persian carpet, the cat lay upon the red plush armchair and, broad white head poised above fat white paws, regarded me with green eyes as round and blank as stones.

———

. . . a softness unfolding at my neck and shoulders and Miss Lizzie's face before me as she tucked the afghan round my body, draped it down my knees. She held a bubble-shaped glass half-filled with brown liquid to my lips. "Brandy," she said. "Drink it, child."

I sipped at it. Bitter, and it burned.

"More," she urged.

I took another small swallow, felt it glide fiery down my core, go glowing out along my being. And, stubbornly, I resented it, hated it, for its invasion of my numbness. When she offered the glass again, I shook my head. To this day, despite having tried to do so, even while surrounded by friendship and love, I cannot abide the taste or smell of brandy.

Miss Lizzie stood, looked down at the glass, then raised it to her lips and drained it. She said, "I'll return in a moment.

———

. . . suddenly, and lit so garishly that it might have been sprawled beneath a photographer's flash, the scene in the guest room returned to me, and I saw again the gore-splashed walls, the stains and spatters, that awful *thing* of meat and bone sprawled along the bed, hacked and smashed and battered. The obscene white glimmer of bone, the black thickening sheen of blood.

My mind wrenched itself away, spun back, and I toppled into the safety of my solitary, empty Winter.

———

. . . Miss Lizzie again, striding across the carpet to her telephone, one of the few of these luxuries possessed by summer boarders. She looked older and paler and somehow thinner, as though her body had compacted itself against her frame. Before lifting the earpiece, she glanced at me. I could not tell, from within my stupor, what was in that glance, whether pity or compassion or horror. Perhaps all of them; perhaps none. I realized only later that she had gone Up There, into the guest room next door, and seen what I had seen.

She looked away. For a moment she stood with her hand atop the telephone, resting upon it, leaning her weight upon it. Then, abruptly, she lifted the receiver, waited for the operator, and then asked for a number in Boston.

I was staring at the floral pattern in the Persian carpet. I heard her give her name, "Miss Lizbeth A. Borden." From then on, I heard fragments only as I drifted up to and then below the surface of my Chill. "Someone here in town . . . The best, you say?" Then, explosively: "Of course not, don't be daft." I heard her mention Father's name, and the brokerage firm for which he worked. "Who was the doctor again? . . . Yes. . . . Yes, *immediately*, do you understand? . . . At my cottage, yes. . . . Good-bye."

She seated the receiver in its cradle, momentarily rested upon it once more, then lifted it again. She asked the operator for a Dr. Bowen.

I heard: ". . . Shock, yes. . . . As soon as possible, if you don't mind. . . . Miss Lizbeth A. Borden . . . One-

Oh-Two Water Street. . . . Borden. . . . Miss *Lizbeth* A. *Borden* . . ." Snappishly: "Are you there, you silly girl?" Somewhat mollified: "Yes, I shall be most grateful." She slammed the phone into the cradle and spat out: "*Idiot.*"

She stood there for a moment, breathing raggedly. I stared at the carpet.

"Only one more," she said.

I looked up sluggishly, saw that she was speaking to me. I nodded even as I wondered what she meant.

She lifted the telephone, waited again, and then asked for the police. A pause. Then: "This is Miss Lizbeth A. Borden. I should like to report a murder."

———

. . . Miss Lizzie sitting beside me, unspeaking, her left arm along the sofa's back, behind my head. I could smell her comforting sachet smell of citrus and spice; but, beneath my Snow, I was having no more of comfort now.

———

. . . a rap of heavy knuckles at the front door, a sound that in the stillness of the house came as a jolt, sudden and peremptory. Miss Lizzie touched me once, lightly, upon the shoulder; and then, with another rustling sigh of petticoats, moved away.

———

. . . the door opening, a voice other than Miss Lizzie's, heavy-timbered, hard, Irish, determinedly masculine. Miss Lizzie's voice, hushed. Another male voice, softer than the first, placating. The first voice again, harsh, aggressive. Miss Lizzie's voice, temporarily overriding his, growing gradually louder in protest. The second male voice interrupting hers, polite and deferential, but very firm. Miss Lizzie, tired and resigned.

Footsteps thumping on the carpet.

———

. . . a blue uniform, the slacks neatly pressed, the black shoes carefully polished. I saw that the sole of the shoe on the right had a notch in it, as though a small wedge of leather had been nicked away by a knife. The man squatted onto his heels before me, his cap held in both hands, his elbows braced against his knees. "Hello, sweetheart," he said softly.

In his early thirties, he had a tanned face and closely cropped blond hair parted on the left. His eyebrows were also blond, and so was his mustache, which ended exactly at the well-defined creases—smile lines, Father always called them—that curled down from a slightly aquiline nose and bracketed a finely shaped mouth. What saved the face from being entirely *too* handsome was a tiny raised round mole, chocolate brown, lying at the curve of one chiseled cheekbone. Still, it was an extremely good-looking face, a face that one would be most gratified to see smiling stalwartly down as its owner, with a single deft sweep of his pocket blade, sheered the coils that bound one to the cold train tracks, already humming now to the vibration of the fast-approaching and relentless 9:05.

The owner of the face said to me, "My name is Officer Medley." Then, as though embarrassed by the formality, he grinned. Sheepishly, engagingly, charmingly. "But you can call me Tom. Most folk do, hereabouts. What's *your* name, sweetheart?"

I looked at Miss Lizzie, who stood off to one side, her hands folded Mandarin style into the loose sleeves of her black dress. Her lips were set in a thin suspicious line. Older and wiser, she was no doubt less susceptible to the allure of looks and charm; and perhaps especially, given her background, when they were being demonstrated by a representative of the Law. But, fractionally, she nodded.

I looked back at Officer Medley. "Amanda," I said. My voice still sounded distant, alien; but, warming to the man, I could feel myself begin, slowly, to rise up from the depths into which I had tumbled.

He nodded, smiling. "And your last name is Burton," he said, "and you're from Boston. Isn't that right?"

I nodded. "But how did you know?"

He smiled his stalwart smile. "We're supposed to know stuff like that, it's all part of our job. Boston, eh? It's a lovely city, even for such a great big place. I've been there many times myself. Sometimes I'll sit at one of the benches along the grass and watch the boats go sculling up the Charles. Did you ever do that, Amanda?"

I nodded. "With Father."

"That would be Mr. Burton, the stockbroker."

I nodded.

"And I suppose he'd be back in Boston now? For the week, that is?"

I nodded.

"Well," he said, and tapped me gently on the knee, "we'll be in touch with him directly, sweetheart, and I know he'll be here as soon as he can."

Miss Lizzie said stiffly, "I have already made arrangements to apprise Mr. Burton of the situation."

Officer Medley looked at her and smiled his charming smile. "Very good, ma'am. Thank you. That was considerate of you."

Miss Lizzie gave him a curt nod.

He turned back to me and thoughtfully pursed his lips. "Now, Amanda," he said, "I know you're upset right now, and believe me, I feel very bad for you. But I understand there's been a terrible accident next door, at your house, and it's also part of my job to ask you some questions about it. Do you think that'd be all right?"

I said, "No accident."

He nodded, his handsome face serious. "Of course not, sweetheart. Your mother?"

I shook my head. "Stepmother."

"Do you have any idea, Amanda, who might've done this thing?"

I shook my head.

He nodded. "I wonder if you saw anyone about the house today, on the lawn or in the street, who was acting strangely-like?"

Again, I shook my head.

"And you were where, yourself, this morning, Amanda?"

"Upstairs. Sleeping. The heat."

He nodded. "Didn't you have breakfast, then?"

"Earlier."

"And your stepmother ate with you?"

"Yes."

"And when might this've been?"

I was about to answer when suddenly more footsteps, heavy and hurried, came pounding on the carpet, and then another policeman, cap still perched atop his head, exploded into the parlor. Shorter than Officer Medley, he was a heavyset man in his late forties with a round shining face and a bulbous nose. His skin would normally (I later learned) be florid with the ruptured veins and shattered capillaries of the valiant drinker, but now only two spots of color were visible, bright red splotches, clownlike, against the pallor of his face. His clothes were considerably less dapper than Officer Medley's, and considerably less well fitting: the circumference of his shirt, in particular, lagged several inches behind his girth, and a button had popped undone at his belly to reveal a diamond-shaped expanse of taut white undershirt.

"Jesus-Mary-and-Joseph, Tommy!" he cried in a horrified brogue, his eyes wild. "You should see what the evil bastards *done* to her! Blood all over, *buckets* of the stuff!"

"Frank," said Officer Medley, slowly, patiently, but with a rising note of warning in his voice that even I could hear.

The other policeman, however, was too appalled, and too excited, to listen. "Like a slaughterhouse it was! My God, Tommy, I've never seen the like, never in me life! They hacked her up like an old *heifer*, bones pokin' through and brains spillin' out across the *bedsheets!*"

In a rush, everything came hurtling back to me—the walls, the bed, the gore, the mutilated human wreckage that had been my stepmother—and, with a gasp, I drew up my knees, wrapped my arms around them, and dug my face into the afghan, my entire body clenched as tightly as a fist.

I sensed, more than heard, Officer Medley spring from his crouch. "God *damn* it, Frank!"

Almost simultaneously from Miss Lizzie: "You clod, you *oaf*! You insensitive *cretin*! How *dare* you?"

"Now hold on there just a minute, lady," said the second oficer. Nothing brings a policeman to his senses, reminds him of his significant position within an ordered society, more swiftly than a reproach of any sort from a civilian.

But Miss Lizzie overrode him: "Don't you *dare* tell me

what to do, you insufferable lout. This girl has had a dreadful shock, and you come blundering in here like some comic opera *buffoon*. It will not do, it will not do at all. I'll thank you to leave my house at once."

"Listen, lady, you don't seem to understand who it is, exactly, you're talkin' to." And then, growing heated as he fully appreciated the intolerable indecency of it: "I'm the *police*, lady, the *police*, and there's been a horrible murder committed here, and if anyone's to be doin' any orderin' around, it'll be *me* that does it!"

"*Frank*," said Officer Medley. "Let it go."

"Did ya *hear* her, Tommy? Orderin' me about like a bloody drill sergeant? I'll have none of that from her, by God, not when likely she's the one herself that did the old lady in."

"Frank—" said Officer Medley.

"Bloody, Miss Lizzie *Borden*, and *bloody's* the name of the game all right, where Miss Lizzie *Borden* is involved."

"I think," said Miss Lizzie, and her voice was chill, "that we have had quite enough of this. I am entirely aware of my rights, and of the child's. A lawyer will be here presently, and I feel constrained to warn you that I shall be—"

"A bloody *lawyer*, is it now!"

"Damn it, Frank!"

"—shall be discussing with him not only the legal means requisite to protecting the interests of the child, but also such matters as harassment and, of course, slander."

"Slander! *Slander*, is it? Tommy, the whole *world* knows she whacked her ma and pa!"

"*Jesus*, Frank."

"Unless you propose to make an arrest," said Miss Lizzie, "I must ask you—" She broke off for a moment abruptly, and then said in a tone that was, if possible, even more chilled, "And *who*, might I ask, are *you*?"

"Da Silva," said a voice, an altogether new voice. "The chief of police." And the voice was so commanding, it seemed to resonate with such absolute authority, that even Miss Lizzie was for the moment speechless.

I looked up from the afghan. Miss Lizzie, Officer Medley, and the officer called Frank were all staring toward the parlor door. I turned.

The man who stood there was not exceedingly tall, perhaps a shade below six feet in height, but he seemed much taller because he held his body in a posture so stiffly upright that he might have been a Doric column. Beneath short curly black hair threaded with gray were two thick black eyebrows; and, beneath these, eyes of a color so dark that they too seemed black. A hawklike nose thrust out above broad sensual mouth. The dark face was square and hard, as though it had been sculpted from a single block of granite, a visage of flat planes and sharp angles. He had no mustache; the sculptor had not, perhaps, dared attempt one.

He was, I would have said, in his mid-fifties; but he seemed immensely fit: broad shoulders, broad and muscular chest, a stomach as flat as a slab of marble. He wore civilian clothes—black shoes, black trousers, white shirt, black tie—but he wore them as a military officer might, starched and pressed, all the creases razor sharp. One expected, almost, to see a swagger stick wedged beneath his arm.

It would have been wedged, of necessity, beneath his right arm—for he had no left. The left sleeve was neatly folded back and pinned to itself just above the spot where his elbow should have been.

If you browse through any popular magazine of those

years following World War I, you will discover countless advertisements for ingenious and "undetectable" prosthetic devices: hands, arms, feet, legs. Before antibiotics and microsurgery, infection was almost invariably lethal, amputation a commonplace. And as a nation we had left more than the dead behind us at the Somme, the Marne, the Argonne.

But in the case of the man before us, one felt that for him a missing arm, particularly his own, was a thing to be noted and then totally ignored. One felt that he knew he could accomplish more with one arm than any other man might attempt with two.

He made a small formal nod toward Miss Lizzie and then turned to Officer Medley. "Medley," he said. "Report."

Unconsciously or not, Officer Medley had drawn himself up into something like a position of military attention. "The station received a notification from Miss Borden"—he indicated her with a nod—"that a murder had been committed at One Hundred Water Street and that a relation of the deceased was present at this cottage. Patrolman O'Hara and I were dispatched. I sent Officer O'Hara to investigate the murder scene while I attempted to interview young Miss Burton here, the stepdaughter of the deceased."

"Alleged deceased," said Da Silva. "Have you viewed the murder scene?"

"No, sir. Officer O'Hara has."

Da Silva turned to the other policeman and frowned. It was a flicker of movement only, cold and hard but quickly gone. "O'Hara," he said. "Your uniform is unkempt."

"Sir?" said Officer O'Hara, who also stood at attention. Looking down, he spied the loose button. Sucking in his paunch, he promptly fumbled it back into place. He looked up again. *"Sir."*

Da Silva said, "You visited the murder scene?"

"Yes, *sir.*"

"Report."

O'Hara's military bearing deserted him. His stomach collapsed against his shirt and he shook his head heavily. "Oh, sir, it was horrible, sir, *horrible*. Blood all over and bits of her scattered about, *horrible*, sir. Like someone had gone at her with a cleaver or"—he glanced quickly at Miss Lizzie, glanced away—"or with an axe, like. Sir."

Da Silva nodded. He turned to Miss Lizzie and for a moment stood appraising her. Then he smiled. His smile was as restricted and as cold as his frown. "So," he said. "Been up to our old tricks again, have we, Lizzie?"

Miss Lizzie was, in her turn, appraising him, peering at him intently. Now, puzzlement in her voice, she ignored the familiarity of his tone and said, "Do I know you?"

Still smiling his small cold smile, Da Silva nodded. "You did once. A long time ago. I was a patrolman then. The one who examined the loft in your barn."

"Da Silva," said Miss Lizzie, and her voice went flat. "The Portuguese."

Chapter
FIVE

SUDDENLY WE HAD become transformed, all of us, no one actually willing it, into antagonists and audience. The two of them stood watching each other, neither speaking, Da Silva smiling that faint smile which had no warmth to it, Miss Lizzie expressionless. Silent, the rest of us watched them. Someone, probably, sooner or later would have said something; although I cannot imagine who, or what. But then, all at once (and it came as a kind of deliverance) we heard voices at the entryway and a rapping at the front door, still open, presumably, after Officer O'Hara's appearance.

Without taking his eyes off Miss Lizzie, Da Silva flicked his head toward the entryway. "Get that, Medley."

Miss Lizzie said, "This is *my* house." She drew herself up as tall as her stocky body would allow, and I was reminded of photographs I had seen of the British queen, Victoria. "And *my* door. If anyone is to answer it, it will be I."

Da Silva, his smile unchanged, made another small formal bow. "As you wish."

No one spoke as she left.

Swiveled slightly on the sofa, I stared at the chief of police. He must have felt my scrutiny: his glance darted toward me, and he stared back. In his eyes, dark as obsidian, I could read neither fondness nor dislike, neither concern nor malice nor curiosity, no emotion at all.

Miss Lizzie returned, followed by two men.

One of them, I knew instantly, was the doctor. A short tubby man in a rumpled black suit, a few sparse white hairs lacquered over his gleaming pink scalp, he carried a battered squat leather satchel in his right hand. His eyes blinking rapidly behind thick horn-rimmed glasses, he was chattering away to Miss Lizzie: ". . . quite a coup for me, you know, half the town dying all summer for a peek inside this place, clucking away like hens, and here I am, eh? old Dr. Bowen, the lucky one . . ."

Miss Lizzie was expressionless still.

". . . Ah," exclaimed the doctor, spotting Da Silva and extending his hand toward him, "good to see you, Chief. How's the arm, eh? Still no problems?"

Da Silva released the doctor's hand. "None."

"Good, good, glad to hear it, they can do first-rate work, those army surgeons. Not always, mind—butchers, some of them, pure and simple, lobbing off arms and legs and whatnot like pruning hedges, eh? H'lo there, Tom, keeping out of mischief, eh? Frank, you're looking a mite peaked, need more iron in your diet, blackstrap molasses be just the ticket. Well, to work, to work, eh? Where's the patient?"

"Miss Burton," said Miss Lizzie. "On the sofa."

This I barely heard; I was staring at the second man. He stood now with his arms folded across his chest, his shoulder canted casually against the jamb of the parlor door. He wore a suit of white linen that was spotless and, defying the heat, decidedly unrumpled. He sported too a pair of white patent leather shoes, a pale-blue shirt of some shiny material that could only be silk and whose white collar was clasped together with a gold collar pin, which helped hold in place a dark-blue regimental tie. In his late twenties, sharp featured, his black hair combed straight back from a broad, intelligent forehead, he was rakishly, elegantly, handsome—years later, when I read the line of Edward Arlington Robinson, "clean shaven and imperially slim," I thought immediately of this man.

His mouth was formed into a lazy and ironic smile— at Dr. Bowen, at the situation, perhaps at life itself. His eyes were green, like those of Miss Lizzie's cat; but, beneath lids that were half shut, as though he might doze off at any moment, they glittered with shrewdness and a private amusement.

He nodded to the two officers. "Medley. O'Hara." And, still smiling ironically, nodded to Da Silva. "Chief."

Da Silva nodded back, no longer smiling himself. "I see that Miss Borden has spared no time, and no expense, obtaining counsel."

The man raised his eyebrows in mock surprise. "But surely that's her right, old man?"

Ignoring this, Da Silva said, "O'Hara?"

O'Hara snapped to attention. "Sir?"

"Get back next door and stand watch."

O'Hara blanched. "Uh, beggin' your pardon, sir—"

A faint cold frown of impatience. "You don't have to go inside. Just wait there and keep the vultures away until Hardesty and Dr. Malone arrive. And Freeling, the photographer. No one else is to be admitted."

"*Sir*," said O'Hara; and, transparently relieved, he marched from the room.

Dr. Bowen, who sat beside me on the sofa, burrowing through the clutter of his bag, now at last produced a flat wooden tongue depresser. "All right, my girl," he told me cheerfully, "open wide and say *ah*."

"She is suffering from shock," said Miss Lizzie, "not from laryngitis."

"Ah, to be sure, to be sure," said Dr. Bowen, blinking. He put his palm against my forehead, and I caught a whiff of Bay Rum. "Hmmm, definite clamminess, indeed, yes. Let's have your wrist, eh?" I gave him my arm and he tugged a gold watch on a gold chain from his pocket, sat blinking at its face as he held his fingers against my pulse. Finally he looked up and announced to the room at large, "Shock, yes, no doubt about it." And then, to me: "Warm liquids, some chamomile would be just the ticket, eh? and lots of bed rest. And to help us sleep, eh? a teensy weensy sedative."

Da Silva said, "We'll have to ask her some questions first."

"Afraid not, old man." This from the slender young man leaning against the door jamb.

Da Silva turned to him. "Slocum," he said patiently, "there's been a murder committed next door, and so far this girl is the only witness we have, possibly the only witness we'll ever have. We need to question her."

"And so you shall," said Slocum with a small nod. "But at the proper time."

"This *is* the proper time."

"Oh, no, no," Slocum said lightly, shaking his head. "I shouldn't think so, old man. You heard the good doctor. The girl's in shock."

"That doesn't mean she can't answer a few questions."

"Perhaps she could. But consider for a moment how it might appear in court. Consider how a jury might react when they learn that this poor girl, still in a state of trauma, was badgered—"

"I do not badger witnesses," Da Silva said. No anger there, only a passionless certitude.

Slocum arched his eyebrows, a token of astonishment. "Of *course* you don't, old man. *I* know that. Most of the fair folk in town know that. I'm simply suggesting what some defense lawyer—one lacking any scruples, naturally—might imply to those twelve men sitting in the box. Surely you wouldn't wish to cast suspicion upon the verity of any testimony you've obtained?"

Da Silva's eyes were narrowed. "Just exactly who is it you're representing here, Slocum?"

"Why, Miss Borden and young Miss Burton, of course. But I've been remiss." He eased himself from the door jamb and nodded pleasantly to Miss Lizzie. "Darryl Slocum, Miss Borden." Then, moving with feline grace, he crossed to the sofa and held out his hand to me. "Darryl Slocum, Miss Burton. How do you do?"

I took the hand. "It's Amanda," I said. "Very well, thank you."

He smiled suddenly, a dazzling smile totally without irony. "Amanda," he said. "Delighted." And then he made, over my hand, a quick, supple, continental bow. I felt my face flush and my eyelids flutter. I hoped no one had noticed. But concurrent with my embarrassment came the immediate conviction that this was the man I would one day marry.

The funeral meats had not even been baked and already I was furnishing the marriage tables. I like to believe, from the forgiving vantage point of the present, that this was not simple callousness on my part, not simple indifference. I was in shock still. In the normal course of things, the human mind can accept only so much horror. Faced with more, it will divert itself or it will wink altogether out. Mr. Slocum's dazzle provided, momentarily, the diversion a stricken soul required.

"Look, Slocum," said Da Silva, "you can't represent them both."

"Of course I can," said Mr. Slocum, releasing my hand (which hovered there, tingling, for a moment) and turning to the chief of police. "Unless I learn that so doing would constitute a conflict of interests."

For a moment Da Silva only stared at him. Then he smiled his small tight frown. "Very well," he said. "We'll question the girl later. Miss Borden—"

"Miss Borden," interjected Mr. Slocum, "is naturally entitled to confer with counsel before answering any questions."

"We can," said Da Silva, "request that Miss Borden accompany us to the station and make a formal statement."

"Certainly you can," Mr. Slocum agreed amiably. "But as her lawyer, I should advise her against complying. A woman of Miss Borden's character and position need not, I suggest, suffer that indignity. And you can't force her compliance without putting her under arrest. For which, I need hardly add, you have no charge."

"Slocum—" began Da Silva.

The lawyer turned to Miss Lizzie. "Miss Borden, have you any information whatever that might assist the police?"

Miss Lizzie raised her jaw slightly. "I have not."

Mr. Slocum turned back to Da Silva and shrugged. "There you are, old man."

A muscle rippled along Da Silva's cheek. "There's

been a *murder* committed, Slocum. Someone has taken a human life. Doesn't that mean anything to you?"

Beside me, Dr. Bowen shifted uncomfortably on the sofa.

"Of course it does," snapped Mr. Slocum, and the lightness was gone from his voice. "I'm an officer of the court, just as you are. And I understand your determination to locate the person responsible. But supposing," he said in a tone of great reasonableness, "supposing we do this. We permit Miss Burton and Miss Borden—for I feel certain that Miss Borden, too, has undergone considerable distress—we permit them both their rest, their time to recover from all this. And let us all convene here tomorrow afternoon at, say, two o'clock. Both of them, I expect, would be happy to provide you with a statement then. Is that agreeable to you, Miss Borden?"

"It is," said Miss Lizzie.

Mr. Slocum turned to me. "Amanda?"

I nodded.

"Chief Da Silva?" said Mr. Slocum.

Da Silva stood there. His glance flicked from Mr. Slocum to Miss Lizzie, back to Mr. Slocum. "A guard will be placed upon the house." He smiled that small hard smile. "For the protection, of course, of Miss Borden and Miss Burton."

Mr. Slocum nodded. "Agreed."

"Neither of them to leave the town."

"Without prior notification," amended Mr. Slocum.

Da Silva considered this for a moment and then nodded. "Without prior notification."

"Agreed," said Mr. Slocum.

"No press," said Da Silva. "No reporters."

"Agreed."

Da Silva nodded. "Two o'clock, then. Medley?"

"Sir?"

"Come along."

————

As Officer Medley departed through the parlor door behind Da Silva, he looked back over his shoulder and favored me with a quick intrepid grin. I smiled back, but automatically, reflexively; my allegiance had shifted. Officer Medley's stalwart charm was no match, so it seemed to me then, for Mr. Slocum's flair. And, besides, Medley was on Their Side, Mr. Slocum was on Ours, mine and Miss Lizzie's.

Miss Lizzie turned to him. "I thank you," she said rather stiffly, as though unused to being in another's debt.

Mr. Slocum waved a hand. "Nothing. When Felix telephoned from Boston and explained the lay of the land, I thought it best to trot on over."

"I am grateful that you did. I know that I, alone with that man, should not have been so politic." She bobbed her head daintily, almost shyly. The movement, too, seemed to be something to which she was unused; something that perhaps she had not done since she was a young girl. It had, at any rate, a tentative, girlish quality to it; and I remembered the sketch of the young Miss Lizzie, done before the murders had changed her. "You are most kind," she said.

The ironic smile came back to Mr. Slocum's lips. "I suspect that Chief Da Silva would disagree with your assessment of my character."

For the first time that day, Miss Lizzie smiled. "I suspect that Chief Da Silva would disagree with any of my assessments."

"Oh?" said Mr. Slocum, left eyebrow rising. "You know him, do you?"

She nodded curtly. "From many years ago."

"Ah," said Mr. Slocum. "Of course. Fall River. I'd forgotten that Chief Da Silva hailed from there. You knew him at the time of your"—his brief hesitation took much less time than it takes to mention it—"trouble?"

"Yes," she said, the word clipped and brusque. She turned to the doctor, as though she had suddenly re-called that he was there. He still sat beside me on the sofa, and he (like I) had been following this exchange with great interest. "And, of course, I am grateful to you as well, Dr. Bowen, for arriving so promptly."

"Wouldn't miss it for the world," said the doctor, blinking happily. "Make me the most popular party at the bridge game, eh?"

Smiling, Mr. Slocum said, "I know I needn't remind you, Doctor, of the principle of confidentiality."

"No, no, course not," said Dr. Bowen, blinking. "Course not. Mum's the word, eh, my boy?"

"You said something," said Miss Lizzie, "about a sed-ative for Miss Burton?"

"I did indeed. Got it right here." Head bent, he rum-maged through his bag. "Somewhere. Ah." He took out a small amber-colored glass bottle, opened it, tapped four small white tablets from it onto his palm. "Here you are, my girl." He handed them to me. "Two of these right away, and there's two more for tonight, if you've got a problem sleeping."

"Thank you," I said.

"Chamomile tea," he said. "And lots of bed rest, eh? Be good as new in the morning. Right as rain."

"Thank you, Doctor," said Miss Lizzie. "Please be good enough to send me the bill."

"The wife makes up the bills," he said. "Should get quite a kick out of this one, eh? I mean, well, considering. . . ." Neither Miss Lizzie nor Mr. Slocum said anything. Blinking, Dr. Bowen cleared his throat. "Yes, well." With a small grunt of effort he stood from the sofa. "Have to be going. No rest for the wicked, eh?"

Mr. Slocum said to Miss Lizzie, "Shall I show the doctor out?"

"Thank you, Mr. Slocum," she said, nodding.

As the two men left the parlor, she approached the sofa. "How are you feeling, Amanda?"

"Tired," I said.

"Would you like to lie down?"

"I think so, yes. If it would be all right?"

"Of course it would. You'll use the spare room, upstairs. Ah, Mr. Slocum. Let me just help Amanda get settled, and then you and I can talk."

Mr. Slocum nodded, then said to me, "The doctor's right, Amanda. You'll feel better after you get some rest."

His teeth, I noticed, were perfectly uniform; and, even in the dim light of the parlor, they actually sparkled.

Upstairs, Miss Lizzie refused to let me help her make the bed. She insisted that I sit down on the small wooden chair set against the wall while she fussed with the sheets, drawing the lower so taut it could have served as a trampoline. Finished, she stroked them smooth. "There. You get into bed now, dear, and I'll fetch you your tea."

I wanted to ask her about her earlier experience with Chief Da Silva in Fall River, but I felt it would be an imposition, an intrusion. Instead I asked, "Do you think my father will be coming soon?"

She reached out and stroked my hair. "I'm sure he will, dear. When I spoke to my lawyer in Boston and asked him to send along someone here in town, I told him to call your father's office and let him know what had happened. I'm sure he's on his way right now. I'll send him up to see you as soon as he arrives. Now into bed with you."

She bustled off, shutting the door behind her.

After putting Dr. Bowen's pills on the nightstand, I undressed slowly, crawled into bed, and pulled the sheet over me. It smelled of mothballs.

Whether through shock or through mere exhaustion, my mind was finally beginning to wink out. Tucked now in a protective cocoon, I felt extremely weak and infinitely tired.

Within perhaps fifteen minutes, Miss Lizzie returned carrying a tray that held a glass of water and a cup steaming with chamomile tea. She set it on the nightstand and sat down beside me on the mattress.

"These are the tablets that Dr. Bowen gave you?" she asked, picking them up.

"Yes," I said. "Do I really have to take them?"

She smiled. "Yes, dear, you do. They'll help you sleep. Two of them, he said. Here. And here's your water. Very good. Thank you, Amanda."

I said, "How old do you think Mr. Slocum is?"

"Mr. Slocum? I don't know, dear. Twenty-seven? Twenty-eight? Why do you ask?"

I shrugged beneath the sheet. "I don't know. Just curious, I guess. He seems awfully clever, doesn't he?"

She smiled. "Awfully. Now you get some sleep. I promise that as soon as your father gets here, I'll send him up."

"Thank you, Miss Lizzie."

She stroked my hair again. "And don't you worry, Amanda. I promise, I'll take care of everything."

"You've been really kind, Miss Lizzie."

"Hush," she said. "Sleep now. I'll check in on you later."

She stood and turned, walked to the door and opened it. She turned back to me and smiled. "In ten years, when you're twenty-three, he'll be only thirty-seven."

I blushed. Was I so ridiculously obvious?

"Sleep well, dear." She smiled and slipped through the door and pulled it shut.

Ten years, I thought.

In only a few minutes I fell into a deep, dreamless sleep that lasted until the morning of the following day.

Chapter
SIX

I AWOKE IN the unfamiliar bed to the smell of camphor, a closed-in, claustrophobic smell. The air was hot and still, as dense as broth, and my cotton chemise clung to my damp skin like a mustard plaster.

A blade of sunlight lanced between the lace curtains behind me, sliced aslant across the room, glinted off the glass-covered walnut cabinet on the opposite wall. On the far side of the dusty glass stood rows of stiff porcelain figurines: shepherds and shepherdesses, rotund grinning burghers and their rotund grinning wives, all their tiny glazed eyes staring idiotically into mine.

To my right was a dressing table with a clouded mirror set in an ornate but chipped oval of dark wood. To my left was a squat oak writing desk, its worn surface bare, its cubbyholes empty. And there, before it, slumped in the straight-backed chair against the wall, his white-shirted arms folded across his chest, his tie loosened at his neck, his head bowed, one lock of brown hair hanging limply down his forehead, sat Father.

"Daddy?" I said. "Daddy?"

His head snapped up and he looked at me. "Amanda," he said. He stood up so slowly, with such difficulty, that he seemed to be aching with the effort. His shoulders stooped, he crossed the floor and sat beside me on the mattress. His cheeks were sunken, his blue eyes rimmed with red. "How are you, baby?" he said, and his hand moved forward to touch my head.

"Oh, Daddy," I said, and I reached out and he drew me up to him, arms tight around me, and, for the first time since I had seen the body of my stepmother, grief clotted in my throat and tears came scalding between my eyelids.

"Oh, Daddy," I sobbed. *"Daddy."*

He held me, his hand patting me softly on the back. "Baby," he said. "Baby."

He held me, and all at once I felt against my face a drop, and then another, of my father's tears. Each trembled there for a moment and then trailed wet and ticklish down my cheek and mingled with my own. I had never seen my father weep before. And then I was sobbing for him, for his loss and for his hurt and even for his gladness at holding me. I held him, and he held me, and together, silently, for a long time we cried.

————

After a while, when my sobs had subsided to sniffles and deep ragged sighs, he sat away from me and, breathing through his mouth, scraped at his eyes, first his right and then his left, with the fingertips of his right hand. It was a gesture that I found, in its masculine abruptness, as touching as his tears. He reached back into his rear pocket and plucked from it a neatly folded white cotton handkerchief, opened the thing, and handed it to me. I wiped my puffy eyes (I have never been one of those fortunate and possibly mythical women whom tears make more appealing) and then put it to my nose and trumpeted into it. I looked at him and said forlornly, "I must sound like a goose."

He smiled, blinking away a shimmer. "Like a silly goose."

I honked into the handkerchief again. "I'm all plugged up," I said, and frowned.

"Me too."

I gave him back the handkerchief, and he blew his nose, more discreetly than I, sniffed once, blew again, and then returned it to his pocket.

I said, "Daddy, it was awful."

He nodded. "I know, baby. I saw her."

"You *saw* her?" That torn flesh and splintered bone; those awful splatters of blood. "The police made you look?"

"Down at the hospital." He inhaled deeply. "Someone had to identify her."

"Oh, Daddy." I put my hand on his.

He covered it with his other hand. "It's all right now, Amanda. It's over now."

"That rotten Chief Da Silva. That *rat*."

Squeezing my hand, he shook his head. "No, Amanda. It's the law. Chief Da Silva was only doing his job."

"I don't like him."

"He's a hard man, but I think a fair one."

"I still don't like him. Daddy?"

"Yes?"

"Who could've done that to Audrey?"

He shook his head. "A madman. A maniac. I—"

Someone knocked at the door. Father called out, "Come in."

The door swung open and Miss Lizzie entered, holding upright a tidy stack of clothing. "I heard you talking. I don't mean to interrupt."

She was not apologetic, exactly; I should have a hard time imagining Miss Lizzie apologetic in any circumstances. I believe she was uncomfortable dealing with the obvious intimacy between Father and myself. But whatever the reason, she was subdued, almost businesslike.

Father said, "Not at all, Miss Borden."

She turned to me. "And how are you today, Amanda?" In her voice was that crisp, bright, artificial heartiness with which most adults speak to children. Her manner had none of the closeness and warmth of yesterday: it seemed to imply that the two of us were merely acquaintances and not, as I had come to believe, friends. And, as only a thirteen-year-old can be, I was stung.

"I'm all right," I said, my voice sulky.

She nodded. "I've brought some of your things from next door. If you'd like to bathe, the washroom is just down the hall."

"Thank you." I kept my voice cool, noncommittal.

She set the bundle of clothing on the writing desk and turned to Father. "Have you told Amanda yet about the meeting?"

"Not yet," he said.

"With the police?" I asked.

"With the lawyer," he said. "At noon." He smiled faintly. "A Council of War before we talk to the police."

"The lawyer?" I said. "Mr. Slocum?"

He nodded. "And a Pinkerton man. Miss Borden feels

he may be necessary." From his tone, I gathered that he did not share this feeling.

"A real private detective?"

He smiled. "A real private detective."

"Well," said Miss Lizzie, "I'll leave the two of you alone." She turned to me. "You're quite welcome to stay as long as you like, Amanda." She glanced around the room, disapproval tightening her mouth. "The furniture isn't mine, of course. It's the sort of sorry odds and ends you find in any summer rental. We could do something about that, if you like. Bring in some nicer things. Those Dresdens"—with a frown at the figurines—"are particularly odious."

"No," I said, "that's all right, Miss Lizzie. The room is fine."

"Well, let me know if you reconsider." Then, as though suddenly remembering something, she said, "Are you hungry, child?"

I discovered, to my surprise, that I was famished. "A little," I admitted.

Her face softened. "Good. I'll bring something up for you."

At once I felt guilty for my earlier coolness. "No, Miss Lizzie, really. You don't have to go to any trouble."

"It's no trouble at all," she said. "And you need to maintain your strength." She turned to Father, gave him her businesslike nod. "Until later, then."

As she made to leave I called out, "Miss Lizzie?"

She looked at me, eyebrows raised. "Yes?"

"Thank you," I said. "For everything."

She smiled then and at once became the Miss Lizzie I remembered, bright gray eyes and dimpled cheeks. "You needn't mention it, child. It's been my pleasure." With another nod to Father she turned and left.

I looked at him. "She's been wonderful, Father." The moment I spoke the word I realized that we were no longer *Daddy* and *baby*; Miss Lizzie's visit had served as a reminder of a world other than ourselves. I felt a small quick stab of regret.

"I know she has," he said.

"Would it be all right if I stayed with her for a while?"

"Well, Amanda," he said, and stroked his mustache. "I thought we'd get you a room at the hotel, maybe the one next to mine. At least until all this is over with. You'd have a bathroom all to yourself, and the restaurant's right downstairs." He made himself smile. "And they've got maids to keep the room clean. You wouldn't have to worry about tidying up."

I realized that if Father were trying to appeal to my slovenliness, which within the family was legendary, he must be displeased for some reason by the idea of my staying with Miss Lizzie.

I said, "Father, she's my friend. I don't know what I would've done yesterday, if she hadn't been here to help me."

He looked at me for a long moment. Finally he said, "All right. We'll see how it goes." Then he gave me another forced smile. "After all, if she's your friend, you can't desert her, now can you?"

"No," I said, and grinned, pretending, as the situation obliged me to, that his smile was real. "Thank you, Father. What about William? Is he staying at the hotel?"

The smile faded and he shook his head. "No, Amanda. We can't find him. I was hoping you might have some idea where he's gone."

"He said yesterday that he and Andy were going up the coast in Andy's car."

He shook his head again. "The police talked to Andy. William never showed up yesterday. No one's seen him."

———

The Council of War was to take place in Miss Lizzie's parlor. At a quarter to twelve, we were all waiting there for the Pinkerton man to arrive.

Father and I sat on the sofa. He was wearing his tie and suitcoat now—a gentleman did not wear shirtsleeves in mixed company—but he looked no less haggard, no less drawn.

I had not told him yet about the argument yesterday between Audrey and William. He had received enough bad news already, I thought; and, besides, bringing it up would have meant revealing my part in it, and the secret I had been keeping from him all summer. Families are held together as much by what they do not say as by what they do.

I was wearing a lightweight blue poplin frock trimmed along its hem and cuffs with lace. Audrey had brought it for me in Boston, before we left for the shore. It was a very pretty dress, but the hem fell only five inches from the floor, and for months I had been pleading with her to let me take it up to a more reasonable height. She had maintained that I was still growing, and that sooner or later the hem would catch up with fashion. (Which would happen, I told her, at exactly the same time the cuffs caught up with my elbows.) And so the dress, lovely as it was, had languished all summer long in the closet. I wore it today as a kind of apology for my stubbornness.

Miss Lizzie, who wore her invariable black, sat in one of the red armchairs, a copy of *Harper's* on her lap. Pince-nez in place, she leafed idly through the magazine, now and then lingering over a page; but eventually, inevitably, she would look up and glare, her mouth in a thin grim line, off toward the parlor window.

Somewhat back from the window—through whose lace curtains he could see the street without himself being seen—stood Mr. Slocum, his hands in his pockets, a small thoughtful frown upon his lips. He wore another linen suit today, this one the pale yellow of aged ivory, and with it a light-green shirt and a lime-green tie.

Father, querulous with fatigue and tension, suddenly said, "Haven't they got anything better to do?"

"I shouldn't think so," said Mr. Slocum, still gazing out the window. "I should think that none of them has ever had anything better to do. Certainly nothing so soul stirring." He turned to Father and smiled faintly. "Given what passes for souls in those circles."

They had begun to gather, Miss Lizzie had told me, early last evening while I was asleep. At first they had been only a silent motionless few; but gradually they had been joined by others, and at midnight, Miss Lizzie said, there must have been two hundred of them. Over the course of the night their number had dwindled; and then, with the dawn, had begun to grow again.

Now, despite the flat white glare of midday and the oppressive heat that lay like a woolen blanket over the town, a great many more than two hundred stood out there. They choked Water Street, spilled over onto the side streets, blocked every sort of traffic. There were children and there were old people. There were pale clerks in business suits, terra cotta–faced farmers and weathered fishermen in overalls, housewives in drab calico wrappers and shopgirls in modish skirts, many of these holding gaily colored parasols to shield their fair skin from the implacable sun. They milled about, grouping and regrouping with seeming aimlessness, moving as though in a trance, without expression, sometimes looking off, down the street, up at the fierce white sky, over to their fellows; but always looking back again in dull stupefied fascination at the house where Lizzie Borden lived.

None of them had broached the white picket fence. Perhaps they were kept at bay by the presence of Officer O'Hara, who sat on the porch's swaybacked wicker loveseat, scowling as he thwacked his nightstick rhythmically against his palm. But more likely, I believe, they were held in check by their own fathomless dread.

Occasionally one of them, braver than the rest, would shout something—*"Show us the axe, Lizzie!"*—and another would whoop, and then a ripple of laughter, at once shocked and relieved, would wind through the crowd; and then this would slowly fade, fall off to a murmur which itself slowly died away until all that remained, once again, was that heavy, mindless hush.

Father said, "You'd think that sooner or later they'd get tired of this."

Looking up from her magazine, Miss Lizzie said, "They never get tired of this."

(She had told me, earlier, that the telephone had rung all morning, until finally she had called the exchange and demanded that they change her number. She expected, she said, that she would be forced to change it again, possibly several times; and she was.)

Mr. Slocum leaned slightly forward. "I believe our Pinkerton has landed."

We heard mutterings from the crowd, then a spiteful voice calling out, then a clamor as if some great beast were stirring itself, awakening from slumber.

Mr. Slocum turned to Miss Lizzie. "I'll just see him in, shall I?"

"Thank you," she said, and put aside the magazine.

He turned and strode from the parlor. Outside, the crowd rumbled and growled.

I said to Father, "What do they want?" They frightened me, those blank empty faces.

He ran his hand back through his hair, shook his head. He sighed. "I don't know, Amanda. I don't think I want to know."

I looked at Miss Lizzie. She seemed about to say something, but then she merely tightened her lips and looked away.

We heard the front door open and close, heard footsteps; and then Mr. Slocum entered the room with the Pinkerton man. "This," announced the lawyer, and his ironic smile had returned, his green eyes were glittering again with that private amusement, "is Mr. Boyle."

Chapter

SEVEN

I AM NOT really sure what I expected. Pinkerton men, I knew, were a bit like sleuths and a bit like sheriffs: They foiled the fiendish schemes of tenement gangsters and they tracked down, on the backs of relentless horses, mustachioed desperadoes who plundered trains. A Pinkerton man should look rather like a cross between Sherlock Holmes and Buffalo Bill; should wear a deerstalker cap and, beneath a silver-buckled belt festooned with sixguns, a pair of gleaming leather chaps.

He should not look like a short, overweight, middle-aged former prizefighter. He should not be balding. He should not have, shadowing his jowly cheeks, at least two days' worth of salt-and-pepper stubble. He should not be wearing a brown suit (even I knew that brown suits were worn only on hayrides), especially one that appeared to have been slept in, frequently, and by several insomniacs at once.

"Call me Harry," said the Pinkerton man. "Sorry I'm

late. Had to dump the fliver a couple blocks away. Vultures are pretty thick out there."

"No problem, old man," Mr. Slocum said expansively, clapping him on the back. (I imagined I saw a small cloud of dust puff off Boyle's shoulders.) "Here, let me introduce you."

He led the man around the room, first to me and Father. I nodded and Boyle nodded back. "Please ta meetcha." Father shook the man's hand; Mr. Boyle nodded back. "Please ta meetcha."

Miss Lizzie, to whom Slocum referred as "Miss Lizbeth A. Borden," sat stiffly upright, staring at Boyle with her gray eyes startled wide behind the pince-nez. She had, perhaps, been expecting the same dazzling hybrid as I.

"How do you do?" she said quite formally, and nodded without offering her hand.

"Swell, thanks," said Boyle. "Please ta meetcha." He showed no awareness whatever that this was the famous Lizzie Borden. While I would, of course, have instantly scorned any such reaction, I felt (scornfully) that his failure to provide it was further proof, should any be required, of his utter uselessness. At that point, so far as I was concerned, Boyle really could not win.

"Sit down, old man," said Mr. Slocum, smiling, "and I'll fill you in."

Boyle chose the chair opposite Father and only a yard to Miss Lizzie's right. She seemed to shrink slightly away from him, as though trying, without actually rearranging the furniture, to maximize the distance between them. Mr. Slocum sat in the chair to Miss Lizzie's left.

Boyle turned to Miss Lizzie. "Okay if I smoke?" he asked, slipping a crumpled pack of Fatimas from his shirt pocket.

"Certainly," she said, starch in her voice. "The ashtray is over there." This in case he had overlooked it, or had failed to recognize its obvious purpose.

As Boyle stuck a cigarette between his lips, Mr. Slocum began: "I've waited until you were here, Mr. Boyle, so that I need cover the ground only once."

"Harry," said Boyle. Leaning forward, the cigarette bobbing as he spoke, he dug both his hands into his coat pockets, searching for something.

"Yesterday," said Mr. Slocum, "Mrs. Audrey Burton was murdered in the house next door. It was young Amanda here, her stepdaughter, who found her."

Boyle stopped digging and frowned around his Fatima. "Hey, kid," he said sadly, "that's a tough one."

I did not know what to say. I had not liked him—he had been one of those sudden slapstick clouts that Reality delivers to the face of Imagination—and yet he seemed genuinely concerned.

Stretching out his leg as he continued the search in his pants pocket, he turned to Mr. Slocum. "The part about the lady, Mrs. Burton, I got that from the newspapers. It made the Boston rags already. There's a couple of their snoops outside, mouth-breathing with the other boobs." He had at last found what he had sought: a wooden kitchen match. When he snapped it alight with his thumbnail, I glanced at Miss Lizzie to see if she had noticed this, a gesture that might give her a feeling of kinship with Boyle. Evidently it had not; she was staring at him as though she had spied a serpent lazing atop the meringue.

Boyle tossed the match into the ashtray and sat back, exhaling a billow of blue smoke. "So what's the scoop? What're the cops up to?"

"Fair enough." Mr. Slocum nodded, still smiling—he

seemed to have taken a fancy to Boyle. He reached down to the floor and pulled up his alligator leather attaché case. He opened it on his lap and eased from it a sheath of papers, tapped them against the case, straightened them with tapered fingers, and then lay them carefully atop it. "First of all," he said, "I have the results of the preliminary autopsy." He turned to me, his face kindly, and said, "Amanda, you don't have to listen to this, you know."

I shook my head. "I'm all right." Earlier, Father had explained what an autopsy was, and had said much the same thing. I believed that hearing the facts might in some way diminish the horror of what I had seen. I was also, of course, morbidly curious. Death, despite the horror of yesterday, was as exotic and distant as Siam.

"If you're certain," said Mr. Slocum.

I nodded. Father covered my hand with his and squeezed it. "You're sure, Amanda?"

"Yes."

Miss Lizzie pursed her lips. Boyle, not looking at me, tapped his cigarette against the rim of the ashtray.

Father said to Mr. Slocum, "I know we can count on Mr. Slocum's discretion."

The lawyer nodded, then scanned the top sheet. "Well. Mrs. Burton's death was caused by a series of blows from a heavy, sharp-edged object, probably a common household hatchet. There was a total of, um, twenty-five blows. At least five of these would have resulted in immediate loss of life."

Twenty-five, I thought, stunned. How could someone have hated Audrey, have hated anyone, that badly?

Mr. Slocum was reading to himself. "Hmmm," he said. "I think we'll just skip that." He turned over the sheet, peered at the next, looked up and said, "From the, ah, contents of Mrs. Burton's stomach, the medical examiner has determined that she died approximately two hours after eating."

I remembered the oatmeal congealing in the saucepan atop the stove, thought of it lying in Audrey's stomach; my own stomach squirmed.

"How good is this guy?" asked Boyle. "The M.E."

"Dr. Malone?" said Mr. Slocum. He shrugged. "Competent enough, I imagine. But certainly no genius."

"So he could maybe be off by an hour or two."

"Possibly, yes. But Miss Borden tells me that Amanda discovered the body at just a little after twelve o'clock. The police and Dr. Malone examined it fairly soon after that. Malone's certain that the, ah, various details at the scene fit in with the same time of death. And the police have the testimony of a Mrs. Esther Mortimer . . ." He riffled through the sheets.

Mrs. Mortimer, I thought with a start. Mrs. Mortimer had *been* there, she had *seen* that awful fight between Audrey and William. Had she told the police? I looked at Father. He was staring down at the floor, tracing the pattern in the Persian carpet as though it might lead him somewhere, into the past or into the future. He must have felt my gaze, for he looked up, smiled, and squeezed my hand again. Comforting me when clearly he was in need of comfort himself.

"Here we are," said Mr. Slocum, sliding a sheet to the top of the pile. "These are only notes, you understand," he told Boyle. "I didn't have time to make complete copies of her testimony."

Boyle nodded. He lit a second Fatima from the glowing butt of the first, then ground out the first in the ashtray.

Mr. Slocum said, "Mrs. Mortimer testified that she'd

eaten breakfast with Mrs. Burton at eight-thirty that morning. So you see the stomach contents do tie in with the other indications."

"So she got"—Boyle glanced at me, sucked on the cigarette, exhaled—"so it happened around ten-thirty?"

"Sometime between ten and eleven, yes."

"Cops got the weapon? The hatchet?"

"No weapon was found."

Boyle raised his eyebrows, turned down the corners of his mouth. "Okay," he said. "So who do they like for it?"

"Well," said Mr. Slocum, sitting back with a smile, "some of them are convinced that the murder was part of a radical plot."

This was not so unlikely a possibility as it might appear. In 1920, only a year ago before, the U.S. Attorney General, Mr. Palmer, had corralled over five thousand suspected Communists (none of whom had committed any crime) and deported them. In September of the same year, a bomb had exploded on Wall Street, near J.P. Morgan and Company, killing thirty people and wounding hundreds more. And approximately two weeks before my stepmother's death, less than a hundred miles away, a court had convicted two obscure Anarchists, Bartolomeo Sacco and Nichola Vanzetti, of murder.

"But those who incline toward this theory," said Mr. Slocum, "are the same people who believe that the Pope is a Bolshevik."

Pale-blue smoke streaming from his nostrils, Boyle nodded. One could not tell, from his expression, what he felt about Bolsheviks or about the Pope, or about any possible connection between the two.

Mr. Slocum said, "One or two of the policemen to whom I spoke felt that Mrs. Burton might've been murdered by a madman, a stranger. But most of them tend to discount this notion. First, because it would mean, essentially, a motiveless crime, which could prove impossible to solve." He smiled. "Itinerant madman, as I'm sure you know, are notoriously difficult to locate."

Boyle shrugged. "Could of happened, though."

"It could've," Mr. Slocum agreed. "But, second, as again I'm sure you know, most murders are committed by someone close to the victim, someone who knows him. Or, in this case, her."

Boyle said, "So they're looking at family and friends."

"Occam's razor," said Mr. Slocum. "Simplify. And the police are great simplifiers. Just now, they feel that there are four likely suspects." He turned to Father, frowning. "The first of them, I'm sorry to tell you, Mr. Burton, is your son."

Father shook his head. "William would never."

"No," said Mr. Slocum diplomatically. "I'm sure he wouldn't. But according to Mrs. Mortimer's statement, which was apparently given with much reluctance, your son and Mrs. Burton had something of an altercation yesterday."

That *ninny*! (*Bitch* was a word that had not, unfortunately, yet entered my vocabulary.)

Father shrugged. "An argument. It happened sometimes. Sometimes Audrey could be a difficult woman."

"Blows were given," said Mr. Slocum.

"That's impossible," Father said firmly. "William would never strike a woman."

"Apparently Mrs. Burton was the one who did the striking."

It took Father, who had never raised a hand to his children, a moment to assimilate this. At last he said, in disbelief, "She hit him?"

"According to Mrs. Mortimer's statement."

Father looked at me.

"It's true, Father," I said. "I was there."

"Audrey *hit* him?" It was as if he were remembering William not as the young man he had become, but as a small helpless child.

"She was in a terrible mood," I said. "She was angry, she was—"

"But why didn't you *tell* me, Amanda?" He seemed more wounded than angry. I would have preferred his being angry.

"At any rate," Mr. Slocum said smoothly to Boyle, "Mr. Burton's son has been missing since yesterday."

"Cops got a warrant yet?" Boyle asked him.

"No, but the Boston police have been notified and asked to keep an eye out for him. The state police too."

Father looked at me, frowned sadly, and looked away.

Nodding, Boyle blew two plumes of smoke from his nostrils. "Who else they got?"

"Second in line," Mr. Slocum said, "is you, Mr. Burton."

Father turned to him, surprised.

Mr. Slocum smiled. "Husbands are always suspects in the murder of a wife. But so long as someone can substantiate your statement, you needn't worry about it. You were in Boston, I believe you told them, conferring with a client."

"Yes," Father said.

Mr. Slocum nodded. "Their third choice," he said, smiling ironically as he turned to Miss Lizzie, "is you, Miss Borden."

Miss Lizzie smiled back with an irony that mirrored his. "Only third?"

"Ah." He smiled. "But first in the heart of Chief Da Silva." He turned to Boyle. "Our chief of police was a patrolman in Fall River when Miss Borden's parents were murdered. He worked on the case."

"Da Silva," said Boyle. "Right. The cop in the loft."

So he *had* known about Miss Lizzie after all. And evidently a good deal more than I had. That loft again. What was its significance?

I looked at her and saw that she was looking at Boyle with one eyebrow slightly raised behind the pince-nez, as though she were reappraising him.

"Yes," said the lawyer. "He thinks that Miss Borden was unfairly acquitted for those earlier crimes and seems determined to prove her responsible for this one."

"They got any evidence?" Boyle asked. "Witnesses? Anything?"

"Nothing."

Boyle nodded, tapping his cigarette into the ashtray. "You said four."

"Four." Mr. Slocum nodded. He turned to me and smiled. "Some of them seem to think that Amanda killed Mrs. Burton."

"That," said Miss Lizzie, "is absurd."

"Come on now, Slocum," Father said impatiently. "Not even the police could think that a thirteen-year-old girl did *that*."

Boyle simply sat there, smoke drifting up from his nose, his eyebrows raised quizzically as he waited for my response.

My response, when I heard the words, had been immediately to recognize their truth.

I knew, of course, that I had not actually murdered

my stepmother. But if, as the priests maintained, intent were as wicked as act, then I stood condemned as surely as if I had picked up the hatchet and smashed out her life.

Had I not, with my thousand casual brutalities, been killing her day by day, piece by piece, since I met her? Had I not, a thousand times, wished her *gone*: from me, from Father and William, from our home, our lives: away, vanished, disappeared: nonexistent?

Yesterday, while she raved and screeched and sputtered through the kitchen, her mouth agape, her loose body shuddering as she clubbed at my brother, had I not truly wished the woman dead?

The police were right. I was guilty. And, as a consequence, I was doomed.

I surprised myself by the stoicism with which I accepted this, a fate of eternal hellfire. An image flickered for an instant before my mind's eye, of myself shrieking and writhing in the flames; and I regarded it not with fear and trembling, but with a detached, almost nonchalant, curiosity. *So this is how it feels*, I thought, *to be damned.*

Mr. Slocum was still smiling. "Amanda," he said gently, "we all know you didn't do it."

And I felt a stab of sorrow then, bittersweet, for his kindness, so misplaced, so *wrong*. I deserved no kindness, least of all from him; for by my wickedness I had lost him, and the choirs of cherubs, and the galleries of harps, forever.

"The police," he said reasonably, "have to suspect everyone who had the means and who might've had a motive. And so, you see, I really think you ought to tell us what happened yesterday."

Father's hand tightened over mine. His blue eyes no

longer looked wounded. But how would they look when he learned I had kept a secret from him all summer long?

I realized that I must postpone, for the moment, any further consideration of my brimstoned future. I could take it up again later, on a direct basis, one to one, with God himself.

I looked at Miss Lizzie. Her head bowed, her mouth pursed, she was peering at me over her pince-nez. She nodded once. I looked at Boyle. And he confounded me by giving me a broad, slow wink.

I took a deep breath.

Chapter
EIGHT

TELLING FATHER ABOUT Miss Lizzie and the magic turned out to be, as anticipated events frequently are, anticlimactic. With all the others watching on, keeping any trace of whimper from my voice, I said, "I would've told you before, but I was afraid you'd think it was, I don't know, wrong or something."

"No, Amanda," he said. "I do wish you'd told me, but I don't think it was wrong." He squeezed my hand and smiled. "You'll have to show me one of these tricks Miss Borden taught you."

"Shall I go get some cards?" Wait till he saw my Whispering Queens or my Siamese Twins.

He smiled again. "A little later, maybe. You go ahead with your story."

When I mentioned Marge Grady and the small cardboard box Audrey had produced, no one said anything. Father and Mr. Slocum only exchanged glances, while Boyle continued to sit back and watch his cigarette smoke wind upward in the hot, still air. Miss Lizzie sat as stiffly erect in her chair as she had when I began.

I finished, and Mr. Slocum said, "All right, Amanda." He had been gentle throughout, his irony abandoned, his smile considerate as he eased the account out of me with tactful questions and patient encouragement. "Let's go back a bit. Back to the argument in the kitchen. From what you say, Mrs. Mortimer probably didn't hear those last words of William's to your stepmother, out on the back porch."

You'll be sorry, Audrey.

"I don't think so," I said. "She was in the hallway, on her way out of the house."

Father said to Slocum, "It's not in her testimony?" His voice sounded hesitant, diminished.

"No. Now, Amanda, you *are* certain that while you were upstairs in your bedroom, you heard no noise, no sound at all?"

"I was asleep," I said.

He nodded. "When you came downstairs afterward, was the back door open, from the kitchen to the porch?"

"Yes. Audrey usually kept it open during the day."

"The screen door from the porch to the outside. Did that have a lock?"

"A latch."

"Was the latch set?"

"I don't know. I don't remember."

"Was the door normally kept latched?"

I nodded. "Audrey was afraid of hobos."

"The windows in the house were open?"

"Yes."

"Do they all have screens?"

"Yes."

He turned to Father. "Locks on the screens?"

"Not locks," he said. Glad, I think, to be certain of something, and able to contribute it. "Hooks and latches."

"On the inside."

"Yes."

"All right. Amanda. When you came downstairs from the guest room, after you found your stepmother, was the front door opened or closed?"

"Closed."

"Locked?"

"I don't remember."

"Was it usually kept locked?"

"Usually."

He turned to Father again. "What kind of lock is it?"

"A Yale."

"It slam-locks automatically when the door is shut?"

"Yes," Father said. "And there's a bolt too. You set it with a small knob on the inside, or with the key outside."

Mr. Slocum asked me, "You don't remember if it was bolted?"

"No," I said. "Is it important?"

"It could be."

"Why?"

He smiled. "Well, suppose someone wanted to get in, and the back door was latched. Suppose whoever it was didn't want to cut the screens. If the front door was *unlatched*, he could've used a strip of celluloid to slide back the tongue of the lock."

Father said, "And that wouldn't work if the bolt had been set?"

"No," said Mr. Slocum.

"Are you talking about a burglar?" Father asked him.

"It's a possibility."

"But I thought most burglaries took place at night."

"As a matter of fact, most of them take place in the daytime, when the householders are away."

Still gazing idly at the streamer of blue smoke, Boyle said, "You get a lotta burglaries round here?"

Mr. Slocum frowned, shook his head. "Not a great many, no."

Boyle watched the smoke. "Anything taken from the house?"

"Not according to the police," said Mr. Slocum, and looked at Father.

"They asked me to look," he said. "Audrey had some jewelry in our bedroom dresser, and we kept some cash in a cookie jar in the kitchen. They were both still there. But maybe there was a burglar, and maybe he got frightened off before he could find them."

Boyle stopped watching the smoke and looked at Father. "Maybe," he said. "But why did he go to the guest room first?"

Mr. Slocum said, "What do you mean?"

Boyle sucked on the cigarette. "Why would he go up there before he finished the downstairs? Most burglars, they know the loot in the house is gonna be in the bedroom or in the kitchen. They know all about cookie jars. And most burglars, what they're thinking the whole time they're in there is getting out. Someone comes in while he's upstairs, the burglar's gonna be trapped up there. Doesn't it make sense he'd check out the kitchen first?"

"But maybe this man wasn't a professional," Father said. "Maybe he hadn't thought all that out."

Boyle shrugged. "Maybe not." He inhaled on his cigarette, sat back, exhaled, and watched the smoke drift upward.

Mr. Slocum said to me, "You say that your stepmother usually took a small nap after breakfast?"

"After breakfast and after lunch," I said. "She said her feet hurt her." Guilt nudged me, and I added, "Her feet really did hurt, I guess."

"And she usually took her naps in the guest room?"

"Yes, so she could hear the doorbell if anyone came."

"You can't hear the bell," Father said, "from the back of the house, upstairs, where our bedroom is."

Slocum nodded. To me: "And when you found her, did she look as though she might have been asleep when it happened?"

"I guess so. Yes."

"She was lying on the bed," Mr. Slocum said to Father, "and according to the police report, there were no signs of a struggle anywhere in the room. Presumably she *was* asleep. And Amanda was asleep as well. A burglar *could* have entered the house. How many keys are there to the front door?"

Father frowned. "The police asked me the same thing last night, you know."

"I'm sure they did."

"Well," Father said, "I have one. Audrey has—Audrey had one. Mr. Cutler, the owner of the house, has at least one. And William has one. Four that I know of."

"Where did Mrs. Burton keep her key?"

"On a nail in the kitchen."

"When you went over the house with the police, did you notice if it was there?"

"No. It didn't occur to me."

"Did they ask you about it? Where it was kept?"

"Earlier, yes."

He turned to me. "Amanda, you don't have a key?"

"No."

He sat back, his face thoughtful. No one spoke for a few moments.

At last Boyle said, "So what happens now?"

Mr. Slocum shrugged. "Amanda and Miss Borden give their statements to the police. And we try to locate your son, Mr. Croft. I'd like to speak with him before the coroner's inquest. That'll be on Monday. It's basically a formality. Unless the police discover anything new, its findings are essentially a foregone conclusion."

"Yeah," said Boyle. "Doesn't sound like she committed suicide."

I astounded myself by producing an explosive giggle. Clapping my hand over my mouth, I blushed furiously.

No one spoke; Mr. Slocum was smiling his ironic smile.

Boyle glanced around the room. "Whoops," he said. He held out his hands, palm up, to Father and Miss Lizzie. "Sorry."

Father nodded abruptly. Miss Lizzie attempted to press her lips even more tightly together.

Boyle turned to Mr. Slocum and, evidently trying to get the conversation back on track, said, "So where do I fit in? You want me to sniff out the brother? This William?"

"That," said Mr. Slocum, "is up to Miss Borden."

Boyle looked at her.

"I should like you to stay close to hand," she said, some resistance to the idea visible on her face. "Mr. Burton may wish to engage your agency in the search for his son, and I would suggest to him that he do so. But I believe you'd perform a more useful function conducting your investigations here in town."

"Which investigations?" Boyle asked.

Mr. Slocum said, "Miss Borden feels that the local police, in their rush to judgment, may overlook something."

"I have," said Miss Lizzie, "placed an advertisement

in the local newspaper today, offering a reward for information leading to the arrest and conviction of the person responsible for Mrs. Burton's murder. If anyone comes forward with information that seems promising, I should like you to pursue it."

"What kind of a reward are we talking here?" Boyle asked her.

"Five thousand dollars."

Father shook his head. "Miss Borden, I really can't allow you to—"

"I appreciate your concern, Mr. Burton," she said, "but it is, after all, my money."

"Yes, but surely—"

"Really, Mr. Burton. My mind is made up."

"Miss Borden," he said. "Please. At least let me contribute some part of it."

She cocked her head, nodded it. "If you insist."

Boyle said, "That's a lotta cash, Miz Borden."

She nodded again. "I am aware of that."

"You're gonna get a lotta loonies crawling out of the woodwork, they hear about it."

"Possibly. But possibly we will uncover something that the police would not."

"Probably uncover a lotta things."

"That's as may be."

"And it's an open case. Police aren't gonna be too thrilled, I start poking around in it."

"Does that bother you?"

He shrugged. "Not a whole lot."

"And bear in mind," she said, "that should you unearth any such information on your own, you will yourself be entitled to the reward."

Exhaling smoke, Boyle shook his head. "Not allowed

to take it. Against the rules." He shrugged. "And besides, money like that, it just complicates things."

Miss Lizzie raised both eyebrows now, in surprise or disbelief. "But can we count on you? Will you accept the job?"

Boyle smiled. "Dunno if you can count on me. But sure, I'll take the job."

I said to Mr. Slocum, "Will I have to tell them?"

"Tell whom, Amanda?" he said. "Tell what?"

"The police. About what William said. On the porch."

"If they ask you, Amanda. Yes. I'm afraid so."

———

"Try," said Officer Medley. "Try to remember if the door was bolted."

"I can't," I said. "I really can't remember."

Officer Medley and Chief Da Silva, when I mentioned Marge Grady and the cardboard box, had exchanged the same sort of quick complicit looks that Father and Mr. Slocum had. And they had seized upon, as I had feared they would, and they had made much of William's parting words to Audrey, nodding and passing Dark Significant Looks. Now they hammered, stubbornly, at the front door.

"Come on, Amanda," urged Medley, who had been doing most of the questioning. He demonstrated his winning smile. "Give it a try."

"She's already explained," said Mr. Slocum with bland patience, "that she can't remember."

"It's pretty important, sir," Medley told him earnestly. Officer Medley was capable of a wonderful earnestness.

Across the room the police stenographer, a remarkably short young woman, to all intents a dwarf, sat poised in a gingham dress over her notebook. Her name was Miss Mullavey.

Chairs had been moved by Boyle, Medley, and Mr. Slocum from the dining room into the parlor. Few objects are as intractable as a dining-room chair; willful, it resists any major relocation. Even the usually adroit Mr. Slocum had seemed ungainly and comical (although endearingly so) as he wrestled his charge into position atop the Persian carpet. All eight of us were distributed around the room in an irregular circle; with cups and saucers on our laps we might have passed for a (fairly motley) afternoon tea.

I was desperately tired by now of all these questions. First from Mr. Slocum and then, with less tact (but heaps of earnestness) from Officer Medley. I tried again, however. I remembered tottering, almost tumbling, down the stairs, remembered that awful coppery stink in my nostrils. Remembered reaching out, seeing my hand move toward the door. . . .

"If she can't remember," Mr. Slocum said to Officer Medley, "she can't remember."

Fingers going for the bolt . . .

"She's undergone an enormous strain," he said.

"It was *bolted*," I cried. And then, more calmly: "It was bolted, I do remember."

Medley's glance skipped to Da Silva, then back to me. He grinned. "That's swell, Amanda. That's terrific. You're sure?"

"Yes," I said. "I'm sure."

Slowly, with an air of having achieved something of supreme importance, Officer Medley sat back.

Mr. Slocum was slouched down in his chair, hands in his pockets, the ankle of his lime-green sock perched atop his white linen knee. His brow furrowed, his lips in a reflective pucker, he mulled over this new development. Boyle blew slow streamers of smoke toward the ceiling. Da Silva was, as he had been throughout, expressionless.

Miss Lizzie had not changed her own expression, primly aloof, since the police arrived. Nor had she spoken. Now she said, "Was the door on the back porch latched?"

"Yes," said Officer Medley.

"Do you have her key?"

Medley frowned. "What?"

"Mrs. Burton's key to the front door. Do you have that?"

Medley glanced at Da Silva, then back to Miss Lizzie. "Mrs. Burton's key."

"I believe that's what I said."

"Well," said Officer Medley, clearly hesitating.

"Ah," said Mr. Slocum with a sudden smile. "So you haven't found it."

"Not yet," said Medley, by his staunch tone implying that the thing would doubtless materialize at any moment.

"I see," Mr. Slocum said, and nodded pleasantly. "And what about witnesses? Have any turned up?"

Officer Medley looked again at Da Silva, apparently uncertain whether he was permitted to answer questions as well as pose them.

Da Silva said flatly, "No."

Mr. Slocum's left eyebrow arched. "Really? Someone commits a murder in broad daylight and then goes marching merrily down the street, no doubt covered with gore, and no one sees anything?"

"We don't know," Da Silva said, "that the murderer went down the street."

"Ah," said Mr. Slocum. "Yes. Probably he lolled about on the beach for a time, and then swam away."

"We don't know what the murderer did," said Da Silva. "The beach was deserted yesterday. For the same reason that everyone on the street was inside, with their shades drawn. The heat."

"What about forensic evidence? Did you find anything in the house that might help?"

Da Silva produced his quick cold frown. "Nothing."

"But there must be something, old man. I mean, you don't commit a crime like that without leaving evidence about. In the room. On your person."

"The drains," said Miss Lizzie.

Everyone looked at her.

Over her pince-nez she asked me, "Is there a wash-room upstairs? On the guest-room side of the house?"

I nodded. "A small one. Just a shower and a sink. And a toilet."

She turned to Da Silva. "Have you looked in the drains?"

The chief glanced at Medley, who gave a small quick shake of his head. Da Silva turned to Miss Lizzie. "And why, exactly, would we do that?"

She said, "It's obvious, surely. He was probably stained with blood. Wouldn't his first thought be to wash it away before he went outside? Some it may have remained in the trap below the drain. If it did, I imagine there was very little he could do about it."

Da Silva was smiling that hard small smile that was as cold as his frown. "*He*, Miss Borden?"

Chapter
NINE

DURING THE INTERVIEW with Miss Lizzie, it was Chief Da Silva rather than Officer Medley who asked the questions. Once again, the rest of us became an audience. None of us spoke, except for Mr. Slocum, who interrupted from time to time, acting almost as a referee. And none of us moved, except for Mr. Boyle, who puffed quietly away, one by one, at a chain of cigarettes; and for the diminutive police stenographer, whose pen darted with swift metronomic efficiency across the pages of her notebook.

> *Chief Da Silva:* Miss Borden, how long have you been residing at One-oh-two Water Street?
>
> *Miss Borden:* Since the beginning of May.
>
> *Chief Da Silva:* You rented the house for the summer?
>
> *Miss Borden:* Yes.

Chief Da Silva: Did you know the deceased, Mrs. Audrey Burton?

Miss Borden: I did not.

Chief Da Silva: But you were aware, were you not, that Mrs. Burton resided at One Hundred Water Street, next door to you?

Miss Borden: Yes.

Chief Da Silva: Did you ever speak with her?

Miss Borden: No.

Chief Da Silva: Come now, Miss Borden. You expect us to believe that you lived next door to the deceased for several months and never once spoke with her? Not even to say hello?

Miss Borden: What you believe, or disbelieve, is of very little interest to me.

Mr. Darryl Slocum: Miss Borden has answered your question, Chief Da Silva. Perhaps we can go on.

Chief Da Silva: Miss Borden, you notified the police, by telephone, that Mrs. Burton had been murdered. Is that correct?

Miss Borden: Yes.

Chief Da Silva: How did you know this?

Miss Borden: Miss Burton, young Amanda Burton, her stepdaughter, came to my front door and told me.

Chief Da Silva: What time was this?

Miss Borden: About twenty minutes after twelve.

Chief Da Silva: At approximately twelve-twenty on the afternoon of August the second, is that correct?

Miss Borden: Yes.

Chief Da Silva: And what, exactly, did Miss Burton say?

Miss Borden: That someone was dead and that there was blood all over.

Chief Da Silva: Those were her exact words?

Miss Borden: As I recall them.

Chief Da Silva: Did you ask her who was dead?

Miss Borden: I did.

Chief Da Silva: And what was her reply?

Miss Borden: That it was her mother.

Chief Da Silva: How did she appear to you?

Miss Borden: She appeared to be in shock.

Chief Da Silva: Have you had any medical training, Miss Borden?

Miss Borden: No.

Chief Da Silva: Then what, exactly, qualified you to diagnose Miss Burton?

Mr. Slocum: Hold on, old man. You asked her how the girl appeared to her. It seems to me that she's answered that question.

Chief Da Silva: What were the symptoms of this shock you diagnosed?

Miss Borden: She was quite pale. Her speech was disjointed.

Chief Da Silva: What form of treatment did you prescribe?

Miss Borden: Are you asking me what I did next?

Chief Da Silva: Yes.

Miss Borden: I took her inside and tried to comfort her.

Chief Da Silva: How?

Miss Borden: I wrapped her in a shawl and gave her some brandy.

Chief Da Silva: What is your relationship with Amanda Burton?

Miss Borden: She is a friend.

Chief Da Silva: Do you often give her brandy?

Miss Borden: No.

Chief Da Silva: Have you ever given it to her before?

Miss Borden: No.

Chief Da Silva: Are you aware, Miss Borden, of the Volstead Act?

Mr. Slocum: We're wandering a little far afield, aren't we? If you want to arrest everyone who's got a spot of medicinal brandy in the cupboard, you'd have to arrest half the town, including, I daresay, most of the police department.

Chief Da Silva: We'll leave it for the moment. Miss Borden, why would Miss Burton come to you?

Miss Borden: I am her neighbor and, as I said, her friend.

Chief Da Silva: She's visited your house before?

Miss Borden: Yes.

Chief Da Silva: Often?

Miss Borden: Yes.

Chief Da Silva: On a daily basis?

Miss Borden: I shouldn't say that often.

Chief Da Silva: Once a week? Twice a week? Three times a week?

Miss Borden: Perhaps three times a week. Perhaps four times.

Chief Da Silva: And what did the two of you do on these visits?

Miss Borden: We played cards.

Chief Da Silva: What sort of cards?

Mr. Slocum: Surely that's irrelevant?

Chief Da Silva: I'm trying, *counselor*, to establish the relationship between Miss Borden and the girl.

Mr. Slocum: You've established it. They're friends and they played cards together. Whether they played gin or whist, or poker for that matter, has no bearing on the matter at hand.

Chief Da Silva: Thank you for your advice, counselor.

Mr. Slocum: Don't mention it, old man.

Chief Da Silva: Miss Borden, what did you do after you comforted Miss Burton with your brandy?

Miss Borden: I went next door.

Chief Da Silva: You mean to the Burton residence?

Miss Borden: Yes.

Chief Da Silva: Why?

Miss Borden: To verify what Amanda had told me.

Chief Da Silva: I see. And what did you find?

Miss Borden: I found Mrs. Burton.

Chief Da Silva: What do you mean, you found her?

Miss Borden: I found her in the guest room, dead.

Chief Da Silva: How do you know she was dead? Did you examine her?

Miss Borden: It was obvious from the nature of her wounds.

Chief Da Silva: Did you touch her body?

Miss Borden: I did not.

Chief Da Silva: Did you touch anything in the room?

Miss Borden: No.

Chief Da Silva: But you did enter the room.

Miss Borden: I took a step into the room. It was obvious even from the doorway that the woman was dead.

Chief Da Silva: You found her in the guest room?

Miss Borden: Yes.

Chief Da Silva: You proceeded from your residence to the Burton residence and went directly to the guest room?

Miss Borden: Yes.

Chief Da Silva: How did you know she was there?

Miss Borden: Miss Burton had told me.

Chief Da Silva: But you say you went *directly* to the guest room. Had you ever been in the Burton residence before?

Miss Borden: No.

Chief Da Silva: Do you mean to say that while Miss Burton was in a state of shock, she gave you directions as to how to locate the guest room?

Miss Borden: No, I do not mean to say that. Had I meant to say that, I should have done so. Miss Burton told me some three weeks ago where the guest room was.

Chief Da Silva: Why would she do that?

Miss Borden: We were discussing the similarities between our two houses. They are, for the most part, identical. She told me then where the guest room was.

Chief Da Silva: And you remembered this three weeks later?

Miss Borden: Do you find that remarkable?

Chief Da Silva: I find it impressive.

Miss Borden: That does not surprise me.

Mr. Slocum: I think we've covered this point sufficiently, don't you, old man?

Chief Da Silva: What did you do after you discovered the body of Mrs. Burton?

Miss Borden: I returned to my house.

Chief Da Silva: And then?

Miss Borden: I made a telephone call.

Chief Da Silva: To whom?

Miss Borden: To my lawyer, in Boston.

Chief Da Silva: You didn't telephone the police?

Miss Borden: You know quite well that I did.

Chief Da Silva: But only after you telephoned a lawyer.

Miss Borden: Yes.

Chief Da Silva: Why is that, Miss Borden?

Miss Borden: I wanted to protect Miss Burton's interests.

Chief Da Silva: What led you to believe her interests might be in jeopardy?

Miss Borden: I have had some small experience with the police before.

Chief Da Silva: And when might that've been, Miss Borden?

Mr. Slocum: I don't see that my client has any reason to answer that question.

Chief Da Silva: Why not? Does she have something to hide, Mr. Slocum?

Mr. Slocum: Any experience that Miss Borden may've had with the police would be a matter of record. And it would also be totally irrelevant to this inquiry.

Chief Da Silva: Miss Borden is not under arrest, counselor.

Mr. Slocum: Ah. I thought that perhaps that small fact had escaped your notice.

Chief Da Silva: Would you like to answer the question, Miss Borden?

Mr. Slocum: As her lawyer, I advise Miss Borden not to answer it.

Chief Da Silva: Miss Borden?

Miss Borden: Yes.

Chief Da Silva: Would you like to answer the question?

Miss Borden: I think not.

Chief Da Silva: You refuse to answer the question?

Mr. Slocum: She just said so. Does memory serve me correctly, or didn't you say something yesterday about not badgering witnesses?

Chief Da Silva: Slocum, I'm growing a bit tired of you.

Mr. Slocum: And here I thought we were getting along swimmingly.

Chief Da Silva: And so, Miss Borden, you telephoned your lawyer. What was the result of that call?

Miss Borden: He told me he would telephone a local lawyer, Mr. Slocum here, and ask him to come to my house.

Chief Da Silva: Which of course, being the conscientious soul he is, Mr. Slocum immediately did.

Mr. Slocum: Nicely phrased, old man.

Chief Da Silva: Miss Borden, how many other telephone calls did you make before you called the police?

Miss Borden: One.

Chief Da Silva: To whom?

Miss Borden: To Dr. Bowen.

Chief Da Silva: For what purpose?

Miss Borden: Miss Burton was in shock. I felt she needed a doctor.

Chief Da Silva: And then, finally, you called the police.

Miss Borden: Yes.

Chief Da Silva: Do you have any idea who might've murdered Mrs. Burton?

Miss Borden: None.

Chief Da Silva: Can you tell us anything further that might help?

Miss Borden: No.

Chief Da Silva: Nothing?

Miss Borden: Nothing.

Chief Da Silva: Thank you for your cooperation, Miss Borden.

The stenographer sheathed the nib of her pen in its cap and flipped her notebook closed.

Mr. Slocum said to Da Silva, "Before you go, old man, I wonder if you'd agree to increase the police guard outside Miss Borden's house."

Da Silva was frowning, annoyed. "I have only a limited number of officers, Slocum. Half of them are already occupied with this case, and the rest are doing twice the work they should be."

"I realize that," Mr. Slocum said. "But you've seen that crowd outside. They're only a single sluggish thought away from turning into a mob. Far be it from me to tell you your job, but imagine how it will look in the newspapers if something were to happen to Miss Borden or young Miss Burton."

Da Silva smiled. Briefly. "What would I do, Slocum, without your concern for my good name?"

"Think nothing of it, old man."

Da Silva nodded. "Very well. Two more officers."

"Thank you," said Mr. Slocum.

Da Silva stood. Then Medley stood, then the stenographer, then the rest of the men in the room.

"After Miss Mullavey has transcribed her notes," said Da Silva, "someone will bring the statements here for Miss Borden and Miss Burton to sign."

"I have every confidence in Miss Mullavey," said Mr. Slocum, smiling gallantly at the short stenographer. (I knew that he was only being pleasant, but I wondered why he would bother for such a mousy, drab little thing.)

Da Silva's glance flicked to mine, and I looked into his dark unfeeling eyes. "Do you happen to remember, Miss Burton, what clothes your brother was wearing yesterday?"

I looked at Father. He nodded.

"He had on a white shirt and white pants," I said. "And white shoes." I remembered him bursting into the kitchen as bright and handsome as a movie star, grinning hugely and moving, despite his size, with an effortless grace.

Da Silva was nodding to Officer Medley. "That corroborates Mrs. Mortimer's description."

Father said to him, "How is that you haven't found him yet?"

Da Silva turned to him. "We've been looking for him, Mr. Burton, for only a day now. But we'll find him." These last words were spoken with such a finality that neither Father nor I could draw much comfort from them.

"He had nothing to do with what happened to Audrey," Father said. "I know that."

"Then," said Da Silva, "the sooner we find him and eliminate him as a suspect, the better for everyone."

Father said nothing, merely took a long deep breath.

"One more thing," said Da Silva, and turned to the Pinkerton man. "I'm sure you realize, Mr. Boyle, that this is an active murder investigation. If I learn that you've obstructed our work in any way, I'll be very disappointed."

"Wouldn't think of it, Chief," said Boyle.

"See that you don't. I can make life extremely unpleasant for you."

"I got the message, Chief. Count on me."

"We'll see our own way out," Da Silva said to Miss Borden.

After Medley and Miss Mullavey had trooped out behind Da Silva (Medley forgetting to reward me with another stalwart grin), the men sat down and Boyle said, "Nifty guy. What does he eat for breakfast? Baling wire?"

Mr. Slocum smiled. "He's a good policeman."

Boyle said, "Wasn't all that good, him missing those drains." Grinning, he turned to Miss Lizzie. "I don't think you put yourself in real solid with the chief there, Miz Borden."

Miss Lizzie smiled dryly. "No, I expect not."

"He assumed Medley had checked the drains," said Mr. Slocum. "As Medley should have. But this is the first real homicide investigation those people have handled. Da Silva's the only one on the force with any real experience. Don't underestimate him. I don't think he'll be making any more assumptions. He's very smart and he's very dedicated."

"Yeah," said Boyle, "he seems pretty thrilled with you too."

"Ignorant armies"—Mr. Slocum smiled—"clashing by night."

Father spoke. "What does it mean, Slocum, their not finding Audrey's key?"

Mr. Slocum offered a small shrug. "I really don't know. Obviously, the police don't either. But I can tell you what one of its consequences is. It weakens their case against your son. If William had a key, there'd be no reason for him to take Mrs. Burton's. But someone else, our hypothetical burglar, *could've* taken it and used it to bolt the front door."

"I don't have a key," I said. "Does that mean they think I took it?"

"No, Amanda," Mr. Slocum said, and smiled. "They didn't ask you, did they? And besides, if they really wanted to make any sort of case, they'd have to *prove* you took it. You didn't, did you?"

"Uh-uh. No."

"Okay," said Boyle. "So what's next?"

"Well," said Mr. Slocum, "what I suggest we do, all of us, is get some rest. We can meet back here tomorrow at, say, eleven o'clock. By then, I'm sure, enough fair citizens of the town will've seen Miss Borden's advertisement and suddenly found themselves spurred by an inexplicable sense of duty. If it's acceptable to you, Miss Borden, Harry and I'll round them up and bring them over."

Miss Lizzie nodded. "Perfectly acceptable."

I asked Mr. Slocum, "Can I listen?"

He frowned. "I don't think, Amanda, that you'd find it an especially edifying experience." He shrugged. "But of course it's up to your father."

Father looked up. "What? Oh. Well, Amanda, yes, I suppose so. If you really want to."

He had been lost in thought; worrying, I believed, about William.

I was worrying about him too. Where on earth had he gone?

Chapter
TEN

MR. SLOCUM LEFT for his office. Father and Harry Boyle left for the Fairview, to get an early dinner, Father promising he would return to say good night before he went to sleep. He had fallen in with Miss Lizzie's suggestion that he use the Pinkertons to help locate my brother; Boyle would take down whatever information Father provided and transmit it, by telephone, to his agency in Boston.

Miss Lizzie's sitting room—in which, as in most sitting rooms of the period, no one ever actually sat—lay on the north side of the building, and from its window I could clearly see our own summer rental. Less than an hour after Da Silva and the others had departed, I watched through the curtain as another detatchment of police arrived. With much honking of horn and ringing of bells, their black van slowly shouldered aside the reluctant crowd before my house.

Four in all, the policemen tumbled from the van like

Keystone Kops and leaned their way through the swarm, which was buzzing now, aroused from its lethargy. Armed with wrenches, hacksaws, sledgehammers, and an empty metal bucket, they rattled up the walk and clattered across the porch to disappear into the house. Behind them, the crowd moaned, hissed, applauded.

Over the next hour or so I paced back and forth between the sitting room and the parlor, where Miss Lizzie sat at the coffee table practicing glides and palms. (During the time I stayed with her, she never practiced her magic when anyone other than I was present. Nor did she smoke her cigars.)

Finally the policemen reemerged onto the street, looking morose and secretive, something at which policemen are expert. Two of them wore their shirtsleeves rolled back, displaying forearms calico with grime, and one of these carried the metal bucket, covered now with a towel and, by the way he held it, gingerly, away from his body, no longer empty. The crowd clustered around, murmuring and mumbling, but the policemen shook their heads at jabbered questions, jerked themselves free from clutching fingers. One of them buffeted his way to the front of the van and cranked it astart. Then he and the officer who had towed the bucket drove slowly from the house, backing out down Water Street. The other two officers jostled through the crowd and came along the sidewalk to join Officer O'Hara at the front porch.

I wandered back to Miss Lizzie. She looked up, cut the deck, and held it out to show me an ace.

I said, "There are two more policemen on the porch."

"Was that the noise I heard? The arrival of the Pretorian guard?"

"And I think they found something next door. In the

drains." I felt a small shiver, not entirely unpleasant, curl up my spine as I imparted this melodramatic bit of news.

"I imagine they did," she said, looking down to give the cards an overhand shuffle. She seemed unreasonably blasé, considering that a search of the drains had been, after all, her idea. "I'm sure Mr. Slocum will find out about that and let us know." She split the deck, then riffle-shuffled. "How would you like to learn the Nikola system?"

"What's that?"

"It's a stacked deck invented by a man named Louis Nikola. It's really quite wonderful. Here, sit down and I'll show you."

Briefly, the Nikola system is a method of prearranging the cards. Every position in the deck from one to fifty-two is assigned a name. Each card is also given a name. The name of all clubs except for face cards begins with the letter C; of all hearts, with the letter H; et cetera. The two of clubs, for example, is called *can* and is located at position twenty-two, which is called *nun*. One remembers this by picturing the jolly image of a nun drinking from a can.

Although not (quite) as complicated as it might at first seem, the system does require a good deal of rote work. I spent a week on it before I had the mnemonics down. Once mastered, however, it allows one to perform a range of rather spectacular effects. And, additionally, the first twenty-one cards are stacked for poker, while the entire deck is stacked for whist or bridge. I have made a point, since I learned it, of always carrying a Nikola deck with me. In the Yucatan once, twenty years later, it saved my life.

But that afternoon, Miss Lizzie had hardly begun explaining how it worked when she was interrupted by a sudden knock at the front door.

She set down the cards and frowned at me. "You'd best stay here, Amanda," she said, and stood up.

I waited until she was out in the hallway before I followed her.

From the entrance to the parlor, I watched her lean toward the door, cock her head, and call out, "Who is it?"

"Officer O'Hara," came the answer.

"What do you want?" Miss Lizzie called.

"To borrow the use of the facilities, if ya'd be so kind."

Miss Lizzie hesitated for a moment, then turned the bolt. She eased open the door as though she were ready, indeed eager, to slam it shut.

Both of them were careful not to touch each other. Officer O'Hara edged into the hallway and deferentially adjusted the brim of his cap; Miss Lizzie backed away. "Ma'am," said O'Hara.

"Down the hallway, on the left," Miss Lizzie said over her shoulder.

"Thank ya, ma'am," he said, and adjusted his hat brim again. Then, turning and seeing me, he adjusted it once more. "Miss Burton. Uh. And how are you today?"

"Fine, thank you."

"Glad to hear it. Well now"—his glance darting between us rather like a cornered bear's—"if you'll just excuse me, I'll be gettin' out of your way." And then, with a brave, rolling, pigeon-toed gait, he sauntered down the hallway.

Miss Lizzie shut the door, shot the bolt, and turned to me. She made a sour face. "If I didn't let him in, he'd just go round back and use the yard."

I said, "Do you think he'll tell us what they found next door?"

"I doubt he knows. Why would anyone tell *him*?" She saw my disappointment and said, more softly, "Is it really so important for you to know, Amanda?"

"Yes."

"Why?"

"I'm not sure," I said. I suspect it had something to do with wanting to understand the fragments of what had been, until only yesterday, my life. Chaos had suddenly shattered it, my stepmother murdered, my brother missing; and I think I felt that if I could examine the pieces of rubble, grasp their meaning, then somehow I might be able to restore not my life as it had been, but at least its underlying order. The same belief, that order *can* ultimately be discovered, is the force that drives policemen and physicists and a large percentage of paranoiacs. "I just want to *know*," I told Miss Lizzie.

She smiled sadly. "All right, child," she said. "Ask him, then. The Irishman. I'll be inside. Just make sure you come to get me before you open the door."

"Thank you, Miss Lizzie."

She touched me lightly on the cheek with her fingertips and rustled past me into the parlor.

A few minutes later Officer O'Hara came rolling down the hall. I stood before the door, effectively blocking it.

"Officer O'Hara?" I said.

"Yes?" His small eyes were blinking and he was getting his cornered look again.

"What did they find?"

The eyes narrowed. "What d'ya mean?"

"In the drains next door. At my house."

"Well, now," he said, and I think he was trying to be avuncular, "I don't believe that's somethin' a little girl ought to trouble herself about."

"I'm not a little girl," I said. "I'm thirteen. And I've already heard worse. And seen worse," I reminded him.

He blinked at me, then frowned.

"Well, ya know," he said, scratching at his bulbous nose, "I've been meanin' to talk to ya about that. And now I see I've got me chance. What it is, I figure I was a mite inconsiderate yesterday, rushin' in like I did and blabberin' away like a bloody idiot. I owe ya an apology, and there's no man alive can say that when Frank O'Hara owes a thing, he don't pay it up. So I'm here to tell ya, young Miss Burton, that I'm sorry."

I blushed. It was, I thought, awfully generous of him. I was old enough to realize how seldom adults apologized to children. But I was also old enough to take advantage of it.

"Thank you," I said, smiling as sweetly as a Borgia. "But really, Officer O'Hara, couldn't you tell me what they found next door?"

He hesitated. "I'm not so sure, ya know, it's a good thing to be talkin' about."

"Mr. Slocum, the lawyer, will find out tomorrow anyway. He'll tell me, I know he will."

He frowned in disapproval.

Perhaps Mr. Slocum had been the wrong tack to take. Back to fundamentals: "*Please*, Officer O'Hara?"

He glanced at the front door as though spies might be loitering outside, then, lowering his head and his voice, he said, "Well now, they had the devil's own time gettin' at the trap, I'll tell ya. The trap, that's the bendy part in the pipe, ya see, just below the drain thing. Jimmy tells me they had to rip up the tiles and all from the floor of the shower. And the wood too, no less. They had to smash it all up with the hammer. Took 'em forever, Jimmy says. And I guess it'll take 'em nearly that long to fix it up all proper again."

It was taking him nearly that long to tell it; but you never hurried a gift.

"And then, when they got to it, ya see, they couldn't just wrench it out—rusted, it was, from the humidity of it all. They had to use the hacksaw, Jimmy tells me, and even then it was no piece a cake, no, not by a long shot. And in a cramped narrowy space like that, ya see—"

I hurried the gift. "But they *found* something."

He nodded with great gravity. "They did that. They found something."

"Was it blood?"

"It was indeed. It was blood. I'm sorry to say it was your poor stepmother's own life's blood they found."

———

Miss Lizzie shut the front door on Officer O'Hara and turned to me. "You look pale, child. Would you like to lie down?"

"No," I said. "No, thank you." But I was *feeling* pale, wispy and insubstantial, as though a light held behind my back might shine straight through me, organ, flesh, and bone.

It was all very well to speculate, enjoying the shuddery *frisson*, about what might be in the drains. But the thought that Audrey's blood had actually been found in there, trapped with bits of hair and a gray scum of soap, had made me suddenly faint, light-headed. And even now, as we stood there, my stepmother's "own life's blood" was slapping against the sides of a tin bucket in the police van, gurgle and slosh. . . .

"They found it," Miss Lizzie said.

"Yes."

"Come sit down, dear. I'll make you some chamomile."

She made me some chamomile, brought it to me, and asked if I thought I could eat anything. I told her no, thank you, but said that if she was hungry she should by all means eat. She would have a little something later, she said, and hoped I would join her then. She asked if I'd like to continue with the Nikola system. I told her that just now I thought I would read for a while.

And so we sat there, Miss Lizzie on the sofa working her card tricks, me in the chair using the *Harper's* as an excuse for silence.

The drains had proved that the murderer had washed himself clean after killing Audrey. And, to me at least, they had also proved one thing more. That William had not killed her.

I had never believed he had. But now I saw the argument against his guilt as overwhelming, a kind of hierarchy of impossibilities.

William hated even the *idea* of killing. Once, four years ago in Boston, when he was thirteen and I was nine, he made himself a slingshot. To try it out, he went to a park along the Charles. The very first time he used it, he aimed at a strutting pigeon and hit it. He carried it home in tears. When Father told him there was nothing anyone could do, that the bird was far beyond the stage where it could be nursed back to life, William had buried it at the base of an elm tree on the street, saying prayers and erecting a small cross, sniffling the entire time.

So, William would not have killed Audrey.

I knew that William had a temper—I had seen him pick up a model schooner and hurl it across his bedroom to smash it against the wall, all because, after hours of trying to fit it into place, one single delicate spar had snapped. But his remorse, afterward, was as sudden as his anger. And, unprompted, he had gone to Father and apologized for ruining the gift Father had given him.

He was not a brooder, not one to coddle his anger silently over the hours and days, nursing it with bitterness and hate.

So, if William *had* killed Audrey, he would not have done it in the guest room, so long after the argument in the kitchen.

William possessed an innate sense of fairness. He was a Greco-Roman wrestler, the best in his weight class at school. Once, during a state championship, both his shoulders had touched the mat, for only an instant and unseen by his opponent, the crowd, or the referee. William could have continued; but he stopped the match and conceded the point and, with it, the championship. Later, when I asked him why, he looked at me as though he did not understand the question. Because I lost, he said. Yes, I said, but no one *knew*. But Amanda, he said as though he still could not grasp what I meant, *I* knew.

So, if William *had* killed Audrey, he would not have done it while she was lying there asleep and vulnerable.

Naturally, I did accept the (extremely remote) possibility that even such a paragon, even one so gentle, brave, and honorable as William could suffer a brain storm, could inexplicably, without warning, go insane. But suppose he had. Suppose some wild demon had taken him over, suppose some lunatic bubble had burst and sent venom foaming through his mind. Suppose he had found a hatchet, returned to the house, climbed up to the guest room, and hacked Audrey to death. *He would not, afterward, calmly walk into the shower and sluice himself clean.*

But if he was innocent—and, as I say, I *knew* he was —why had he not come forward after Audrey's death was discovered? (A question the police were doubtless asking themselves.)

I could see only one reason. He did not know that Audrey was dead.

Which meant that he was no longer here, in town. Had he been here, it would have been impossible for him *not* to know.

But if he left the town, presumably right after the fight with Audrey, where had he gone?

He would not have run to Boston, not to complain about Audrey to Father: He was too proud. Oh, he might have gone there, to the house, for money or clothes, but it would have been in stealth, no one the wiser.

Had he gone to any of his friends' houses, one of them would have told him about Audrey's murder; Boyle had said that the news had made the Boston papers.

So, wherever he had gone, it had to be a place where there were no people, and no newspapers, to tell him what had happened.

And, suddenly, I believed I knew where it was.

Chapter
ELEVEN

THE HOUSE OF my grandparents lay in the country-side some miles to the west of Boston. After my father's remarriage, William and I often spent summers there. Father would appear on weekends, usually without my stepmother, who declared herself allergic to an inventory of vegetation that at one time or another, or so it seemed to me, had included every species known to man. (For this reason, the houseplants in our Boston home were cunningly crafted of silk. Which provided the additional benefit that they required little attention and less affection, needing only an occasional dusting now and then.)

But her reluctance to visit, I thought then and I think now, lay more with her sentiment that Father's parents disapproved of her. In this she was correct. Although they were too polite ever to display outright distaste, they included her in conversation only belatedly, as though discovering, with a start, that this dowdy woman had actually been present in the room all along, and then obliged by etiquette, however reluctantly, to acknowledge that puzzling fact.

In any event, beyond the flat green expanse of grass strung with badminton nets and booby-trapped by croquet wickets, small rectangles of white wire that, during lawn parties, often snared a tipsy guest, my grandparents' house was flanked on three sides by a forest of maple and elm and oak. To me the forest had always seemed dank and deep, limitless, as impenetrable as any jungle in Africa and as teeming with probably carnivorous and certainly odious wildlife: snakes and lizards, wolves and bears. And other things lurked there too—the spirits of skulking red bepainted savages, and of the innocent and unsuspecting and presumably bewildered settlers tomahawked by these. I wanted never to enter it.

And then one summer—I was ten, William fourteen—I saw that my brother entered it on a regular basis. I watched from the glass-enclosed stone porch at the rear of the house as, every day, soon after lunch, he would stroll across the lawn, hands in his pockets as though he were taking a constitutional. When he reached the border of the forest, he would glance back once, quickly, furtively (I would duck), then slip like an Indian behind the black ragged trunk of a towering oak, and vanish.

I had no idea what he might be doing in there. Perhaps exploring, playing at Stanley in the Congo. Perhaps meeting a girl. His attitude toward girls, except of course toward myself, had changed over the past few years. Where before he had sneered and sulked whenever in their presence, now he seemed at once fascinated and abashed.

Seeing him disappear regularly into the forest, I pictured him kneeling on the banks of a small bubbling brook, beside a pretty shepherdess who in fact resembled those who, three years later, were frozen in perpetual pertness behind the glass in Miss Lizzie's guest room. Her hair fell in blond ringlets to her bare white shoulders, and she sat demurely on the grass with her hands atop her lap, the immaculate white skirt of her peasant dress unfolded all around her like an opened blossom.

From where she came, out of what fragments of fantasy and forgotten memory I invented her, I cannot say. I had at that point never seen a Dresden figurine, and at no time during our summers had I seen, or heard, or heard tell of, sheep in the vicinity.

One day, I resolved to follow him. I knew that the lawn was too broad for me to wait at the porch while he walked across it: by the time I myself arrived at the forest, he would be gone. So at lunch that afternoon, I made some remark to my grandparents about feeling poorly, no-nothing-serious-just-an-upset-stomach, and trudged up the front stairs toward my bedroom. I stood outside it, listening for a moment, then bolted along the corridor, scrambled down the back stairs, scampered silently out the porch, and sprinted across the lawn. I found an oak of my own, and I waited.

Birds twittered, insects buzzed. The forest behind me began to move closer, Birnam woods to Dunsinane, yet still I waited. Back there, snap of twig and slither of leaf said that animals, drawn perhaps by my scent, were on the move; yet still I waited.

At last William came around the house and began his ramble across the lawn. He might have been humming to himself, so nonchalant was he. Then suddenly, where the lawn ended, he dipped behind his oak.

I tarried for only a moment, then cantered over to

the tree. Poking my head around it, I watched him as he ambled twenty yards ahead down a shaded path. When he had gone another fifteen yards, I started to stalk him.

Another hundred yards in, he turned to the right. When I reached the spot, I saw that here the path met a crumbling stone wall, one built back in colonial times, probably, by settlers in their pre-tomahawk stage. The irregularly rounded black rocks were splotched with gray lichen and furred with a moss so green it seemed to glow.

And there was William, bounding from stone to stone atop the wall, skimming from shade to light down the tunnel of trees. And then, abruptly, he sprang off to the left.

Hurrying now, afraid I had lost him, I ran awkwardly along the stones, squinting through the foliage. And saw it, off to the side: a flutter of white among the trees. William's shirt.

I rushed down the path till I had him in sight once more and then, relaxing for the first time, began to notice that the forest was not so dim and dark after all; not so grim, so monolithic. It was open and inviting; it was luminous. All around me, gold danced with green. Sunlight wheeled down through the treetops, splashed against the leaves, washed across the grasses and the wildflowers. Butterflies floated and swooped; slim slight dragonflies with iridescent eyes hovered and darted and hovered again. The pale-brown leaves atop the ground, speckled bright yellow by the sun, looked soft enough to sleep on.

More trees lived here than I would have believed possible. I would not know all their names until much later, but I saw hickories as tall and straight as the masts of ships, gnarled crabapples, shaggy sycamores, delicate dogwoods and their white flowers, each petal tipped with a droplet of dark brown. (The blood of Jesus, my grand-mother said.) There were thickets of mountain laurel and honeysuckle. Silver birches, their peeling bark as fragile as onionskin, arched skyward and then dipped their branches toward the earth as though (so Mr. Frost has pointed out) they had been ridden there by the exultant swing of laughing boys.

It was, in short, an Enchanted Place, and, like any other princess in such a locale, I very shortly became lost. William was no longer in sight, and I was no longer certain that the path I followed was the one he had taken. I made tentative forays in several directions; but no William. At last, giving way to panic, I called out his name. No answer. Called it out again. No answer.

The forest closed in again around me, and a low cloud with a black underbelly and an impeccable sense of tim-ing went grinding across the sky and blotted out the sun.

I plopped down hopelessly to the ground and learned that dead leaves, sunspeckled or otherwise, are not soft. They are crumbly and prickly, they make bare legs itch, and they cling to a white cotton dress as though stapled there.

My dress! Somehow it had gotten stained with green, smeared with gray. Grandmother would have a fit!

But then Grandmother would never see me again, nor the dress. Not until next spring, when some hearty woodsman (boots, overalls, hefty axe slung over broad plaid shoulder) stumbled upon the bleached little skel-eton lying amid the leaves and the branches and the yellowed cotton tatters.

There would be a funeral, of course, tiny brittle bones rattling in the tiny casket, and everyone would weep at the young life so soon snuffed out. I pictured Grandmother's grief, and Grandfather's, and Father's, and William's (his mingled with an overwhelming and, one hoped, suicidal sense of guilt), and I began to cry.

A rustle in the forest. The woodsman? Already?

It was William, a look of annoyance on his face. "What are *you* doing here?"

I stopped crying. "Looking for you."

"What for?"

"I wanted to see what you were doing."

"None of your business."

"I'll tell Daddy."

"Oh, yeah? Tell him what?"

"That you've got a secret in the woods."

He gave me a shrewd look. "What kind of secret?"

"I don't know, but I'll tell him you come in here every day and you're hiding something."

"Hiding what?"

"I don't know, but Daddy will find out."

He scowled. "Amanda, how come you're such a brat?"

"I am *not* a brat. Come on, William, please tell me what it is?"

He hesitated. I saw my advantage, and pressed it. "Oh, William, *please*? Just show me. I won't tell anyone, I promise. Cross my heart and hope to die."

He was wavering, indecision on his face.

"I swear I won't. I *swear* it."

His eyes narrowed. "Swear it on a Bible?"

"We haven't got a Bible."

"They've got a whole bunch of them at Grandma's."

"All right, I will. I'll swear on one of those."

"Swear that if you tell, you'll go to hell and burn in fire forever?"

"Uh-huh. I swear."

"I'll get a Bible, you know, and make you swear on it." (He did.)

"That's okay. I swear it, I really do."

"Well. Okay. Follow me."

I think that, judging by his pride, he had wanted all along to show someone.

It was a fort. He had built it two years before and had, since then, continually made improvements. It was constructed of branches, each about two inches thick and seven feet long, nailed to either side of a long over-hanging limb of oak to form a sort of A-frame eight feet in length and five feet, at the base, in width. A canvas tarp was slung over it, to make it waterproof; and atop this, leaves had been piled to provide camouflage. (Indeed, from four feet away the structure was invisible.) A small clearing extended before it, in the center of which lay a semicircle of fire-blackened rocks. The fort, William told me, was designed as a family shelter, to be used in the event the Huns invaded Massachusetts. (The War was still in progress: grown men in the United States had devised schemes no less preposterous than William's refuge.)

"Can I go inside?" I asked him.

"Okay. But don't touch anything."

Inside, the floor of hard-packed earth gave off a woodsy smell of loam and mushroom. (To this day I cannot eat morels without recalling William's fort.) Against the far wall he had built shelves of rocks and planks, and these were lined with cans of peas, carrots, corn, corned beef, honey, jam, marmalade. There was no sign, however, none at all, of Little Bo Peep.

I clambered back outside. "William, all that food. You took it from Grandma's pantry."

"I only borrowed it," he said. "And besides, when the Huns come, Grandma and Grandpa will get to eat it."

I eyed the fort skeptically. "We're all going to live in that?"

"We'll build additions."

"What about when the food runs out?"

"We can eat roots and berries. They're all over the place. And we can trap rabbits."

"Rabbits? Oh no, William!"

"Only if we have to. To survive, I mean."

"What about water?"

"There's a stream just over there."

"What about the animals?"

"What animals?"

"You know. Bears and things."

"There aren't any bears around here."

"Yes, but snakes. . . ."

"Animals," he said with absolute conviction, "don't bother you if you don't bother them." Over the years I have learned that, with the exception of sharks and human beings, he was quite right.

I looked at the fort, looked back at William. "Can I come here?"

"What do you mean?"

"When you're not here. Can I come and play inside?"

"No, of course not. It's mine."

"You said it was for everybody, for the whole family."

"Yeah, but only when the Huns come."

I could hardly count upon the Huns; they were notoriously unreliable. "What about when you're not here? What about when you go over to the Bromptons' house? Sometimes you stay there for days. Someone could come along and find it."

"It's been here for two years, and no one's ever found it."

"Yes, but part of that was in wintertime and no one was around. I could guard it for you. If anyone came, I could go up to them and tell them I was lost, so they'd have to take me to Grandma's. They'd never find it then."

He considered this.

"Please, William? I *promise* I'll never tell anyone."

He had the grace to forbear pointing out that the threat I implied—of actually telling—was empty; I had already sworn an oath.

"Well, okay. But only when I'm gone. And no dolls or anything."

(I did bring my dolls—reasoning that if William had actually known them personally, he would have wanted them to share the fort—but I never told him.)

He looked over the fort, as pleased as Carnegie admiring his first library, then turned to me. "Do you like it?"

"William," I said, "I love it."

He beamed.

———

I watched Miss Lizzie as she turned over the middle card of three that lay atop the coffee table. It was the ace of spades. She scooped up the cards, shuffled them, used her thumbnail to split the deck, and, holding one-half in each hand, spread them simultaneously into perfect fans. Then, flawlessly, the cards rustling like leaves in a breeze, she melded them together. She glanced up, saw that I was watching, and smiled. "Can I get you something, dear? Some more tea?"

"No, thank you, Miss Lizzie. I'm all right." But I was thinking of the fort.

We had spent last summer at our grandparents', and the fort had still been there, still stocked with provisions, although William no longer went there every day—at sixteen he had other things on his mind, chiefly girls. (In two years his shyness had dropped away, possibly because, with the faulty taste that only one's older brother can possess, the girls he chose to court were so simpering and witless.)

Now, a year later, might he not have gone there once again? Had it not been designed, after all, as a refuge?

But I had sworn an oath, under pain of hellfire, never to tell anyone about the fort.

On the other hand, logically speaking I was already damned. Throughout the day, idly, I had been examining the image of Amanda amid the flames, turning it round and about as one might a bright shiny aggie or a gleaming shard of costume jewelry. There was, in the end, only one eternity; you could not be sentenced to it twice.

Yet violating the oath somehow seemed so much worse than wishing Audrey dead.

"Miss Lizzie?" I said.

She was palming the king of hearts. Distracted, she said, "Yes?"

"What do you think hell is like?"

"I don't know, dear. Pittsburgh?" Then, looking up, she saw by my frown that I was serious. "Why do you ask, Amanda?"

I shrugged. "Just curious, I guess."

"Well, child," she said, kindness in her tone, "I think that perhaps that's a question you should ask your father."

"I will," I said. Fat chance. "But I wanted to know what you thought about it."

She smiled. "What I think may be very different from what your father thinks."

"That's all right. What *do* you think?"

"Well," she said, "this is only my opinion, mind, but I really don't believe that hell exists. At least not the way the books and the Billy Sundays talk about it."

For a moment I was speechless. Startled not so much by what she said—startling enough—as by her saying it, *thinking* it, without being snatched from the face of the earth and hurled at once into that very place. Stammering, I said, "But—but where would we *go* then? Afterward? I mean the bad people. Where would they go?"

"I don't think they go anywhere. I think they stay here on earth."

"You mean like ghosts?"

"No, not like ghosts." She smiled faintly, thoughtfully. "Well, some of them, perhaps." I thought then of her mother, her father. Had they haunted her, hacked and bleeding? Had they come to her on lonely moonlit nights?

She said, "I think most of us stay here, through our actions, through the events we set in motion. Through the people we've known."

"But what about our soul? What about our spirit? Where does my *me* go when I die?"

She smiled. "Where was it before you were born?"

I thought about that. "In the Mind of God?"

She nodded. "All right. Yes. The Mind of God. That's as good a way as any of putting it."

"And we all go there?"

"We all *are* there, I think. We're all pieces of it, expressions of it. Everything is. If you look into the eyes of a dog or a cat, any animal, you can see it there, that Something, that Force. The Mind of God."

"Even bugs?"

She laughed. It seemed like weeks since I had heard her laugh. "If our own eyes were clear enough, yes, I think we could see it even in theirs."

"But what about—" I stopped, listening to the sudden murmur from the crowd outside. I looked at her.

"Perhaps it's your father coming back."

A pounding at the front door.

I think we both knew that it was not Father.

Once again I followed her, once again she held her face to the door and called out, "Who is it?"

"Officer Medley."

She unlocked the door, opened it. Medley stepped inside and she closed it behind him.

Officer Medley seemed grim. "I'm looking for Mr. Burton."

"He's not here," Miss Lizzie said. "I believe he's at the Fairview."

Medley shook his head. "I checked. He's not there."

"What is it?" I said. "Is it about William?"

Medley turned to me. His mouth tightened.

"Is it?" I said. "Is it about William?"

"Yes," he said.

Chapter
TWELVE

I STOOD IN my nightgown at the open window of the darkened room, staring past the lace curtains at the empty beach. The tide was low, and by starlight I could see broad fingers of flat gray sandbar curling out into the black glossy sea. I had been standing there for some time.

Officer Medley had told us only that William was still missing. He refused, stalwartly, to reveal what new information the police had obtained and insisted, earnestly, that he must speak with Father.

After he left, Miss Lizzie had made some mutton sandwiches, the meat cut from a roast in her icebox; but neither of us had eaten much. By ten o'clock, Father had still not returned. Miss Lizzie suggested I try to get some sleep, assuring me that the moment he did appear, she would send him to my room.

I had lain for a while, breathing in the smell of camphor, but sleep had not come.

What had the police found? Evidence, as Mr. Slocum would have said. But evidence of what?

Had they found him? Had they somehow located his fort? To get to my grandparents' from Boston, he would have had to hitchhike or take a train. Had someone seen him, reported him?

Worry, like sadness, feeds upon itself. After a while, lying there fretting in the dark, another thought occurred to me. For the first time since the murder (such is the protective power of self-absorption) I asked myself, if William had not killed Audrey, then who had?

Who had sneaked into our house with a hatchet, skulked up into the guest room, and chopped at her *twenty-five times*?

If he was a madman—and who but a madman could have made those wounds?—then he could be anyone, anywhere. He could be lying awake at this very moment, a few blocks away, gloating, plotting another kill. He might have been one of those anonymous faces in the crowd outside Miss Lizzie's house. I could imagine him letting his face go slack to mimic the dull fascination of those around him, all the while laughing inwardly and hugging his secret to his poisonous heart.

Whoever he was, he must have *known* that Audrey had been up there, in the guest room. Otherwise, he would have gone up the stairs at the back of the house, looking for her in Father's room, or in mine—

But perhaps he had. Perhaps he *had* crept up the back stairs, had peered into my parents' room, then opened the door to mine and seen me lying there. If I had not been asleep, if I had opened my eyes just then, then perhaps I would be as dead now as Audrey. I shuddered. It was not a comforting thought.

Whoever he was, he had killed my stepmother while I was lying *only ten or fifteen feet away.*

There were no connecting doors between the upstairs rooms at the front of the house and the upstairs rooms at the back. But the walls were thin, and there had been times when I was in my room, and Audrey in the guest room, that I had heard her moving about. Why had I not heard her murderer?

Murder, the act itself, should shriek so loudly that it awakens even the dead. But it did not, apparently. Apparently one could lie asleep in dreamy ignorance while, a few paces away, a human being was smashed, slashed, shattered.

Who had done that to her? And why?

The questions, all of them, would not stop drumming at me. Finally I had thrown back the sheet, rolled from the bed, and crossed over to the window. I stood and stared at the sea, as though somewhere out there beneath the skein of stars, between the black velvet and the black glass, the answers might lie. They had not.

Suddenly I heard, downstairs, the front door open and shut. And voices, low, indistinct, Miss Lizzie and a man. Father? Yes! Footsteps on the stairs. I padded quickly to the bed, hopped in, and whipped the sheet over me.

A gentle tapping at the door. It cracked open and a bar of light unfolded across the room. Father's voice called out, softly, almost a whisper, "Amanda?"

"I'm awake, Father."

The door swung open, and he stood silhouetted by the glow of the hallway lamp. From the sag of his shoulders I saw how tired he was.

"Shall I turn on the light?" He sounded raspy, worn.

"No, that's all right."

Leaving the door slightly ajar, he moved slowly, heavily, to the bed. He and the mattress sighed together as he sat upon it.

"William?" I said.

He shook his head. "They haven't found him yet."

"But they've found something, haven't they? Officer Medley was here."

"I know. He told me. I was at Mortimer's tavern, with Boyle."

"What did they find?"

"I called Mrs. Dougherty"—our housekeeper in Boston—"this morning and told her to let the police go through William's room. I thought they might find something that'd tell us where he's gone."

"Did they?"

"Mrs. Dougherty could see that someone had been in there. She'd dusted the room just a few days ago. Some of William's clothes were missing. And a rucksack."

The fort, I thought. He's gone to the fort.

Father took a deep breath, let it slowly out. "And they found his clothes on the floor of the closet. The clothes he was wearing yesterday. A white shirt, a pair of white pants."

"Yes?"

"They were stained with blood."

I shut my eyes against the image, shook my head. "No," I said. "No, Father, he didn't do it."

"I know, baby, I know." His hand found mine. "The Boston police are examining the stains. They've got tests now, chemical tests, that can prove it wasn't Audrey's blood. But if it wasn't . . ."

"If it wasn't Audrey's," I said, "it was William's blood."

"Yes, but it probably wasn't anything serious, Amanda. He was well enough, mobile enough, to get to Boston.

Maybe he cut himself, or he got a bloody nose somehow."
I knew I was not the only one that Father was trying to
convince.

"Father—"

"There's something else, Amanda."

"What?"

"Last night, when I talked to the police, I didn't tell
them the truth."

Father lying? "What do you mean?"

He was looking toward the window, out at the night,
as though he, too, sought answers there. "You're going
to hear about it anyway, I'm afraid. You might as well
hear it from me."

He had me worried now. "Hear *what*?"

He took a deep breath and turned to face me. "I told
the police I'd been in conference with a friend of mine.
Tad Garrison. We had an arrangement, Tad and I. If
anyone asked about me on certain days, Tad would say
I'd been with him. But I never expected *this*. And I can
hardly blame him for not lying for me."

"Lying about *what*, Father?"

Another deep breath. "I have a friend, Amanda. A
woman. In Boston. I was with her yesterday."

Vastly relieved, I said, "Is that all? What difference
does that make?"

He shook his head and smiled ruefully. "No, baby.
You don't understand. In the eyes of the police, in the
eyes of the church, what she and I were doing is adultery."

Adultery. I had heard it spoken of without ever really
knowing what it was. Something Bad, according to the
priests. But then, according to the priests, most things
were. And obviously, as Father had committed it, it could
not be terribly so.

"Is she a nice person?" I asked him.

He surprised me by laughing, a low laugh, softened by melancholy. "Amanda," he said, "it's a sin. And in Massachusetts, as Chief Da Silva was kind enough to remind me, it's also a crime."

A sin perhaps, but almost certainly a venial one, three Hail Marys and off you go. Couldn't be much of a crime either; and Da Silva was a bully. "But *is* she?"

He sighed. "Yes. Yes, she is. She's very nice. Very smart, very kind. It was wrong of me, being involved with her the way I was, but I love her."

This, now, was serious. Except briefly, at the beginning of their marriage, I had never seen Audrey as a threat to my father's love for me.

"What's her name?" I asked him. As though by knowing it I could gauge the menace she represented, and contain it.

"Susan."

Far too nondescript, I thought, to be dangerous.

"Susan St. Clair," he said. "I think you'd like her very much."

I doubted that. Not with a name like St. Clair. It conjured up visions of the gay Parisiennes of whom Miss Lizzie had spoken, loose women who pranced across a stage and kicked ruffled skirts toward the ceiling to display their fancy knickers.

Rather bravely (I thought) in view of the situation, I asked him, "Are you going to leave us for her? Me and William?"

His hand tightened on mine. "No, Amanda. Of course not. I'll never leave you. But I had to tell the police about Susan. And now that they know about her, they've got even more reason to suspect me for Audrey's murder. They think I had a motive."

That was ridiculous. If the police were so addled that they suspected Father and required a motive, Audrey's personality, all by itself, would have provided one. I could deal later with the threat represented by the St. Clair strumpet. At the moment, there was a more important consideration. Even if it meant an eternity of brimstone for me, I had to tell him about the fort.

"Father," I said, "I think I know where William is."

———

As best I could, I told Father how to find William's fort. He left Miss Lizzie's, to telephone my grandparents' house and, afterward, to begin the long drive up there.

My life had all at once become extremely cluttered; I could not sleep. I worried about William, and I worried about Father driving when he was so exhausted—he had not slept for two days. I wondered who had killed Audrey, and I wondered why. And periodically, throughout the night, images of Susan St. Clair in her cancan outfit went high-stepping across the shadowed room.

For a long time I held a serious discussion with God. I explained that I was perfectly willing to accept his sending me to hell, if that was what he *really* wanted. But perhaps we could, between us, work out some kind of arrangement—two or three centuries of merely purgatorial suffering in exchange for a lifetime among the nuns or the lepers. (I would have opted, given a choice, for the lepers.) I reminded him that there had been mitigating circumstances both in the case of my violating the oath (William might be hurt right now, and in need of help) and in the case of my wishing Audrey dead (she had been, rest her soul, a witch). I asked him to bear all this in mind before arriving at a possibly precipitate Judgment; and suggested, in passing, that he keep an eye on this St. Clair woman, who might very well be a gold digger.

I asked for a Sign to indicate that my message had reached him, but there were no visitations, no burning bushes, not even a breeze to stir the limp lace curtains.

Finally, early in the morning, I fell asleep.

———

I stood at the guest-room door, and I saw before me a tall, dark figure bending over Audrey. His back to me, he wore black trousers and a long black Edwardian coat. I saw him raise his arm, saw the gleam of the hatchet's head, saw his arm swing down and turn the metal to a blur, heard the wet *crunch* as it smashed into flesh and bone. He raised it again, swung again, and again came the brittle snapping sound; and he raised it again and again, and blood was flying now in spurts across the room.

I cried out in horror, and he wheeled about and saw me, and I saw him, *and I recognized his face.*

. . . I awoke with a whimper in my throat, and the face vanished. I tried to will it back, desperately tried to recall those familiar features; but the face was gone.

Gray light seeped through the window. The tide was coming in: I could hear the waves wash against the shore. But they did not sound like sand and water; they sounded like the scrape of steel on gravel, the slow plodding measured beat of someone filling in a grave.

I lay there, the room gradually forming itself around me, until I heard Miss Lizzie begin to move about.

———

Miss Lizzie made griddle cakes, and we ate them in the dining room. The crowd outside the house was much smaller today. Officer O'Hara, who had come in earlier to borrow the use of the facilities again, told me that these were "only the riff-raff, the town scum," which did not, as I fancy he intended, much comfort me.

I looked up from my plate and asked Miss Lizzie, "What about the good people?"

She appeared puzzled. "What, Amanda?"

"Do you believe there's a heaven they go to?"

She smiled. "I think that the good people, the truly good people, are already in a kind of heaven."

"And the truly bad people?"

She paused, her teacup raised halfway to her lips. "The truly bad people, yes, are already in a kind of hell." She took a sip of tea, set the cup down, touched the napkin to her mouth, and said, as though to herself, "I really must get out today and do some shopping."

"But Miss Lizzie! All those people outside. . . ."

"Rabble," she said lightly. "What can they do to me? Gawp and stare? No, I've let them have their way entirely too long."

"But Mr. Boyle and Mr. Slocum are coming. With the people who answered your advertisement."

She pursed her lips. "Afterward, then. I refuse to be kept a prisoner in my own house."

But the first visitor to Miss Lizzie's that morning was neither Mr. Slocum nor Mr. Boyle, nor any of their entourage of potential witnesses.

Chapter
THIRTEEN

"THERE'S A YOUNG gentleman," said Officer O'Hara, poking his ruddy face around the edge of the door, "to see Miss Amanda."

The time was just a little before ten o'clock; we had been in the parlor when he heard the knock on the door. Now as Miss Lizzie looked at me, I looked at Officer O'Hara and asked him, "Who?"

"Carl Drummond's son, Roger." To Miss Lizzie he confided, "He's a fine lad, works at the candy store, you needn't worry about *that* one."

"It's up to Miss Burton," she said. Officer O'Hara's approbation cut very little ice with Miss Lizzie.

"Would it be all right with you?" I asked her.

"Of course, child." To O'Hara she spoke as though she were addressing a servant. "Please show the young man in."

The face folded into a sour frown, ducked away, and a moment later Roger stepped through the door.

With all that had happened over the last few days, the thought of Roger had never entered my mind. Now I wondered why.

Still tall and dark and lean (although neither so tall nor so lean as Mr. Slocum), and still as handsome as Heathcliff (although not so handsome as Mr. Slocum), he wore a natty seersucker suit, a white shirt, a black tie, and black high-topped boots. He grinned at me, showing all his teeth. "Hi, Amanda."

"Hello, Roger." I introduced him to Miss Lizzie. Both of them were stiffly formal, Miss Lizzie, I imagined, because by then she would be wary of any stranger; and Roger—well, I would learn shortly why Roger was so restrained.

"I was wondering," he told her, "if I could talk to Amanda."

"Certainly," she said. To me: "Amanda, why don't you and your guest talk in the parlor." To Roger, politely: "Would you care for some tea?"

"No, thanks." After a second's hesitation, he added, "Ma'am."

Miss Lizzie told me, "If you need anything, I'll be upstairs in my room."

I thanked her and, as she left, showed Roger into the parlor. I felt quite assured and adult, rather as though the room, the house, were my own, and Roger a gentleman caller come to ask my hand.

He sat down on the sofa and, with a glance toward the parlor door, said, "So that's her, huh?"

I sat opposite him in the armchair. "Yes. She's been really wonderful, Roger."

He leaned forward. "She's a psychopath, Amanda."

"What's a psychopath?"

"A crazy person. A loon."

I laughed. "Oh, Roger, she is not. She's one of the nicest people I've ever met."

"She killed her parents."

"She did not," I protested. "The jury said so. She was innocent."

"The jury said she wasn't guilty."

"That's what I *said*."

He shook his head. "It's not the same thing. Look, do you know anything about the trial?"

"I know they found her innocent, or not guilty, or whatever. They let her go."

He glanced toward the door again, leaned closer, and lowered his voice. I noticed, as I had before, how long his black eyelashes were, longer and finer than my own. (It seemed unfair that a boy could have lashes like those.) Maybe he was not so handsome, so dashing, as Mr. Slocum, but through my sins I had lost Mr. Slocum, and Roger, with his dark-brown liquid eyes, his poetic cheekbones, would make a not-altogether unpleasant alternative. "I've read all about it," he assured me. "They've got books in the library and copies of the *Boston Herald* from the time the trial took place. And I've talked to people who were there."

"What people?"

"Chief Da Silva, for one."

"Chief Da Silva doesn't like Miss Lizzie."

He snorted. "I'll say. He doesn't like her because he knows she did it, and she got away with it."

"She *didn't* do it."

"Look," he said. "Did you know the murders took place in August, on the hottest day of the year?"

"So what?"

"Well, for one thing, the number of homicides goes up whenever the temperature is over ninety-eight point six. Body temperature. People get irritated. People who are a little bit crazy get even crazier."

"Who says so, Roger?"

"It's a scientific fact. And for another thing, the Bordens had a barn in their backyard, okay? It was just a little carriage house, really, but they all called it a barn. They were like that."

"Like what?"

"You know. Stuck up."

"Who says?"

"Everybody." He waved a hand dismissively. "It doesn't matter, okay? They called it a barn. And the barn had a loft."

The loft, I thought. Perhaps now I would learn what all this talk about the loft had meant.

"The loft had one entrance," Roger said, "a trapdoor at the top of a stairway up from the barn, and it had one window, and that was glass, and it was locked. Now at the trial, when they asked her where she'd been that morning, Lizzie said she'd gone up into the loft to get some pieces of lead. She was going to Marion in a few days, she said, and she wanted to use the lead for sinkers on a fishing line."

"Roger, I don't see the point to all this."

"Let me finish. First of all, when she went out to the barn, her mother had already been dead for two hours. The medical evidence proved that. Lizzie said she thought her mother was out. Her father was lying down, she said, in the sitting room, asleep. He'd just gotten back from downtown. Okay, she goes up to the loft to get this lead, and she stays there, she says, for fifteen minutes. She *says*"—sarcasm curled around the word—"that she stood at the window and ate a few pears."

"What's wrong with that?"

"On the hottest day of the year? In a closed-in loft? She stood there for fifteen minutes eating *pears*?"

"Maybe she couldn't find those pieces of lead, and she was trying to remember where they were."

"Come *on*, Amanda," he said, scorn twisting his face. It made his cheekbones seem a good deal less poetic. "There was a box with some lead in it, but it was *downstairs*, not in the loft."

"But there *was* lead in the barn."

He rolled his eyes theatrically. "All right. Chief Da Silva was only a constable in Fall River. But he was one of the first cops on the scene. While the neighbors and the other cops were talking to Lizzie in the house—"

"Stop calling her *Lizzie*."

He looked at me, surprised. "What *should* I call her?"

"Miss Borden."

He laughed. Scornfully. Roger was looking less and less a likely marriage prospect.

I said, "It sounds nasty the way you say it. *Lizzie*. She's not your friend. It's rude."

"She kills her parents with an axe, and I'm the one who's rude?"

"She *didn't* kill them."

He sighed elaborately. "While the other policemen were talking to *Miss Borden* in the house, Da Silva went into the barn. He went up into the loft. He stood there at the trapdoor and he held his head at eye level with the floor. He looked all around. There were no footprints in the dust, Amanda. None. And there was plenty of dust—even *Miss Borden* admitted at the trial that no one in the family had been up there for months. *There were no footprints*."

"So why didn't Da Silva say so at the trial?"

"He did. And the defense brought in two kids who

said they'd been playing in the loft that morning, *before* all this happened. Which naturally made Da Silva look like a liar, because if the kids *had* been up there, they would've left footprints all over the place."

"So Da Silva *was* a liar."

"Amanda," he said, with that heavy patience which intentionally fails to disguise its opposite, "the kids had been paid off. Like Bridget, the Bordens' maid, had been paid off."

"By who?"

"By whom, you mean." He smiled. Insufferably. "By your friend, *Miss Borden*."

"That's crazy. If Da Silva wasn't lying, he just made a mistake. He didn't see the footprints."

"He's a good cop, Amanda. He knew what he saw up there. There were no footprints. Why do you think he left Fall River? Because he *knew* she'd done it, and he knew that by paying off those kids, she'd made him look like a liar or a fool."

"Roger," I said, "give me one good reason why Miss Lizzie would kill her parents."

"Sex," he said, and sat back triumphantly, like someone who had just cut an ace from a blind deck.

"Sex? What are you talking about?" Sex was a thing, like adultery, about which my information was inadequate. It was much in the news, with priests and ministers across the nation denouncing the lax morals of the postwar generation; but no one had ever explained precisely in what direction this laxity lay. In school I had heard tales of petting parties and something called French kissing; but, as naughty and vaguely intriguing as they had sounded, I could not imagine why everyone made such a fuss over them.

Roger shrugged casually. "She denied her sexual impulses, and because they didn't have any way to release themselves, they turned violent. It's a classic case of repression."

"Repression?"

"If you'd already read your Freud, you'd know all about it."

"My Froyd?"

He smiled smugly again. "Sigmund Freud," he said. "He's a German doctor who's discovered everything there is to know about the subconscious." He crossed his legs like a professor about to elucidate an especially thorny problem to a well-intentioned if somewhat dense undergraduate. "The human mind, see, is divided into these three parts. There's the libido, which is your primitive, animalistic energy. There's your ego, which is what you get from your parents. And then there's your superego, which is what you get from society. Now, if your superego's too strong, then your libido gets blocked, okay? Your natural impulses get twisted, and you get hysteria and craziness and in some cases even murder."

"He's a doctor, this Sigmund Freud?"

"One of the greatest who ever lived. He's revolutionized psychology."

"He sounds like a screwball to me."

"That," he announced, "is because you don't know what you're talking about." Roger, alas, was definitely out of the running as a spousal candidate.

"This superego thing," I said. "Just how do you get it from society?"

He shrugged. "From the rules and codes of the social group."

"So it's like a conscience."

"Well, yeah," he said. "Sort of. But naturally it's a lot more complicated than that."

"But how does it become a part of your mind?"

Impatiently, he waved his hand. "That's not important, Amanda." He uncrossed his legs and leaned toward me once again, his forearms resting on his knees. He *did* have nice long fingers; it was a pity he was such a dope. "The important thing is that repression leads to violence. And your friend Lizzie Borden is repressed. She's been repressed all her life. She never got married, she was a thirty-two-year-old spinster when she killed her parents."

"She *didn't* kill her parents. Roger, there are *thousands* of thirty-two-year-old spinsters, *millions* of them, probably, and they don't all go killing their parents."

He shrugged again. "Some of them just can't stand the strain."

"How many of them kill their parents?"

"Geeze, Amanda, it only takes one, you know. Look, there's no question she did it."

"There is for me."

He sat back and shook his head, disgusted. "You don't get it, do you?"

"No," I said. "I don't."

Once more he leaned toward me. His dark eyes peered intently into mine, Svengali-like. "Listen to me, Amanda. *Listen* to me. Did you know that your house next door is almost identical to the Bordens' house in Fall River? The same number of rooms? The same arrangement?"

"So what?"

"So *listen*. Your stepmother was killed in August, on the hottest day of the year. Did you know that Lizzie Borden's mother wasn't really her mother? She was her *stepmother*. And did you know that she was murdered upstairs, in the front room on the left side of the house?

The *guest room*, Amanda. And *your* stepmother was killed in the guest room."

"Oh, Roger, *really*. You're not saying—"

He nodded. "Yes I am, Amanda. She killed your stepmother."

Chapter
FOURTEEN

"THAT'S IMPOSSIBLE," I said.

"It was the heat, Amanda. It got to her, it brought her back to Fall River thirty years ago, and she just went berserk."

"Roger, she didn't even know my stepmother."

"So it would have been *easier* for her to kill her. Don't you see? I mean, she knew her parents and she killed *them*." The logic of this escaped me, but Roger was fervent now, folded forward and jabbing his finger at me. "Look, the police searched all over your house, right? Next door? And they couldn't find the weapon. But did they search this place?"

"Of course not. They didn't have any reason to."

"Oh, they've got reason to, but it's not good enough yet to get a warrant. But I'll bet you, Amanda, I'll bet you that hatchet is lying right around here somewhere." He glanced around the room as though he might spot it on the end table, tucked beside the cloisonné vase. He looked back to me. "And the thing is, she could go berserk again any minute, you know. The weather's still hot, the temperature's still over ninety-eight point six. She could go off any time, like a bomb."

"Roger," I said, "I think *you're* a psychopath."

He sat back. "Hey, I'm not the one living in a house with an axe-murderer. Understand? You're not safe here, Amanda. You could be next."

I cocked my head. "Is that why you came over here? To warn me?" Wrongheaded as he was, his heart, at least, might be in the right place.

"Partly," he said.

I hid my disappointment. (And yet why, I asked myself, would I be disappointed? The boy was a boob.) "What other reason?"

"I'm doing an article for the paper." I had forgotten that he was a journalism student. He grinned, excited, proud. "This'll be my first real scoop, Amanda. I'll get a byline and everything."

"But you can't do that!" I said. "Mr. Slocum, the lawyer, he promised Chief Da Silva that none of us would talk to the newspapers."

He waved an airy hand. "I've already interviewed Da Silva. He knows what I'm doing."

"Yes, and he's letting you do it because he knows you'll write what he wants you to."

"Hey," he said, affronted, "I don't write what anyone *wants* me to. I write the truth as I see it." Even at eighteen, he was able to make this vibrate with the dreary self-righteousness of the crusader.

"Well, you can't write anything *I* said," I told him. "I won't let you."

"Amanda," he replied, in the now-familiar tone of patient superiority, "it's a free press, part of a democratic society."

"If you write anything bad about Miss Lizzie, she'll sue you, you know. And the newspaper. For slander. How many articles do you think they'll let you write then?"

"Slander is spoken," he said. "Libel is written." But the pedantry was distracted, automatic; and he was frowning.

Once again sensing an advantage—a thirteen-year-old girl can be as ruthless as a Mongol—I pressed it. "You'll probably never be able to write anything for anybody, ever. None of the newspapers will touch you with a ten-foot pole."

"No one can stop a free press," he said, and I think he meant it to sound like a ringing declaration, but it came out strained and querulous, almost petulant.

"Well," I said—and just then came the sound of someone knocking at the front door. Miss Lizzie was upstairs; I would have to answer it myself.

"Well," I snapped at him as I stood, "you just remember that the free press won't have you as a part of it if you write anything bad about Miss Lizzie." And I turned and flounced from the room, having got the last word and very well pleased with myself.

At the front door, I held my face against it as I had seen Miss Lizzie do. "Who is it?"

"Darryl Slocum."

I unlocked the door, opened it; the lawyer and Mr. Boyle passed by me into the entranceway. Mr. Slocum was wearing another stylish linen suit, this one pearl gray; the Pinkerton man wore the same rumpled brown thing he had been wearing yesterday.

"Miss Lizzie's upstairs," I told them. "I'll go get her."

As I was closing the door, Roger emerged from the parlor. "I've got to be going," he said to me. He spoke rapidly, uneasily, a small boy nearly caught with his hand in the jam jar.

"Hello, Roger," said Mr. Slocum. "How's your father?"

"Fine, Mr. Slocum. Excuse me, I've—"

"Roger," I said to Mr. Slocum with an innocence as sweet and genuine as saccharine, "is going to write an article about Miss Lizzie for the newspaper."

Mr. Slocum smiled. "Good for you, Roger."

Roger scowled at me, then said to Mr. Slocum, "Well, sir, it's not all that big a deal—"

"Roger thinks," I said, still with that heartless innocence, "that Miss Lizzie killed Audrey."

"Does he now," said Mr. Slocum, raising an eyebrow. "Well, Roger, you're entitled to your own opinion, of course. Opinions are wonderful things, like collar stays. Everyone should have a few. But you want to be careful with them, you know. Don't want to poke yourself."

"Yes sir," said Roger, and laughed. A bit shakily, I was pleased to note. There were also a few gratifying beads of sweat along his upper lip. "That's a good one, sir. Ha-ha. Collar stays. I'll have to use that some time."

Smiling, Mr. Slocum bowed his head. "Consider it yours."

"Yes sir, thank you. Well, yeah, I guess I better be going. Good-bye, sir." He turned and nodded uncertainly toward Boyle, to whom he had not been introduced, then turned to glare at me. "Good-bye, Amanda." Coldly, flatly.

"So long, Roger," I said pleasantly, holding the door open for him. "Do come again, whenever you can."

He scowled, then slipped through the door. I shut it behind him, smiling.

Boyle turned to Mr. Slocum. "Looks a little young for Richard Harding Davis."

"Oh, Roger's all right," said Mr. Slocum. "A tad overenthusiastic, maybe. I'll have a word with Benedict, the owner of the *Sun*, and make sure he and his people understand the merits of discretion." He turned to me. "Well, Amanda, how are you today?"

"Fine," I said. "And you?" He was certainly an extremely handsome man.

"Not at all bad. Do you think you could find Miss Borden for us? Our prize witnesses should be arriving soon to rake in their just deserts."

"I'll get her." And then, remembering my manners, I said to Boyle, who was digging a pack of Fatimas from his shirt pocket, "How are you, Mr. Boyle?"

"Swell, kid. You holding up okay?"

I told him I was, and went off for Miss Lizzie.

———

The witnesses—three of them—were waiting in the sitting room. Mr. Slocum, Boyle, and Miss Lizzie would interview them one by one in the parlor, behind closed doors. I was merely a supernumary, a witness to their witnessing.

The first of them, led in by Mr. Slocum, was a stocky woman carrying a gray carpetbag and wearing a flowing white silk dress that reached almost to the soles of what looked like white satin ballet slippers. It was an unusual dress, a composite that resembled an ancient Greek gown, Empire waisted, onto which a seamstress with nothing better to do had stitched a pair of loose triangular sleeves. It gave her a vaguely hieratical air and might have made her seem almost imposing, had she not been shorter than I and nearly as short as Miss Mullavey, the police stenographer. When she sat, draping the carpetbag across her ample lap, her plump tiny feet hovered just above the floor.

She did not seem, initially, an attractive person. A helmet of brown hair, laced with gray, lay close to her scalp in tight determined curls. Beneath a broad forehead and bracketing a slightly upturned nose, her small brown eyes were deeply set between horizontal folds of flesh. On either side of her wide meaty mouth were slack jowls that, in conjunction with her bright-red lipstick and bright-red rouge, gave her rather the look of an effeminate bulldog.

But her smile, when Mr. Slocum introduced her, was one of those, like Miss Lizzie's, that immediately transforms the face from which it shines, making it younger and sweeter and causing a flicker of guilty confusion in the observer. And her voice, as she said her *hello*s, was low and musical; disconcertingly so, when what one half-expected was a canine growl. Her name was Mrs. Helene Archer.

"Now, Mrs. Archer," said Mr. Slocum, "I understand you have some information about the death of Mrs. Audrey Burton."

"I do, Mr. Slocum," she said in those soft melodious tones. "I spoke with Mrs. Burton only last evening."

Mr. Slocum sat back and crossed his right ankle over his left knee. "I see," he said, and nodded sagely. "You do know, of course, that Mrs. Burton died two days ago."

She smiled back. "I prefer to use the phrase *passed over*."

"Ah," said Mr. Slocum. "And why might that be?"

"Because it describes more accurately the active nature of the soul's condition. After, that is to say, the cessation of activity in the physical being."

"I see," said Mr. Slocum. "I take it that you're a believer in spiritualism."

Mrs. Archer smiled again. "Yes. Of course."

Boyle, slumped down in the chair to Mrs. Archer's left, blew a perfectly round smoke ring that sailed out above the coffee table, trembled there for a moment, then twisted round itself, feathered, finally unraveled.

I looked at Mrs. Archer and felt a wrinkle of scorn twitch across the back of my mind; Father had told me about spiritualists, with their ectoplasms and their table rappings, and (like him) I heartily disbelieved in them all.

"I see," said Mr. Slocum, and it seemed to me he sighed. "You're acquainted, I gather, with my secretary, Mrs. Coyne."

She nodded. "I've been fortunate enough to assist Mrs. Coyne in a number of her inquiries. Her late husband, Albert, passed over during the War, you know."

"Yes," the lawyer said. "I know. You are *Madame* Helene, are you not?"

She nodded graciously. "It is an appellation which many of my clients use."

"Yes. Well, Mrs. Archer, Mrs. Coyne is an extremely capable secretary, and I think it's safe to say that I've always respected her . . . religious beliefs, but I believe that in this case she may've misunderstood my intent. What we're looking for here, I'm afraid, is specific information about Mrs. Burton's murder."

Mrs. Archer cocked her heavy head, making her jowls quiver. She smiled. "But what could be more specific than the information provided by Mrs. Burton herself?"

Mr. Slocum glanced at Miss Lizzie as though asking

her to step in and dismiss this woman. She surprised him, I think, by saying "Since Mrs. Archer has taken the trouble to come here, perhaps we should take the time to listen to her."

Mrs. Archer nodded pleasantly to her. "I realize that you're a skeptic too, Miss Borden, and I appreciate your kindness."

"Not at all," said Miss Lizzie. "You say that Mrs. Burton spoke with you last evening?"

"It would be more accurate for me to say that Mrs. Burton spoke *through* me last evening. Mrs. Coyne came to my house after dinner last night and explained the situation. She suggested that I might be able to aid Mr. Slocum in his quest for Truth. I agreed that it was possible, and with Mrs. Coyne's assistance I was able to reach Barnard."

"The college?" asked Miss Lizzie, frowning.

"The Spirit Guide," said Mrs. Archer. "He's been most helpful to me over the years. He's a very wise and very compassionate soul. Wisdom, as I'm sure you know, is inevitably compassionate. And time, if only we keep our hearts open, brings wisdom to us all. Barnard has had literally eons of time to develop his. He was a warrior, you see, in old Atlantis."

"Before it sank, presumably," said Miss Lizzie.

"Of course," said Mrs. Archer. "His physical being was drowned during the inundation."

Boyle blew another trembling blue smoke ring. Idly watching it wobble away into nothingness, Mr. Slocum tapped his index finger against the leg of his slacks. Both men had the resigned appearance of late-night passengers in a deserted depot, waiting for the morning train.

Miss Lizzie said, "Barnard helped you locate Mrs. Burton, did he?"

"Yes. As I say, he's been most helpful."

"And what did Mrs. Burton have to say? Once Barnard had located her."

"She extended her affection to her stepchildren, William and Amanda." She gave me a sweet smile, and, unaccountably, I felt a chill go shuddering along my body. "And she extended her forgiveness as well."

"Forgiveness?" said Miss Lizzie. "Forgiveness for what?"

"She didn't specify, I'm afraid. They're all a bit confused, you see, when they first pass over."

"Understandably," said Miss Lizzie.

"They're not used to the astral plane as yet, and sometimes they don't realize that our vision isn't as wide as theirs has become. Often they assume that those of us on this side possess knowledge which in fact we do not."

"A common enough mistake"—Miss Lizzie nodded—"even among those of us on this side."

Boyle spoke for the first time. "She happen to mention who bumped her off?"

Mrs. Archer smiled at him. "Who killed her, you mean? No, I'm sorry, she didn't. I asked her, of course, but she doesn't know. She was asleep when it happened, you see."

Boyle nodded, his face blank. Mr. Slocum smiled at the woman. "That was in the newspapers, Mrs. Archer."

Mrs. Archer returned the smile. "Was it? I wouldn't know. I seldom read the newspapers, I'm afraid."

Boyle blew another smoke ring, this one toward the ceiling.

"What else did Mrs. Burton have to say?" asked Miss Lizzie.

"Well, as I told you, she extended affection and forgiveness to her stepchildren." I had gotten over my initial shock, had already begun denying to myself that it had ever happened; and now I was skeptical enough to note that death had brought about a marked improvement in Audrey's attitude. "And she mentioned something about a key," added Mrs. Archer.

"A key?" said Miss Lizzie.

Miss Archer nodded. "When I asked her about the murder, her exact words were, 'The key is the key.' "

Excited, my disbelief momentarily suspended once again, I asked her, "The key to the front door?"

Mrs. Archer smiled at me. "I wouldn't know, my child. I can only relay the information that the souls are kind enough to impart. I cannot, alas, interpret it."

"The key is the key," said Mr. Slocum, as though to himself, and then looked down at the floor and smiled.

"Yes." Mrs. Archer nodded. "Those were her words."

"Did she say anything else?" Miss Lizzie asked.

"No. We lost contact with each other."

Mr. Slocum looked up from his reverie. "A bad connection?"

"A disturbance in the ether. It sometimes happens."

"Ah."

Miss Lizzie asked, "Is there anything else you can tell us, Mrs. Archer?"

She smiled. "No, not about Mrs. Burton. But if you like, we could get together one day and I could attempt to contact her again. I'm entirely at your disposal."

Smiling, Mr. Slocum asked, "And what might be your fee for that, Mrs. Archer?"

"Oh, there's no set fee," she said. "No, that would be improper. I ask only for a contribution, you see, to help me continue my work. Whatever the donor can afford and wishes to give."

He nodded. "I see. Well, perhaps we'll be in touch with you."

She nodded. "Thank you." She turned to Miss Lizzie. "There is one other thing, Miss Borden. I have a message from your father."

Miss Lizzie raised an eyebrow. "Indeed."

"Yes. He wanted me to tell you that he still wears your ring."

Miss Lizzie's eyebrow dropped and her face suddenly went very pale.

Chapter
FIFTEEN

MISS LIZZIE'S SHOCK, if such it was, lasted for only a moment. Within a few seconds, color filled her face again and she was smiling at the spiritualist, a smile as ironic as Mr. Slocum's. "You say my father wanted me to know that," she said. Both Mr. Slocum and Boyle were watching her with interest (as was I).

Mrs. Archer nodded. "Yes. He seemed very firm about it."

Her smile unchanged, Miss Lizzie nodded. "Yes. He would be. Thank you for relaying the message. And if he should stop by again, do thank him for me, would you, Mrs. Archer?"

She nodded. "I'd be happy to."

"And I thank you for coming," Miss Lizzie added. "It's all been most instructive."

"You're quite welcome, I'm sure."

"She's fairly impressive at first glance," said Mr. Slocum as he returned to his chair after showing Mrs. Archer to the door. "But there was nothing in what she said that she couldn't have learned here in town." He sat down.

"What about the key?" I asked him, unsure just then whether I was skeptic or believer. "Audrey's key? It *is* missing."

He smiled. "The whole police force knows about that key. And small towns being what they are, I imagine that everyone living within a five-mile radius does too."

I looked toward Miss Lizzie. From her pallor, even though it had been only momentary, Mrs. Archer's "message" had obviously affected her. Mr. Slocum and Boyle were looking, I noticed, in the same direction.

"My father wore a ring I'd given him," she said, smiling at me. "My high school graduation ring. He was buried with it. For a moment I wondered how Mrs. Archer could've known that. But it was something that was mentioned in all the newspapers. Anyone could've known about it."

I remembered Roger telling me that the local library carried issues of the *Herald* dating back to the time of Miss Lizzie's trial. Mrs. Archer could easily have gone there and learned about the ring. I was relieved and I was also irritated at myself: relieved, because like everyone I preferred not to have my beliefs—and my father's—called into question; irritated, because it was I myself who had called them into question, and because it was *not* I who had worked out how the trick had been performed.

"Still," said Miss Lizzie, smiling now at Mr. Slocum, "I thought she brought it off rather well."

"Oh, she's good," said the lawyer. "She's taken my secretary for several hundred dollars."

Boyle sucked on the Fatima, exhaled a billow of smoke, and said to Mr. Slocum, "Who's up next?"

———

Miss Clare Hammill was one of those people (rare, but implacable when met, usually at cocktail parties and on ocean cruises) who suffer from an overabundance of presence. With her short mauve crepe de chine dress (not really the thing for afternoon wear), her bobbed and hennaed hair, her rouged cheeks and painted lips, her bright animated brown eyes, and her mobile mouth, she occupied the parlor in the same sense that the American Army, after the Armistice, had occupied Coblenz. She filled the room, and its boundaries seemed to tremble with the effort of containing her.

Even sitting, she was constantly in motion. She snapped her chewing gum; fluttered her thick eyelashes; arched and dipped her plucked eyebrows; crossed and uncrossed her long legs, shiny with white silk hose; stabbed at the air with her cigarette, holding it between two taut slender fingers, waving it like a conductor's baton to punctuate her narrative. I remember thinking that she could be only seven or eight years older than I, just across the border of her teens into her twenties and safely situated in the mysterious realm of adulthood; and, far from feeling disapproval, I felt a kind of awe at what I took to be her singular sophistication.

"I was with Bobby Childers in his father's Packard coupe, you've seen it, probably, it's the only Packard in this whole one-horse town, and we were parked out past the fish market, you know that little alleyway there? This

was a couple weeks ago, a Thursday. I remember because I just got back from New York the day before,
Wednesday, me and my friend Annabelle went down
there to see some plays and pick up some culture, you
know? I mean, there's nothing going on in this burg,
nothing. Honestly, sometimes I think I'm going to *suf-
focate*. Why my father thinks it's such a big deal I haven't
got the faintest. A beach is a beach, you know? Sand
is sand."

"You were parked with Bobby Childers," Mr. Slocum
reminded her.

"Right, yeah," she said, exhaling a tumbling cloud of
smoke. "Bobby thinks he's this big sheik or something,
because of the Packard, I guess, and that's not even *his*,
he only gets to use it a couple of times a week. I mean
really. Anyway, he gets sexy all of a sudden, you know?
Hands everywhere I looked, it was like being jumped
by an octopus." Here she did something that endeared
her to me forever: She looked at me and gave me a
conspiratorial wink, as though I knew (which of course
I did not) exactly what she meant.

Then, to Mr. Slocum: "I mean I've been around and
everything, but I'm not that kind of girl, at least not with
a creep like Bobby Childers who doesn't even own his
own car, you know? Anyway, I just get him settled down
and all, cooled off, you know, when I notice that there's
this woman watching us. She's standing kind of in the
shadows, right next to the pharmacy? Just standing
there and watching us. It was pretty spooky. I mean
there was nobody else around, it was dinnertime, I guess,
and everyone was home. So I tell Bobby to get the heck
out of there, I don't want to hang around with this weird
woman *staring* at us like that, you know? So Bobby hits
the gas and we get outta there."

"And the woman was Mrs. Burton?" asked Mr. Slocum.

"I'm coming to that," she said, holding up her palm like a traffic policeman. "See, what happened was, the next day I'm at Drummond's, you know, the candy store? And this same woman comes up to me and says she'd like to talk to me, she says it's something real important, it'll be worth my while to hear her out. I figured what do I have to lose, at least it'll be something to *do*, you know? So I go outside with her.

"Well, it turns out she knows my name, she calls me Clare like we've been friends for years and years, and she tells me it'd be real unfortunate if Dr. Hammill— that's my father—if Dr. Hammill learned about what I was doing in parked cars."

Mr. Slocum frowned.

"Well, I could see plain as day where she was going, she wanted money, naturally, but she never got a chance, because I just laughed in her face. I told her, and it's the truth too, that my father would rather hear that I was spooning in some car than find out I was off at a gin mill somewhere getting blotto."

"And what was her response to that?" Mr. Slocum asked.

"She just got a tight little nasty look on her face and said, 'We'll see,' real mean and cold, like it was supposed to scare my socks off."

"But she never actually asked you for money?"

"Like I said, she never got a chance. But that's what she was after, all right."

"Did she ever speak with your father?"

"Not really speak to him, no. But about four days later when I got the mail there was a letter addressed to him, and the writing on the envelope was all straight lines, like someone made them with a ruler? And it was mailed from here in town, and the rest of our mail is always forwarded from our address in Boston. So I opened it." She inhaled on the cigarette, clearly enjoying the air of melodrama that filled the pause she had created.

"And?" said Mr. Slocum.

"The letter was written the same way as the address, like it was done with a ruler? All block letters and everything, and it said that maybe Dr. Hammill would like to know that his daughter spent her evenings carrying on in Fred Childers's Packard with his son Bobby. I mean, she actually said *carrying on*. Can you *believe*? Is that corny or what?"

"Did you keep the letter?" Mr. Slocum asked her.

Her plucked eyebrows soared up her forehead. "I only *look* dumb, okay? And I'm definitely not crazy. I mean, my father's progressive and all, but why take chances, you know what I mean? I threw it away."

"Were there any more letters?"

"Uh-uh. I guess that she figured she'd already done all the damage she was gonna do."

"And the woman who spoke to you, that was Mrs. Burton?"

"Yeah. See, what I did, after she pulled that little number on me outside Drummond's, I went back inside and asked Roger—he's the son, he's sort of cute but he's not really my type—if he knew who she was. He said she was Mrs. Burton, the stockbroker's wife." If she thought Roger was cute, I wondered what she would make of his friend, Dr. Freud.

Mr. Slocum nodded. "Did she ever speak to you again?"

"I only saw her one more time, and that was on the street, just passing by. She didn't even look at me. I almost said something to her, something nasty, you know? But I figured the best thing to do was let sleeping dogs lie."

"Probably the wisest thing, under the circumstances. Let me ask you this, Miss Hammill. Do you have any idea who might've killed Mrs. Burton?"

"Well, I mean it's pretty obvious, isn't it? She was blackmailing somebody, or trying to, just like she tried to do to me, and he got ticked off and he killed her."

Mr. Slocum nodded.

She plucked a flake of tobacco from her lower lip. "So what's the story on this reward? I mean, it's not like I'm greedy or anything, but we can all use a little extra spending money, you know?"

Mr. Slocum smiled. "If your information proves helpful, we'll be getting back to you."

She frowned. "It wouldn't have to be in the papers or anything, would it? I mean, you wouldn't have to use my name, or all that stuff about Bobby Childers?"

Mr. Slocum shook his head. "I think it's safe to say that we can guarantee you anonymity."

She nodded. "Anonymity. That would be good. And the money would be cash or check?"

Mr. Slocum looked at Miss Lizzie, smiled, looked back at Miss Hammill. "I imagine we could arrange a cash payment."

"Good," she said. "Great."

"Thank you for coming, Miss Hammill."

"Don't mention it."

———

Mr. Slocum showed Miss Hammill out, returned to his chair, sat down, looked at Boyle, and said, "Blackmail?"

Boyle shrugged. "From what Clara Bow says, the lady never got to mention money. But it sure sounds like it, doesn't it?"

Mr. Slocum frowned again. "Somehow I have a hard time accepting the idea of Mrs. Burton as a blackmailer."

Boyle grinned. "You think blackmailers wear striped shirts and little black masks, like those burglars in cartoons?"

Mr. Slocum smiled. "But a middle-aged woman who's more than financially secure? Why would she bother?"

"Blackmail isn't always about cash. Sometimes it's about the kick you get from messing around in other people's lives."

"So you think Hammill was telling the truth."

Another shrug. "Sounded like straight dope to me."

Mr. Slocum turned to me. "Do you know anything about this, Amanda?"

"No," I said. "I don't."

Miss Lizzie leaned toward me. "Do you think your stepmother could have done anything like that? Like what Miss Hammill described?"

I remembered Audrey's pettiness, her preoccupation with both money and scandal. "Yes," I said.

Miss Lizzie nodded. To Mr. Slocum she said, "I tend, as Mr. Boyle does, to believe the Hammill woman." She smiled. "But I confess that she's a type with which I'm wholly unfamiliar. That dress of hers, and those cosmetics. And she possesses a self-involvement I can only describe as heroic."

"A new breed," smiled Mr. Slocum. "The flapper. F. Scott Fitzgerald invented it."

"Then I think he should return to the drawing board, in posthaste. But, as I say, I believe her. Unfortunately, if she's correct, and Mrs. Burton *was* blackmailing someone else, it will be a difficult thing to prove. Whoever he was, he's hardly likely to come forward and admit it."

"Even if he didn't kill her," said Boyle.

"But it is," she told him, "the only possible line of approach we've discovered so far. Perhaps you could talk to Mrs. Burton's friends and acquaintances, and try to determine whether any of them knew about this."

"Needle in a haystack," said Boyle.

"Perhaps," she said. She smiled. "But surrendering their needles is, after all, the purpose of haystacks."

Grinning, Boyle shrugged once more. "It's your nickel, Miz Borden."

Miss Lizzie turned to Mr. Slocum. "Who else is waiting to talk to us?"

Chapter
SIXTEEN

THE THIRD AND final witness was a man in his forties. His face was square, weathered by the sun, creased with age or effort. A pair of thick black eyebrows bristled below (and not very far below) a thatch of wiry black hair. His eyes were brown, small, set close to a broad flattened nose; and his wide, thin-lipped mouth was downturned at both ends, as though he had once been displeased by something and had resolved to make his displeasure permanent. Atop heavy sloping shoulders was a gray cotton work shirt, somewhat the worse for wear, and over this lay the straps of his dark-blue denim overalls. His shoes were black brogues. Taller than Boyle but not so tall as Mr. Slocum, and wider than either, he was a very large man.

He moved across the room with the slow stolid comfortable walk of someone who depends on his body for his livelihood and knows that it will never fail him. Mr.

Slocum, who had led him from the sitting room, introduced him as Mr. Hornsby. He introduced the rest of us and said, "Have a seat, Mr. Hornsby."

Mr. Hornsby eyed the plush red velvet chair for a moment as though it might be an elaborate trap, then lowered himself into it and crossed his arms over his chest.

Mr. Slocum said, "Now, Mr. Hornsby. You say you have some information about the murder of Mrs. Audrey Burton."

Hornsby said, "The nigger did it."

For a moment none of us spoke; even I knew that this was not a word used in polite discourse.

"I see," said Mr. Slocum at last. "And which Negro, exactly, did you have in mind?"

"The old one. Old nigger lives out at the edge of town with the rest of 'em. Charlie, they call him."

"Old Charlie?" I said. I looked at Miss Lizzie. "He's the man who brings the chickens. He wouldn't hurt a fly." He was an old man, stooped and white-haired, terribly sweet, with a wide ready grin that showed black spaces between nubs of yellow teeth. (Audrey, whenever pointing out the perils of improper dental hygiene, had always used Charlie as an example.) He had talked with me, joked with me, whenever he came to deliver the chickens Audrey had ordered. From the first I had wanted, but never dared, to ask him to teach me a spiritual or two. Everyone understood that all Negroes knew an infinite number of spirituals.

"What makes you believe," Mr. Slocum said, "that this man might be involved in Mrs. Burton's death?"

"Saw him," said Hornsby. "Saw him comin' out of the place next door to this one. That's the Burton place, right? He had blood on his shirt. I could see it plain as day. And he was carrying somethin' in a paper bag. Walked right on past me down Water Street."

There was more in his voice than the familiar Yankee twang, some other sort of accent, but I could not identify it.

"Mr. Hornsby," said Mr. Slocum, "if we're talking about the same person here, Charlie Peterson, he's a man who raises and butchers chickens. It wouldn't be unusual for him to have blood on his shirt. Or to be carrying something in a paper bag. A chicken, for example."

"Saw him coming out of the Burton place. With my own eyes."

"Actually saw him coming out of the house?"

"Coming down the porch. Bold as brass at first, and then he saw me and got all shifty-eyed the way they do. Wouldn't look me in the face when he passed me. I knew right away he was up to no good."

"Does he know you?"

"Course he does."

Mr. Slocum turned to me. "Amanda, do you know if your stepmother ordered a chicken for Tuesday?"

"I don't think so. But Charlie could've come by to see if we wanted one. He did that sometimes. Really, he wouldn't hurt anyone."

Mr. Slocum asked Hornsby, "Have you told the police what you saw?"

"Not yet. I will, though. You can bet on it. Then I saw in the papers yesterday about the reward. Thought I might as well do myself some good while I do my duty. Someone's gotta do something. Take a stand."

"Against what?" asked Mr. Slocum.

"The niggers. All they do is cause trouble. Look at

Chicago." Two years before, Chicago had been torn apart by a race riot that began when white bathers had stoned a young black boy who swam, unwitting, across the invisible line that segregated the Lake Michigan beach. The boy had drowned. Over the next week, fifteen whites and twenty-three blacks were killed, and the U.S. army was called in as a peace-keeping force.

"They come floodin' up here from the South like locusts," said Hornsby. "They want our jobs, they want our women."

"According," said Miss Lizzie, speaking for the first time, "to whom?"

Hornsby looked at her. "Common knowledge."

She pursed her lips. "Common indeed."

"Mr. Hornsby," said Mr. Slocum, "you wouldn't be, by any chance, a member of the Invisible Empire?"

"I'm a Kleagle," said Hornsby. A Kleagle (as Mr. Slocum later explained) was a representative of, and sold memberships in, the Ku Klux Klan. "And proud of it. Someone's got to do something to save this country from the niggers and the Jews. The nigger population, right here in town, has doubled since before the war."

"Yes," said Mr. Slocum. "From ten to twenty. And correct me if I'm wrong, Mr. Hornsby, but aren't you from the South yourself?"

"So what?" Hornsby said. "I came up here to get away from their kind. Raise my family where the living was clean and pure. And now look. Niggers everywhere. Killing white women in broad daylight."

"I think," said Miss Lizzie, "that we've heard enough. Thank you for coming, Mr. Hornsby."

Hornsby uncrossed his arms and put them along the arms of the chair. He looked at Mr. Slocum, at Miss Lizzie, at Boyle, who smiled pleasantly at him, smoke trailing from his nostrils. "I shoulda known," Hornsby said. "I shoulda known you'd try to screw me outta the money."

Mr. Slocum calmly said, "Thank you for coming, Hornsby."

Hornsby glared at him. "You a nigger lover, Slocum? I hear you Harvard boys are like that, when you're not too busy lovin' each other."

Boyle put his cigarette carefully into the ashtray, then stood up. "Okay, ace," he said. "Time to get back to the padded room and count your toes."

Hornsby stood to face him. "Whatta we got here? 'Nother nigger lover?"

"Nah," said Boyle. "I'm a nigger. I'm passing." He jerked his head toward the door. "Out."

"You gonna make me, fatboy?" His knobby hands opened and closed.

Boyle smiled sleepily. He was a head shorter than Hornsby. "That'll be swell," he said. "I haven't stomped a moron before lunch in almost a week."

Hornsby swung his big right fist. I have never seen anyone move as quickly as Boyle did then. He stepped forward, caught Hornsby's swing on his left forearm, then smashed his own right fist, swiftly, twice, at Hornsby's face, driving the big man back. His left arm slipped away from Hornsby's right and the fist crashed down on Hornsby's jaw. The big man's head jerked back and he sat down, legs asprawl. His nose was bleeding and his eyes were dazed.

Boyle came around, grabbed him by the left arm, tugged him effortlessly to his feet, and held him there. "Gotta watch those carpets, ace. They slip, you can take a nasty fall."

Hornsby had his hand to his mouth. He said, "You knocked a tooth loose, you son of a bitch."

"Put it under your pillow," said Boyle. "Maybe you can pick up some pocket change."

Hornsby yanked his arm free. "You gonna be sorry, fatboy."

"Sure. See you in the funny papers." He stabbed his thumb over his shoulder. "Be missing."

Hornsby, his eyes narrowed, looked around the room. "You people all gonna be sorry."

Boyle took a step forward. "You looking for some more change?"

Hornsby edged back, still unsteady on his feet. He glanced around the room again, then turned and walked, swaying slightly, to the door. He opened it, looked back to Boyle, and said, "I'll see you again, fatboy."

Boyle smiled. "Be a treat, ace."

——————

As Hornsby left, Boyle returned to his chair. He sat down and stared at his right hand while he flexed it for a moment, opened and closed, opened and closed, as if making sure that everything still worked. Apparently, everything did. He shook it once, as though it were wet, then plucked his Fatima from the ashtray and said to Miss Lizzie, "Sorry about that. Didn't look like he wanted to go."

Miss Lizzie smiled. "No apology is necessary, Mr. Boyle. I'm very grateful that you handled it as you did. And for doing so without damaging any of the furniture. You do have," she added, "a very nice jab."

Boyle grinned behind a cone of smoke. "Thanks."

I said, "You were great, Mr. Boyle."

"Nah," he said, shaking his head. "A lucky punch."

"I'd like to add my thanks as well," said Mr. Slocum, smiling. "For your springing so quickly into action in defense of my honor."

"Hey." Boyle grinned. "No sweat, counselor. Professional courtesy." He looked at Miss Lizzie. "Okay. Where do you want me to start?"

"I think, as I said before, that you should begin with Mrs. Burton's friends here in town. I'm sure Amanda can give you a list of them. I realize that it's going to be difficult, but perhaps one of them does know something about this blackmail."

"Alleged blackmail," said Mr. Slocum.

She nodded. "If you like."

Boyle asked her, "You want me to talk to this Charlie, the guy Hornsby was gassing about? The chicken guy?"

"I think it might be a good idea, yes. From what I know him of him, Amanda is right. He couldn't have been responsible for Mrs. Burton's death. But according to your good friend Mr. Hornsby, Charlie was in the neighborhood at the time. It may be that he saw something."

"According to Hornsby," said Boyle, "Charlie wasn't the only guy in the neighborhood at the time."

"Yes," said Miss Lizzie. "I realize that. Hornsby has admitted, obviously, that he was there himself. But can you think of a single reason why he might kill Mrs. Burton?"

"Not yet," admitted Boyle. "But I'll keep working on it."

———

After the meeting, Mr. Slocum returned to his office, Miss Lizzie went upstairs—to read, she said—and Boyle sat with me in the parlor, writing down in his notebook the names of Audrey's acquaintances. There were not many. Mrs. Mortimer; Mrs. Sheehy, the local milliner; Mrs. Maybrick, who was spending, with her banker husband, her first summer at the shore; and Mrs. Marlowe.

"But Mrs. Marlowe hasn't come by much lately," I told him.

"Why's that?" Boyle asked, looking up from the notebook.

"I don't know. Maybe she hasn't been feeling well. She's real old, almost eighty, and she has a hard time moving around."

"Who is this Miss Marlowe?"

"She's sort of the important lady here in town. She has a big lawn party every year, at the end of the summer, and everyone wants to go. Do you know what I mean?"

He nodded. "The big cigar. Your stepmother ever go over to her house?"

"She used to, at the beginning of the summer, but I don't think she's gone there for a while."

"How long a while are we talking?"

"I'm not sure. Maybe a month. Do you think it's important?"

"Dunno. Have to find out, looks like. Anybody else you can think of?"

"No, not really. Audrey didn't have too many friends."

"Yeah." He folded the notebook, slipped it into his inside jacket pocket. "Okay, kid, thanks."

"Mr. Boyle?"

"Yeah?"

"Do you think you can find out who killed Audrey?"

"I dunno, kid. Gonna give it a try. But usually, see, it's the cops work these things out best." He took a drag of his Fatima.

"But they think my brother did it."

"Because he took off," he said, exhaling. "Someone takes off, right after a murder, the cops gotta get concerned. Only natural. But don't sweat it. Soon as he turns up again, he'll set 'em straight."

"Do you really think so?"

"Sure I do. Seen it happen a million times."

I nodded, grateful for the reassurance. "I guess you've been a Pinkerton man for a long time."

"Forever," he said, and sucked on the Fatima again.

"Did you ever shoot anybody?"

"Shot *at* a guy or two. Never hit 'em. Not much good with guns."

"You're a really good boxer, though."

"Nah."

"But I saw you, with that man Hornsby."

"Hornsby's not much. Ten years ago, maybe. Right now he's coasting on history."

"But he looks really strong."

"Maybe. But he's not tough."

"They aren't the same thing?"

He shook his head. "Strong is outside. Tough is inside."

"You mean a person can be tough without being strong?"

"Happens all the time." He grinned. "Miz Borden now. Not all that strong, probably, but tough as a bag of nails."

"She's really been good to me."

He nodded. "She's a piece of work, all right."

"She didn't do it, *did* she, Mr. Boyle?"

He inhaled on his cigarette. "Do what?"

"You know. Back in Fall River."

He shrugged. "Jury acquitted her."

"But some people still think she did it."

He shook his head again. "You can't worry about that stuff. You gotta deal with people the way they deal with you. They treat you fair, you treat them fair. Simple."

"What about if they *don't* treat you fair?"

"Then you treat 'em the same way."

I considered this for a moment. "I guess," I said, "you've got to be pretty tough to do that."

"Sometimes." He smiled. "Sometimes you just gotta be smart."

"Do you think Mr. Slocum is tough?"

He leaned forward, tapped his cigarette into the ashtray, leaned back. "I think he's smart," he said. He shrugged. "Being tough isn't something lawyers gotta worry about, generally. Small town like this, subject probably never comes up."

"You think he's not tough just because he lives in a small town?"

He grinned. "Hey. I didn't say that. Maybe he's tough, maybe he isn't. No way of telling."

"You can tell if Miss Lizzie is tough or not."

He laughed. "You'd make a good lawyer yourself, kid. I guess you like him, huh?"

"Like who?" I could feel my face flushing elaborately.

Laughing again, he said, "Don't worry. Secret's safe with me. I—"

He looked off to the left. Someone was knocking at the front door.

I sprang from my seat. "Excuse me," I said. "I've got to see who that is."

Boyle jammed his cigarette into the pile of butts filling the ashtray, then stood up, still grinning. "That's okay. I gotta go anyway. Come on, I'll walk you to the door."

Out in the entryway, he twisted the knob of the lock, pulled the door open, and stepped back.

In gray twill pants and a plaid workshirt, summer clothes he wore when we were at my grandparents' house, Father stalked into the hallway.

"Father!" I cried. "Was he there? William? Was he at the fort?"

Lips compressed, he nodded. "Yes. But the police have him now."

Chapter
SEVENTEEN

"LET'S ALL SIT down," Boyle said to Father. "Sounds like you got a lot to talk about."

We went into the parlor. Father stood straighter than he had yesterday; his movements were quick and abrupt, impatient, and his face was grim. Anger, I realized, had replaced his exhaustion.

He and I sat on the sofa, Boyle in one of the chairs.

"Okay," said Boyle, getting out his cigarettes. "You found your son. Where was he?"

"Near my parents' house, up in the Berkshires. He was in the woods." He winced. "And dammit, I should've left him there."

Boyle snapped a match alight. "Wouldn't of helped any."

"At least the police wouldn't have him right now."

Boyle tossed the match into the ashtray, inhaled on the Fatima. "Maybe. Maybe not. He was in the woods?"

"In a lean-to he built a few years ago. Amanda told

me about it. She thought he might there, and she was right. I found him there early this morning. About five o'clock."

"Was he all right?" I asked.

He put his hand on my knee. "He's fine, Amanda."

I asked, "Where did the blood come from?"

He sat back. "It was his. He was hitchhiking to Boston, and he got into a fight with the man who gave him a ride." I made a face, and he shook his head. "It was just a bloody nose, baby. Nothing serious."

Boyle said, "You're talking about the blood on his clothes. The ones the police found in Boston."

Father looked at him, surprised. "You know about that?"

Boyle shrugged. "My job. Crime lab in Boston should have the results by now. Okay. You found him. Then what?"

"I took him to my parents'. We talked."

"He tell you why he left town?"

"He was angry and humiliated. That argument with Audrey worried him. Confused him. He wasn't really running away—I tried to tell that to the police. He didn't even know Audrey was dead until I told him. He just wanted to go someplace where he could be alone and think."

"What time did he leave?"

"Before ten o'clock, he said. He said he got the ride about ten."

"So he's alibied for the time of the murder." His brow furrowed. "Hold on. Why'd he fight with the guy?"

Father frowned, glanced at me, said to Boyle, "The man made advances."

Boyle sighed. "Terrific," he said.

I asked Father, "What does that mean, he made advances?"

He shook his head. "Later, baby."

"Your son happen to get his name?" Boyle asked.

"Smith," Father said sourly. "Jim Smith."

"Uh-huh. What about the car? What make?"

"A Ford."

"Great," said Boyle, nodding. "Perfect. You know how many Fords are out there on the road?"

"It had Massachusetts license plates. William remembers that."

Boyle nodded glumly. "Okay. Why was the guy traveling between here and Boston?"

"He was just motoring, he told William."

"Motoring." Boyle nodded. "Keeps getting better, doesn't it. He tell your son where he lives?"

"Boston. He lives in Boston. William said he seemed to know the city well."

"So *maybe* he lives in Boston. Maybe he *used* to live in Boston." He shook his head. "Never mind. We'll find him. Okay. Your son can describe this guy?"

"Yes, of course. He's given the description to the police."

"Okay. I get it from him, or from the cops, and send it on to the agency. Now. Anyone see your son in Boston?"

"No. No one he can remember."

Boyle nodded. "How'd he get from Boston to your parents' place?"

"The train. Listen, someone *had* to have seen him on the train."

"What time's the train leave Boston?"

"Five in the afternoon."

Boyle shook his head. "Doesn't help much. Okay. At your parents' house. You and William talked. Then what?"

"We slept for a while. Both of us. We both needed it."

"What time the cops show up?"

"Ten this morning. It was that policeman. Medley. He must've followed me last night. I never saw him till he showed up at the house this morning, with a state trooper."

Boyle nodded. "Out of his jurisdiction. Needed the state cops to pick up the warrant and make the pinch."

"He explained all that."

"Nice of him. Okay. So where's your son now?"

Father frowned. "In the jail."

"Here in town? They already booked him?"

"Yes. I think that's what they've done."

"Took his prints? His picture?"

Sighing, Father nodded. "Yes."

"Hey," Boyle said. "Don't worry about it. Couple years from now, it'll be a big adventure. Nick Carter stuff. Something to brag about to the coeds."

Father frowned again. "I hope you're right."

"Sure I am. Okay. Let's go down to the cop shop and see what we can do."

Father nodded, then turned to me. "Amanda, you wait here. I'll be back as soon as I can."

"But I want to see William," I complained, a whine nearly creeping into my voice.

"Tomorrow, baby. I promise. Right now we've got to let Mr. Boyle do his job. All right?"

"It's not *fair*."

"I know it's not. I know that. But what we've got to

do now, all of us, is concentrate on helping William. Don't you think?"

Reluctantly, I said, "Well . . . yes. I guess so. But I can see him tomorrow?"

"I promise."

———

No more than ten minutes passed from the time Father and Boyle left to the time Miss Lizzie came down the stairs and found me sitting dejected on the parlor sofa.

"Amanda?" she said. "What is it?"

"Father was here," I said, not looking up.

"You should've told me, dear. I would've come down to say hello."

Still staring down at the carpet, I said, "The police have got William. He's in jail."

For a moment she was silent. Then she sat down beside me. "They have him here in town?"

"Yes. That sneaky rat Officer Medley, he followed Father all the way to my grandparents' house last night. William was hiding in his fort in the woods."

"Well," she said, "at least you know he's all right."

I looked at her. "But he's not all right, Miss Lizzie. They think he killed Audrey."

"Amanda, everything will work out." She smiled. "Didn't I promise you? You'll only get yourself upset if you keep worrying."

"Everyone tells me not to worry—but how can I *stop* worrying? My brother's in *jail*, and he's never done anything bad in his life. It just isn't *fair*."

She reached up and stroked the back of my head. "Sometimes life is like that, Amanda. Or it seems to be.

But I believe that everyone gets what he deserves, sooner or later." She smiled again, faintly, sadly. "Sometimes a good deal later." The smile brightened and she took her hand from my head, put it on her lap. "But I don't think that's going to happen here. I'm sure that once your brother tells the police his story, they'll understand that he's innocent."

"That's what Mr. Boyle says."

"You see? And Mr. Boyle is an expert."

Reluctantly—my sadness did not wish to capitulate to optimism—I smiled. "He was awfully good fighting with that man Hornsby, wasn't he?"

She nodded. "He was indeed."

"He says it was just a lucky punch."

"We make our own luck, Amanda. But some of us make it more quickly than others. Mr. Boyle makes his *very* quickly."

"I'll say." And I laughed.

Miss Lizzie smiled. "Now listen, dear. While I was upstairs I wrote down the position of all the cards in the Nikola system. Here." She handed me a folded sheet of paper. "So you can take a look at it, if you like, while I'm gone."

"Gone?" It was only then I noticed that she was holding her purse and her bonnet. "Oh," I said, and shook my head. "No, Miss Lizzie. You *can't*."

"If I eat another bite of mutton I shall scream. I thought I'd go down to Mr. McGee's, the fish market, and find us some nice seafood for lunch. Some bluefish, or some crab? Would you like that?"

"I hate seafood," I told her. "Mutton is fine with me. Really. I love mutton."

She nodded. "Then you shall eat the mutton, and I shall eat the crab."

"But Miss Lizzie, they're still out there. They're all still waiting out there."

"Only a few of them. Layabouts and vagrants. They'll not harm me." She smiled. "And your friend Officer O'Hara is out there as well. I'm sure he'll protect me."

"But you *can't*."

"Of course I can. And if I'm going to do it, I should do it now. There's a storm building up, out at sea, and I think we'll finally be getting some rain. So you just wait here, and I shan't be long at all." She stood up, put on her bonnet, and stepped over to the circular mirror that hung above the escritoire. "I do hope it rains," she said, adjusting the bonnet. "This heat is intolerable."

"Miss Lizzie," I said, and this time the whine did insinuate itself into my voice. *"Please."*

"I'll be perfectly all right, dear." She returned to the sofa, picked up her purse, and tucked it under her arm. "So which is it?" she said. "The fish or the crab?"

There was obviously no point in arguing further. And so, with little grace, pouting now, I admitted, "Crab."

She smiled. "Crab it is." She turned and then, bent slightly forward, as resolute as I remembered her, she marched off toward the door.

As soon as I heard it shut, I pushed myself off the sofa and rushed toward the window. By wedging my body against the sill and craning my neck, I was able to see Officer O'Hara and Miss Lizzie through the screen. Despite his being only inches taller, he somehow made himself appear to tower over her as his florid face twisted in outraged protest. I could not hear what he said, for though he seemed to be shouting, he must actually have been whispering.

But his theatrics proved as futile as my whining. Miss Lizzie gave him a firm little shake of her head, turned away, and started down the porch steps. O'Hara slapped both his palms against his legs and rolled his head skyward, a dog baying at the moon.

The crowd, small a few hours ago and now smaller still, consisted of only twenty or thirty people, all of them men. For a moment, as Miss Lizzie strode down the steps, they seemed to draw back from the picket fence, as though the sight of her—at last, after all the shuffling and waiting and jeering—had startled and perhaps even frightened them. And for a moment, I thought she would do it: that, cowed by her determination, they would keep backing away, would fall aside to let her pass.

And then, just as she left the steps and reached the flagstone walk, someone called out, *"Hey, Lizzie!"* and from the corner of my eye I saw a flash of movement, an arm slicing through the air above the gathered heads, and I saw the blur of the projectile as it hurtled toward her. *"No!"* I cried, but it was too late.

It struck her shoulder, and her body rocked as the thing exploded with a flat dull *splat*, spraying red everywhere. *Blood*, I thought, horrified. But it was not—another missile sailed toward her, missed, and splashed red against the sandy lawn. Tomatoes.

Barks of laughter shot from the crowd, and Miss Lizzie stopped moving forward. Another tomato flew through the air, and then another, and someone whooped with wild hysterical glee. As the first smacked against her, and then the second, Miss Lizzie stood immobile. Another flashed by her head, a miss, and still she did not move. I believe to this day that if I had been in front of her, facing her, I would have seen that throughout all this she did not once blink.

Then Officer O'Hara was slamming down the steps

and across the walk, waving his nightstick and shouting, "Here now, stop, *stop!*" With a speed and agility I would not have thought possible, he sprang over the fence and stormed into the crowd. *"Idyots! Ya bloody idyots! Get the hell outta here, ya hear me!"*

This time the crowd, alarmed, did fall back. It splintered into clusters, pairs, individuals; it fractured, dissipated, before the fury of Officer O'Hara. He blustered and screamed, he wailed, he bellowed. He nabbed one straggler by the shoulder, swung him round, sent him reeling off down the street. He snatched another by the collar and roared into his astonished face, *"Git the hell outta here, O'Hanlon, before I break yer thick Irish skull!"* then hurled the backpedaling man away.

And they left: some running off, giggling like adolescent pranksters; some strutting, sneering back over their shoulders to demonstrate the tenacity of their valor; some skulking like beaten dogs. But they left, all of them, and Officer O'Hara stood there alone in the hot empty street, his back to me, panting with anger and struggle, slapping his nightstick against his palm—as though hoping for, *daring*, them to return.

I looked at Miss Lizzie. She turned and, her head lowered, she walked up the porch steps.

I raced to the entryway, twisted the knob at the lock, jerked the door open, and stood back.

She entered the house, pushed the door shut with her back, and remained there, leaning against it, holding her purse with both hands below her stomach. The front of her dress was splotched and splattered with tomato, bright yellow seeds and an ooze of shiny red liquid pulp. It was in her hair and on her face and it was dripping from both her arms. As she stood there against the door, her breast rising and falling with short quick sibilant breaths, a wet chunk of it fell from her hip and plopped against the carpet.

I had heard Miss Lizzie when she was angry, when Officer O'Hara had burst into her parlor and babbled about my stepmother; but my head was hidden in her afghan, and I had not seen it. Now I did.

Her eyes were narrowed, her lips white and so thin they had almost vanished. Blotches of reddish purple blossomed like evil bruises along her pale forehead and cheeks.

She closed her eyes. *"Poltroons!"* she hissed, her nostrils flaring. *"Bumwipes!"*

She opened her eyes and those gray eyes, darker now, stared at me. Or, rather, toward me; or through me; for I do not think she recognized me at all.

She blinked once, and then, without another word, she pulled herself off the door and stormed past me down the hall. She disappeared round the corner and I could hear her feet *thump thump thump* against the stairway as she pounded up the stairs.

Someone's knuckles were rapping at the front door. I turned, called out, "Who is it?"

"O'Hara!"

I opened the door.

"Bloody woman!" he cried, his eyes wide, his face dark red. "Had to have her own bloody way!" He twisted his nightstick like a washerwoman wringing a wet towel. "I *told* her. But did *she* listen? Oh no, not Miss bloody-minded Lizzie *Borden*. I *tried* to stop her, I *did*, ya know, before any o' this *happened*."

"I know," I said. "I saw you."

"But *no*. Not *her*. She had to go to McGee's and get her bloody *fish*." He looked down, shook his head. *"Fish!"* He looked up. "And just how is she now?"

"She went upstairs. She was . . . awfully upset."

"And can ya blame her? Ignorant fools peltin' her with tomatoes? Bloody *idyots*." He turned to scowl at the empty street, then turned back to me. "What sorta fish was it she was after, exactly? What I could do, I was thinkin', is send young Timothy down to fetch it."

"Crab," I said. "She wanted some crab."

He raised his eyebrows. "Crab, is it? Now ain't that a bit—" He shook his head, as though suddenly remembering he was in the middle of a kindness. "Never mind. We'll fetch her the crabs."

"I've got some money—"

"You just keep it, young Miss Burton, and you buy yourself some candy or some nice chocolate cake. I'm no pauper to be takin' money off a young girl." He hesitated, looked off down the hallway, then looked back at me and said softly, "I'll tell ya one thing, though, between you and me and the lamppost. She may be a horrible murderer, that Lizzie Borden of yours, but God knows she's as brave as a bull."

With that, he nodded his good-bye and turned away.

I shut the door. I looked down at the carpet at the spatters of tomato, then looked up toward the upper rear of the house, where Miss Lizzie was.

My mind had been skittering away from one particular thought since the moment I saw her face. Now the thought came back to me. As she stood there, her face mottled, her body tight with rage, Miss Lizzie had quite literally looked angry enough to kill.

Chapter
EIGHTEEN

MISS LIZZIE CAME back downstairs an hour later. I was sitting on the sofa, hunched over the coffee table, where I had arranged a deck of cards in the pattern of the Nikola system.

She had bathed and changed her dress, washed and dried her hair and wrapped it again into a chignon. She smiled at me. "I see that someone has cleaned all the vegetable puree off the floor. Could that've been you?"

I shrugged.

"I thank you," she said. "And I apologize to you for letting my temper get the better of me."

I felt that awful lumpishness which overtook me whenever I became embarrassed. "You don't need to apologize, Miss Lizzie."

"Of course I do. That was a disgraceful exhibition, and I'm thoroughly ashamed of myself."

I would have much preferred that she pretended (as I wanted to) that the incident had never happened, so we could return as soon as possible to being the people we had been before. Brightly I said, "Do you still want some crab? Officer O'Hara brought us some. I put it in the icebox."

"O'Hara?" she said, bemused. "Did he? Well, that was really very kind of him, wasn't it? I'll have to repay him. Is he still outside?"

"I think," I said, "well, I think that he'd be happier if you didn't, Miss Lizzie. I think it would just make him, you know . . . sort of upset."

She looked at me for a moment, and then she said, "The diplomatic corps will be the loser when you become an aviatrix, Amanda." She smiled. "You're right, of course. But do you suppose that it would be terribly improper for me to go outside and thank him for his kindness?"

She said this with such a gentle irony, affectionate and teasing, that I had to smile myself. "I think that would be nice."

"Good. I'll just do that. And then you and I shall have a crab soufflé. How does that sound?"

"It sounds really good."

She nodded. "Then that's settled."

———

Miss Lizzie had been right about the rain. As we ate our lunch on the back porch, the storm lumbered in across the water, growling and flickering. The sea was black out there, below the bloated clouds and the dark draperies of rain; closer in, it was a drab slate gray, feathered with froth, ragged where the wind rattled over it. Along the shore the waves were growing larger: They smacked and hissed and sucked against the sand and left dull white streaks of foam slithering behind.

After the flat stagnant heat of the past few days, the gusts that swept through the screens were at first deliciously cool. When we finished the meal, Miss Lizzie lit a cigar and we sat there in silence and watched the squall roll toward us; both of us, I believe, savoring that heady mixture of humility and exaltation that only a top-notch thunderstorm can produce.

But such feelings require the detachment of distance. Not long after Miss Lizzie lit her cigar, perhaps ten minutes later, the wind was whipping bits of ash from its tip and snapping at her dress, and at mine. We gathered up the plates and scuttled with them into the house. Far off, thunder boomed and rumbled.

The rain began as we stood at the kitchen sink—Miss Lizzie washing dishes, me drying them—and it continued to drum against the rooftop all through the evening and long into the night. Father came by after dinner, water streaming off his topcoat. He hooked the coat and his hat on the hallway clothesrack, then sat down in the parlor and drank tea with us while he related what he and Boyle had learned.

The crime lab of the Boston police had completed its examination of William's clothing and determined that the stains were of Type A blood, the same sort as William's. They were also, unfortunately—according to the medical examiner, Dr. Malone—the same sort as Audrey's.

The local police had interviewed the employees at the Hotel Fairview and the attendants at both of the town's automobile service stations; but no one remembered the man William had described. Boyle had arranged with his agency for another operative to arrive in town tomorrow; the new Pinkerton would try to locate someone who might know the man or who might have seen him.

Father had spoken with Mr. Slocum, and the lawyer

had recommended another local attorney, a Mr. Spencer, with whom Father had consulted. Mr. Spencer felt that, despite the apparent evidence, the state's case was weak. Tomorrow, he thought, it should be possible for William to be released on bail.

Seeing Mr. Spencer had obviously cheered Father. For the first time since Audrey's death, he was his old self, loose and relaxed. (We did not discuss the possibility of Audrey's being a blackmailer, and neither of us mentioned Susan St. Clair.)

He asked me, after some fairly broad hinting on my part, to show him a magic trick; and, when I (flawlessly) performed my Knock Out Speller, he was suitably knocked out.

So knocked out, in fact, that he seemed a bit uneasy, as though a part of him wondered why on earth a daughter of his might be bothering with something so outré as sleights of hand. But he put the best face he could upon things, which in this case was an uncertain smile; and to himself, I think, he merely hoped for the best. It was a reaction with which I would become familiar over the years, and not only from Father.

But he was too pleased about the prospect of William's release to be unsettled for long. Soon he was smiling happily again, and even joking, something he had not done, it seemed, for weeks.

He left around nine o'clock, promising that he would come pick me up at the same time tomorrow morning, to go see William. Shortly afterward, Miss Lizzie and I cleared up the parlor and went upstairs. The wind had died, but rain still pattered against the roof and the air was cool, so she tugged a quilt from the hallway closet and forced it on me before she smiled good night.

I undressed, flipped the quilt over the mattress,

scooted into bed. How luxuriously comfortable it was, after those long sweltering nights, to snuggle up in a warm dry bed while the rain rustled overhead and the sea rustled against the shore. The day had been a long one, but it had ended well, and I felt cozy and secure. Miss Lizzie had apparently forgotten about those nincompoops with their tomatoes; Father was rested and happy; and William would be released tomorrow.

I remember thinking that the police would soon find out who had actually committed the murder, and I remember anticipating how pleased I should be to learn that it was someone about whom I knew nothing and cared less. Someone, for example (just picking a name at random), like Susan St. Clair, she of the flounced skirts and black net hose.

But she, I glumly recalled, had been huddled with Father at the time.

Well, even so, they would find someone, and it would not be William.

Things, it seemed, were finally beginning to work out.

———

I awoke with a shock as sudden as if I had been hurled into icy water. Dread coiled in my chest and sweat lay chill and dank along my skin. For a moment I lay there, heart rapping against my ribs, and tried to understand what had happened, why I had scrambled so panicky from sleep.

It was late; two or three o'clock, one of the darker corners of the night. The rain had stopped, the sea was still, the house was silent. I could hear only the steady metallic dripping of runoff from the roof's gutter as it plopped to the puddles below.

Then I smelled it.

Smoke.

Today I do not know why, nor did I then, but immediately I assumed that the men who had been outside Miss Lizzie's house, the men who had pelted her with rotten tomatoes, had returned and set the house afire.

I threw off the covers, swung my legs off the mattress, and stood up. I picked up my robe from the back of my chair and wrapped it around me. I tiptoed over to the door, cracked it open, held my ear to the opening. I heard nothing. Opening the door farther, I saw that Miss Lizzie's door, across the hall, was ajar, and that a light glowed beyond.

The smoke was drifting from her room, and I recognized it at now as cigar smoke.

Had she fallen asleep with the light on and a cigar burning? If she had, ought I not do something?

I had never been inside Miss Lizzie's room. She had never invited me in, and during the day she kept the door shut. Perhaps it was locked; I had never tried it, and never asked. Doing either would have been, I thought, a violation of her privacy.

Now, tentatively, I crossed the hall. Without touching the door, I leaned toward it and whispered, "Miss Lizzie?"

Nothing.

I pushed the door open gently and stepped inside.

She had told me she had hired a team of movers to help her transport furniture from her house in Fall River to the shore. As I stood in the doorway, I wondered how many of them had wrestled with the enormous four-poster that sprawled across the room at the far wall. It was a behemoth of dark wood, canopied with pale-pink silk, and it looked solid enough to go sailing across the seas; forever, like the Flying Dutch-

man. By the light of the kerosene lamp on the nightstand, I could see that someone had lain in it; but it
was deserted now.

Then I looked to my left and saw—my breathing
stopped, my entire body went cold—two strange women
sitting there. They did not move, they did not acknowledge my intrusion. In the flickering lamplight, they had
a peculiarly somber and melancholy quality, a pair of
specters waiting with infinite patience, but virtually no
hope, for some final decision: a ransom, a pardon. Had
I not been frozen with surprise, I think I would have
run from the room. And then, after a moment, I realized
that they were a doubled Miss Lizzie, the woman herself
and her reflection in the mirror of a wide mahogany
dressing table.

I barely recognized my friend. I had seen her only
when she wore her black mourning and her hair was
clenched in a chignon, Now her hair tumbled in thick
white curls to her shoulders, and she wore a lavender
silk dressing gown, belted, on each lapel of which was
embroidered a large red rose. Her legs were crossed,
right over left, and her head was canted slightly forward.
Her hands were in her lap, folded round a balloon glass
of dark liquid.

To her right, on the dressing table, sat a tall opaque
green bottle and rectangular teakwood jewelry box. Beside them, in a square black ashtray, a cigar sent smoke
spiraling up to the ceiling.

I stepped forward. "Miss Lizzie?"

Her glance swung up into the mirror, and she saw
me.

"Amanda," she said tonelessly, watching me in the
glass.

"Are you all right?"

She shifted in her chair, cleared her throat. "I couldn't sleep."

"Can I get you something?"

"No," she said, and looked down. "No." She turned, looked at me directly, and said, "No, dear. Thank you."

To her left stood a small stool whose red leather matched that of her chair. I walked over to it, sat down, and looked up at her. "Are you okay, Miss Lizzie?"

She raised the balloon glass to her lips, sipped at the liquid. "I'm fine, Amanda. I'm just thinking."

I glanced into the mirror. It made me uncomfortable, made me feel that there were too many of us in the room. I asked her, "Are you sure? I could make us some tea."

"I'm sure," she said. She picked up the cigar, puffed on it, blew a small cloud of smoke. Then she frowned at me. "Amanda? Why are you up so late?"

"I think I had a bad dream. I woke up and I was scared."

She smiled faintly, one of her inward-looking smiles. "Yes," she said, and put the cigar back in the ashtray. "That sounds like a bad dream."

"I don't remember it, though. Usually I remember the bad ones."

Looking off, she nodded slowly. "It would be good, wouldn't it, if we didn't remember any of the bad ones." She sipped again from her glass.

"Are you still upset?" I asked her. "About those men yesterday?"

"No," she said. "No. They were nothing." She moved the glass in a slow wave of dismissal, and the liquid sloshed against its sides. "A ripple of anger. Hatred." She shook her head. "Nothing. It passes and the surface is still again."

I did not know what she meant by that, and I did not know what to do. She seemed to me profoundly unhappy, and I had nothing to offer her. But I did not want to leave her alone. Quickly I glanced around the room. For want of anything better to say, I volunteered inanely, "That's a really pretty jewelry box."

She looked toward the box. "Yes," she said. "Thank you. It was a gift from my father." She shifted the glass to her left hand, reached out with her right and lifted the lid. A clockwork mechanism was hidden somewhere inside. Music suddenly filled the room, as tinny and as paltry and as poignant as only a music-box tune can be.

"What song is that?" I asked her.

"It's the music someone wrote for a poem. 'Hame, Hame, Hame.' It's a Scottish word. It means *home*."

We listened to the tune play, light and lilting at first, then steadily exhausting itself as the device wound down. The notes grew hollow, leaden; they slowed, faltered, died; and left in the room, all at once, a silence louder than themselves.

In nearly a whisper, looking off again, Miss Lizzie recited, " 'When the flower is in the bud . . . and the leaf is on the tree . . . the larks shall sing me hame . . . in my ain country.' " She looked at me and smiled, and gave me a small soft shrug, as though in apology, as though she were embarrassed by the quality of her reading, or of the poem itself. "It was his favorite song," she said.

I had noticed that two items lay on the top shelf of the jewelry box, a strand of pearls and a gold-framed picture, portrait sized, facedown. Nodding to the box, I said, "Is that his picture?"

She looked at the box, shook her head. "No." She reached out, carefully lifted the picture off the velvet lining, and handed it to me.

It was a photograph of a young woman, taken sometime toward the end of the last century. She wore a light-colored dress, its sleeves long, its skirt pleated, its waist sashed; and over it a matching, tightly fitted jacket whose short ruffled sleeves were bordered with lace. Her blond hair was parted in the middle and pulled back into a bun, a few tendrils escaping artfully at her temples. She stood sideways to the camera, looking into it, holding a bonnet behind her back, a pose that demonstrated to best advantage an excellent, almost a voluptuous, figure. The pose, with the lighting and the expression on her face, seemed to be striving for, while not quite achieving, a soulful esthetic delicacy.

Possibly her face was at fault. Her eyes were set too deeply and too far apart; her mouth was a shade too narrow, a shade too thin. It was a face that suggested some small but potentially troubling weakness of character: willfulness, perhaps, or pettiness.

For all that, she was a very pretty woman, and I said so to Miss Lizzie.

"Yes," she said, and took another sip from her glass. "She was very pretty."

"What happened to her?" I asked.

"I killed her," she said.

Chapter
NINETEEN

MY FACE MUST have shown my shock, for Miss Lizzie smiled and said, "No, not out here, not in the real world." She gave the word *real* a slight sarcastic emphasis. "No. In here." She gestured with the glass toward her breast. "In my heart."

"Why?" I asked her. "Who was she?"

She pursed her lips and raised her eyebrows speculatively. "Who was she." She sipped at her drink, then shrugged lightly. As though it answered the question, she said, "She was an actress."

This I found not especially illuminating. "An actress?"

"One of the best," Miss Lizzie said simply, and I could see her lassitude begin to fall away. "She was brilliant. I've seen Eleanora Duse and Sarah Bernhardt, and neither of them could hold a candle to her."

She picked up her cigar, puffed at it, put it back down. "I saw her first in 1904 at the Colonial in Boston. Lady Macbeth. Do you know *Macbeth*?"

I shook my head.

"Lady Macbeth is a difficult role, you see. She's not a very nice person. She goads her husband into killing the King of Scotland so the two of them can take over the kingdom. She's tremendously ambitious. A monster, in fact. And many actresses play her that way. Gnashing their teeth, sweeping their arms about, tearing out their hair. Unredeemed evil."

She sipped at the drink. "But Nance had a gift. It was an instinctive thing—she'd had no formal training. But she was able to make the audience feel that even monsters have depth. And really, why shouldn't they? Few people, including monsters, account themselves evil in their own minds."

"But that doesn't mean they aren't," I said.

She smiled sadly. "No. It doesn't. . . . But what Nance was able to do was give you a sense that there was something behind Lady Macbeth's villainy. Something vulnerable and frail. Something you couldn't identify precisely but knew was there. . . . And it made you feel that if you'd ever been able to understand it, you'd have been able to understand the evil too."

She paused, shook her head. "I'm not doing this well. What I'm trying to say—well, perhaps the audience at the Colonial said it best. For the first time that I'd ever seen, an audience felt genuinely sorry for Lady Macbeth."

"Even though she was evil?"

"Evil is a failure of empathy. What Nance did was make the audience empathize with the failure." She shrugged. "It's a trick, you see. Like the Whispering Queen or the Knockout Speller."

"Is that when you met her? When she played Lady Macbeth?"

She shook her head, took another sip. "Not then, no. About six months later. At a party in Tyngsboro. She was opening at the Tremont in *Judith*. We talked, and we became friends."

"What was she like?"

"Like fire," Miss Lizzie said. She smiled. "Like smoke and rain. She was an elemental, a force of nature. Quite different, I needn't tell you, from anyone I'd ever met."

"And so what happened? How come you stopped being friends?"

She shrugged again, lightly. "The brightest blaze leaves the coldest ashes. We were friendly for a while, intensely friendly, and then we weren't."

"But what happened? You said you killed her in your heart."

She sipped at her drink, frowned.

"That's okay," I said. "It's not really any of my business, I guess."

Miss Lizzie smiled. "You'd make a good actress yourself, you know."

"What do you mean?" I asked her, but my face was flushed.

Miss Lizzie laughed. "At least you have the grace to blush." Another sip of her drink. "Nance wouldn't have blushed. Laughed, perhaps. She usually laughed when she was caught out."

"I only meant," I protested innocently, "that you don't have to to to tell me if you don't want to."

"You only meant," she said, smiling, "that since you were sensitive enough to realize that it wasn't your business, I ought to be sensitive enough to reward you by making it your business."

I laughed; I could not help it.

"There, you see," she said. "Caught out." She sat back

and regarded me for a moment, then said, "You do rather remind me of her."

"Of Nance?" I was unsure whether this was a compliment.

"Physically, I mean. You're a much better person. Kinder. But you carry yourself in much the same way. And you have the same oval face. The same hair. The reviewers were always calling it *flaxen*."

I looked down at the photograph. "She has a small mouth."

Miss Lizzie laughed. "You're an improvement, then, upon the original."

Her laughter pleased me, despite its having my vanity as its cause. "Nance wasn't kind?" I asked.

Miss Lizzie smiled. "And you don't give up. She didn't either." She leaned slightly forward. "Do you really want to know about Nance?"

"Yes," I said. "Of course."

"All right." She sipped at her drink, and then she nodded. "All right. When I met her, she was having financial problems. She was in debt to a theatrical manager in Chicago, she was being sued by another manager in Boston, and she'd just purchased a farm in Tyngsboro. And as a touring actress, a star, she was responsible for the expenses of the company. Everything came out of her profits.

"But Nance didn't care about money. It didn't have any reality to her. Not much did. Not money, not people, not anything from the drab day to day. I think the only thing that was truly real for her was the magic she produced on stage."

A sip of her drink. "Off stage, back in the real world, she was like a child. Wild, irresponsible, flamboyant. And thoughtless, of course. But brave too—immensely brave. Back then, that sort of behavior took real courage, even for a woman of the theater. I remember her telling me that when she was a little girl, about your age, she'd written in her diary, *Better an outlaw than not free.* And that was exactly the way she lived."

"But if she was so wild, how come you two got to be friends?"

Miss Lizzie picked up the cigar again, puffed at it, placed it back in the ashtray. "Well, as I say, I'd never met anyone like her. She was a revelation. And I know I was flattered that she wished to have me with her, as a companion. We went to parties in Boston and we took the train down to New York for openings. We went to restaurants and nightclubs, and it was all very gay. Bright lights and music. She was beautiful and she was famous, and wherever we went, the men would turn and stare. The women would look away and—you could see it in their faces—they would simply give up. They would stop trying."

She took another sip. "As for what drew her to me," she shrugged, "she thought she recognized me. The roles she liked best as an actress were those of women who lived their lives alone, by choice or by circumstance. I was . . . well, I was alone then, most of the time, at any rate, and I think it intrigued her to be with someone she imagined was like the characters she played."

"But what happened?" I asked her.

"Well, as I said, she was in financial trouble when I met her. I gave her some help—the money wasn't much and I was glad to be able to provide it."

"Did she pay you back?"

Miss Lizzie smiled. "Some of it. But remember, money meant nothing to her, and she assumed it mean nothing to anyone else. And, really, in her own way she was always very generous. When she was playing in New York and I went down to meet her, we'd dine at Delmonico's, and she'd always refuse to let me pay for my meal."

Another sip from her drink. "But then, two years after I met her, she got into more financial trouble. If she didn't have seven thousand dollars, she'd lose the farm in Tyngsboro. She asked me for it, and I told her I didn't have it. The truth was, I didn't. I could've raised it, but not without a substantial loss. Even if Nance were to pay me back, which didn't seem likely."

A puff at her cigar. "Well, we argued. I said some things I shouldn't have. She said some things she shouldn't have. She was much more accomplished at it than I—never argue with an actress, Amanda. They have a spectacular repertoire of invective. She showed a level of cruelty, of malice, that I'd never experienced before. At least not from her." She hesitated for a moment and then shrugged again. "And that was the end. I left the room—this was in Boston, I remember, at the Bellevue Hotel—and we never spoke again."

She put down the cigar and lifted the glass to her lips.

I asked, "She didn't try to make it up to you?"

She shook her head. "She was a very proud woman."

"And you never saw her again?"

"Never." She took another sip, emptying the glass. "I closed my heart to her, sealed it shut. I was proud as well, you see." She set the glass on the dressing table, lifted the bottle, uncorked it, and poured herself some more of the liquid. The label on the bottle said it was cognac.

"What happened to her?" I asked.

She corked the bottle, picked up her glass. "She lost her farm. For a while, things went badly for her."

"And afterward?"

"As it turned out, she did quite well for herself. David Belasco took her on. Then, for a few years, she appeared in the cinema. She came back to the stage last year. In *The Passion Flower*." She smiled her inward smile, sipped at the cognac. "It was a triumphant return, from what I read."

"You didn't see it?"

She shook her head. "I haven't gone to the theater in a very long time."

"Didn't you ever want to be friends again?"

The same smile. "Not at first. But after a while . . . I did, yes."

"Then how come you didn't do anything?"

She sighed. "By then there was nothing I could've done. Too much had happened. We were both older, we were both different people." She frowned. "She got married, I understand, six or seven years ago."

"But I still think that maybe if the two of you had gotten together—"

"We would've been cordial, and pleasant, and perhaps we would've felt a sort of fondness for each other. But the . . . affection that we had was gone. We'd trampled on it, both of us. And in a way, standing there with pleasant smiles on our faces, chatting pleasantly away, would make things even worse. For me, at any rate. It would be as though both of us were denying the existence of something so much more . . . important."

She sipped again at her drink.

I said, "It sounds like a shame to me."

"Yes," she said, and her smile seemed like a wound. "To me as well."

We talked for another half an hour, Miss Lizzie and I. She had consumed quite a lot of brandy; and although she continued to enunciate as clearly as ever, she began to speak more slowly, more deliberately, as though the words had somehow gained physical weight and must be used cautiously lest they tumble from her lips and shatter on the floor. Finally, giving me a weary smile, she suggested we both get some sleep.

The next morning was bright and clear and pleasantly warm. Miss Lizzie, wearing her mourning once again, moved throughout the house with a slow underwater precision, like a soldier through a minefield. She explained that she had acquired rather a bad headache. At breakfast, she set down her teacup, frowned, and abruptly said, "Amanda, I do apologize for keeping you up last night."

"Oh no, Miss Lizzie," I told her. "I enjoyed it."

She nodded primly. "Thank you for saying so. But please, dear, try not to attach too much importance to the ramblings of an old woman."

"I didn't think you were rambling at all. I really had a good time."

She frowned again. "Yes, well, I think your father would be most distressed if he learned I'd been so remiss. Let's keep it our little secret, shall we?"

"Sure," I said. I thought she overestimated Father's distress, but with the truth of the card tricks revealed, and the existence of the fort, my fund of secrets was much depleted. I was delighted to share one with Miss Lizzie.

She smiled. "Thank you, dear."

Father showed up at nine, and, when the two of us

went outside, I saw that although there were people moving about in the street, none of them seemed especially interested in us or in the dwelling we had just left. The crowd was gone. Perhaps Officer O'Hara's rage of yesterday had frightened them away. Perhaps last night's rain had discouraged them. Perhaps, with William in jail, they had discovered a new source of fascination. Whatever the reason, the siege of Lizzie Borden's house had been lifted.

Book
THREE

Chapter
TWENTY

SEEMINGLY WITHOUT A care in the world, his legs crossed, reading a copy of *Collier's* he held braced against his chest, William was lying on the swaybacked bottom mattress of a double bunk. He looked away from the magazine, saw me standing at the bars, and grinned. "Hiya, kiddo. How're you doing?"

"I'm fine, William. How are *you?*"

"Not bad." Putting the magazine aside, he sat up and swung his long legs off the mattress.

He appeared absolutely unchanged. I had thought that his journey to my grandparents', his stay in the fort, his trip back in Officer Medley's custody, his night in the jail, that each of these would have left its mark. But none had; not superficially, at least. His black hair was neatly combed, his black mustache neatly trimmed. His nose—which according to Father had been hurt—seemed exactly as it always had, straight and regular, with the same small cleft at its tip.

He stood up, looking strong and vibrant and very much at ease, and sauntered over to the bars. He was wearing not the seedy prison costume I had half expected, ill-fitting and grimly striped, but a white tattersall plaid shirt, pleated tan slacks, and a pair of brown-and-white saddle shoes.

"Well," I said, "you're acting awfully calm about all this."

He grinned. "What should I do? Roll around on the floor and scream and shout?"

"William," I said, and put my hands on my hips, "do you know how worried we all were?"

He leaned against the wall and folded his arms over his chest. "It's funny," he said, smiling, "you sound just like Audrey."

"Well, thanks a *lot*. Father and I worry ourselves *sick* about you, nobody gets any sleep, Father drives all the way up to *Grandma's* to get you, and all you can say is I sound like *Audrey*?"

He grinned. "See what I mean?"

"William—"

"Look," he said, smiling patiently. "I'm sorry you and Dad were worried. I told him so last night. And I want to thank you for figuring out where I was. I mean it. If you hadn't remembered about the fort, everyone would still be out looking for me. But I'm okay now. Really. And everything's fine."

"William," I said, "you're in *jail*."

He shrugged again. "It's not so bad. I've got a room of my own"—he smiled—"and Dad brought a bunch of magazines. And they're letting me order in food from the Fairview. I had steak and eggs for breakfast."

I looked around the "room." Sallow green cement-block walls with one tiny barred window high overhead, a single bare electric bulb in the ceiling, a gray concrete floor, two gray metal bunk beds. Cobwebs drooping from the upper corners, out of reach. Over to the right, a dented gray metal bucket beside an open toilet. The air was motionless and crowded with smells: the sting of disinfectant, the reek of stale urine, the sad wood-smoke stench of stale sweat. I wanted to cry.

"Hey," he said, "I hear you're real chums now with Lizzie Borden."

"Miss Lizzie's been very kind to me."

"Yeah?" He grinned. "Well, I wouldn't go out chopping any wood with her, if I were you—"

"That's nasty, William. You don't even know her."

"—Not unless *you're* the one with the hatchet."

"*William.*"

He laughed, put up a hand. "Okay, okay."

"Father wouldn't let me stay there, at her house, if he didn't like her."

"I *said* okay." He smiled.

I looked to my right down the corridor. Beyond the steel door, Father waited with the new Pinkerton man, a Mr. Dick Foley. I leaned closer to the bars. "Did you know that Father has a girlfriend?"

"Sure," he said, and shrugged again. "Susan St. Clair. He's been seeing her for a long time."

Astonished, I said, "How long?"

"A couple of years."

"A couple of *years*? How do you know that?"

"Last year I found a letter she wrote. In one of the books in the study."

"Last year? What were you doing in the study?"

"Looking for something to read." He grinned. "Is that a crime? You want to send me to jail?"

"That's not funny," I said. "How come you never told me?"

"I figured it was Dad's business."

"But *you* knew about it."

"That doesn't mean I had to tell *you*."

"What did the letter say?"

"I told you. It's Dad's business."

"*You* read it."

"By mistake."

"But William, she could've been the one who killed Audrey. She could be after Father's money. She could be a gold digger."

He smiled scornfully. Over the past few days, while I had been listing William's many virtues to myself, I had neglected (with what I perceived as an extreme nobility of spirit) to recall his vices. Foremost among these, perhaps, was fraternal scorn. "Amanda," he said, "she's rich. Really rich. She's got more money than Dad has."

"How do you know *that*?"

He waved his hand vaguely. "I found out."

"How?"

"I just found out, okay?"

No point questioning him further: he was as stubborn as I.

"She's a nice lady," he said. "Everybody thinks so."

"What does she look like?"

"She's pretty."

"So you've *seen* her?"

"Yeah, I've seen her. So what?"

"Where? Where'd you see her?"

"Downtown. On the street. They were driving around in her car. She's got a Packard."

"What does she look like? Is she a blonde or a brunette? Is she tall?"

"She's blonde. What difference does it make?"

"Well," I said, "maybe someone here in town would recognize her. So far the police don't have any witnesses. But there must've been *someone* who saw *something*. There *had* to be. Maybe we could get a picture of her, and the police could show it around to everyone. Not just here, I mean, but at all the places between here and Boston."

He had been listening to this with pursed lips and furrowed brow. Now he shook his head. "Amanda, Susan St. Clair didn't kill Audrey."

"But how do you *know* that?"

He smiled. "Because I killed her."

"That's not funny," I said. My fingers were tight around the bars.

"It's not supposed to be." He slid his hands into his pockets. "It's the truth."

"It is not, William. Stop it. You're lying."

"I'm not lying. I killed her."

"Oh, really? So how'd you kill her?"

"With a hatchet."

"Where'd you find it?"

"What difference does it make?"

"*See?* You don't even know where you found it."

He grinned. "In that old shed by the swamp."

"What were you doing in there?"

"That's where I went after we had the fight. I was just sitting there and I saw it lying under some boards."

"Where is it now?"

"I threw it in the swamp. Afterward."

"Where in the swamp?"

"I don't remember. I was running away. I was in a hurry."

"They'll look in the swamp, you know. The police."

He shrugged. "Then they'll probably find it."

"All right, William." I crossed my arms over my chest. "*Why'd* you kill her?"

"I was sick of her. Her dumb whining and complaining. The way she treated Dad, the way she treated us. I was tired of the way she looked at me, and her fat white hands, and the way she touched me sometimes."

"What do you mean?"

He stopped himself before he answered, and he frowned. "Look, I was just sick of her, okay? Everything about her. And I was angry, really angry. I saw the hatchet lying there and I picked it up. I walked back to the house along the beach."

"With a *hatchet* in your hand?"

"I shoved it into my pants. It's only a couple hundred yards from the swamp to the back of the house, and there wasn't anyone around."

"How'd you get into the house?"

"The back door was latched, so I came around and used the front door."

"Was the front door locked?"

"No. I just walked in. I looked for her up in her room, but she wasn't there, so I came downstairs—"

"You went upstairs first? The *back* stairs?"

"Yeah, but she wasn't up there. So I came down and then I went up the front stairs. She was asleep in the guest room." He shrugged. "And I killed her."

I shook my head. "You're lying, William."

"I'm not lying."

"Did you look in my room?"

"No."

"Why not?"

"I didn't think she'd be in there."

"*I* was, you know."

"So? I never looked inside."

"How come I didn't hear you?"

He shrugged. "I was walking on tiptoes."

"I still should've heard you."

"But you didn't." He smiled as though taunting me.

I took a deep breath. "So what did you do after you killed her?"

"I had some blood on me, so I took a shower in the washroom, and then I wrapped the hatchet in the dirty towel and came downstairs and left."

"With the hatchet and the towel."

"Yeah."

"And you threw them both in the swamp?"

"Yeah. Separately. The towel first, then the hatchet. And then I walked up the path along the creek for a mile, up to the road, and I hitchhiked a ride to Boston."

"Who was the man who gave you the ride? The man you had a fight with?"

"I made that up. Because of those stains on my shirt. I tried to get them out in the washroom, but some of them were still showing."

"So who gave you a ride?"

"Some guy. I don't remember."

"What did he look like?"

"Just a guy. Short. He had a mustache."

"William, you're *lying*."

He shook his head. "Nope. Sorry, Amanda. I'm not lying. I killed her."

"You did *not*."

"It doesn't matter whether you believe me or not. I did it."

"When you left the house, did you lock the front door?"

"I don't remember."

"It was *locked*."

"Then I guess I locked it." He smiled again. "Give it up, Amanda. Forget about it. I killed her."

———

"He's *lying*, Miss Lizzie," I said. "I know he is. Father must've told him all that stuff, and he's using it now to say that he killed Audrey. He was making it all up as he went along."

She frowned. "It does sound almost as though he were trying out the role, doesn't it? Trying it out on you before he tried it out on the police. Like a New York show going first to Boston."

"But he *is* going to tell the police."

"Did he say why he hasn't told them already?"

"He said he didn't want Father to know. But now he sees that he's got to tell, he says, no matter what."

"And you say you left your father at the police station?"

"Yes. He doesn't know yet."

"You didn't tell him about this?"

"William made me promise not to. He said it was his responsibility."

She nodded.

We were sitting at the table on her back porch, a cup of her universal panacea, chamomile tea, resting before each of us.

"The thing that bothers me," I said, "is that towel he was talking about. He said he wrapped the hatchet in a towel before he left. Maybe there really is a towel missing, and if there is, how did William know about it?"

She smiled. "Just because you and I didn't know about it doesn't mean that there wasn't a missing towel. Very possibly, whoever used the washroom did take a towel with him, so as not to leave it as evidence. And the only way the police could've determined that was by asking you or your father. If they did ask your father, he could easily have told your brother."

"That's it!" I said. "That must be it! He got it from Father, just like he got everything else."

"So it would seem. Did he mention anything about the key? Your stepmother's key?"

"The one that's missing? No." I leaned toward her. "Miss Lizzie, we've got to *do* something."

"Yes," she said, and frowned. She looked down into her teacup.

I stood up and crossed over to the screen that faced my house. From there I could see through the tattered privet hedge that divided the two properties, Miss Lizzie's and ours. I could make out the beach behind our house, most of our sandy yard, and the weathered gray stoop at the back porch, where, just three days ago, my stepmother and William had fought with each other.

"If I'd only been standing here on Tuesday," I said. "Then I could *prove* that William didn't come back like he says he did."

Behind me, Miss Lizzie said softly, "There are no *ifs* in the world, Amanda, I'm sorry to say."

I turned to her. "Why is William *lying*? What's he *doing* it for?"

"Well," she said, "I can think of several reasons." She smiled. "But let's not worry about them right now. The important thing, it seems to me, is to prove that he *is* lying, and I've got an idea or two as to how we can do that. Mr. Boyle called earlier and said he'd stop by after lunch. We can discuss it with him. How would that be?"

"Okay," I said. "I'll be back by lunchtime."

She frowned. "Where are you going?"

"To the swamp."

Chapter
TWENTY-ONE

MISS LIZZIE DID not want me to go alone—"I don't think it's safe, dear"—and for a while she threatened to come along herself. I had visions of her trudging across the hot sand, a strained intrepid smile on her lips, her black dress billowing like a banner in the breeze; and I knew that for her (although neither of us would ever admit it) the trip I was planning would be difficult and uncomfortable. Finally, when I promised to get Annie Holmes to accompany me, she agreed to let me go. It was eleven o'clock when I left, and I assured her I would be back by one-thirty.

Annie's house lay a block north of ours on Water Street. Her family, like mine, lived in Boston, but this was their third summer at the shore. She knew more about the neighborhood than I did, as she had often pointed out, and she might even know whether there had ever been a hatchet somewhere in the old shed by the swamp.

Annie opened the door, saw me, and suddenly, without actually withdrawing, seemed to shrink back behind it, using it almost as a shield. "Uh, hello, Amanda."

"Hi, Annie." I had expected a more exuberant reaction; but perhaps the past few days had left her feeling a bit awkward. "Come on out, okay? Let's go for a walk."

She hesitated. "Um, well, I don't feel very good." Annie was a poor liar; and now, quite clearly, she was lying. I knew it, and she knew I knew it. She looked down at her shoes, her eyelids fluttering. "I guess not."

"What is it?" came the voice of Mrs. Holmes, and then she was standing in the doorway, a big-boned officious woman wearing a flowered apron over a brown cotton dress. "Amanda," she said, her face tightening as she put her hand protectively on Annie's shoulder. "Annie's not feeling well. She needs her rest."

Annie was, except for Miss Lizzie, my best friend at the shore; her mother had always treated me with kindness. Now they were shutting me out, both of them. Their faces were taut and empty, a pair of blank masks; but what lay beneath them, what revealed itself in their eyes, was fear.

I felt open and exposed, as though my skin had been flayed away to reveal the hot raw flesh beneath.

For a moment I could not breathe, could not find my voice. I swallowed, and weakly I said, "Yes."

"We'll see you some other time," said Mrs. Holmes. She forced a brittle smile. "All right, dear?" As though she wished me to ratify the humiliation.

"Yes," I said meekly, but already she was closing the door.

The rims of my eyes stung like the lips of a wound. I turned and walked down the stairs, my body clumsy. I will not cry, I told myself. *I will not cry.*

I stood for a moment in front of Annie's house, blinking back the acid, wondering what to do. I almost returned to Miss Lizzie's. I had an excuse: I had told her I would make the journey only if Annie came with me. But I remembered how Miss Lizzie had stood up to the crowd yesterday while they taunted her and hurled their idiotic vegetables. *She* had not run away. *I* would not either, not at least from bulky boring witchy Mrs. Holmes and her sniveling treacherous backstabbing daughter. Anger, as it often does, had replaced pain.

A large part of it was directed at myself, for agreeing so quickly, with such cowardice, to my own dismissal; for lacking the courage to call them, to their faces, the bitter names I silently called them now.

Very well, I told myself. I did not need them. If I could live without heaven, I could live without traitors and rats like Mrs. Holmes and Annie. I could live without anyone.

But because the heat wave had ended, all the people were back on the beach, clusters of murmuring adults and giddy children; and as I passed by them, I could hear their whispers and giggles, feel their stares prickle the small of my back. I might believe today that I imagined all this, had I not heard, behind me, a shrill childish voice start to chant, "Lizzie Borden took an axe—" Then the sharp *smack* of palm against skin, followed by a thin high wail.

The tide was up and the breeze was mild, the sun was shining. It was a beautiful day, almost certainly. I really did not notice. I was trying to keep my shoulders squared and maintain my head upright atop a suddenly fragile stalk of neck. For the first time I understood Miss Lizzie's determined walk, that slow relentless march of hers.

———

The shed, which I believe had once belonged to a fisherman, was simply a shed, abandoned and ramshackle, smelling of dust and sun-scorched wood. As William had said, there were boards scattered about, and empty tin cans and other bits of rubbish. At one corner, an old *Police Gazette* lay curled in a rictus. But along the dust that lined the floor there was no convenient silhouette of a hatchet. I do not know what I should have done if there had been.

Just beyond the shed was the swampy inlet that led to the mouth of the creek. The swamp was about a hundred yards wide and a hundred yards deep. The air seemed thicker here, and smelled of rot and mold. Small dense clouds of midges hovered above the clumps of skunk cabbage and the thickets of marsh grass, nasty stuff with long narrow blades as sharp as swords.

Amid the brackish water and slick black mud were small weeded islands, and between many of these someone had slung old boards to form a sort of meandering passageway. I picked up a stick and stepped out onto one. It sagged beneath me and dipped down into the muck, *smack*, and clammy water gushed in over the tops of my shoes. I shuddered. A pair of pallid fiddler crabs scuttled away, into the grasses.

Carefully, I slid the stick down into the water, into the mud. Water striders skimmed off across the surface. The stick went two feet deep before it stopped.

If a hatchet *had* been thrown in there, somewhere in those five or six acres of slough, no one would ever find it. And last night's storm would have snatched away anything like a towel that might have been floating about.

I left the stick in the glop and stepped back onto solid ground. My shoes were soaked. I sat down on an old stump, untied the laces, took them off. I stripped off my socks, wrung out the yellow swamp water, wrestled them back on, and then tugged on the shoes. They looked perfectly presentable, but felt terrible against my feet, cold and damp.

I looked around the swamp. Except for the shifting swarms of midges, everything was still. But I knew that behind the quiet, down where the blades of marsh grass poked through the sodden earth, the place was slithering with life. Rats and snakes, leeches and slugs, chiggers and beetles and centipedes.

And then, out of the corner of my eye, I saw a sudden quick flicker of movement. Off to my left, in the woods.

I might have imagined it. But just then, as the fear shivered along my skin, I did not think so. Over there, in the shadows between the trees, something had moved. Or someone.

And I cannot say why, but I was certain that it was Audrey's murderer.

I saw him, in my mind's eye, watching from behind a tree, hatchet in hand, waiting for his chance to come at me. He had passed me over when he slaughtered Audrey, but now he would correct that mistake.

And then, from the same part of the woods, another flutter of movement: The branches of a small tree trembled.

Suddenly I felt very much alone. The swamp was silent and the woods were abruptly darker, abruptly thicker. I was far from the nearest help. And out of earshot: If I were to scream, no one would hear me. If he killed me here, hacked at me, shattered me with his weapon, he could push my body deep into that black, foul-smelling ooze, and no one would ever find it.

I stood up and began to walk back along the path toward the beach, my shoes squishing beneath me. I walked calmly, slowly—I did not want to alert him, to let him know that I was aware of him. But I *was* aware, acutely so; I could feel the weight of his stare all along my body.

When I got back to the beach and saw the people up ahead, the same people whose whispers had disturbed me earlier, I was shamelessly glad to see them. And by the time I reached the street again, heading for the police station to talk to Father about William, I had convinced myself that I had imagined that presence in the woods, that no one had actually been there. That the movement I saw had been, at most, a squirrel; perhaps a rabbit.

But, as I later learned, I was wrong. Someone *had* been in the woods that day; someone *had* been watching me.

———

The policeman sitting behind the big desk in the lobby of the police station, a middle-aged fat man with a shiny bald scalp, told me that Father had gone to Boston. When I asked to see William, he seemed suddenly embarrassed. "Well now, he says he don't want to see nobody."

"But I'm his sister."

"I know that, miss. But he don't want to see nobody, he says. Even a prisoner's got his rights, see. He don't wanna see nobody, he don't see nobody."

"Is the chief of police here?"

"He's a busy man, the chief is."

"Can I see him?"

He frowned. "He's talkin' with Tommy Medley just now."

"Please? Could you ask him? It won't take long."

He shrugged. "I'll check. But I can't promise nothin'. On account of he's busy, see, like I said."

He got up from the desk, walked over to a door on his right, knocked on it, waited, opened it and stuck his head in for a moment. Leaving the door open, he returned to the desk. He shrugged again, defeated or surprised or both. "He says to come ahead."

In his single-sleeved starched white shirt, Chief Da Silva sat starchly upright behind the desk. Officer Medley, who had been sitting in a chair to my left, stood up. "Hi, Amanda." He grinned earnestly.

"Hello." This was the man who had dragged my brother from my grandparents' house: he would get from me nothing more than curtness.

He said, "I guess it's been a rough week for you, hasn't it?"

"Yes," I said, and turned to Da Silva. "Could I please talk to you?"

Da Silva nodded. "Certainly. Have a seat." He turned to Officer Medley. "I'll expect to hear from you by tonight, then."

"Yessir. Bye, Amanda." Another grin.

"Good-bye," I said. *Rat.* I sat down.

Medley left, closing the door behind him, and Da Silva said, "Now. How can I help you?"

"My brother didn't do it."

He nodded noncommittally, his dark eyes as unreadable as ever.

"He wouldn't do something like that."

He nodded again. "I agree."

I had been about to continue; caught off guard, I said, "What?"

"I don't believe he killed your stepmother."

Indignant: "Then what are you keeping him here for?"

He made his small quick smile. "One. By all the evidence, he left town shortly after the time the murder occurred. Two. He didn't come forward voluntarily. Three. An article of his clothing was proved to contain bloodstains that matched the blood group of the deceased—"

"But they match *his* too. He's got the same kind of blood."

"I'm aware of that. Four. He's confessed."

So William had actually done it. The fool. The silly, silly fool. "But he's lying," I said.

He nodded. "I agree. But so long as he maintains that he killed her, I can't do a thing. All the evidence in our possession suggests his guilt. He had motive, means, and opportunity."

"But you *know* he didn't do it."

He gave me a small brisk shake of his head. "I *believe* he didn't do it. I learned a long time ago that what I believe and what a court accepts as evidence are two completely different things."

"But it's not *fair*."

"It's the law."

"Then the law *stinks*."

He smiled briefly. "It's all we have. It's the one thing that keeps us all from behaving like animals."

"It doesn't stop some people. It didn't stop whoever killed my stepmother."

"No. But God willing it'll allow us to prevent whoever did it from doing it again."

"But my brother's the one in jail, and he *didn't* do it."

"None of us want to see your brother convicted. We're still making inquiries. We're still looking for evidence. I believe that sooner or later we'll have a case against the person who was actually responsible."

"And meanwhile my brother is stuck in jail."

"I know." For a moment I imagined that the granite of his face changed slightly, that the hard planes softened. "I'm sorry."

I looked at him. "You still think it was Miss Lizzie, don't you?"

If it had indeed momentarily softened, his face was suddenly all granite once again. "As I said, what I believe doesn't matter."

"She didn't, you know. I know you don't like her. From before. I heard about the dust and stuff up in her loft, back in Fall River. But what if you were wrong about all that? What if you made a mistake?"

He smiled the cool remote smile. "I made no mistake."

"How do you *know*?"

"There was other evidence."

"Then how come you didn't use it at the trial?"

"It didn't present itself until after the acquittal."

"What was the evidence?"

He shrugged his heavy shoulders, which had the effect of drawing my eyes to his empty sleeve. "It doesn't matter now. That was a long time ago."

I did not believe that the long-ago trial did not matter to him. And I did not believe that there was any other evidence. "Can I talk to William?" I asked him.

He shook his head. "He requested that he get no more visitors. That's his right."

"Just for a minute?"

"I'm sorry." I imagined no softening this time.

I had no hope whatever of swaying him. I said, "Does my father know that William confessed?"

"Yes."

Poor Father. One sad thing after another for him. "Why did he go to Boston?"

"I don't know."

Once again, I did not believe him.

———

I was passing by the Woolworth's, on my way to Miss Lizzie's, when someone called my name. I turned and saw Roger Drummond.

Chapter
TWENTY-TWO

SURPRISINGLY, ROGER SEEMED even happier to greet me than he had been to leave me, yesterday, at Miss Lizzie's. He was grinning, his eyes alight, as he waved a folded newspaper under my nose. "Hey, did you see my article? It just came out."

"Roger," I said, "I really don't have time right now. And besides, why would I want to read a nasty old article about Miss Lizzie?"

"No, no, it's not like that," he said, the words coming out in an excited rush. "Come on, I'll show you. You're in it too. We'll go into Woolworth's, I'll buy you a soda."

I had enough things on my mind without worrying about Roger's silly article. But he was so obviously pleased with himself that it would have been cruel to refuse him. Besides, he was the first boy who had ever offered to take me to a soda fountain, at Woolworth's or anywhere else. Whatever the circumstances, one tries not to let a milestone opportunity slip away.

As we sat down on the stools at the counter, Roger to my right, he said, "Hey, I heard about your brother. I'm sorry. I really liked him."

"*Liked* him? What do you mean, Roger? He's not dead or anything."

"No, no, I know that. I just meant it's a tough break for him, being in jail and all." He opened the newspaper on the counter.

"He didn't do it," I said.

"Hey, I'm not arguing with you." He had not yet heard, obviously, about William's confession; and he would not hear about it from me. "Here, look," he said, pointing to the page of newsprint. "See that. *By Roger Drummond, Special Correspondent*. Pretty neat, huh?"

The waitress came over and Roger, frowning with impatience, ordered a cherry phosphate. I ordered a cup of coffee with cream and sugar, and felt rather pleasantly wicked.

"I didn't know you drank coffee," Roger said, picking up the newspaper as the waitress left.

"Oh," I said, "now and then."

He shook his head. "Too bitter for me."

"You put sugar in it," I explained.

But Roger was already reading, his head hidden behind the paper. " 'The entire town was shocked to learn last Tuesday of the brutal murder of Mrs. Audrey Burton of One Hundred Water Street. According to police reports, Mrs. Burton—' " He lowered the paper, looked up at me, blinked, frowned, and said, "Well, that part doesn't really matter. Let me get to the good stuff. Let's see. . . ." He ducked behind the paper again. The waitress brought the phosphate and the coffee and set them down on the counter.

"Hello, my child," said a low musical voice to my right.

It was Mrs. Archer, the spiritualist. She wore a white dress identically strange to the one she had worn yesterday, and she smiled sweetly, brightening her bulldog face. "How are you feeling, Amanda?"

"I'm all right. This is my friend Roger. Roger, do you know Mrs. Archer?"

Impatient again, Roger was eyeing her over the rim of the newspaper. "Hi."

"How do you do," said Mrs. Archer, then turned back to me. "It's so good to see you out and about, my child. You mustn't grieve, you know. Your stepmother is completely happy to be where she is."

Which, if true, would have been a first for Audrey.

Mrs. Archer leaned toward me, eyes narrowed confidentially between folds of flesh, as though she were about to impart a great Secret. "I've spoken with her again, by the way."

"Yes?" I said.

Beyond her, Roger rolled his eyes and disappeared behind the newspaper.

"She sends her love," said Mrs. Archer.

"Oh. Okay. Thanks." I tasted my coffee.

"If I can be of any help, my child, I want you to call upon me. Do you have my card? Here, let me give you one." She opened her carpetbag, which was at least as long as she was tall, and removed from it a white business card. She handed it to me. In spidery raised script it said MADAME HELENE, VOYAGER, CONSULTANT, and gave her telephone number.

I thanked her.

"Not at all." She smiled. "Please don't hesitate to come

to me. I'd be very happy to help you with any problem you might have. There'd be no charge, of course. Well, I must be going. The demands of the corporeal world, you know. So good to see you again. And a pleasure to meet you, Roger."

Roger's head poked above the newspaper. "Sure. Me too."

When she was out of earshot, I said, "Roger, that was rude, reading the paper while she was standing right there."

He grinned. "You think I should've laughed right in her face?"

"Well," I said, and sipped at my coffee, "it was still pretty rude."

"She's nuts," he said. "I've heard about her. Talks to ghosts. Bunkum."

I teased him: "I wonder what Dr. Fraud would say about her."

"Very funny. It's *Freud*, and from what I hear about Mrs. Archer, she's one of the people who could *use* a little repression."

"What does that mean?"

He waved his hand. "Doesn't matter. C'mon, let me finish this."

He read through the article, and it was much kinder and more objective than I had expected. Nowhere was there the slightest suggestion that Miss Lizzie was guilty of anything. She was described as short, white-haired, and dignified. I was described as the young, attractive daughter of the victim. Basking in the glow of the second adjective, I allowed myself to admire the arc of Roger's cheekbones, the curve of his lashes.

He finished up: " 'With the current flurry of opinion, it behooves all of us to remember that opinions are somewhat like collar stays. Everyone should have a few, but when trying them out, we must be careful not to poke ourselves.' "

"Roger!" I said. "That's not fair. That's what Mr. Slocum said."

He grinned. "He told me I could use it. And I changed it, I added some stuff. I improved it. When you do that, it belongs to you."

I shook my head, dubious.

"Really," he said. "Everybody knows that." Eagerly he raised both eyebrows. "So what do you think? About the article?"

"I think it's very nice."

He grinned. "Yeah?"

"Yes. I think it's really very nice."

He looked down at the newspaper, studied it silently for a moment, then looked up, grinning once more. "Yeah, it's not bad at all, is it? You want this copy?" He folded the newspaper, held it out to me. "I've got a bunch of them."

"Thank you," I said, and took it. "I'll bring it back to Miss Lizzie."

The animation left his face. "You mean you're still staying there?"

"Of course."

"You ought to get out of that house, Amanda. Seriously. She's not normal."

I shook my head. "Honestly, Roger. I thought you'd gotten over all that. I mean, the article—"

"Mr. Benedict and I, he's the editor, we talked about it and we decided we had to be careful. For the sake of fairness and all. But I'm telling you, she killed her parents."

"You and Chief Da Silva, Roger. You don't give up, do you?"

"That's because he knows the same thing I do. That she did it."

"It's not fair," I said. "Now he even says there's some kind of evidence that proves she did it. Something that came in after the trial."

Roger nodded. "Yeah. The letter."

"What letter?"

I felt a light, tentative tap on my shoulder and swung around on the stool.

"Oh, hello, Mrs. Mortimer," I said. "How are you?"

Clutching her purse in both hands, she said hello to Roger, then turned and smiled sadly at me, cocking her head with a quick birdlike motion. "Amanda, I can't tell you how sorry we were to hear about this awful thing. Are you all right, dear?"

I was moved. So far, she was the only person in the whole town who had come forward to say this. "Thank you, Mrs. Mortimer. I'm okay, I guess. How's Mr. Mortimer?"

"He's fine, dear. And he's just as concerned for you and your father as I am. And your brother too, of course. Is there anything we can do?"

"No, really. But thank you very much. Everything is—"

" 'Scuse me," said the waitress, across the counter. "You want some more coffee?"

"Yes, please," I told her. She poured it.

Mrs. Mortimer was watching with a small uncertain frown. "Are you really sure, dear, that you should be drinking that?"

I smiled. "It's okay. Really. Father lets me. My stepmother was the one who didn't. And I used to steal it from her all the time."

"Steal it?"

"When she wasn't looking. I was kind of a sneak, I guess. I even stole some last Tuesday . . . you know, after the argument."

She frowned, perhaps felt a flicker of pain at the memory, and she reached out a thin hand to touch my shoulder. "I know, dear. It's probably best not to talk about it."

"I'm really sorry you had to be there to see that."

"I know, I know. Poor Audrey was so . . . difficult sometimes. She was such a good woman, but her pride. . . ." She gave a small sad shrug. "And believe me, Amanda, I'm truly sorry about William. I don't for a minute think he had anything to do with what happened. I hope you know that."

"Yes, sure, of course."

"It's just that the police, they were so *persistent*. They wanted to know everything, they kept *hounding* me. They wouldn't take no for an answer! There just wasn't any way I could avoid telling them. About the . . . argument."

"I understand, Mrs. Mortimer. It wasn't your fault."

"Well, I wanted you to know how I felt. And I don't want you to be a stranger, all right? If you need anything, someone to talk to, anything at all, you just come and see us, all right?"

"Okay, I will. Thank you."

"All right, dear. Good-bye now. Good-bye, Roger."

Roger and I said good-bye, and she stalked off, tall and angular, her shoulders slightly stooped, her head bobbing atop her long thin neck as though she were searching for slim metallic fish down at her feet, down at the bottom of a shallow lake.

"You're getting to be pretty popular," Roger said.

"Not everywhere," I said. "What about this letter?"

"What letter?"

"The one you said Chief Da Silva was talking about."

"Oh. Yeah. It was a letter from a banker. What it said was, he knew for a fact that on the day of the murder, Andrew Borden, Lizzie's father, was planning to transfer a piece of property. It was a house, and it had belonged to Lizzie, but he was going to give it to Lizzie's stepmother. I guess it had been set up for a couple of weeks, the transfer."

"Who was the letter sent to?"

"The chief of police in Fall River. And it was sent after the trial, after Lizzie was acquitted. So he couldn't do anything about it. You can't try someone twice for the same crime."

"Why not?"

"It's just the law. Anyway, according to the banker, Lizzie's stepmother was supposed to meet Andrew at the bank at ten-thirty. Well, naturally, she didn't show up, because right then she was lying upstairs in the guest room, all chopped up—"

"*Roger.*"

He grinned, then suddenly frowned—remembering, I think, my stepmother. "Oh. Yeah. Sorry. Anyway, Lizzie's father went home early. Usually he didn't go till lunchtime, around one o'clock. He was looking for his wife, obviously. At the trial, Lizzie said she told him that her stepmother went out, that she'd gotten a note saying someone was sick. But whoever wrote the note never turned up. Because there wasn't any note."

"You don't know that."

"Her story was in the newspapers, Amanda. The whole town knew the cops were looking for whoever wrote the note."

"Maybe he didn't read the newspapers."

"Hey. The murders were the biggest thing that ever happened in Fall River. You think that *everyone* wasn't reading the newspapers?"

"Okay," I said. "Forget about the note. What was so important about this house?"

"What was important, see, was that Lizzie was really possessive about property. A real capitalist. Five years before all this happened, her father had done almost exactly the same thing. He'd taken another house that had belonged to Lizzie and given it to his wife."

"Why?"

"How would I know? Anyway, just to make things right, her father bought Lizzie *another* house, so she could get the income from the rents. But even that didn't make her happy. She never spoke to her stepmother again. Never stayed in the same room with her, never ate meals with her."

"And you think that because her father did the same thing again, Miss Lizzie would go and kill her stepmother? *And* her father?"

"Look," he said. "Here's what I think happened—and Chief Da Silva agrees with me." He sucked some cherry phosphate up through the straw. "To start off with," he said, "Lizzie was always sort of weird. She was repressed, like I said, really repressed, and once in a while she had these fits. Fits where she didn't know what she was doing. That's in the record.

"Okay. It seems like her father was trying to keep the transfer a secret from Lizzie. Which stands to reason, if you remember the way she acted last time. But she *does* hear about it."

I said, "How do you know?"

"Because it's the only thing that makes sense. Just hold on a minute, okay?"

"It doesn't make sense to me."

"Just wait. So Lizzie gets more and more desperate. She *hates* her stepmother. She can't *stand* the idea that the woman's getting another piece of Lizzie's property. And so finally, on the day when she knows her stepmother is supposed to go downtown to sign the papers, Lizzie goes crazy. She has one of her fits and she grabs an axe, goes up into the guest room, and she kills her. Maybe she doesn't even know what she's doing. She probably doesn't. Not while she's doing it.

"But as soon it's over, she does. Her stepmother's dead, and Lizzie's got to do something. She washes up and she gets dressed to go outside. So she can say she wasn't there when it happened.

"But her father comes home *early*, see, before she gets a chance to go out, and he asks where Mrs. Borden is. Lizzie tells him about the note, but she knows it's not going to make any difference. Sooner or later, someone's going to find the body, and her father's going to know that Lizzie's been there all morning. He's going to know that she's the *only* one who could've killed her. So Lizzie gets out the axe again, and she kills him."

"Someone else could've come into the house."

"When? Either Lizzie or the maid, one or the other, was downstairs all morning. And the front door was locked. So how'd he get in? And *after* he got in and killed Mrs. Borden, where'd he hide until he killed Mr. Borden? And *why* did he kill either one of them?"

"Wait a minute. You said there was a maid?"

"Yeah," he said. "Bridget Sullivan." Smiling, he shook

his head. "But that won't work, Amanda. She didn't have any reason to kill anyone."

"How do you know? Maybe she was stealing or something, and Mrs. Borden caught her. And maybe Mrs. Borden was going to tell the police. And so the maid killed her."

"Why would she kill Mr. Borden?"

"For the same reason you said about Miss Lizzie. Because he'd know that she did it."

"Then why didn't she kill Lizzie? Lizzie would've known it too."

"Maybe they were friends, and she knew Miss Lizzie would protect her."

"Even if Lizzie was going to be executed?"

"Like I said, maybe they were friends."

"You'd have to be pretty good friends with someone to let yourself get executed for something they did."

"It could happen."

"Look," he said. "Bridget Sullivan had been working there for years. You're trying to say that she gets caught stealing, and she kills both of them, on the same day that *Lizzie* has a good reason to kill them?"

"That could happen too."

He grinned. "So you *admit* that Lizzie had a good reason to kill them?"

"You're just trying to be clever now. I didn't admit anything. And besides, I have to go." I stood up off the stool.

He laughed. "Yeah, sure," he said.

"I do. I promised I'd be back by one-thirty. Thank you for the coffee. And for the newspaper."

Smiling, he said, "She did it, you know."

Chapter
TWENTY-THREE

"FIRST THING IS," said Boyle to Miss Lizzie as he exhaled a cone of blue cigarette smoke, "you were right about the bank. I talked to the manager this morning, and she *did* have another account."

"What bank?" I asked Miss Lizzie.

It was two-thirty, and the three of us were back in Miss Lizzie's parlor. Over lunch, she had told me that Father had telephoned before leaving for Boston and had promised to telephone again when he arrived. He had not, she said, explained why he had left town in such a hurry. ("I barely had a chance to speak with him," she told me, pursing her lips and seeming rather nettled by this unseemly haste.)

Now she turned to me and said, "Well, dear, it occurred to me that if your stepmother were actually blackmailing someone, she might need a place to keep the money. If it had been in your house somewhere, the police would have found it when they searched. And so this morning, when Mr. Boyle telephoned, I suggested he inquire at the bank, to determine whether she had an account there."

"She *did* have an account," I said. "Father opened one up when we first came here."

"She had two accounts," said Boyle. "Joint account with your father, another in her maiden name, Richards." He slid his hand into his suit coat, pulled out a small notebook, flipped it open. "Joint account got opened at the end of May. Other one on the fifteenth of June." He looked down at the notebook. "She deposited a hundred dollars in cash to open it. Then another hundred on the seventeenth of July."

"Was that in cash as well?" asked Miss Lizzie.

"Yeah."

"Is this a savings or a checking account?"

"Savings. The July deposit was the last one she made."

Miss Lizzie turned to me. "You have no idea from where the money came?"

"No," I said. "Like I said before, she was always complaining she didn't have enough."

She nodded and looked at Mr. Boyle.

I asked her, "Does that mean she really was a blackmailer?" In a perverse way, I rather hoped she had been. It would have made her more wicked than I had believed; but also more interesting.

"We don't know yet, dear," said Miss Lizzie. "But I *should* like to know the source of that money." To Mr. Boyle: "You spoke with the women on the list Amanda provided?"

"Yeah." He turned over a page in his notebook. "Mrs. Sheehy, Mrs. Maybrick, Mrs. Marlowe, Mrs. Mortimer. Just got finished with Mrs. Mortimer. None of them knows anything, not about blackmail anyway. So they tell me. Except Mrs. Marlowe, maybe, and she won't tell me what it is."

"She informed you that she knew something?"

Boyle smiled. "She informed me that if Miss Borden desired to know anything about Mrs. Burton, Miss Borden could request the information herself. Quote unquote." He closed the notebook. "Doesn't talk to lackeys, is what she means."

"I see. Then I *shall* speak with her myself. Did the others seem surprised by the notion?"

"All of 'em. Mrs. Mortimer told me it was crazy."

Miss Lizzie nodded. "Have you spoken with the Negro man, Charlie?"

"Stopped by his place, but he was out. I'll go by again later today."

"Very well. Now, as to the matter of Amanda's brother. Did you know that he's confessed to the crime?"

Boyle sucked on the cigarette, glanced at me, nodded to Miss Lizzie, exhaled. "Heard that, yeah."

"Amanda believes, and I'm inclined to agree with her, that the boy is lying. Your associate, the other Pinkerton man, what exactly is he doing at the moment?"

"Foley?" He shrugged. "Don't know. Kid's confession probably took the wind out of his sails."

"Well, it seems to me he ought to be proceeding on the assumption that William's first story is the true one, and attempt to identify the man who drove him to Boston."

Boyle nodded. "Be a good idea, sure. But how's he gonna do it? Kid said the guy was just out motoring. Even if Foley went up to Boston, take him forever to locate one particular guy who owns a Ford."

"In my experience," said Miss Lizzie, "the sort of people who own Fords do not go motoring about on a weekday."

Boyle cocked an eyebrow, interested. "Yeah?"

"It's at least a possibility that the man was a tradesman, a commercial traveler calling upon some business account here in town. Your Mr. Foley might do well to canvass the local retailers. He has a description of this man, no doubt?"

"No doubt," said Boyle, and grinned. "You ever need a job, I can get you one with the Pinkertons."

Miss Lizzie smiled. "Thank you. I'll bear that in mind. So you'll discuss this with Mr. Foley?"

Boyle nodded. "Maybe do a little poking around myself."

"If you like. But I do think you should interview this Charlie person."

"Right. Has Slocum turned up anything else? Any more action on that advertisement of yours?"

"I spoke with him earlier this afternoon. Apparently a few more people have come forward, but none, according to Mr. Slocum, seem to know anything of substance."

"How's Mr. Slocum?" I asked.

She turned to me and smiled. "He's fine, dear. He sends his regards."

Boyle stubbed out his Fatima and stood. "Well," he said, "I'll go find Foley and wind him up."

────────

"I don't think so, dear," said Miss Lizzie, sitting beside me on the sofa. "I don't think it's a good idea."

"But I *know* Mrs. Marlowe," I said. "I *like* her." The

latter statement was less true than the former, and the former was true only marginally.

"Yes, I know," she said, "but you saw those men yesterday. You saw the way they behaved. I don't feel it's safe for you to go with me."

"But they're not there anymore, Miss Lizzie. They're not going to bother you again. Everyone thinks William is the one who killed Audrey."

"Amanda," she said, and her voice was soft, her eyes kindly behind the pince-nez, "the way they acted yesterday has very little to do with your stepmother. It has to do with me, dear. With who I am, or who they think I am. Do you understand? If we go out together, you'll be associated in their minds with me. It's not fair to you. I won't let it happen."

"Miss Lizzie," I said, "they already know in their dumb old minds that I've been staying with you. And I don't care what any of them think. Really I don't. They're not my friends, none of them. I don't even live here, and I never will, and I'll probably never see any of them again as long as I live. But even if we were in Boston, even if we were right in my own neighborhood, I'd still want to go out with you. Because you *are* my friend."

The wide gray eyes eyes blinked for a moment, and then she cleared her throat. Her hand reached out, covered mine, squeezed it. "Very well," she said. She nodded once, then looked away.

———

We walked up Fremont Street in the shade of the elms and maples and the sycamores. The day was still beautiful, warm and clear, the cloudless sky stretched overhead like the taut skin of a huge blue balloon. The smell of fresh-cut grass and the purple scent of clover curled across the air. Here and there, despite last night's rain, sprinklers swished silver spray over bright-green lawns and discovered rainbows hanging there. The houses, all set back from the street, all large and substantial, were hushed and serene, a row of plump burghers dozing away their untroubled afternoon.

We saw no one until we reached Main Street. Here we turned right and walked for a while past the shops and stores. People bustled by. Heads turned, stares danced away; chatter became silence, silence became chatter. Miss Lizzie marched along beside me, her purse swinging rhythmically from her folded arms.

One of the largest in town, Mrs. Marlowe's house was a rambling white Victorian affair strung with ornate cornices and topped with a pair of slender cupolas. Sprawled as it was along a rise in the wide green sweep of lawn, it resembled a stately old paddlewheel riverboat, beached there by a floodtide.

We walked up the cement walkway, up the broad white wooden stairs to the front door, and Miss Lizzie tugged on the bellpull. A muffled chime sounded within. Lace curtains, limp and yellowed, hung behind the large rectangle of etched glass set in the door, and through them, after a moment, I saw a flutter of movement.

The door opened and an elderly man stood there, tall but stooped, his cheeks sunken, his sparse hair exactly the same sallow hue as the curtains and combed back from a high freckled forehead. He wore a black butler's livery as though he had worn it since birth.

"Good afternoon," he intoned, his voice as mannered as a butler's in a play. "How may I help you?"

"Good afternoon," said Miss Lizzie. "If Mrs. Marlowe is receiving visitors, we should like to speak with her." The butler nodded. "And who may I say is calling?" "Miss Lizbeth Borden and Miss Amanda Burton." "Very good. Please step this way." He stood stiffly aside for us to pass, closed the door, led us stiffly into the parlor, and told us stiffly that he would inquire of madame whether she was receiving.

The parlor, dark after the sun-splashed outdoors, was at least twice the size of Miss Lizzie's, and packed with enough heavy antique furniture to stock a good-size house or a small municipal museum. All four walls were covered with framed paintings and engravings of clipper ships, schooners, cutters, sloops. And everywhere—atop every square inch of surface space, tables, cabinets, bookshelves—stood bric-a-brac and knickknacks of the sea: ships in bottles, ships' bells, bos'ns' whistles, conch shells, small fans of coral, whales and walruses and dolphins whittled from wood and ivory.

"Mrs. Marlowe's taste leans rather toward the nautical, it would seem," said Miss Lizzie, glancing around at the jumble.

"Gosh," I said. "I guess so."

The air was threaded with a mixture of smells: musk, citrus, a faint fragrance of jasmine, a fainter one of pitch. (Many years later, I found precisely this combination of scents embroidered across the air of an empty Buddhist temple in northern Thailand, and instantly I was transported back to Mrs. Marlowe's cluttered parlor. Almost anything, alas, can serve as a *madeleine*.)

I was examining an ebony statuette of a harpooner, intricately carved, his tiny pointed teeth made from shell, when the butler returned. "Madame will see you," he announced.

We followed his stooped spine through the hallway (more pictures of ships bedecked the walls, and a brace of harpoons crossed like swords), up a long flight of carpeted stairs, down another hallway (more ships) at the end of which was an open door. He stepped through it, turned to his right, and said, "Your guests, madame." He turned to us and nodded us in.

The room was large and airy, lit by the buttery sunshine slanting through the windows. Only one wall displayed a painting, a large four-master running before the wind, clouds scudding overhead, swells feathering into foam; and directly opposite it, propped up by pillows in a large four-poster bed, sat Mrs. Marlowe.

"Amanda," she said, and nodded. Her voice, as always, was raspy and parched, as though it had been dusted with talc. She nodded to Miss Lizzie. "Miss Borden."

The bed's golden silk comforter was drawn up to her chest, and on her lap lay a leatherbound book, opened facedown. She was tiny, almost elfin, and quite old, her round face creased and gullied. Her thin white hair was pulled back against her scalp so tightly it had lost the texture of hair and become seamless. She wore gold wire-rim glasses and a long-sleeved white flannel nightdress, its lace-trimmed front buttoned up to the wiry cords of her neck.

"Tea?" she said, and beneath her lips her tongue slid across her teeth. "Or sherry?"

"Thank you," said Miss Lizzie. "Some tea, please."

"See to it, Clabber," she told the butler, who turned stiffly and departed. She looked back at us, waved a bony freckled hand. "Sit, sit."

Two slender Hepplewhite chairs flanked a matching table. Miss Lizzie and I sat down, Miss Lizzie placing her purse on the table.

Mrs. Marlowe adjusted her glasses and her bright tiny brown eyes peered at Miss Lizzie. "Knew some people from Fall River. Friends of my late husband's." She folded her hands over the book.

Miss Lizzie politely cocked her head. "Indeed?"

"The Stockwells," said Mrs. Marlowe, watching her.

"Yes," said Miss Lizzie with a marked lack of enthusiasm.

Mrs. Marlowe smiled. I had never liked Mrs. Marlowe's smile. It seemed always to have something of malice in it, a hint of wickedness; and her pale-yellow dentures, large and impossibly regular, reminded me of a mouthful of old dice. "Not best friends, eh?" she said. "Can't blame you. Pair of twits. He died, I heard," she added complacently. "Stomach."

"Mrs. Marlowe," Miss Lizzie said, "we came here to ask you a few questions about Mrs. Burton. I understand—"

"I followed the trial, you know. Yours. In the newspapers. Biggest thing to happen round here till the War. Funny thing, memory." She closed her mouth, slipped her tongue again across her teeth. "Remember exactly what I was doing, where I was, when I heard about the murders. See it now, plain as day. New Bedford. Always stank of fish, New Bedford. Went up there, Carl and I, to look at another old tug he wanted to buy. Riddled with dry rot but he wanted it. An idiot. Always was. Dead now. Heart." She narrowed her eyes at Miss Lizzie. "So why'd you do it, exactly? Why'd you hack 'em up?"

"Mrs. Marlowe—"

The old woman laughed, almost a cackle, and then shook her head. "All you had to do was *wait*, woman. Wait long enough, they die on you. All of 'em. Look at me. Parents, two brothers, a sister, two husbands, three worthless brats. All gone. Hear that noise in the background? Know what it is? Silence. *Silence.* Peace and quiet. Took me seventy years to get it, but it's all mine now." She narrowed her eyes again and seemed genuinely puzzled. "So why on earth didn't you wait?"

Miss Lizzie lifted her purse from the table and said, "Perhaps we should come again, Mrs. Marlowe. Some other time."

Mrs. Marlowe raised her hand and pointed a thin unwavering finger. "You don't want to hear about Audrey Burton and her blackmail? Isn't that why you sent that grubby little man this morning?"

Miss Lizzie said, "Are you saying you do know something about Mrs. Burton and blackmail?"

"Course I do. I know everything. Ah, the tea. What took you so long, Clabber?"

"I heated the pot first, madame," the butler said, and set his silver tray on the table between Miss Lizzie and me.

"Well, pour it, for God's sake," said Mrs. Marlowe. "Three spoons for me."

"Yes, madame." Her poured our tea, carried a cup and saucer over to Mrs. Marlowe.

She took it, saying to us, "Twenty years now Clabber's been with me. First mate. Eh, Clabber?"

"Twenty-two, madame."

"Wife used to be the cook here. Galley, eh? Died a few years back. Liver."

"Heart, madame."

She frowned up at him, querulous. "Dead, though, isn't she?"

"Quite."

She nodded, mollified. "Couldn't cook worth a damn. Slop she put together probably did Carl in." She cackled again. "Suppose I owe her one, come to think." She looked up at the butler, frowned. "Clabber, don't hover."

"Sorry, madame."

She waved a hand. "Out, out, out."

As soon as he left the room, she showed us her teeth again. "Thinks he's in the will. Thinks he'll be rolling in cash when I go. New car, trips to Boston and New York. Wine-women-and-song. Not a chance. It all goes to the D.A.R. Every penny. Besides, he's sick. Always has been. Heart. Etta's food again, I expect." She cackled. "I'll outlast him too."

"Mrs. Marlowe," said Miss Lizzie, "about—"

"They never found it, did they? The axe you used."

Miss Lizzie sighed and set her cup and saucer on the table. "Mrs. Marlowe, thank you for the tea. I'm afraid we really must be going."

Mrs. Marlowe sipped at her tea. "Sidney Chatsworth," she said, and smiled her wicked smile.

"I beg your pardon?" said Miss Lizzie.

"The man Audrey was blackmailing." Behind the round lenses, her brown eyes glittered. "Isn't that what you wanted to know?"

Chapter
TWENTY-FOUR

"AND WHO," SAID Miss Lizzie, "is Sidney Chatsworth?"

Mrs. Marlowe sipped at her tea. "Don't know Sidney, eh? Family's famous in these parts. Been here for ages. Not as long as the Lorings, of course. My people. Old man Chatsworth and my father never got along. First-class swine, old Chatsworth was. Womanizer. Got our housemaid in the family way. Rosa. Not much upstairs but tolerable looking, in a vulgar way. She told Mr. Loring, my father, and he went out and found the pig. Took a horsewhip to him." She cackled. "On Main Street. Broad daylight, no less. Hah!" She shook her head, smiling happily. "Little Sidney never did forget that."

Miss Lizzie said, "You say that Mrs. Burton was blackmailing Mr. Chatsworth?"

"His wife's a cripple. Keeled over one day, ten years

ago, *bang*, and that was that. Stroke, they said. Legs gone, been in bed ever since. She's a Cooper, of course. Bad stock. The grandmother was loony, the aunt ran off with a blacksmith. Can you imagine?" She cackled. "A *blacksmith*? No wonder Bessie turned out the way she did. In bed all day with her morphine and her ghosts."

Miss Lizzie said, "And Mrs. Burton learned about the morphine and used that knowledge to blackmail Mr. Chatsworth?"

Scornfully: "Don't be dense. Whole town knows about the morphine."

"Then why—"

"You answer *me* a question," said Mrs. Marlowe, and smiled.

"What question?" asked Miss Lizzie guardedly.

"Amy Stockwell said you tried to buy poison for two whole weeks before the murders. Prussic acid. Couldn't find anyone to sell it to you. That true?"

"Surely if it *had* been," said Miss Lizzie, "it would have been revealed at the trial."

"Bilge. You had the best lawyer in the state. Ex-governor. Same man who gave the judge his job. *Your* judge. They worked a deal at the trial, Amy said."

"No deal was worked."

"So you deny it? The Prussic acid?"

"I don't see that I have to."

Mrs. Marlowe displayed her yellow teeth. "Cool as a cucumber, eh? Good, good. But you should've waited, woman."

"About Mr. Chatsworth," said Miss Lizzie.

Mrs. Marlowe cackled. "Cool as a cucumber. You want to know about Sidney? All right. Sidney's been"—Mrs.

Marlowe glanced at me, looked back at Miss Lizzie—"carrying on with that table-rapper. That Madame Whosis."

"Mrs. Archer?" said Miss Lizzie, surprised. "The spiritualist?"

"Can't imagine what he sees in her. Face like a bucket of worms. Course, Bessie's no prize herself, and never was. Always looked like she was standing around waiting for someone to slap a saddle on her back." Another cackle. "No accounting for tastes, eh?"

"They were . . . involved?"

Mrs. Marlowe frowned. "Didn't I just say that? And Audrey found out about it. And she told Sidney she knew. Said she wanted a little money to keep her mouth shut."

"And Mr. Chatsworth paid her?"

She grinned. "Didn't have any choice, did he? Crippled or not, addled or not, Bessie's the one with the money. She finds out Sidney's having at it with her pet table-rapper, she'll drop him like a hot potato. Write him clean out of the will. And her brother, he'd make it stick. He's their attorney, and he never did like Sidney. No one did." Another cackle.

"You know that for a fact?" asked Miss Lizzie.

"Course I do. He's a blockhead."

Miss Lizzy smiled wearily. "Do you know for a fact that Mrs. Burton threatened to inform Mrs. Chatsworth, and that Mr. Chatsworth bought her off?"

"For an absolute fact. Told you, I know everything. People tell me things." She pointed to the telephone on her nightstand. "Greatest invention of all time."

"And someone must've told things to Audrey Burton."

Mrs. Marlowe blinked. "What d'you mean?"

Miss Lizzie sipped from her cup. "Mrs. Burton was a stranger here in town. How could she possibly have learned about an affair between two local people, a relationship that both of them, presumably, were keeping secret, unless someone had told her?"

Smiling comfortably, Mrs. Marlowe said, "Someone did, I expect. Town is crawling with busybodies and snoops. Makes a body sick to think about it."

"And which one of them, do you suppose, would be spiteful enough, poisonous enough, evil enough, to provide that piece of information to Mrs. Burton?"

Mrs. Marlowe's smile had faded and she was glaring through her wire-rims. "Why ask me? How would I know? What Audrey did was her own damn business. Not my fault she was a bitch. Evil? If anyone was evil, it was Audrey. Isn't that right, Amanda? *You* know that. *Tell* her."

Miss Lizzie set down her tea cup and saucer. "Come along, Amanda. Time for us to leave."

As we stood, Mrs. Marlowe said, "But one thing I'll say for Audrey." Her face was red. Her thin arms were at her sides, her tiny fists clenched. "She never killed *her* parents. She never picked up an axe and hacked *her* mother's head off."

"Thank you for the tea," said Miss Lizzie.

We were moving out the room, down the hall, but Mrs. Marlowe was shouting after us: "She never killed anyone! She never spilled *blood*! *Spill* it? She never splashed it all over the house! She never *wallowed* in it! *She never chopped anybody up and got away with it!*" She started to cackle then, and we could still hear it from far off, the wild brittle rattle of her laughter, when we let ourselves out the front door.

I could hear Miss Lizzie breathing heavily beside me, but neither of us spoke as we walked down the walkway. When we reached the sidewalk she put her hand on my shoulder, stopped moving, and said, "Are you all right?" Concern furrowed her brow, narrowed her eyes.

"I'm okay, Miss Lizzie. Are you?"

"Yes." She took a deep breath. "Yes." Suddenly she smiled. "But rather glad to be out of there."

"She's not a very nice lady, is she?"

"No. Not very nice at all."

We moved off down Main Street.

After a while I asked her, "I guess Audrey really was a blackmailer."

She looked at me and nodded, her lips compressed. "If Mrs. Marlowe is telling the truth."

"Maybe she isn't, you mean?"

"We'll find out, Amanda."

"Are we going to ask Mr. Chatsworth?"

She smiled. "I think we'll leave that to Mr. Boyle. I've had quite enough of the local gentry for a while."

"If she *was* blackmailing him, he could've been the one who did it. To get rid of her."

She nodded. "Possibly."

Two cars passed us, both heading into town.

I said, "So you think it was Mrs. Marlowe who told Audrey about Mr. Chatsworth?"

"Assuming that anything she said is true, yes. And, again on that assumption, it must have been Audrey who told her about the blackmail."

"Why?"

"From what she said, she and Mr. Chatsworth aren't

on the best of terms. *He* wouldn't have told her, certainly. And who else is there?"

"Mrs. Archer?"

"I rather doubt that."

"But how do you think Mrs. Marlowe knew in the first place? About Mr. Chatsworth and Mrs. Archer?"

"Perhaps Mr. Chatsworth has servants, and one of them talked to someone else's servant. And someone overheard and told someone else, and sooner or later it reached Mrs. Marlowe."

"Why do people gossip so much?"

"Gossip is like glue. It holds people together."

"How?"

"Well," she said, "when two people gossip about someone else, they're proving to each other, and to themselves, that they're alike. That they have the same terribly weighty concerns, and the same terribly impeccable standards."

"But sometimes gossip isn't very nice."

Miss Lizzie smiled. "If it were nice, it wouldn't be gossip."

We were coming into the business section once again.

I looked at her. "So I guess Mrs. Archer was Mr. Chatsworth's girlfriend?"

She looked at me. "I suppose so. But let's not worry about it any more, shall we? What would you like for dinner tonight? Shall we stop at Hanrahan's and pick up a nice bit of steak?"

"Sure. Can we have baked potatoes too?"

She nodded. "I think we deserve them, don't you?"

I laughed. "Yes."

A Ford Model T stopped across the street. Its horn honked and the driver waved. "Miz Borden!"

It was Boyle. He opened the door, stepped out, and crossed the street, hands in his pants pockets. He still wore the rumpled brown suit he had worn when we first met him.

He told Miss Lizzie that Mr. Foley, the second Pinkerton man, was talking to all the shopkeepers in town, trying to identify the man William had described. Miss Lizzie told him what the two of us had learned from Mrs. Marlowe.

When she finished, Boyle smiled. "You don't need me, Miz Borden. You're gonna put a lid on this thing all by yourself."

Miss Lizzie smiled back. "I think you should be the one to speak to Mr. Chatsworth."

"Soon's I get done with Charlie. On my way to his place now."

"Can I go with you?" I asked him. I am not really sure why I asked. Perhaps I merely wanted to see again a face that had, before Audrey's death, been friendly.

He shrugged. "Okay with me." He looked at Miss Lizzie.

She frowned. "It's getting near to dinnertime, Amanda."

"It won't take long. Will it, Mr. Boyle?"

Boyle shrugged again. "Shouldn't."

"Dinner will be at eight," she told him.

Boyle took a watch from his pocket, glanced at it. "Over two hours. No problem."

"You'll keep a close eye on her?" she asked him.

"Sure."

To me: "All right, dear." To Boyle: "Before eight o'clock, then."

Boyle's car smelled like Boyle, which is to say, like cigarette smoke. He sat back comfortably on the seat as he drove, his left elbow hooked out the window, his right hand at the top of the steering wheel, Fatima notched between first and second fingers.

I asked him, "Do you think Mr. Chatsworth could've killed Audrey?"

"Coulda, yeah." He shrugged. "Coulda been Mrs. Archer. Coulda been anyone, at this point."

"Mrs. Archer? But she's *tiny.* She's smaller than me."

"Big enough to hold a hatchet."

"But then why would she come to Miss Lizzie's like that? If mean, if she was the one who did it."

Boyle took a drag from the cigarette. "Two ways to find out what someone knows. One, you ask him questions. Two, you let him ask *you* questions. If we'd of asked Mrs. Archer about the murder, she would of known, maybe, that we thought she did it."

"But nobody asked her anything."

He nodded. "And now she knows we *don't* think she did it. *Damn.*" He jerked the steering wheel, but too late: We hit a rock and the Ford jumped. It landed with a thump, its body rattling, and skittered to the left.

"Not much of a road," said Boyle, easing up on the gas pedal, slowing down the car. He brushed cigarette ashes from his pants.

The road was dirt, potholed and badly rutted. Along its sides sat small clapboard houses, most of them painted white, each surrounded by a small plot of lawn. Some of the houses were ramshackle, their dingy paint flaked and blistered, their roofs sagging; the sunburned yellow grasses in front were as high as my waist. The windows of these were open, and the front doors too, all leading into an interior darkness that seemed to be not so much the absence of light as the presence of something else, something palpable and oppressive. As though to escape this, the people sat out on the porch steps under the lengthening late-afternoon shadows, black men and women and children.

When we drove by in the Ford, they suddenly stopped whatever it was they were doing. Husbands stopped talking to their wives; old men stopped laughing with each other; a young girl, my age, brown legs lean and strong below a frilled pink skirt, stopped skipping rope in the dusty footpath that led down to the road. They stopped and they looked at us, not with hatred or fear or resentment, not even with curiosity, but with a kind of blank watchfulness: as though they were waiting, all of them, to learn what this intrusion signified before they would commit themselves to any particular emotion.

We passed other houses as well, these set on small, neatly trimmed lawns bordered with whitewashed picket fences and carefully tended flower gardens, chrysanthemums and carnations gay against the green of grass. But the people on those steps watched us in the same way; and the houses themselves, neat and trim and brightly painted as they were, still seemed guarded, suspicious, still seemed to be marking time until we left.

It was in front of one such house that Boyle brought the car to a stop. Flowers grew in a rectangular plot on the left of the lawn, tomatoes and lettuce and runner beans in a plot on the right. Behind the building was a small patch of corn, slender pale-green stalks leaning at an angle from last night's storm.

"Here we are," said Boyle.

"Charlie lives here?" I asked him. I had begun to

picture Charlie living, squalid and sad, in a rundown sullen shack like one of those we had passed.

"Yep. C'mon."

I did not really want to come. For the first time, as we drove down that road, I had understood that black people might lead lives in their own right, and not serve merely as adjuncts and background to the lives of white people. Not an especially brilliant insight, granted, but rather a disconcerting one at the time. I did not know what I ought to do with it, did not know where thought and feeling, armed (and alarmed) by this new truth, might lead me. I told myself that by being here we were imposing ourselves upon people who wanted nothing to do with us. But the truth is, their sudden reality was imposing itself upon me; and I had, or so I thought, experienced quite enough of new realities over the past week.

But even if I could have verbalized all this to Boyle, it was too late now to tell him.

We got out of the car and followed the flagstones up to the porch. Pale-blue curtains hung in the windows. To our left, a white wooden swing hung above the floor. They were simple, everyday objects; and yet, just then, invincibly alien to me.

I asked Boyle, "What's that smell?"

"Chickens. Pretty ripe, huh? Coop must be out back."

He knocked on the door. After a moment, Charlie opened it.

He wore polished black shoes, pressed black woolen pants, an opened black vest, a white shirt without its collar. I had never seen him dressed in anything but blue denim coveralls, and those usually stained and smeared.

"Mr. Peterson?" said Boyle.

Charlie looked from Boyle to me.

"Hi, Charlie." I smiled, pleased to see him even if he chose to masquerade as someone else.

He looked down at me, and his face was far from friendly. The black skin tightened around his eyes and curled downward at the corners of his mouth.

Chapter
TWENTY-FIVE

THE EXPRESSION DISAPPEARED from Charlie's face so quickly I was unable to determine what it was, beyond a kind of general unhappiness. He looked back at Boyle and said, "You not the poh-lice."

"Uh-uh. Pinkerton. Harry Boyle. We need to ask you a couple questions about last Tuesday. Won't take long."

Charlie's mouth moved as he sucked at a tooth. He said, "I already talk to the poh-lice."

Boyle smiled pleasantly. "Good. Then this'll just be more of the same. Easy stuff. Could we come in?"

Frowning, Charlie reached up and scratched for a moment at the back of his white-haired head. Then he said, "We talk out here. Don't want to disturb Mrs. Peterson. She ailin' some right now." He waved a hand— reluctantly, I thought—toward the swing.

Boyle and I sat down on the swing. Charlie leaned back against the low wall of the porch. He did not seem to know what to do with his knobby hands. For a moment

he put them, large and gnarled, one atop the other on
his lap, and then he crossed his arms and held them
underneath, long fingertips flat against the curve of
his ribs.

"We interrupting something?" Boyle asked him.

"Gettin' ready for services. Over to the church."

This was a very different Charlie from the man who
had joked and laughed with me. He lived within a quiet
self-possession at which I would never have guessed.
And yet behind it, so it seemed to me, lay the same
guarded watchful quality, the same wariness, I had
sensed since we arrived in his neighborhood.

"This won't take long," Boyle assured him.

Charlie nodded. "Yessuh." He had not looked at me
since that first glance in the doorway. Now he did. "Sorry
about your momma, Miss Amanda."

I said, "Thank you, Charlie."

"The good Lord give and he take away. He give you
comfort now, you axe for it."

I nodded.

"Mr. Peterson," said Boyle.

"Yessuh?" Blinking, he shifted his position slightly on
the wall.

"You were on Water Street last Tuesday? Near Mrs.
Burton's house?"

"Poh-lice already axe me that."

Boyle nodded. "And what'd you tell them?"

"I tole 'em the truth. Yessuh, I on Water Street Tuesday."

"Did you go to the Burton house?"

"Yessuh. Goes up and knocks on the door like I do.
See if Miz Burton, she wants to order her a chicken.
Usually she do. Once a week, leastways. But nobody
show up, so I leaves. This just like I tole the poh-lice."

"You see anybody else around?"

"I sees that Mr. Hornsby. Big gennleman works on Captain Hardee's boat. The police, they already know he be there. He the one say *I* be there."

"You talked to the police yesterday?"

"Yessuh. Chief Da Silva come here. And another one. That Mistuh Medley. 'Bout this time of day."

"Where was Hornsby when you saw him?"

"He comin' down Water Street. I goin' up."

"After you left the Burtons' house."

"Yessuh."

"And you were going north on Water?"

"Yessuh. North."

"Away from downtown."

I think that Charlie smiled then, very faintly, very quickly. "Yessuh. North."

Boyle smiled and said, "See anybody else on the street?"

"Nosuh. Only Mr. Hornsby."

"Where were you going, Mr. Peterson?"

"See Miz Cooper, over to Burnside. Had a chicken for her she ordered from me."

"That was the thing in the bag you were carrying?"

"Yessuh. Poh-lice axe me that too. You axe Miz Cooper I didn't bring her no chicken."

Boyle smiled. "Take your word for it. But just so's I get an idea, where's this Miss Cooper live?"

"Three-one-two Burnside. You go ahead, you axe her. She tell you."

"No problem, Mr. Peterson. Burnside is what—two, three blocks up from Mrs. Burton's house?"

"Yessuh. Fremont, and then Sheridan, and then Burnside. Three blocks." Charlie sucked on a tooth. "North, that is."

Boyle grinned. "That'd be away from downtown, I guess, huh?"

Charlie did not smile, but for an instant his eyes seemed brighter. "Yessuh. That direction."

"What did you do after you gave Miss Cooper her chicken?"

"I goes back to Water Street and walks down that till I comes to Grant, and then I goes up Grant to Main Street and gets the buggy."

"Where was the buggy?"

"I leaves it by the Woolsworth."

Boyle nodded. "Okay. So you came back down on Water Street. You passed Mrs. Burton's house again. You see anything this time?"

Charlie glanced at me, glanced back to Boyle. "Nosuh. I tole you. I don't see nothin' at Miz Burton's house."

"You see anything else at all while you were on Water Street?"

"Nosuh. Like I tole the poh-lice."

"Are you sure, Mr. Peterson?"

"Nosuh. I keeps tellin' you, I don't see nothin' at Miz Burton's house."

"But did you see anything along the street? Or on Burnside? Anything strange, anything unusual?"

Charlie cocked his head, his lower lip protruding. "Nosuh. Don't believe so."

"Nothing? Everything exactly like it always is?"

"Yessuh." Charlie shrugged. " 'Cept for the Packard."

Boyle frowned. "The Packard? What Packard?"

"Parked on Burnside, under the trees. Half a block down, across from Miz Cooper's."

"A two-door Packard?"

"Nosuh. Onliest two-door Packard in town, that be Mistuh Childers's from Boston. I know that car, I be bringin' Mistuh Childers a chicken every week. This a four door."

"You're sure?"

"A four-door Packard," Charlie said. "Black. Parked right there on the south side of the street, plain as day."

"You tell this to the cops?"

"Sure." He shrugged again. "They axe me did I see any strange cars. I tells 'em bout the Packard."

Boyle nodded. "Okay, Mr. Peterson. Getting back to Mrs. Burton's house—"

"I tole you, I don't see nothin' at Miz Burton's house."

Boyle nodded. "I remember. But you were standing right outside the front door, right? So while you were there, did you *hear* anything? Anything from inside the house?"

Charlie's glance darted at me again, darted back to Boyle. "Nosuh. Don't hear nothin', don't see nothin'."

Perhaps it was the way he had slipped a look at me— three times now when our house was mentioned—that made me feel he was not telling the truth. "Are you *sure*, Charlie?" I asked him. "It's really important."

He looked at me, his eyes sad. "Miss Amanda, best thing now, you leaves this be. Do your grievin', do your prayin', and then you moves on. Nothin' good come of all these questions."

"But Charlie," I said, "we really want to *know*."

Slowly he shook his head. "Nothin' good come of it." He turned back to Boyle. "Like I tole you, I don't hear nothin', I don'—"

He turned around to look off to his right.

Another Ford came bouncing and bucking down the road, a cloud of brown dust billowing behind. As we watched, it braked abruptly, tires skidding, and pulled in behind Boyle's and lurched to a halt. The doors popped open and four white men spilled out and gathered together at the edge of the lawn, about twelve feet away on the far side of the low picket fence. I recognized the two who had tumbled from the backseat, although I did not know their names. They had been part of the crowd that threw tomatoes at Miss Lizzie. And I recognized the driver, a big man, weaving slightly, a wide grin on his broad face. It was Hornsby.

Charlie had stood away from the wall of the porch and turned to face them. Boyle stood up now, as I did, and Boyle said quietly, "You got a bird gun in the house, Mr. Peterson?"

Charlie said sadly, "Nosuh, I sure don't."

"Uh-huh," said Boyle.

"God*damn!*" Hornsby said, and his broad face was bright with pleasure. "It's fatboy! How you doin', fatboy? Told ya I'd see ya again."

Boyle nodded. "Ace."

Hornsby laughed. He turned to the other three. "This here's fatboy. I told ya 'bout fatboy."

The men nodded and grinned. One of them called out, "Hey, fatboy!" and then doubled over, made helpless with laughter by this witticism. His two friends, evidently sharing the same sense of humor, slapped each other on the back and guffawed. They all appeared quite drunk.

Hornsby said, "I'll tell ya what, fatboy. It's so good to see ya, I'm not even gonna pound your ugly face in." He waved his big hand magnanimously. "You go off and do whatever ya want. We got business to take care of here, me and my friends."

"What kind of business?" Boyle asked him.

Hornsby hooked his thumbs over his belt. "Nothin'

serious. We're just gonna take ole Charlie here for a little ride, ask him some questions."

Behind Hornsby, one of his friends guffawed again.

"What kind of questions, ace?" Boyle asked.

Hornsby laughed. "What *kinda* questions?" Grinning, he turned to the others. "He wants to know what *kinda* questions?"

The three men laughed at this. Boyle turned to me and said under his breath, "Anything starts to happen, you run. All the way home. Got me?"

I nodded.

When Hornsby rounded on Boyle, he was no longer grinning. "I'll tell ya what kinda questions, fatboy. The kinda questions that ain't none of your damn business. This here is our town and we don't need no fat Pinkertons to handle our niggers for us. You just get in your car and take the girl with ya and get outta here before ya get yourself hurt."

Boyle shook his head. "Don't think so, ace."

Hornsby laughed again, harshly, heavily. "You don't *think* so?" His face went cold. "Listen, fatboy, that nigger killed a white woman. He ain't gonna get away with it. Not in *this* town."

"Sounds to me," said Boyle, "like you and your friends got seriously misinformed."

"Sounds to me," Hornsby said, "like you're gonna get your fat ass kicked."

Boyle nodded. "Maybe. Maybe not."

He stepped off the porch. Hornsby turned to the other three men, jerked his head toward Charlie's house, and the four of them moved forward, stepping over the picket fence.

A car horn honked off to the left, and for a moment everyone froze.

A long sleek black Cadillac sailed down the road. It slowed as it purred past the two Fords, and then it swung off the road and parked before them. The far door eased open and Mr. Slocum stepped out.

Tall and slim and (as usual) spectacularly well groomed in another white linen suit, he sauntered around the front of the Cadillac and up to the four men. Two of them, the two I recognized from Miss Lizzie's house, still straddled the picket fence; Hornsby and the fourth stood on the lawn.

"Mr. Hornsby." Mr. Slocum smiled. He stopped walking and he nodded amiably, slipping his hands into his pockets. "What a pleasure." He gazed round at the others. The two at the fence swung their legs over it and stepped back sheepishly, away from the house. Mr. Slocum said, "And Pete Dirkson, and the inestimable Farley brothers. Captain Hardee's entire crew. Are you people by any chance lost? The harbor's in that direction." He nodded toward the east.

Hornsby said, "Get outta here, Slocum."

Still smiling, Mr. Slocum said, "Afraid I can't do that, old man. Have to transact some business with the people up there. Tell you what, though. How about you trot back to town right now, all of you, and then we'll meet later, aboard Captain Hardee's boat, and toss back a pint or two of ale, or grog, or whatever. How's that?"

"You're lookin' for trouble, Slocum," Hornsby said, turning to face him directly.

"Really?" Mr. Slocum smiled. "What gives you that idea, old man?"

The two of them were only seven or eight feet from the porch; consequently, even though Hornsby lowered his voice now, I could still hear him clearly. He said, "Get the fuck outta here, faggot." And then he struck out, straight-armed, palm forward, fingers splayed, and smacked Mr. Slocum in the chest.

His face awry, the lawyer jerked his hands from his pockets as he backpedaled. He caught himself, regained his balance, and straightened up. He smiled mildly. "You know," he said, "I was rather hoping you'd do something like that." Carefully, so as not to crease it, he took off his suit jacket.

Boyle was standing at the entrance to the porch. I scurried over to him. "Mr. Boyle, you've got to stop this."

He shook his head. "Can't, kid. Not now."

Mr. Slocum folded his jacket at the shoulders, brushed it off, and turned to the other man standing on the lawn. "Mr. Dirkson, would you hold this, please? Good man."

He turned back to Hornsby just in time for his face to collide with Hornsby's roundhouse punch.

Chapter
TWENTY-SIX

HORNSBY'S FIST CAUGHT Mr. Slocum square on the left cheek. The lawyer spun away, off his feet, and crashed full length to the ground, rolling twice along the lawn. He lay there, his back to the grass, and for a long cold moment I feared he was dead. My breath stopped; and, I think, my heart as well. Then, slowly, his hands pushing against the ground, he sat up. He looked around himself, mildly puzzled, like someone waking up in a strange room.

Hornsby laughed. "Had enough, Nancy?"

Mr. Slocum rubbed the left side of his face. He glanced down at his hand. From the porch I could see the smear of red along his fingers. His lip was split.

I moved forward, trying to slip around Boyle, who stood at the porch entrance. I cannot imagine what I intended to do; wipe the blood off, perhaps, with my dress. Boyle put his hand on my shoulder and squeezed it once, firmly. "Not now," he said.

"But—"

"Give it a minute," he said, and released me. I stayed where I was.

Mr. Slocum looked at Hornsby and smiled. It was the same bland amiable smile he had smiled before. He drew his feet in and levered himself to a standing position. He took a deep breath, let it out, raised his fists, and began to move them in small tight circles in the air, the left somewhat forward. His spine straight, his head canted slightly back, stepping lightly on his toes like a dancer, he advanced on Hornsby.

Grinning, Hornsby called out over his shoulder to the men behind him, "We got Gentleman Jim here." Mr. Slocum jabbed him in the nose with his left fist.

Hornsby did a little backward jig, blinked his eyes, and shook his head. More startled than damaged, he reached up to touch his nose. Mr. Slocum knifed his right fist into Hornsby's stomach, just below his rib cage.

Hornsby's eyebrows dived downward and his hands clapped at his stomach. Mr. Slocum's left hit him again on the nose, once, twice, three times, very quickly.

Hornsby staggered back. A bright-red trickle ran down his chin. He shook his head again and wiped the blood away with the back of his hand. Suddenly he growled deep in his throat and lunged forward and swung another roundhouse right at Mr. Slocum. Mr. Slocum ducked below it. As Hornsby tried to recover from the momentum of his swing, Mr. Slocum rapped him twice more in the face with his left.

Hornsby flailed out with his right arm, as though to sweep the lawyer off the face of the earth. Mr. Slocum swayed back, dodging it, then leaned forward to swing a fast angled left at the corner of Hornsby's jaw.

Hornsby rocked to the side. Then, all at once, he

lowered his head and rushed toward the lawyer, his hands out, his fingers spread.

Mr. Slocum danced aside and Hornsby hurtled past him.

Hornsby checked himself and whirled around, nearly slipping on the grass. He had his hands up now, closed into fists, and apparently he planned to try beating Mr. Slocum at what was clearly Mr. Slocum's own game. Slowly, eyes wary, he moved toward the lawyer.

Boyle turned to me and said comfortably, "He's gonna try something dirty now. You watch."

I watched. Boyle was right. As soon as he was close enough, Hornsby lashed his foot out, toward Mr. Slocum's groin. The lawyer sidestepped, swerving his torso, but the kick scraped against his thigh. He stumbled, and Hornsby came in.

Mr. Slocum's right shot out and smacked into Hornsby's mouth. Hornsby jerked back, and Mr. Slocum jabbed a fast left into the mouth, and then another. And then the lawyer's right fist, cocked down at his side, shot up like a piston and slammed into the bottom of Hornsby's jaw.

His arms windmilling, Hornsby went back too quickly for his legs to keep him vertical. When he landed flat on his back, I could feel the vibration through the soles of my shoes.

After a moment, it became obvious that Hornsby was not going to get up. Mr. Slocum lowered his hands, stepped over to the man holding his jacket, and took it back. The man merely stood there, staring at Mr. Slocum. The lawyer jerked his head toward Hornsby. "Get him out of here."

Draping the folded jacket over his left arm, he walked up to the porch.

" 'Bout time you finished him off," Boyle said.

Mr. Slocum smiled. He turned to me. "Hello, Amanda."

"You're bleeding, Mr. Slocum," I said. "Your lip is hurt."

He reached up, touched it with his fingertips, glanced down. He shook his head. "Nothing serious."

Mr. Slocum was not the sort of man to swagger, but his standing there, calmly dripping blood onto the grass, was itself a kind of boast. Men enjoy the marks of a victorious battle, their red badges of courage; and I have always found this profoundly irritating. It never occurs to them that physical courage, as opposed to the moral kind, is usually nothing more than a failure of the imagination.

He was also, I think, enjoying the audience. What he really needed was someone to take him home and clean him off and tend to his wounds. And wash his shirt and slacks, both of which were stained with soil and grass.

He looked across the porch. "Hello, Charlie. Sorry about all that." He waved his hand toward the lawn. Beyond the picket fence, the three men were loading Hornsby into the back of their Ford.

"You ain't got no reason be sorry, Mr. Slocum," Charlie said. He was grinning, displaying what remained of his teeth. "That an *exhibition*. You a *boxer*, Mr. Slocum."

Boyle smiled at him. "Wouldn't stand a chance against Jack Johnson, though."

"Different weight," said Charlie. "Jack Johnson, he be a heavyweight."

"If he were a midget," said Mr. Slocum, "he'd still be out of my league."

One of the men cranked the Ford's engine astart, then ran around the hood, climbed into the front seat, pulled the door shut behind him. He glanced back at us as the car pulled away.

"Now," Mr. Slocum said to Boyle. "What was that all about, exactly?"

Boyle said, "Hornsby and his buddies wanted to talk to Mr. Peterson here. Hornsby had this idea Mr. Peterson killed Mrs. Burton."

Mr. Slocum nodded, looked over to Charlie. "Are you all right, Charlie?"

Charlie grinned. "Yessuh, just fine. You ever fight like that again, Mistuh Slocum, you let me know up ahead. We sell tickets, make us a fortune. You thirsty now? I get you a drink? Some lemonade?"

Mr. Slocum smiled, tugging a handkerchief from his back pocket. "You wouldn't happen to have anything stronger, would you?"

"Nosuh, sorry, I sure don't."

Nodding, Mr. Slocum wiped the handkerchief against the knuckles of his left hand. It came away red. *His hand too*, I thought.

"His or yours?" Boyle asked him.

"His, I think."

"What I figured. He never laid a finger on you, champ."

"Funny, though," said Mr. Slocum, dabbing the handkerchief at his lip. "For a moment there, I thought he had."

"Sucker punch," said Boyle. "Doesn't count."

"Ah."

Boyle said, "So what brought you out here?"

"Hmm?" said Mr. Slocum. "Oh. I was just leaving the office, on my way out to Mortimer's for a drink, when Fred Spencer called. It seems that the other Pinkerton,

Foley, may've discovered the identity of the man who gave the Burton boy a ride into Boston."

I had been gazing up at him. Now, suddenly excited, I said, "He found him?"

"Not him, exactly," Mr. Slocum said. "His name. Or what might be his name." He turned to Boyle. "Norton. Wilbur Norton. He sells shoes, works for a wholesaler in Boston. He matches the description, and he was in town on Tuesday morning. In any event, I telephoned Miss Borden to tell her, and she mentioned that the two of you were out here. It's on the way to Mortimer's, and I decided to drop by. I thought Amanda would like to know the news." He smiled at me. The green of his eyes was really quite uncanny. A deep green, the color of emeralds, and lit from within.

I discovered, once again, that I was blushing. "Thank you, Mr. Slocum."

Mr. Slocum held out his hand to Boyle. "My God, would you look at that?" His fingers were trembling.

"Happens all the time," Boyle told him. "Afterwards. No big deal. Just don't do any brain surgery for a while. Tell you what, though. Why don't we head over to Mortimer's and get that drink."

Mr. Slocum took a breath, blew it out. "Yes." He nodded. "Yes, I think that's a splendid idea."

I asked Boyle, "Do we have time?"

Boyle grinned. *"We?"*

"You mean I can't come?" I thought I kept the pout from my voice extremely well. "Annie Holmes has been there. She says it's not really a saloon, it's more like a restaurant."

Boyle glanced at his watch. He turned to Mr. Slocum. "What do you think? Is she ready for Mortimer's?"

Mr. Slocum smiled at me. "So long as she promises not to turn into a flapper."

"I promise," I told him. I would, of course, have promised Mr. Slocum anything.

Boyle said, "And maybe you better not mention this to Miz Borden."

I said, "She'd want me to go. Really."

Boyle laughed. "Okay then."

We said good-bye to Charlie and we walked down the flagstone walk to the cars. As Mr. Slocum was getting into his Cadillac, Boyle called out from beside the Ford, "Hey. Where'd you learn to box like that?"

Mr. Slocum smiled. "Yale," he called back.

Grinning, Boyle nodded. "Figured that was Hornsby's problem. Never had the benefit of a college education."

———

As the Ford rattled back down the road toward Main Street, I said to Boyle, "Do you still think Mr. Slocum's not tough?"

Without looking away from the road, Boyle smiled. "Never said he wasn't, kid. Said I didn't know if he was or not."

"Well, what do you think now?"

Still smiling, he sucked on a Fatima. "Tough as nails."

"I'm *serious*," I said.

"Hey. Me too." He glanced at me, turned back to the road. "He's tough, all right. Lotta guys wouldn't get up from a punch like the one he took. He's got moxie, no question." He inhaled on the cigarette. "Can't help wonderin', though, what he's doin' in a little one-horse town like this."

"What do you mean?"

He flicked his cigarette ash out the window. "Guy like

him, money, brains, what's he doin' out here in Podunk? How come he's not up in Boston, or New York? Philadelphia, even."

"Maybe he just likes it here."

"Maybe. Or maybe he just likes being a big fish in a small pond."

"That's not fair," I said. "You're judging him, and you don't even really know him."

He shook his head. "You don't got to judge people, kid. You leave 'em alone long enough, they show you who they are, all by themselves."

"You don't *like* him." I was less angry than surprised. It was preposterous that anyone could not like Mr. Slocum.

"Hey," he said, and turned to me. "I like him fine. I think he's a peach. No kidding."

"Well then, how come you're saying bad things about him?"

Boyle grinned and shook his head. "I wasn't. I'm not. I really think he's jim dandy. Okay? You two get married, I wanna be best man."

"Married?" I could sense the blush beginning along my cheeks. "Who said anything about getting married?"

"No one," Boyle said, and he laughed. "No one. Look, I really think he's a good guy. I sincerely mean it. Okay? So we still friends, you and I?"

Once again I felt the lumpishness of embarrassment. For most of my life I have been unable to accept a direct offer of kindness or friendship without it.

"Yes," I said.

"Shake on it," he told me. Cigarette between his lips, eyes narrowed against the smoke, he took the wheel with his left hand and held out his right. We shook hands.

———

Certainly, when we were sitting at our table in Mortimer's Boyle seemed to like Mr. Slocum well enough. He and I brought him up to date: Boyle told him what the two of us had learned from Charlie, which was very little; I told him what Miss Lizzie and I had learned from Mrs. Marlowe, which the lawyer pronounced "intriguing." Boyle said that he would have a little chat with Mr. Chatsworth this evening and with Mrs. Archer tomorrow.

And then the two of them started to talk about boxing, Johnson and Dempsey and Carpentier, uppercuts and jabs and crosses. After rather a lot of this, they moved on to a discussion of the acquittal, just two days before, of eight White Sox players on the charge of fixing the 1919 World Series, trading names back and forth—Jackson, Johnson, Comiskey, Rothstein—like boys trading baseball cards. I found all this, despite Mr. Slocum's involvement in it, less than fascinating. There is something about the smell of alcohol and the company of other men that compels otherwise intelligent human beings to revert to preadolescence.

The alcohol, in this case, lay discreetly in the coffee cups sitting before each of them, a scotch and soda for Mr. Slocum, a bourbon on the rocks for Boyle. In my cup lay only coffee; but since it was my third helping of the stuff in one day, more than I had ever been allowed before, I was fairly well pleased with myself.

They moved on to the possibility that the Red Sox, who were apparently in third place, whatever that meant, might this year win the pennant, whatever that was. While they analyzed this, I gazed around me.

The room in which we sat was the dining area. Dark,

low-ceilinged, it held perhaps thirty tables, all of them filled now with couples or families. Off to my right, set into a wall covered with flocked red wallpaper, was a steel door, painted black. Through this, periodically, single men and more couples came and went. It led, so Boyle had told me, to the bar.

Mortimer's was, however, no speakeasy. There were no passwords here, no Charleston dancers, no wild and desperate gaiety. The place was as sedate and ordinary as a Woolworth's. It could have been any restaurant, anywhere, at any time. In this first year of Prohibition, the people who ran it, and the people who came here, were local folk who simply did not believe in the Noble Experiment, and who never had, and who expected a drink or two with their meals.

Presumably, if the establishment had been within the city limits, Chief Da Silva would have done something about it. (Reluctantly, I suspect, for according to Boyle half of Da Silva's police department could be found, at any given moment, behind the steel door.) But it did not, and, as Boyle told me, Mr. Mortimer had an "arrangement" with the local state police barracks. There was in fact no need for the dining-room liquor to be served in coffee cups; this was done, Boyle said, partly as a joke and partly to "give the customers the idea they were gettin' away with something."

I was, as I say, gazing around the room, lost in thought, wondering about William, why he had lied, wondering what had happened to Father, why he had gone so suddenly to Boston, when I heard Boyle say: "So suppose we find the guy, and he clears the kid? What happens then?"

Chapter
TWENTY-SEVEN

SLUMPED BACK IN his chair, one hand idly toying with his coffee cup, Mr. Slocum shrugged. "That's up to Miss Borden. She seems to believe that we can discover who the actual murderer was and somehow prove that to the police." His fingertip tapped lightly against the lip of the cup. "I get the impression, from what she says, that she has some idea, or thinks she does, who it is."

I interrupted. "Does she think it's Mr. Chatsworth?"

He turned to me, and I saw that a bruise was beginning to flower along his left cheek. "She didn't say. It was only an impression, really. Something I picked up from talking to her this evening."

Boyle said, "Guy I'd like to pin it on is Hornsby."

"He's a charmer, isn't he?" said the lawyer with a smile. "You know, I've often asked myself what Mr. Hornsby's precise function might be. In the cosmic scheme of things, I mean."

Boyle took a drag from his Fatima. "So far, looks like

his function is to wander around and get beat up by everybody." He jerked his head toward me. "It's the kid's turn next."

Smiling, Mr. Slocum said, "Pity we can't give him some of his own medicine. Slip him a Mickey Finn and cart him off somewhere, persuade him to tell us what, exactly, he was doing on Water Street last Tuesday."

Boyle sipped at his cup. "Lookin' for someone else to beat him up, probably."

"What's a Mickey Finn?" I asked Mr. Slocum.

"It's—ah, here's exactly the man to answer your question. Mr. Mortimer, good to see you. Have a seat."

Beaming expansively, Mr. Mortimer said, "Don't mind if I do."

He was one of those heavy, hearty, middle-aged men who did nearly everything expansively—sit, stand, talk, listen, breathe. His was a comfortable expansiveness, genial and genuine. I had met him only twice before, but both times I had liked him. Bald, florid, barrel chested and big bellied, today he wore a vested suit of a brown-and-yellow checked material that might perhaps have done better service as a tablecloth. He plucked a large black cigar from between his teeth, grinned happily at Mr. Slocum and shook his hand, grinned happily at Boyle and shook his hand; and then, sitting down, turned to me with a frown of sympathy, broad and awkward but obviously genuine.

"Young Amanda," he said. "Mrs. Mortimer tells me she talked to ya today and told ya to come by if ya need anything. Well, I just want to say to ya, that goes double for Donald J. Mortimer. You need anything, you come to us, me or the missus, and we'll take care of it. That was a terrible thing what happened, terrible, and if folks can't stand together in times of trouble, then what good are they to anybody. Hey?" He stuck the cigar back in his mouth with a flourish: in much the way, I imagine, a medieval copyist might have stabbed the nib of his quill to the parchment at the end of the Sermon on the Mount.

"Yes," I said. "Sure, Mr. Mortimer. Thank you."

"And so how're you doin', exactly?"

"All right, I guess."

"Amanda's got a question for you," said Mr. Slocum, smiling.

"And what might that be?" asked Mr. Mortimer, raising his sandy eyebrows expectantly and removing the cigar once again.

I asked him, "What's a Mickey Finn?"

He grinned. "Now why would a young lady like yourself need to know a thing like that?"

"Why?" I asked. "Is it something bad?"

"Well now," he said, and slapped himself affectionately on the stomach, *clap*. "I s'pose that depends on your own personal point of view." Delicately, using only his middle finger, he tapped the cigar's ash into the ashtray. "What it is, see, there used to be a barkeep by that name, down in New York, in old Manhattan. And he had a habit, whenever one of the customers got a little too obstreperous-like, of putting a little something special in the fella's beer. And what happened was, just a wee bit later the customer all of a sudden ceased being obstreperous. Suddenly he got to be as peaceful as a little babe." He raised the cigar to his mouth and gave it a definitive puff.

"But what did he put in the beer?" I asked him.

"Well now"—Mr. Mortimer grinned—"being the respectable restaurant owner that I am, how on earth would I know somethin' like that?"

Mr. Slocum smiled at Mr. Mortimer. "I thought every barkeep on the East Coast had some of the stuff around." He turned to me. "Chloral hydrate. It's a sleeping drug."

He turned back to Mr. Mortimer. "And just how is the respectable restaurant business doing these days?"

Mr. Mortimer waved an expansive hand, indicating the busy room. "Couldn't be better. Not unless the good Lord himself was making the lobster rolls. This prohibition nonsense, it's the best thing ever happened to me." He punctuated this with another grin and another puff.

"No problems with supply?" Mr. Slocum asked him, smiling. "You didn't, by any chance, have any liquor coming in on the *Henry Marshall*?"

The *Henry Marshall* was a rum-running schooner. Three or four days before, flying the British flag, it had become the first ship ever to be seized by the Coast Guard outside the three-mile limit.

Mr. Mortimer beamed. "No sirree bob, I did not. I saw all this comin' years ago, back before the War. Before I went off to France, I had Kevin, my brother, come down from Boston and run the place. And I told him, day I left, I said, Kevin, you sell everything that's not nailed down, and you and the missus take all the cash outta the bank, and you convert everything we got into bottle inventory." He puffed on the cigar and nodded firmly. "Smartest thing I ever did."

Mr. Slocum nodded. "Admirable foresight."

"Bet your life." Mr. Mortimer grinned and slapped his belly again. "I could show that What's-her-name, Madame Helene, a thing or two, hey? Give her a run for her money."

Exhaling cigarette smoke, Boyle asked him casually, "You know Mrs. Archer, huh?"

"Course I do," said Mr. Mortimer. "Doesn't the missus go to see her once a week, regular, like she was goin' to church?"

Boyle sat back in his chair. "So whatta you think of her?" he asked as though only mildly curious.

"Well, she's a fraud, natcherly. Those mumbo-jumbo seances, talkin' to ghosts and all. Bunkum, pure and simple, hey? Fakery. And tellin' the future? She's no more got a line on what's comin' down the pike than I do. *Less*. Give you an example. . . ."

Leaning forward, he braced his thick elbows on the table and took a puff from the cigar. "Like I say, the missus goes to see her once a week. So this week, this past week, she goes over there, and the silly cow's not even home. The missus, she's got an appointment, like usual see, and so she stands there and she knocks at the door forever. But this Madame Helene, she never shows up. The missus finally just leaves. So *you* tell *me*—how do ya go around sayin' ya can look into the future and all, when ya can't even keep a simple little appointment? Hey?" He puffed on the cigar, shook his head, and then stared at the cigar ash, smiling ruefully. "Not that the missus can see it that way, natcherly."

Boyle asked him, "When was this?"

"Tuesday," said Mr. Mortimer. "This past Tuesday. She always sees her on Tuesday."

"What time?"

"Eleven."

I saw Boyle and Mr. Slocum, both their faces without expression, exchange glances. My stepmother, I remembered, had been killed sometime between ten and eleven.

Mr. Slocum said to Mr. Mortimer, "She's an unusual

woman, Madame Helene. What else do you know about her?"

"Looks like a basset hound," said Mr. Mortimer, and chuckled. "And she's a phony. What else I got to know?"

Looking over his coffee cup as he raised it to his lips, Mr. Slocum asked, "Do you know where she's from?"

"New York. I think I remember the missus sayin' New York. Came here about four years ago."

Mr. Slocum set down the cup. "There must've been a Mr. Archer, sometime, somewhere. What happened to him?"

Mr. Mortimer shrugged his heavy shoulders. "Can't say. Never heard." He chuckled again. "Stuck in a kennel somewhere, probably."

A tall round-faced man in a tuxedo had materialized behind Mr. Mortimer, and now he tapped him on his broad shoulder. Mr. Mortimer turned, the man bent forward and whispered in his ear, and Mr. Mortimer nodded. As the man moved away, Mr. Mortimer turned back to the table. "Got to go. Good to see you. Mr. Slocum. Boyle. And Amanda, you make sure you come by now, visit with me and the missus." He pulled his heavy body out of the chair.

"I will," I said. "Say hello to Mrs. Mortimer for me."

"I'll do that." He grinned and clamped the cigar between his teeth, then turned and lumbered off.

Mr. Slocum said to Boyle, "Perhaps we should have another word with Mrs. Archer."

Boyle nodded. "I was thinking that myself."

———

"So Mrs. Archer," I told Miss Lizzie over the remains of my steak and baked potatoes, "wasn't home when Mrs.

Mortimer went to see her. And that was at *eleven o'clock*."
I delivered the phrase with a portentousness I found
infinitely agreeable.

Miss Lizzie only nodded.

As I had expected, she had received the story of my
visit to Mortimer's not only with calm but even with
curiosity, asking me about the decor, the customers, and
about Mr. Mortimer himself, whom she had never met.

"Perhaps we'll learn something tomorrow," she said
easily, "when Mr. Boyle speaks with her."

This was not quite the reaction I had expected. I said,
"Mr. Slocum thinks that maybe you've got some idea
who the murderer is."

She frowned slightly, puzzled. "I don't recall having
said that to Mr. Slocum."

"He said it was an impression he got."

She smiled. "Well, then. No one has any control, finally, over someone else's impressions."

"But is it true?"

"Is what true?"

"That you've got an idea who it is?"

She shrugged lightly. "Perhaps. But at this stage,
Amanda, I don't really think we should be naming
names."

"Who? Who do you think it was?"

Gently she shook her head. "It wouldn't be right for
me to say. Suppose I were wrong?"

"I won't tell anybody. I promise."

Smiling softly, she said, "Amanda, I'm sorry. It's the
sort of thing one ought not say until one is completely
certain. You understand that, don't you?"

I supposed so, but this did not, of course, stop me
from wanting to know. "But what if you just give me a
hint?"

Looking at me with mock severity over the pince-nez, she intoned, "No."

I sighed elaborately.

"Miss Lizzie," I said. "You're not fair."

"Like life," she said, and smiled again. "Let's clear the table, shall we?"

We were doing the dishes—Miss Lizzie washing, I drying—when the phone rang.

"Can I get it?" I asked her. "It's probably Father."

"Of course, dear. If it is, ask him if I could speak with him for a minute, would you?" She reached out, turned the faucet to shut off the hot water. That particular faucet had been loose for several days now, and, as I scurried from the kitchen, I heard her accuse it: "Stupid *thing*."

It was Father. "How are you, Amanda?"

"I'm fine, Father. Where are you?"

"Still in Boston. I'll be there tomorrow morning, early. Are you sure you're all right?"

"Yes, I'm fine. Really. But how come you're in Boston?"

"I had some things to take care of. Business. But everything's done, most of it, anyway, and I'll be driving back in the morning."

"An awful lot's been going on here, Father. I was all over town today, talking to all kinds of people. I've been out with Miss Lizzie, and with Mr. Boyle—"

"Amanda, I'm sorry, I don't mean to cut you short, but I've got to go. I'm sorry, baby. I only called to make sure you were all right. Try to understand."

Everyone wanted me to understand, but no one seemed willing to tell me what, or why.

"Amanda?" he said.

"Yes." I pouted into the mouthpiece. "I'm here."

"Amanda, I truly am sorry," said the brittle, attenuated voice. "I know I haven't been able to spend much time with you lately. I don't know whether you believe me or not—and I wouldn't blame you if you didn't—but it's been bothering me a lot. It has, Amanda. I'm sorry we can't talk longer, but I hope you'll remember that I love you very much, and that I always will, no matter what happens."

"What do you mean?" I said, suddenly uneasy. "What's going to happen?"

"Nothing, baby, nothing." But I could hear the strain, the tightness, in his voice. "Everything will be all right. And I love you. Okay?"

"Are *you* okay, Daddy?"

He cleared his throat. "Fine, baby, I'm fine. I'll see you tomorrow morning. Say hello to Miss Borden for me. All right?"

"What time are you going to be here?"

"Around nine. I love you, baby."

"I love you too, Daddy."

"Good-bye now."

"Good-bye."

The phone clicked against my ear, a metallic, inhuman sound.

I set down the receiver and stood there for a moment. What was so important in Boston? Was it that Susan St. Clair person again? How could she be more important that I was? Than William was?

And what had he meant by *no matter what happens*?

I heard Miss Lizzie call me from the kitchen.

The sadness, the worry, had lumped together in my throat. I swallowed them away (temporarily) and left the parlor. From the hallway, walking toward her, I called out, "It was Father. He was in a hurry, and he couldn't talk. He says hello."

Bent over the sink, she called back to me, "Amanda, in the hallway closet there's a toolbox. I think there's a wrench inside. Do you know what that is?"

"Yes, sure, of course." I was not an entirely benighted female; back in Boston, I had seen William use one.

"Could you get it for me?"

The closet was halfway between the parlor and the kitchen. I opened the door and looked for a light switch. There was none, but a string dangled from the ceiling. I tugged it, and bright-yellow light filled the narrow recess.

Hanging from the rack were a black poplin raincoat and a lightweight wool jacket, also black. Standing at stiff attention on the floor, a pair of black rubber galoshes and a pair of black walking shoes. The toolbox lay in the corner.

It was gray metal, two feet long, one foot wide, one foot deep, with two metal clasps on the front. I undid these and swung up the top. There were screwdrivers on the first shelf, and neatly arranged cardboard boxes that held screws and bolts and nuts and nails. No wrench.

When I lifted off the shelf to get down into the interior of the box, I saw a rusted crescent wrench lying at the bottom.

And I saw, lying just beside it, the hatchet.

Chapter

TWENTY-EIGHT

THE DAY HAD been an eventful one, and long; but that night, as I lay on the camphor-scented sheets, the image that kept appearing before me was not of Annie Holmes and her mother edging behind their front door, nor of Roger Drummond proudly reading his article, nor of Mrs. Marlowe ranting, nor of old Charlie grinning, nor of Mr. Mortimer and his checked suit, nor of Boyle, nor even of Mr. Slocum. It was of that hatchet.

For a moment, bending over the toolbox in the closet, I had hesitated. Then, not breathing at all, I had reached into the box, taken it by the handle, and lifted it out.

It was old and it was heavy. The handle was dark hickory, its surface as smooth as glass. Except for the sweep of sharp curved blade, the head was coated with a fine powdery black rust. In the harsh yellow light, I could just make out the words engraved at its base, where it met the shaft. *Underhill Edge Tool Co.*

From the kitchen, Miss Lizzie called out, "Amanda? Did you find it?"

"Yes," I called back, and I set the hatchet back in the box, easing it down very carefully, as though it might somehow explode. I picked up the wrench and carried it out into the kitchen.

I stood beside Miss Lizzie as she dealt with the faucet. I had never seen a woman effect repairs before—Audrey, whenever something broke, merely threw it away or called in a team of experts. Miss Lizzie's blunt fingers, so nimble when she manipulated the playing cards, were strong and sure now as she fitted the wrench to the faucet's base.

"It's a good thing the wrench was there," I said.

"Umm-hmmm," she said, concentrating on her work.

"That toolbox," I said. "Did it come with the house?"

"No," she said, twisting the wrench with a firm, swift efficiency. "I brought it with me. You can never tell when things will start acting up on you." She straightened up, turned to me, and smiled. "And I think it's a good idea for people to be able to take care of problems on their own." She tested the faucet. "There. That should do for a while."

She handed me the wrench. "Thank you. Let's finish up the dishes, and then we'll have some tea."

We had finished the dishes, and drunk our tea, and we had talked for a while, I forget now about what. I was distant, distracted, and at ten o'clock, pleading exhaustion, I had gone upstairs to my bedroom. Perhaps half an hour later Miss Lizzie came up the stairs and went down the hall to her room. I barely heard her; only the creak and whisper of a floorboard told me she had passed; she could move almost silently when she wished.

"I'll bet you, Amanda, I'll bet you that hatchet is lying right around here somewhere." So Roger Drummond had said, two days before, when he sat with me in the parlor.

I did not believe that Miss Lizzie had killed my stepmother. I reminded myself of her kindness, her insight, her strength. She was intelligent and, more than that, she was wise. She was, finally, and in a way which few people were capable of being, a truly good person.

And besides, as I had told Roger, she had absolutely no reason to commit an act of such brutality, such mindless, venomous evil.

The hatchet was merely another tool. Probably it had lain in the box for years, gathering rust and dust, entirely forgotten.

I did not believe that Miss Lizzy had killed Audrey. But I spent quite a long while not believing it before I was at last able to fall asleep.

———

When I came downstairs next morning at nine, Miss Lizzie was in the parlor, speaking on the telephone. As I came into the room, I heard her say, "I understand. And you'll ask Mr. Foley to do the other thing? Thank you. Have a pleasant trip. Good-bye."

She hung up the phone and turned to me. "My," she said, and smiled. "Don't you look lovely this morning."

I was wearing my favorite dress, the white organdy trimmed with lace. Beneath it, stiff petticoats made a comforting rustle. My shoes were white patent leather, fastened with straps rather than laces, and the shoes, too, I liked very much.

"Thank you," I said. "Do you really like the dress?"

"I do. You look altogether pre-Raphaelite. Now, what

would you like for breakfast? I picked up some nice smoked bacon yesterday."

We started moving toward the kitchen. "Pre-Raphaelite," I said. "Is that good?"

"It is indeed."

"That wasn't Father on the telephone, was it?"

"No. It was Mr. Boyle. He's going to Boston for the day."

As we passed by the hallway closet, I was suddenly aware of the hatchet inside: as though my skin, magically hypersensitive, was able to perceive the subtle radiation emitted by that thing of wood and iron.

"What for?" I asked Miss Lizzie.

"Two reasons, I gather. Something about his reports, for one. He wasn't very forthcoming, but I think that when he writes them, he tends to be a bit less revealing than his superiors would like."

I smiled. "He's a funny man, isn't he?"

"Yes," she said, opening the icebox door. "And competent as well."

"What's the other reason?"

"The other reason," she said, and she smiled, "is that they've located the salesman, the Norton person who gave William a ride to Boston."

"Really?" I said, excited. "That's great."

"Mr. Boyle thinks it would be helpful if he went up there to speak with him. I agreed. Reluctantly."

"How come reluctantly?"

She set the eggs on the counter beside the white butcher-wrapped package of bacon. "Because I have a feeling that the situation here is going to come to a head fairly soon, and I'd feel more comfortable with him about."

"What makes you think that?"

"I'm not entirely sure. Instinct, I suppose."

She was busy in the cupboard, taking out bowls and plates.

"What about Mr. Chatsworth?" I asked her. "Did Mr. Boyle get a chance to talk to him last night?"

Without looking at me, she said, "He did, yes."

"What did he say?"

She pulled open the silverware drawer.

"Miss Lizzie?"

She turned to me and clasped her hands below her stomach and she sighed. "He admitted it. Your step-mother was blackmailing him."

On the moral map with which I navigated at the time, blackmail did not possess much personal significance. I was even, as I have said, in a way rather pleased that Audrey had found something to do with her life besides complaining about it and making mine miserable. Certainly the fact of her being a blackmailer, after my experience of her character, came as no real surprise. I was not nearly so distressed to learn about it as Miss Lizzie seemed to think I ought to be.

Still, everyone around me—Miss Lizzie, Mr. Slocum, Boyle—appeared to agree that it was an Extremely Bad Thing, and I supposed they were right, and I kept my own council.

As we prepared our breakfast, and then as we ate it, Miss Lizzie told me what Boyle had learned. Mr. Chatsworth, while admitting to being blackmailed, had resolutely denied any involvement in Audrey's death. He had been, so he said to Boyle, in Boston that Tuesday, all day; and he had given to the detective the names of several people there who would corroborate this. Boyle planned to speak with them today.

What about Mrs. Archer? I wanted to know.

Boyle would be talking to her today, before he left town. And he had obtained from Mr. Chatsworth her former address in New York City, and had telephoned the Pinkerton office there to see what they could discover about her earlier life.

We finished eating at around ten o'clock, and, fifteen minutes later, Father telephoned. He was back at the Fairview, he told me, and he would be coming over to Miss Lizzie's in another half an hour or so.

Miss Lizzie, who had asked to speak with him, took the telephone when I was done with it and asked him if the two of us might come to the hotel instead. If possible, she said, she should like to speak with him. He agreed.

———

Overlooking the sea from a broad flat spit of land, the Hotel Fairview was a huge white wedding cake of a building with an air of fading but still finicky respectability. (Father had once taken us all to dinner here, and the only sound in the entire dining room had been the subdued click of silver against porcelain.) Running round its octagonal circumference was a wide colonnaded wooden porch. On sunny days the older guests sat out there in the white wicker furniture, their faces empty, and stared silently across the green lawns, beyond the younger couples lobbing tennis balls, toward the small boats sliding slowly in and out the harbor.

The sky today was overcast, the sun hidden, yet some of them were out there still; a few, despite the heat, bundled in blankets against the breeze that scudded in off the ocean and scattered small flickering whitecaps along the gray water.

We were coming up the wide porch stairway when someone called out, "Hey! Miss Borden!"

It was a short man in a brown suit that was, unlikely as this seemed, even baggier than Boyle's. Below the brown fedora, his face was narrow and pointed, like a fox's. As he scurried toward us across the porch, he whipped a notebook from his coat pocket with his left hand and plucked a pencil from behind his ear with his right.

"Phillips," he announced when he reached us. "The *Tribune*." His sharp chin bobbed as he chewed at a wad of gum. "How well did you know Mrs. Burton?"

Except for Roger Drummond, we had so far been untroubled by reporters and photographers. Those who had gathered outside Miss Lizzie's house during the days of the siege seemed to have dispersed with the rest of the mob. But our luck, evidently, had changed.

"I'm sorry," Miss Lizzie said politely. "But I have nothing to say."

She moved forward, but he sidestepped to block our path.

"Hey, c'mon, gimme a break." It was more a demand than a request.

Miss Lizzie said, "Would you please get out of my way?"

"Whaddy ya think about the cops arresting the Burton kid? You got an opinion on that to share with our readers?"

"I have nothing whatever to share with your readers."

He nodded exactly as though she had answered the

question, and continued, "So what about the possibility it could of been a burglar?"

"If you don't stop pestering us," Miss Lizzie said, "I shall find a policeman and report you."

The man's face puckered with irritation. "Look, lady, I'm only doin' my job."

"Please do it somewhere else."

"Listen," he said, suddenly sincere, "we'll make a deal. You talk to me, exclusive, and I'll keep all the other guys off your back. I guarantee it."

Her voice low, precisely enunciating each word, Miss Lizzie said, "Get . . . out . . . of . . . my . . . way."

The man threw up his hands and stood aside. " 'Kay okay okay," he said, managing to convey by his tone, remarkably, both aggrievement and threat. He nodded at me as we passed him. "That the other Burton kid? I heard the two a you are buddies now." And then from behind us, his voice raised: *"She know about Nance O'Neil?"*

Miss Lizzie marched on, ignoring him; but I craned my neck to look back. The man was standing there, hands on his hips, head back, leering at us while his jaw worked methodically on the chewing gum.

I did not know what he had meant, but I did know that if this was what Roger Drummond wanted to become, he was welcome to it.

Far across the empty lobby, Father sat with Mr. Foley, the other Pinkerton agent, on a long, purple velvet divan bracketed by two small, dispirited palm trees. Wearing a two-piece gray suit, his legs crossed, Father was tapping his hat lightly against his knee. When he saw us, he stood up, smiled and waved, and then walked across the white marble floor. "Hi." He bent down, hugged me, kissed my cheek. As always, his mustache tickled. "How are you, Amanda?" He smiled.

"Fine." After last night's telephone call, I felt tentative, awkward, and still a bit sulky. "How are you?"

"I'm all right." But as he straightened up away from me, his eyes shifted, very slightly. Then his glance found mine and he smiled again. "You look very pretty in that dress."

As pretty as Susan St. Clair? I wanted to say. "Thank you," I said.

He turned to Miss Lizzie. "Miss Borden, how are you?"

"Quite well, thank you." She turned to Mr. Foley, whom she had not met, and who had just come up behind Father.

"I'm Foley, Miss Borden," he said. He was a tall, thin man whose closely cropped hair and neatly trimmed mustache were prematurely white, and he looked very dapper in a pinstriped dark-gray suit and a pair of white spats. "I talked to Harry Boyle. How about I give you a phone call later on?"

"That would be fine," said Miss Lizzie. "Thank you."

Mr. Foley nodded, turned to Father and said, "I'll check in with you too, Mr. Burton."

Father nodded. "Thank you, Foley."

"Bye now," said Foley, and nodded to Miss Lizzie. "Miss Borden."

As soon as he was out of earshot, Miss Lizzie said to Father, "If you've a minute, I'd like to speak with you. In private."

Father pursed his lips—a bit surprised, I imagine, by the need for privacy—and then he nodded. "We can use the library. There's never anyone in there."

Miss Lizzie turned to me. "Amanda, excuse us for just a moment, will you?"

My turn to be surprised; I frowned. Why would she want to talk to Father alone?

She said, "You can wait here, dear. We'll be only a few minutes. I promise."

Father smiled at me. I think he meant it to be reassuring, but it seemed to me forced and uncertain.

"All right," I said.

They walked away and disappeared around the corner at the north end of the lobby. I sat down on the divan, leaned forward, and lifted a *Collier's* from the stack of magazines on the coffee table.

Less than a minute passed before someone sat down beside me and tossed a brown fedora to the coffee table. "Hey, kid." Phillips, the reporter, was perched on the edge of the divan, a few feet to my right. "Too bad about your mom."

"I haven't got anything to say," I told him.

"Here's the deal," he said quickly, his eyes wide and honest. "Just a couple questions and I am-scray, right?" His eyes narrowed and the honesty vanished. "Look, I heard you and your mom didn't get along, and I heard the two a you had a big blowout on Tuesday, before she got chopped. All I wanna know is this—did your friend Lizzie know about the fight? I mean, did she see it happen? Maybe hear it happen?"

"Of course not. And what difference would it make, anyway?"

His glance swept swiftly around the room, came back to me. "What I figure is, maybe she *did* see it, and she's your friend, right? so she decides to fix things up for ya." He winked slyly. "Catch my drift?"

"Well she didn't," I said. "And even if she did, it wouldn't have made any difference."

"Listen, kid, this here is a lady got a history with hatchets." He glanced around the lobby again. "I mean, this wouldn't be a first or anything. You follow me?"

"No I don't, and I think you'd better leave me alone."

"Listen," he said, and looked off, and then grimaced, grabbed his hat, and stood. "Later, kid." He scooted around the coffee table and darted off across the lobby.

He had seen, of course, the return of Miss Lizzie and Father. I set aside the magazine. When they reached me, Miss Lizzie said, "Was that man bothering you, Amanda?"

"I guess he was trying to," I said. "I told him I didn't want to talk to him."

Frowning, Miss Lizzie looked toward the lobby entrance, through which Phillips had escaped.

Father's face was pale and slack. He said, "Amanda, I think we have to talk."

Once again I was suddenly uneasy: I feared he was going to tell me that he planned to leave William and me, and go off with Susan St. Clair. I looked at Miss Lizzie. She said nothing.

I looked back at Father. "Okay," I said.

He took a deep breath. "Let's go to the library."

Miss Lizzie said, "I'll wait here, dear."

Chapter
TWENTY-NINE

AS FATHER HAD said, the library was deserted. It was a small room, perhaps twelve feet square, three of its walls lined with books, the fourth holding a wide casement window that looked out over the porch to the lead-gray sea.

"Have a seat, Amanda."

I sat down in a black padded leather chair, Father in the one next to mine.

He crossed his legs and sat back stiffly, folding his arms across his chest. He took another deep breath. He said, "I haven't been telling the truth."

"What do you mean, Father?" Had he not already told me this?

"I mean I've been lying. To the police, to you, to everyone. To myself."

"About what?"

"About almost everything. I wasn't in Boston on Tuesday morning. I was here in town."

"But I thought you were with Susan St. Clair."

He nodded. "We drove down here in her car."

"Why?" I asked.

For a moment he stroked his mustache, studying me. Then he said, "I was going to ask Audrey for a divorce."

I stared at him. Divorce was a good deal less common then than now, a good deal more momentous. I was perhaps more shocked by this than I would have been if he had told me he had killed Audrey.

He said, "It hadn't been much of a marriage for a long time. We were both just going through the motions, and not even doing that very well."

He shook his head. "I don't know. Maybe, maybe if I hadn't met Susan, I would've kept going through those motions. But I did meet her, and it changed everything. After a while, the situation with Audrey became . . . intolerable."

He looked off, narrowing his eyes. "I actually began to hate her. Hate everything about her. The sound of her voice, the way she breathed, the way she smelled. The sucking sound she made at night, when she was sleeping."

His brow furrowed slightly, as though he were surprised and puzzled by the depth of his feeling. "I've never hated anyone before, not really. It's not a pleasant feeling."

He took another breath, let it slowly out, turned back to me. "I'd been thinking about it for a while now." His voice sounded very tired. "The divorce. I knew it wouldn't be easy. I knew that no matter how generous a settlement I offered Audrey, she'd still be difficult. But I'd reached the point, finally, where I didn't care anymore. I was willing to give her anything she wanted."

"You mean, even me and William?"

His eyes widened as he looked at me, and then he smiled sadly. "No. Of course not. If it'd come to that, I would've given up Susan. Amanda, I love you and your brother more than anything else."

I felt a stinging at the rims of my eyes.

Another deep breath. "Anyway. Monday night, I decided. I just couldn't live with her anymore. On Tuesday, Susan drove down with me. To provide moral support." He smiled faintly. "I needed it. I'm not a very strong person, I'm afraid. And Audrey could be fairly . . . formidable. I nearly lost my nerve there, at the last minute. Just outside town, I pulled over to the side of the road and sat in the car with Susan for a while. You know the big oak tree? In that little meadow by the bridge?"

I nodded.

"That was where we sat. And Miss Borden thinks that was where William saw us. I think she's probably right."

"William?"

"He must've seen us somewhere, and that's the most likely place. If William left town by following the creek up from the swamp, the way he told you he did, he would've come to the road just there, at the bridge.

"I'd wondered about it at my parents' house, when he told me about hitchhiking to Boston. Why hadn't Susan and I seen him on the road? We hadn't, of course, because he was hiding. He must've come up the creek, seen Susan and me, and then walked through the woods, next to the road, until he was out of sight. Probably he thought that if he showed himself, he'd embarrass all of us."

His smile was at once sad, wry, and bitter. "A lovely

coincidence, wasn't it? Perfect timing. If he'd come fifteen or twenty minutes later, he never would've seen us. And he wouldn't be in jail right now."

I said, "I don't understand."

"Miss Borden told me that when you talked to him, in jail, you were saying that the police should show a picture of Susan to the people who'd been along the road that day. Remember? To see if anyone recognized her? Well, William knew that Susan *had* been on the road that day. William had seen her, and he'd seen me. He knew that I'd been here in town, just around the time Audrey was killed. And he knew that I was claiming I'd been in Boston then. He confessed to Audrey's murder to protect me, Amanda. Don't you see? He thinks I killed her."

"But you didn't." On its own, without my intending it to, the statement became a question at the moment it left my mouth.

He looked at me. "No. I didn't kill her."

He squared his shoulders, as though bracing himself, and put his hands along the arm of the chair. "I left Susan there, at the tree. I wanted to drive into town alone. I wanted to get it over with, and yet at the same time I wanted to avoid it. I didn't drive very quickly." He smiled faintly, self-mocking.

"And then, when I reached the house, my nerve gave way again, altogether. I drove around for a while and tried to work up my courage." Looking off again, he raised his eyebrows, pursed his lips. "Maybe if I'd gone straight to the house, right away, I could've stopped whoever it was from killing Audrey. The timing was right. Maybe I could've saved her. I've thought about that a lot."

"Daddy," I said, "it wasn't your fault."

He looked at me sadly. "Maybe not. I don't know." He cleared his throat. "Anyway, I parked the car on Burnside and walked back." I remembered the Packard Charlie had seen parked there. And remembered, for the first time, William telling me that Susan St. Clair owned a Packard.

"The front door was locked," Father said. "I opened it and went inside. There was no one downstairs. I went up to our room, but it was empty. I checked in your room, and you were asleep."

"How come you didn't wake me up?"

A sad smile. "You looked so peaceful, Amanda. You looked so happy lying there. And if I woke you up, I'd have to tell you why I came. Or invent some story. I didn't think I could do either. That's part of it. But mostly, I think, I didn't do it because I was already planning to leave."

He smiled bitterly. "Another fine example of my courage. If Audrey wasn't home, you see, if she was out shopping, I could slip away and not deal with the whole thing for a while. Put it off till tomorrow." He shrugged. "I told you. I'm not a very strong person. I'm not much good at confrontations."

He stroked his mustache again. "I went back downstairs. I was ready to leave, go back to Susan, and then I remembered the guest room. I knew she sometimes took a nap up there. So I went upstairs . . . and I found her."

Again he pursed his lips and looked off. "I stood there for a minute just staring down at her." As he remembered this, his face went slack. "I was ill and I couldn't move. All that blood. The room stank of it." He turned to me. "And I think I was a little bit crazy too. Because in spite of the shock, and the sickness, there was a small part of me that was actually *glad*. There was a little voice in my head telling me, 'You're *free* now. She's *gone*.'" He winced and shook his head. "I don't know if you can understand that."

I said, "I can." Had I not felt much the same myself?

He inhaled deeply once again. "And then, suddenly, I realized that everyone would think I'd killed her. Everyone would *know* I'd killed her, even though I hadn't. I had a motive—Susan."

He shrugged. "And so I ran. I ran down the stairs and into the parlor. I went over to the window and looked out, to make sure no one was out there. And someone was, someone was coming up the walk. Charlie, the old Negro man who sells chickens."

I asked him, "Did he see you?"

"I'm not sure. I think he did." Today I, too, think he did, and that he decided to stay out of an affair of white people. It would have been, finally, his word against Father's.

"Anyway," Father said, "I waited till he was gone, and then I left. I locked the door behind me."

He sighed. "Amanda," he said, and his blue eyes were shiny, wounded. He looked down, looked back up at me. "The thing I'm most sorry about is my leaving you there. Leaving you to find her on your own. To see her torn apart like that. I was so busy worrying about myself that I never even considered you! I'm sorry." He cleared his throat again. "I'm sorry that my cowardice, my weakness, brought that into your life. I'm truly, truly sorry."

"No, Daddy," I said, and leaned over to take his hand. "No, Daddy. Really. It's okay. You were confused."

He squeezed my hand and took a long shuddery breath. "No," he said. "I was gutless. It's something I'm never going to be able to forgive myself for."

"It's okay. Really it is." I wanted him to stop blaming himself, punishing himself; I changed the subject. "What happened afterward? Did you tell Susan St. Clair about Audrey?"

He shook his head. "No," he said. "No, not right away. I told her I hadn't seen Audrey, and I drove out of there like a madman. About an hour down the road, an hour and a half, I pulled over again. I told her then. And then, at the next town, I called the police station here. I don't know who I talked to—whoever answers the phone down there. I started to tell him that I'd heard a fight at the Burton house, and he said the police already knew about it. He wanted to know my name. I asked him about you, and he said you were all right, and I hung up."

"Why did you go to Boston yesterday?"

"I had to see Susan. After he made that confession, William wouldn't talk to me. He refused. I knew I had to tell the police the truth. And Susan was involved—I couldn't go to them until the two of us'd talked, and she understood what I was doing. And I suppose I needed some time with her before I told them."

I felt a familiar flicker of resentment: he had not needed time with *me*. "So you're going to tell them now? Today?"

He nodded. "Amanda, Susan and I stopped at the bridge at ten o'clock. I drove away about twenty minutes later. The police think Audrey was still alive at ten. Do you understand? If William saw us then, he *couldn't* have killed her." He nodded slowly, sadly. "Yes. I'm going to tell them. I have to."

"But Mr. Boyle and the Pinkertons, they've found that man that William got a ride with. They'll make him tell the truth."

"Even if they do, even if they can, the police still have William's confession. I've got to explain why he made it."

"But what'll *happen* to you? What'll the police do?"

"I don't know. I don't think they've got enough evidence to arrest me. Not for the murder. They may charge me with making a false statement, or try to." He shrugged again. "I really don't know. I've got an appointment with Mr. Spencer, the lawyer, at eleven-thirty. He'll come with me to the police station."

"But what happens if they *do* arrest you?"

He smiled, squeezed my hand. "They won't, baby."

"But what if they *do*?"

"Amanda," he said, "everything will work out."

"That's what Miss Lizzie keeps saying. But so far it hasn't."

"It will," he said. He smiled. "She's a very bright woman, your friend Miss Borden. She figured most of this out by herself. If I hadn't already decided to go to the police, I know I would've decided to go after I talked to her." He stood. "Come on. You and Miss Borden can go back to her house. I'll come by this afternoon and let you know how it went."

I stood up and hugged him. "I love you," I said.

His arms came around me. "I love you, Amanda."

——————

By two o'clock, we had not yet heard from Father. Boyle had called from Boston, at one, and told Miss Lizzie that he had been unable to locate Mrs. Archer before leaving town. He had, however, spoken with someone in the New York office of the Pinkertons, and he expected some information from them by this evening.

Having finished lunch, Miss Lizzie and I were sitting out on the porch, drinking our tea. Although the sky was still overcast, the breeze had died and the air was motionless and hot and very damp. It left a thin film of moisture on everything, like the trail of a snail.

"Maybe I should go up to the police station," I suggested.

"I don't think it would help, dear."

"But maybe they're beating him up or something."

She smiled. "I suspect that the police seldom beat up people who can afford lawyers. He may be having a difficult time of it, but I doubt that they're physically harming him."

"Why would he be having a difficult time?"

"The police, I think, tend to feel that when you haven't told them the entire truth, you've committed a major offense against the universe. Of whom they, of course, are the local representatives."

"But you don't think they'll hurt him?"

"No, not at all. And, as he told you, they apparently haven't enough evidence to hold him for anything."

"Yes, but they're still going to think he did it."

She sipped at her tea. "Perhaps. We really don't know what they'll think."

"Everybody else is going to think so too. Aren't they?"

"Whom do you mean?"

"Everybody. Here in town. And back in Boston."

She smiled. "Do you mean the people who gathered out in the street a few days ago? That everybody?"

"Well, yes. But everybody else too. All his friends in Boston. The people he works with."

"If they're actually his friends," she said, "they won't judge him. That's what friendship is, I believe. Not judging someone. If they know him, and like him, they're not going to care what the police in some tiny little town might think. And besides, I'm still convinced we'll be able to determine who actually committed the crime."

"Yes, well, maybe, but I'm awfully glad we don't really live in this town."

She sipped at her tea. "Yes. I can understand that."

It occurred to me then—and for the first time, I think—that after her trial, Miss Lizzie had lived out the rest of her life in Fall River, despite her knowing that many, perhaps most, of the people around her believed she had actually been guilty. For nearly thirty years she had lived in a town that was convinced she had murdered her parents.

Why had she not left? She had money; she could have gone anywhere in the country, or out of it. She could have gone back to Paris. Why had she stayed in Fall River?

"Miss Lizzie?"

"Yes?"

Suddenly I heard a knocking at the front door.

I said, "Maybe that's Father!"

She smiled, sipped at her tea. "Perhaps you'd better find out."

I scooted off the chair and ran down the hallway to the foyer. I tugged on the handle and swung the door open.

And standing on the front porch, wearing a seer-sucker suit and a wide toothy grin, was William.

Chapter
THIRTY

"HE'S REALLY OKAY," William said. "They're only asking him questions. The lawyer's with him, Mr. Spencer."

Now all three of us were out on the porch. After introductions, Miss Lizzie had poured William a cup of tea.

"You're sure, William?" I asked him.

"Positive."

"And they just let you out, and that was that?"

"More or less, yeah. Dad and Chief Da Silva came into the jail, and Dad just says, 'William, I know you saw Susan St. Clair and me last Tuesday. I want you to know that by the time I got to the house, Audrey was already dead.' And Da Silva says to me, 'William, did you see your father outside town on Tuesday morning, at approximately ten o'clock?' And I look at Dad, and he nods, and I tell Da Silva, *yes*, and he says, 'Would you like to retract your confession?' You know the way he is, no expression at all, like a rock or something. And I tell him, *yes*, and he just nods and goes away."

"And then what?"

"Then Dad tells me I was dumb to confess to something I didn't do, but that he understood. We shook hands and stuff." He blinked and looked away for an instant. "And so then Da Silva comes back with the key and he unlocks the cell. And he says to Dad, 'You've got a few minutes together. When you're done, come to my office.' And that was it."

"And you're sure Father's all right?"

"Really, he's fine. He said I should come and tell you not to worry."

We talked for a while longer, perhaps another half an hour, and William told us about his past few days, the bugs, the smells, the dullard of a jailer. Already, at seventeen, he had acquired the exasperating masculine habit of speaking about a past misery as though it were merely an amusing inconvenience.

At three o'clock, there was another knocking at the door.

William stopped talking and looked at Miss Lizzie, who looked at me. "Would you like to get that, Amanda?"

It was Father. He smiled down at me and said, "I've got the car. Why don't the three of us go out for a drive?"

———

We went to Mortimer's. Father drank a scotch and water, William had a beer, I had coffee. William was exuberant, laughing and grinning at nothing at all; Father was only a little less so.

I, on the other hand, felt curiously flat and deflated. I was glad enough that William had been released, and pleased that the police had not held Father; but it seemed to me that both of them, in the pleasure of their freedom, had forgotten that neither the police nor Mr. Boyle had any idea who had actually killed Audrey. And until that person was found, suspicion would be directed at my father and my brother and perhaps even at me.

And, too, I suspect that working somewhere deep inside me, at a level below consciousness, was the knowledge that Father had not only lied to me but that he had, as he admitted, left me to find Audrey's shattered body. Consciously, by a deliberate effort, I avoided the thought: He was my father, and I loved him. But the knowledge was there, and I believe it goes some way toward explaining my listlessness.

I was not unaware either that Father had let William spend another night in jail while he himself stayed in Boston, probably with Susan St. Clair. Perhaps he believed it might be their last night together; I still resented it.

Decades can pass sometimes, and even entire lives, before we forgive our parents their humanity.

But, sitting there, I smiled and nodded and pretended to share their happiness. (I was learning how to be a grownup, a skill that today, I am glad to say, I have long since lost.)

Mr. Mortimer came to our table and made a fuss over William, clapping him on the back and asking him about the food in the "pokey." After buying us another round of drinks, he lumbered off, grinning, to the bar.

We left around five o'clock and went to the Fairview. Father called Miss Lizzie from there, to tell her I would be having an early dinner with him and William. When we finished, William went upstairs to take a bath and

Father drove me back to Miss Lizzie's. By this time, about six-thirty, a light rain was falling, a sad slow drizzle, and a fog was beginning to roll in off the ocean. Pale tendrils of mist slowly whirled across the road, curled against the streetlamps. They scattered as we passed, whipped away by the passage of Father's Studebaker.

Father told me, when he dropped me off, that he would come by in the morning, at nine, to pick me up for church; a reminder, unknown to him, that God and I had so far failed to resolve our dilemma.

———

Miss Lizzie and I were in the parlor, working on the Nikola system, when the telephone rang at eight o'clock. Miss Lizzie answered it.

"Yes. . . . Hello, how are you? . . . Yes? . . . Good, good. I'm pleased to hear it." She began to relate the story of William's release, and I realized that she must be talking to Boyle.

"Yes," she said. "It does. . . . Yes. So there's no question about it? He was in Boston on Tuesday morning? . . . I see. . . . Did they? And what might that be? Indeed. . . . Indeed. . . . It was never solved, then? . . . Yes. I agree. . . . And they're certain it's the same person? . . . No doubt at all. Yes, I understand. . . . I spoke with him this afternoon. . . . Yes, he will. . . . Yes. Thanks very much. You've done a wonderful job. . . . Good-bye."

She hung up the phone and returned to her chair, across the coffee table from my perch on the sofa. "Mr. Boyle," she said. "He was quite a fund of information."

"What did he say?"

"Well, first, he talked to the Norton man, and he's obtained a signed statement from him that verifies William's story. He admits that he picked your brother up just a little after ten o'clock."

"But the police have already let William go."

"Every little bit helps, I should think. Second, he spoke with the people Mr. Chatsworth had mentioned. Apparently Mr. Chatsworth was telling the truth. He was in Boston on Tuesday. Mr. Boyle says there's no question about it."

"So he couldn't have been the one who killed Audrey."

"Evidently not. But Mr. Boyle has received some information from the Pinkerton office in New York City."

"Yes?"

For some reason, Miss Lizzie frowned. "Yes. It seems that five years ago, in Manhattan, Mrs. Helene Archer was arrested for the murder of her husband."

———

I just sat there, stupefied, while Miss Lizzie, still frowning, looked thoughtfully down at the cards arranged on the coffee table.

Finally I said, "She killed her husband? Mrs. Archer did?"

Miss Lizzie looked up. "She was arrested, but the case never came to trial. According to Mr. Boyle's Pinkerton associates, the police were convinced she was guilty, but they never found the evidence they needed."

"But the police can be wrong."

She nodded. She examined the cards again. "Yes," she said. "Yes, they can."

"How did he die?"

"He was stabbed. Mrs. Archer is the one who reported it. She told the police she came back from shopping and found him lying there. In the bedroom. She always maintained that a burglar had killed him."

"Do you think that's possible?"

"Possible, certainly, from what Mr. Boyle says. As to whether it's true or not, I've honestly no idea. The police found out that she and her husband hadn't been getting along. Apparently she was seeing another man."

"Who?"

"Mr. Boyle didn't say. He'll be back here in the morning. He said he'd bring all the information with him."

"Do you think we should tell the police?"

"Mr. Boyle intends to. He's telephoning Chief Da Silva at the moment." She frowned. "I suppose he has a moral obligation to do so."

"You don't think he should, you mean?"

She frowned again. "I honestly don't know, Amanda."

"But if she killed her husband, then it's possible she killed Audrey."

"Yes," she said. "It is." She shook her head abruptly, as though clearing it of thought. "Let's not worry about it now. The police can deal with her." She looked down at the cards. "Now. Where were we?"

———

Miss Lizzie stayed downstairs, reading, when I went up to my room at nine-thirty. I was not especially tired, but I wanted to think. I undressed, put on my night-gown, and climbed into bed.

Mrs. Archer? Madame Helene? Could she really have killed Audrey?

She was strange, yes, wearing that silly pseudo-Grecian gown, talking to spirits; but could she kill? (Had she run out of spirits and decided to create one of her own?)

Her having killed Audrey might explain why she had come to Miss Lizzie's house on Thursday. As Boyle had pointed out, she might have wanted to learn what we knew, and what we suspected, about the murder.

But she could have come, just as easily, because she honestly believed she might help us.

Could she kill?

I did not know. It was one of the many things I did not know. For the past four days I had been discovering that the boundaries of my knowledge were much less far apart than I had assumed, and that the territory which lay beyond them was enormous.

Until last Tuesday, I had believed that life was like a river, silver and clear, carrying me off idyllically toward the (presumably rosy) future. Now I had discovered that below the surface, other, darker currents flowed. And that below these, down at the murky bottom, down among the stones and the weeds and the muck, creatures lived whom I did not understand, but whose grotesque faces, as they rose to the surface, I feared I might recognize.

Downstairs, the telephone rang.

Who, I wondered, would be calling now?

After a few minutes, I heard the floorboard creak outside my room, and then a gentle tapping on the door.

"Amanda?" Miss Lizzie, calling very softly.

"I'm awake, Miss Lizzie."

She opened the door and stood. a silhouette, featureless, in the dim light of the hallway. "I'm going out for a few moments, dear. I wanted to let you know."

"Where are you going?"

"I've some business to attend to. It shouldn't take long."

"What time is it now?"

"A bit after ten. You stay in bed, and I'll be back before you know it."

"Okay, Miss Lizzie."

"And Amanda?"

"Yes?"

"Keep the doors locked. All right, dear?"

"Yes," I said. "All right."

———

Ten minutes later I stood at the window with a new set of questions to wonder about. Who had telephoned? Why had Miss Lizzie left? Where had she gone? And why the admonition about keeping the doors locked?

Below me, the fog had grown thicker. The sea was gone, lost in the murk. I could make out, barely, the gray shape of the hedges that separated Miss Lizzie's property from ours; but everything else was a blur of white.

It was moving, the fog, as though it were alive. Pale streamers would detach themselves from the main body and writhe and coil on their own, twisting about, slowly twirling, and then mysteriously blend back once again with the cloud. Sometimes a patch would open up and I could see through it to the ground, black now against the smoky white.

And then, as I watched, something else moved down there. Off to my left, beside the hedges.

I blinked. I had imagined it; I must have. Staring for so long at the fog, my eyes had amused themselves by inventing a presence that was not there.

But no. It moved again, away from the hedges, skulking, a dark form shrouded by the mist, but obviously human. Because it was dressed in black and appeared to be cowled, I imagined for a moment that it was a monk; and, idiotically, I actually wondered what strange Gothic mission he might be on.

And when the figure trod into a small patch of clear air and raised an arm, I expected to see a lantern at the end of it, or a candle, to light the way.

Instead, I saw a hatchet.

———

Since then, over the years, I have seen that hatchet many times, at night in dreams, during the day on misty streets when wisps of fog parted to reveal a form before me, black arm raised, a form that, after a frozen moment, metamorphosed into something harmless and prosaic and consequently mocking: a streetlamp, or a signpost. For years (and so habituated to it did I become that soon it was automatic) I have avoided standing beside, even looking at, windows when a fog rolled outside.

And for years, too, I have occasionally wondered what might have happened if I had not been standing by that particular window when that form stalked across the yard below. I would be dead, I expect.

At the time, standing there, I did not think that the figure beneath me might be Mrs. Archer, or that it might be someone else. I assigned to it no human identity at all. I knew only, as my heart rolled over in my breast and my blood turned to frost, that the *Thing* down there was the monster that had butchered Audrey and that now It was coming for me.

If I had run from the house, if I had tried to hide inside it (and I do not know, to this day, why I did not), I imagine I would be just as dead as if I had not seen the Thing approaching. Instead, I watched It disappear against the wall, and then, my heart drumming, I glanced frantically around the room for a weapon, for something, anything, I could use to protect myself.

There was nothing.

Think! I told myself. *Think!*

There had to be something. Somewhere in the house there had to be *something* I could use against that beast outside.

Hatchet. Yes. *Miss Lizzie's hatchet.*

And I had to get to it before the Thing got in, before the Thing reached me.

I ran to the door, jerked it open, ran down the hall and down the steps. At the bottom, I swung myself around the corner and raced down the hallway. I tore open the closet door, yanked at the light string, and scrambled to the toolbox. My thumbs fumbled at the latches, and then I clicked them open and I tossed back the lid of the box and I reached inside, grabbed at the shelf, ripped it out and hurled it aside, boxes scattering across the closet floor.

And down there, inside the box, the hatchet was gone.

Chapter
THIRTY-ONE

FOR A MOMENT I just knelt there, staring dumbly down at the toolbox.

It was impossible. The hatchet had been there only yesterday. I had *seen it*, I had *held* it.

Forget about the hatchet. *Do something.*

The telephone.

Call for help.

I sprang up and ran from the closet, ran down the hallway into the parlor to the phone. I snatched up the receiver.

Coming from the earpiece there was nothing, no sound at all. The phone was dead.

It might only be children, I told myself. Children playing pranks.

But it was almost eleven o'clock at night. The children were asleep. This was no prank.

That Thing, that beast, the monster who had hacked Audrey and left her smashed and torn, It was out there

325

somewhere, hiding in the fog. From out there It was watching me, watching every move I made.

Fool, I told myself, and ran over to the light, switched it off.

Standing in the dark, I could hear myself breathing, harsh and quick. My heart was pounding so quickly, so powerfully, that I thought it might tear itself from my chest.

I would wait. I would wait until the Thing tried to get in. Whichever door It tried, front or back, I would run to the other.

I waited, listening.

Nothing.

All at once I remembered the kitchen. The carving knives.

Moving on tiptoe, trying to be absolutely silent, as much to hear the Thing as to prevent Its hearing me, I crept across the parlor toward the hallway.

Suddenly there was a loud *thump*. I froze.

The noise came again. *Thump*.

It had come from the parlor wall, the one facing the street, and it sounded like someone slamming a hand against the wood outside.

Thump.

What was happening?

I had not moved. Now, holding my breath, I edged closer to the parlor door.

Thump.

The sound was getting closer to the window. All I could see out there was the oily whirl of fog.

I moved closer to the door, my stare locked on the window. I took another silent step and, just then, with a suddenness that chilled me, a figure appeared beyond the glass.

I did not recognize it at first. Its chest was black with gore and blood was pouring down its face, streaming past the white startled eyes.

Then I recognized the closely cropped hair, the trim mustache, both bright white against the blood.

It was Mr. Foley, the Pinkerton man.

Suddenly, as though in surrender, he slumped against the window. His mouth agape, his eyes still open, staring intently but seeing nothing, he began to sink toward the ground. In an instant he was gone, and there was only the broad black greasy smear along the glass and the swirling white fog beyond.

I did not stop to consider what Mr. Foley might have been doing outside Miss Lizzie's house. I only ran. Out of the parlor, down the hallway, into the kitchen, over to the cutlery drawer. I heaved it open with such force that it jumped from the cabinet and sent knives flying across the room, scattering along the floor. I saw the long French carving knife smack against the base of the stove. Throwing the drawer aside, I scurried over, grabbed it.

Just as I did, the kitchen door began to rattle, the door to the back porch. It rattled violently, loudly, insanely: someone out there fighting with the doorknob. I could not see through the lace curtains, but It could see in. The Thing was on the porch, less than six feet away.

What I should have done, of course, was run for the front door. I believe I would have escaped. Once outside, I could run downtown; if It followed, I could hide in the fog.

But the image of Mr. Foley lying out there, soaked in blood, those blind white eyes swimming up at me through the fog, made it impossible. Without really thinking, knife in hand, I darted up the stairs. Behind me I heard the crash and tinkle of breaking glass.

I raced down the hall. My bedroom door had no lock; I dashed into Miss Lizzie's room, slammed the door, turned the lock, switched on the light.

The lock looked too flimsy to hold for long. Quickly, frantically, I glanced around the room. I had to move something against the door, form a barricade.

The makeup dresser.

I ran to it, tossed the knife onto it, wrapped my fingers around its far corner, and pulled. It was solid teak; it would not budge.

I heard steps on the stairway.

With a gasp, using all my strength, I tugged again at the dresser. It moved. Only an inch or two, but it moved.

Out in the hall, floorboards creaked.

My nightgown was soaked with sweat; my hair, cold and damp, stuck to my forehead. I tugged again, crying out with the effort. The sharp edge bit into my fingers, and the dresser moved. But again only an inch.

The doorknob turned. Someone pounded once, very hard, at the door, and the wood shook.

The window. *Get out.*

The screen was in place. My fingers, slick and trembling, slipped on the latches. They had been painted over, they would never open. I clawed my nails at the mesh, saw it was useless, ran back to the dresser and seized the knife.

A huge *crash* as something hit the door. A long thin splinter of wood popped off.

I slashed the knife across the screen.

Another *crash*. The wood split, and the head of the hatchet lanced through, black with rust.

I ripped at the screening with my fingers, tore it from the frame.

Crash! A large ragged chunk of wood was sent spinning through the air and left a hole in the door, and a hand appeared there, fingers curled like talons, groping for the lock.

Using both hands, I raised the knife high overhead, ran at the door and, with all the power I possessed, putting all my weight behind it, I slammed the knife down into the hand.

It sliced through flesh and bone and dug into the wood and then, from beyond the door, came a wild, shrill, unearthly shriek.

Panting, sickened, I let go of the knife and stepped back.

And the hand clenched into a fist and jerked downward, and the knife snapped free and fell. The hand moved to the lock, the fingers found it, turned it, and then the door flew open and Mrs. Mortimer stood there in a long black dripping raincoat, her hair dank with fog and rain and sweat, her eyes wide and crazed.

"Bitch!" she screamed at me, and the cords in her neck were taut.

I could not move.

"Bitch!" she screamed, and she stepped into the room.

She held the hatchet raised in her left hand. The right hand hung limp at her side, blood spilling from it and spattering on the wooden floor.

I backed away.

She curled back her upper lip. "You knew all the time, you filthy little bitch. She told you, the fat momma bitch, she told you about me and Kevin. And you knew about the coffee. How'd you know, bitch? Who'd you tell?"

I felt the wall against my back; I had moved away as far as I could. I gasped. "Mrs. Mortimer—"

She took another step toward me. There was a long pool now of bright-red blood spreading along the floor. "Filthy little bitch, slut bitch, you're going to die, bitch, I'm sending you to hell so you can be with your fat bitch momma bitch."

The bed was to my left. I sprang onto it, rolled across the silk comforter, landed in an awkward clatter on my hands and knees. I stumbled to my feet and Mrs. Mortimer began to walk around the bed, inexorable, inescapable.

"Fucking *bitch*," she hissed. "Fucking bitch, you're not going to ruin *my* life, oh no, I'm going to *smash* you, bitch. I'm going to smash your fucking face in."

She took another step and then there was a movement off to my right, at the doorway, and I saw—and I realized that all along I had been expecting this, praying for this—that it was Miss Lizzie.

She wore, like Mrs. Mortimer, a black raincoat that dripped water; and she was holding, as Mrs. Mortimer was, a double-bladed hatchet.

She said, *"Get away from her."*

Mrs. Mortimer wheeled around, her coat swirling like a cape.

"You!" she said.

"Get away from her." Miss Lizzie stepped into the room, her eyes narrowed, the mouth set in a line as thin as a knife edge.

Mrs. Mortimer, her back to me, took a step toward Miss Lizzie. "Did you come home to help your little dyke friend?" She laughed, a high-pitched lunatic bark, frayed at the edges. "Did you come to give her a wet dyke kiss? Did you? You wicked wicked fucking *bitch* dyke."

And suddenly, arm above her head, she ran at Miss Lizzie and swung her hatchet.

Quickly, backhanded, her entire body twisting with the blow, Miss Lizzie brought up her own hatchet. The two blades collided with a loud brittle *clang*, and both women, rocked by the impact, staggered back.

Miss Lizzie was the first to recover. Her teeth bared, the hatchet at her shoulder, she leaped toward Mrs. Mortimer. She swung, and Mrs. Mortimer drew swiftly away, and I heard the *swoosh* of the hatchet as it swept through empty air.

Mrs. Mortimer's hatchet came flying at Miss Lizzie's neck. Miss Lizzie jerked back, and the hatchet whistled past.

They began to circle each other, Mrs. Mortimer moving to her left. Beyond them, in the wide mirror atop the dressing table, another Miss Lizzie and another Mrs. Mortimer performed the same wary, lethal dance.

This could not go on much longer. Miss Lizzie was an old woman, and overweight; Mrs. Mortimer was still losing blood. But each of them seemed fiercely determined, each eyed the other with a frightening, savage intensity. Mrs. Mortimer's lips were still drawn back in that malign, maniacal grin. Miss Lizzie's face was mottled, blotched with purple bruises, exactly as it had been in her speechless fury after confronting the mob.

As they completed a full circle, I saw Mrs. Mortimer's glance dart toward me. A kind of calculation suddenly glittered in her mad eyes. All at once she flailed out at Miss Lizzie, wildly. As Miss Lizzie jumped back, Mrs. Mortimer spun about and rushed round the bed, directly at me.

I think she intended not to kill me, not just then, but

to use me as a hostage, as a means of forcing Miss Lizzie to yield.

I stumbled back, away from her, but she moved too quickly. Hatchet high in her left hand, she snatched at me with her bloodied right. It should have been impossible for her to use that hand. Bones had been split, tendons severed. But she was possessed, driven by rage and madness, and I felt her fingernails slice through my nightgown and knife into my shoulder.

I struck out at her in a rush of horror, smashing the back of my knuckles against her eye. Her face twitched back and her fingers loosened, and I grabbed her hand, my fingers sliding in the blood, and as hard as I could I twisted it, wrenched it away. And, mouth awry, eyes astounded, the woman *squealed*, a sound that even then, in the midst of my terror, seemed childlike and pathetic. And then she was swerving, turning to meet Miss Lizzie, but there was not enough time, not for Mrs. Mortimer, for Miss Lizzie was already there, and Miss Lizzie's hatchet swooped down, overwhelming, inevitable, and the curved blade sank into her forehead with a sudden, final, liquid *crunch*.

She sagged to her knees like a marionette whose strings have been clipped, and then she toppled, face forward, to the floor. Miss Lizzie stood over her, staring down, swaying slightly and breathing through her mouth. She still held the dripping hatchet.

She looked at me. I swallowed, unable to speak. She brought up her hand, looked down for a moment at the hatchet, then lowered the hand and opened her fingers. The hatchet fell and banged against the floor.

She said to me, "Are you all right?" Her voice was raspy, distant.

I nodded. "Yes . . . yes."

She reached out to touch me and I moved to her, and then she was holding me and I could smell the citrus smell of her and I could hear, even through her raincoat, the thud of her heart.

I said, "Is it over now? Is it all over?"

She stroked my hair and she said, "Yes. It's all over."

EPILOGUE

BUT OF COURSE it was not all over. There remained the small matters of motive, means, and opportunity: as the legal profession, and Chief Da Silva, liked to call them.

If this were a mystery novel and not a sort of memoir, a kind of extended and much belated *What I Did Last Summer*, I suppose I could gather all the characters in the library and have them sit there, rapt, over Stilton and amontillado, while Miss Lizzie (a Miss Marple with a hatchet) primly explained what had actually happened over the course of the past few days, below the surface of what had appeared to.

Unfortunately, things did not proceed that way. Some time passed before the truth became known, and, even then, the verifiable facts were few. A truth and a fact, thank goodness, are not the same.

Not that Miss Lizzie, Marple-like, had not determined,

and early on, who the murderer was. From the beginning, she had believed it was Mrs. Mortimer.

"The key," she told me on Monday, two days after Mrs. Mortimer's death. I had just come from the coroner's inquest into Audrey's death. "The missing key. There was really no one else who could've taken it, or who had any reason to."

"Why did she want the key?" I asked her.

Smiling, she looked at me over her pince-nez. "What does one usually do with a key?"

I shrugged. "Open a lock."

She nodded. "Your stepmother kept the front door locked. In order for Mrs. Mortimer to get into the house and kill her, she needed a key. She'd been planning this for some time, I believe, and she was just waiting for the proper opportunity. She found that when you and Audrey were out on the back porch that morning. She simply lifted the key from the hook and pocketed it."

"And then later"—I nodded—"when Audrey and I were asleep, she came back and used it to unlock the front door." (And used it to lock the door again when she left, perhaps out of habit, perhaps further to confuse the police.)

"Yes," said Miss Lizzie. "I imagine she called out, for you or for Audrey, when she got inside. If either one of you answered, you could say that she'd picked up the key by mistake and that she'd come back to return it. She could say she'd knocked at the door, no one answered, and she'd come in to put the key back on the hook."

"No one answered because we were both unconscious from the chloral hydrate."

Miss Lizzie said, "She had no reason to believe you

were in the house. No reason to believe you'd been drugged. I imagine that when she discovered, later, that you'd been there, she was horrified. She had no way of knowing what you might've seen or heard."

It had been Chief Da Silva, not Miss Lizzie, who had worked out the chloral hydrate. Although there was no proof, it appeared more than likely that Mrs. Mortimer, before or after stealing the key, had put the drug in Audrey's coffee that Tuesday, to make certain she took her usual guest-room nap. Mr. Mortimer had admitted to Da Silva that he kept the chemical in his house and that his wife had access to it.

My taking chloral hydrate, in the few sips of coffee I stole from Audrey's cup, would explain why I had slept through Audrey's murder and, shortly afterward, Father's visit.

By mentioning the stolen coffee to Mrs. Mortimer, and later that same day asking her husband, purely by coincidence, about chloral hydrate, I had caused her to believe that I knew what she had done. Presumably, this is what she meant when she babbled about "the coffee" during that dreadful scene in Miss Lizzie's bedroom.

In Da Silva's opinion, Mrs. Mortimer had believed herself safe so long as William was in prison. The moment he was released, she realized that the police would once again start searching for the murderer. And I had shown—or so she thought—that I knew about the chloral hydrate, which suggested that the murderer was she. She decided to kill me, using a hatchet, as she had on Audrey, to throw suspicion on Miss Lizzie. That Saturday night she telephoned Miss Lizzie from the Fairview, anonymously, promising information about the killing, luring her out of the house so she herself could get in and reach me.

She was quite mad, I believe.

If she had not been insane before, then worry over her safety had surely driven her insane by Saturday night. Otherwise, I doubt she would have killed Mr. Foley, the Pinkerton man.

Mr. Foley was out there that night because Boyle could not be. Ever since the police guard had departed, Boyle had been watching over me like a guardian angel. Miss Lizzie, knowing that I had been in the murder-house at the time of the killing, and feeling that Mrs. Mortimer might see me as a threat, had wanted someone to keep an eye on me. She had given Boyle the job.

On Friday, when I went off to examine the shed by the swamp, Miss Lizzie had somehow, using the telephone, tracked him down and sent him after me. He had picked me up at Annie Holmes's house and followed me. His was the presence I had sensed in the woods, his was the stare I had felt along my skin.

At night, too, he had watched the house. I do not know when he slept, or if he managed to sleep at all.

But on Saturday Boyle had been forced to go to Boston, and so Miss Lizzie had conscripted Mr. Foley.

As a precaution, it had not been very successful. Mr. Foley had been killed and so, very nearly, had I.

Now, as we sat there in Miss Lizzie's parlor (for the last time, as it happened), I said to her, "How do you think Audrey found out about Mrs. Mortimer and Kevin?"

After talking to Kevin Mortimer in Boston, Boyle had verified that during the War, while his brother was fighting in France, Kevin had conducted an affair with Mrs. Mortimer.

Miss Lizzie said, "I don't know. Perhaps Mrs. Mortimer told her herself."

"Or maybe it was that Mrs. Marlowe."

"That may be. We'll never know for certain, I'm afraid."

"Do you think Audrey was blackmailing Mrs. Mortimer? For money?"

She frowned. "Again, I doubt we'll ever know. But I suspect, from what we know of your stepmother, that whether money came into it or not, she was using the information as a form of power over Mrs. Mortimer, a way of controlling her. Perhaps Mrs. Mortimer couldn't stand it any longer. Or perhaps your stepmother's threats to tell the story had become more serious."

"I guess," I said, "that there's a lot we'll never know."

Miss Lizzie smiled. "I guess," she said, "there is."

———

We left that night for Boston, Father and William and I. Neither my father nor my brother wanted to return to the shore; I did, but I was outvoted. When I telephoned Miss Lizzie to tell her, she told me that she was leaving as well, going back to Fall River. We would see each other, she said, we would visit; but although we sent cards and letters to each other for a few years, we never did.

Officially, no one in Fall River ever learned of what happened between Miss Lizzie and Mrs. Mortimer. Chief Da Silva and the rest of the local authorities hushed up the entire thing. Two axe murders within a week were fairly bad publicity for a resort town.

During that last week, unbeknownst to me, as were so many things during that week, Father had arranged for Audrey's body to be shipped to Boston. The funeral services were held on Wednesday, two days after we returned to the city. It was there, for the first time, that

I met her parents. A sad silent pair with an air of resigned disappointment, they returned afterward to their
home somewhere in Nebraska, and I never saw them
again.

I met Susan St. Clair within a month after our return
to Boston. Nothing like I expected, she was a bright,
lovely, capable woman, totally unaffected (and not at all
French). Even before she and Father married, we had
become friends. It was she who explained to me the
mysteries of Sex (some of them, anyway; no one knows
them all). Had I known about them that summer, I
should have begun to understand the relationship between Father and Susan, between William and Marge
Grady, between Mr. Chatsworth and Mrs. Archer. And
perhaps begun to understand the relationships that
(perhaps) existed between Audrey and William, and between Miss Lizzie and the actress, Nance O'Neil.

When I began this account, several years ago, I wrote
to an old friend in the States and asked for any information he could obtain about Nance. He was able to
verify all that Miss Lizzie had told me and to provide
some additional facts.

A leading lady of the stage at the turn of the century,
beautiful and immensely talented, she became in the late
twenties and early thirties a well-regarded character actress in films. Among many other roles, she played Felice
Venable in the cinema version of *Cimmaron*. During the
early 1960s, she lived on 34th Street in New York (less
than two blocks, as it happened, from where I, un-
knowing, lived at the time), and she died at the Actor's
Fund Home in Englewood, New Jersey, in 1965.

There were many other deaths before hers. One by
one, all the people I knew that summer walked off the
edge of the world and disappeared. William went first.

He died in 1937 in Spain, fighting with the Abraham Lincoln brigade. Father died in 1938, and Susan in 1952. Roger Drummond became a reporter and finally a bureau chief for *Time* magazine, and died in 1960.

Harry Boyle and I wrote letters to each other until he died of lung cancer in Florida, in 1943. I wrote the first letter in care of the Boston Pinkerton office, asking him where Mrs. Archer had been that last Saturday. She had been in New Haven, he wrote, seeing still another "boyfriend."

There is one final loose strand.

Miss Lizzie died in 1927, in Fall River. We had not corresponded for some time; like most other people, I read of her death in the newspaper.

In 1930 I was living on West End Avenue in New York while I attended Columbia Law School. One hot August afternoon I received a special delivery package, heavy, perhaps eight inches wide and deep, and sixteen inches long.

I carried it into the kitchen, set it down on the table, and opened the wrapping. Inside was the teak jewelry box, trimmed with gold, I had seen on Miss Lizzie's dressing table eight years before.

Taped to its top was a note addressed to me in my married name. I opened it and read:

As you may know, Miss Lizbeth A. Borden died in 1927. The bulk of her estate was bequeathed to two different animal shelters, but litigation between the two has delayed the distribution of the estate's remainder. I am pleased to say, however, that this issue has now been resolved and that Miss Borden's last wishes may finally be honored. Miss Borden personally requested to me that you receive the enclosed.

Please acknowledge receipt at your soonest possible convenience.

It was signed Peter M. Wilburforce.

When I opened the box, suddenly from inside it rose a thin metallic tune I had not heard for eight years. Some hand, at some earlier time—Mr. Wilburforce's? Miss Lizzie's?—had wound the mechanism. The music played, and repeated itself, and slowly died.

Inside the box, lying on the shelf, was a single playing card. I carried the box and the card into my husband's study and set the box, closed, on his desk, then lay the card beside it.

He had been sulking for an hour or so; our usual disagreement: He hated New York. Now he looked up, his green eyes puzzled, and he said, "It's very pretty, but what is it?"

"It's from Miss Lizzie," I told him. "She left it to me in her will."

He picked up the playing card, turned it over, turned it back. "Six of hearts. Is that significant?"

I shook my head. "Only a reminder."

Slowly, thoughtfully, he tapped the card against the lid of the box. "Imagine," he said, "if she didn't do it, didn't kill her parents, how lonely she must've been."

I stroked the back of his head, the black hair beginning now to gray. "Imagine how lonely she must've been if she did."

There was one thing I had never told Darryl. It was something that happened that night eight years ago, when Miss Lizzie drank brandy in front of the dressing-table mirror. Toward the end of it, her speech slurred slightly, she had looked at me and said, "Life. People. The mind of God. That's the important thing, Amanda.

Not wood or steel or land. Not property. I chose property over people once, and I shall always suffer for it."

Until Roger Drummond told me about the transfer of land from Miss Lizzie to her mother, I had thought she meant the farm of Nance O'Neil.

I had always wondered whether she ever actually told anyone—Nance, perhaps. I had always wondered if, in some isolate, wounded part of her being, she had wanted to tell, had wanted to confess.

It had been a hatchet, of course, that Miss Lizzie had reflexively chosen as a weapon that night when she went off to meet the anonymous caller—Mrs. Mortimer.

In the Nikola system, the mnemonic pair of images for the position of the six of hearts are a *mother* and a *hatchet*.

———

I left Darryl to his work and carried the box into the bedroom and rested it on my own dressing table. I opened it, lay the card on its shelf, and stared down at it for a long while. And when at last I brought down the lid of the box and sealed the card away, I felt the same sense of ending, of completion—although I knew that Miss Lizzie and all the others from that summer would be with me forever—that one feels when one finishes the final chapter and, with a smile or perhaps a sigh, closes the book.